Stef,

Texas Tornado

by

LANI LYNN VALE

Lani Lynn Vale

Text copyright ©2014 Lani Lynn Vale

All Rights Reserved

The purchase of this E-book allows you one legal copy for your own personal reading enjoyment on your personal computer or device. You do not have the rights to resell, distribute, print, or transfer this book, in whole or in part, to anyone, in any format, via methods either currently known or yet to be invented, or upload to a file sharing peer to peer program. It may not be re-sold or given away to other people. Such action is illegal and in violation of the U. S. Copyright Law. If you would like to share this book with another person, please purchase an additional copy for each recipient. If you are reading this book and did not purchase it, or it was not purchased for your use only, then please return it and purchase your own copy. If you no longer want this book, you may not give your copy to someone else. Delete it from your computer. Thank you for respecting the hard work of this author.

This is a work of fiction. Names, characters, businesses, places, events, and incidents are either the products of the author's imagination or used in a fictitious manner. Any resemblance to actual persons, living or dead, or actual events is purely coincidental.

Dedication

This book is dedicated to the members of the military and their families that support by them. The ones that made it possible for you to sit down and enjoy this book. You have sacrificed a lot for us, and the thanks you all receive is not nearly enough.

I'd also like to give a shout out to the authors Jessie Lane, and Chelsea Camaron for supporting me in writing this series. Thank you, Jessie, for answering my unending questions, and being a good friend. You've done some kick ass covers and done so much for me that I cannot say thank you enough. I'd mow your lawn for you if you lived closer.

To my editor Asli, thank you so much for working with me and editing my babies. You'll never know how much your kindness means to me.

Finally, to my family. To my husband, who took the kids outside to play, cooked dinner, and cleaned up around me while I finished writing a scene in my book. To my kids for spilling that coke in my lap and then running away (I love you anyways!) To my mom and sister for reading my books and telling me they were the shit. I love you all!

Him

James had plans for his life. Those plans were derailed by the surprise arrival of his daughter. His life revolved around her. Then *she* arrived with her beautiful brown hair that was made to wrap around his wrist, and a butt that was to die for in a tight pair of jeans. Nevertheless, he didn't need any more drama in his life. His ex-girlfriend was stirring enough of that up for ten women. Yet, there was something about her that soothed his soul.

Her

Shiloh's made it her life's mission to protect the innocent children she can from the big, bad, scary things that lurk in the darkness. She has an inane curiosity for life and craves knowledge. Which is why when she starts poking around in her father's business, she inadvertently starts something in to motion that threatens her very existence. Her father, the one man that was always supposed to be there for her, drops her off with a brother she never knew she had and leaves. Making her question the father she obviously never really knew at all. Then she meets *him*, and she doesn't think her life's so bad after all. The sexy biker turned SWAT officer sets her nerve cells to igniting, and she relishes in every single second of it.

Him

He knew life could change in an instant. One soul crushing instant.

When he's presented with the aspect of losing Shiloh before he's ever even had her, he decides it's time to grab life by the handlebars and ride it like he stole it. Then that threat not only touches his woman, but his daughter. And there's no power on God's green earth that can protect them from a father's wrath.

Chapter 1

You can tell a woman's mood by watching her hands. For instance, if she's holding a gun, she's probably angry.

-Earl Dibbles, Jr.

Shiloh

I sat in the wooden chair twiddling my thumbs. I was cold, tired and hungry...not to mention a tad bit angry. Glancing down at my watch and realizing I'd been here for nearly an hour and a half with still no sign of him, I finally gave up and stood to leave. Work came first or I didn't pay my bills.

Hesitantly, I started to leave.

Except I didn't get too far.

"Hold her." Winter said as she thrust the tiny little baby in my arms when she came barreling into the office.

Winter was the wife of one of my brother's men, Jack.

Jack and Winter got married when they were both young, and were ripped apart after only being married for a month.

She had a shock of red, curly hair, and she was a paramedic for the Kilgore Fire Department.

Following the frazzled woman, I entered the office and stared. I'd been in there earlier, but with no one answering, I felt uncomfortable about staying inside and I sat on the chair that was propped outside the office instead.

Texas Tornado

Once her hands were free, she started pacing like a caged, rabid porcupine ready to attack with the phone to her ear. If steam were anatomically possible in a human's body, it'd be coming out of all her orifices right about now.

The sound of a big truck backing up filled my ears, and I glance to the side and stilled.

"Holy cow! What happened to that bike?" I asked

Winter's eyes flicked from the paper she was reading to the window, studying the tow truck that was bringing in the mangled hunk of metal.

"I haven't the slightest idea. What the heck do they expect Free to do? They're mechanics, not miracle workers."

Cat stirred in my arms at the sound of her mommy's voice, but with a little jiggling and bouncing, she slipped peacefully back into sleep once again. "I've got to go, Winter."

The sound of my voice was booted out into left field when Winter's voice rose to an almost too high octave.

After listening to a few seconds of her conversation, I surmised that she had a reason to be pissed. Winter was currently on the phone with her cable provider while trying to sort out why five hundred dollars' worth of porn was charged to her monthly account.

"No, you listen to me, jack wad. I've never watched a porn in my life. I don't need porn with the hunky piece of man flesh I have in my bed. If I'm in the mood for porn, all I have to do is watch him move for 2.4 seconds and I'm gone. I have no need for ..." She said picking up the bill that was crumpled and scrunched up from her tirade. "Throbbin' Hood, or an Edward Penis Hands."

I stifled my giggles, or at least tried to, but I wasn't successful. Winter's glare in my direction didn't relieve me of them either. Only made me laugh all the more.

I stopped when Cat started to squirm, but the smile stayed on my face.

Winter made a shooing motion with her hand telling me to go while she listened to the man on the line. Winter's face got darker at whatever the man said, and I decided now would be a good time to leave since she looked like she was ready to lose her shit.

Grabbing Cat's blanket from the chair, I wrapped it around her tight and then cradled her close to my chest as I exited the office into the fresh morning air. Today was a nice day for Texas at sixty-two degrees, but I knew it wouldn't last long. It never did.

Texas had two seasons. Summer, and not summer. For October, this was fairly normal temperature at seven thirty in the morning. By noon, it'd likely be in the nineties. The black clouds in the sky also had something to do with the temperature. We were in for one heck of a storm according to the Channel 7 weatherman, Mark Scirto.

I'd gotten a Thundercall from them not even ten minutes prior telling me that the storm was headed for my neighborhood. I'd been ecstatic when I found out that the local news did that. Back in Galveston, they had something similar, but still different enough that it was a novelty.

In Galveston, they'd call when the hurricanes were approaching.

Texas Tornado

The sharp crack, crack, crack of the tow truck's bed being pushed up and lowered to the ground drew my attention, and I watched and winced as they let the motorcycle practically drop to the ground.

"This where you want it?" The operator asked from the controls.

James, the unbearably hot man I'd had a crush on since I met him eight months ago, came from the other side of the tow truck grumbling, and my heart started pounding a mile a minute. That man was sexy.

Today, he was in coveralls that were only half way on, tied by the arms at his trim hips. The bottom parts of the coveralls were covered in grease, which clearly showed that he'd done quite a bit of work today already. A black wife beater showed off his excellent upper body, allowing the tattoos on his muscular arms to be seen perfectly. His hair was a deep rich blonde that was cropped closely to his head, and he had a beard.

Although it didn't look like much, it had to be as long as his hair all the way around. Normally I didn't do beards, but this man sure could pull one off with excessive ease.

"Well, since you already dropped it on the ground, guess it's there to stay, isn't it old buddy?" James rolled his eyes as he wiped his hands with a red rag.

"Sorry, man. It's not like I can do much with this one. No wheels. Ya know?" He shrugged.

"Yeah, I do know." James said gruffly.

Turning away from the emotion I saw on his face, and totally avoiding thinking about what the man did to me, I walked further into the garage, studiously ignoring the sign that said 'Personnel Only.' and kept scanning the garage looking to see if my brother was in there.

He wasn't, but Jack was, and I settled for him instead.

Jack was Winter's husband.

He fought alongside her brother, and was intimidating as hell.

He was tall with the sexiest arms she'd ever seen on a man.

His nearly black eyes were sharp and all consuming, and always a little frightening to look into.

Walking in his direction, I avoided a car that was on the closest rack, and then two motorcycles in the process of being painted.

He looked up when he heard my approach and beamed when he saw I had his daughter in my arms.

Cat was six weeks old, and he was even more proud of her now than he was when she was born. Although I hadn't been there for the birth and subsequent celebration with everyone afterwards, I did see him once they were home from the hospital, and could tell he was so very proud of not only Cat, but Winter as well.

As for why I didn't attend the celebrations, I still wasn't quite sure where I fit in with everyone. Although Sam was my brother, I didn't feel like I belonged. Sam wasn't trying any harder to get to know me now than he had eight months ago when I'd met him. The men took their cues from Sam and treated me as a nuisance, even though I'd done nothing to deserve it.

The wives were nice enough, but I felt so awkward around them that I avoided them like the plague. Winter was the only one who'd even said more than two words to me in the past month, which completely surprised me.

Once I reached him, I glanced down at his dirty hands and sighed. "I have to go, and Winter is yelling at someone in the office. She handed me Cat, and normally I wouldn't complain about holding a pretty little baby, such as yours, but I have to go to work in less than twenty minutes."

His black eyes flicked to mine, and then went back down to his daughter, then his hands, and finally his clothes. "Can you hold her for a few minutes and let me go change or something?"

I nodded and he left, hurrying in the direction of the bathroom. I'd never been further than the bay doors. I knew that further beyond there was a down room, but nothing more.

The night I came home with Sam, he rented me a hotel room and dropped me and my shit off, and nothing more. Not a single word came out of his mouth. Which wasn't surprising since he'd done the same the whole ride home.

Once I realized that he didn't like me, I was careful not to say anything the rest of the way home. Normally, I didn't have a problem making friends, but Sam seemed to hate me just because he hated our father.

Which was so beyond unfair that I didn't even want to think about it.

The day after I'd been dropped off in the hotel, I'd walked to a local diner to eat, and ended up leaving with a job and, even better, an apartment above the diner. It took me nearly five months to earn the money for a car, but I did it and was now the proud owner of a used Chevy Blazer.

Yes, it was twenty years old, rusted, and had an exhaust leak (so I've been told), but I was super excited that I didn't have to walk three miles to the grocery store and back. Groceries were heavy little bastards when you had to hump it that far, even if they were only cereal, milk, bread, and peanut butter.

I'd made an appointment with Sam to have my car tuned up, and he reluctantly set a time for six forty five this morning. I should've known he wouldn't keep it. He'd spurned every single attempt at trying to get to know me. He didn't even want to talk to me.

There was only so much that a person could take before she just didn't care anymore. Even if it was her brother.

A loud boom startled me from my reverie, and I jumped. Lightening danced across the sky, followed quickly after by another deep boom of thunder. Cat started wailing after the second one, and I started cooing and rocking her to calm her down.

When nothing soothed her, I started singing 'You are My Sunshine.'

I'd just finished the last few words in the song, looked up, and noticed boots clomping towards me.

Jack was back with a soft smile on his face. "Sorry about that. She doesn't like the thunder very much. You did well. Normally, I can't get her to stop crying when we have a big storm like this."

That wasn't surprising with the sheer amount of storms we'd been having over the past three months. There'd been more rainfall in the

Texas Tornado

past couple weeks than we'd seen all of last year according to the weatherman.

Handing the tiny little baby to Jack, I smiled. "No problem. See ya."

Turning on my heels, I hurried past the two motorcycles, and ran hard to get to my truck before the rain soaked me.

I wasn't successful.

My white dress was now soaked all the way through. Cursing, I yanked open the door and jumped inside, slamming it hard behind me.

Shivering, I stuck the key in the ignition, and said a quick prayer that the beast would crank. It took so long to start that I started to get nervous. Finally, the engine caught and I let out my held breath.

"Shew," I said feeling extremely relieved, and reached for the wipers.

They didn't flip on, and my stomach sank. Beating on the dash, I yelled. "Come on, don't fail me now."

The most beautiful sight in the world appeared before me, making the swish swish sound of water being squeegeed off the windshield. "Thank you!" I squealed and clapped my hands.

I didn't want to be here anymore. I really just wanted to go home, crawl back into my bed, and cry. In fact, I wanted to do one better. I wanted to go home to Galveston, crawl into my bed, and cry.

Except none of those things were going to happen because my dad royally fucked me over. My brother hating me was only icing on the giant fuck-me cake.

But I'd survive, because that's just what I did. I didn't need anybody. I didn't need my no show dad, nor my unstable mother. I didn't need anybody. I just needed myself. That was the only thing you could rely on anyway, because everyone let you down eventually.

Even my other brother, Sebastian, had let me down. It'd been months and months since I'd spoken to him, and if I didn't hear from him within the next week, he'd be on my shit list, too.

Chapter 2

After watching copious amounts of crime shows, I concluded that serial killers only target young attractive women with matching panty and bra sets. I feel much safer now.

-Life lesson

James

I looked at the twisted steel and grimaced. I didn't want anything to do with this stupid hunk of metal, but I'd made a promise to an old friend, and would do it whether I wanted to or not.

A flash of white brought my attention from the twisted hunk of junk to Shiloh as she left the office with Cat in her slender arms. She headed straight for Jack, bypassing me completely, which she seemed to do anytime there was an option of me or another person.

Today she was wearing a white dress that hugged her curves beautifully. The sandals on her feet displayed her cute toes.

And they were cute.

Her toenails were painted a bright pink with tiny little flowers interspersed all over. Her feet were tiny, just like her hands. A dragonfly tattooed on her left foot added to the cuteness with its bright cheery colors.

She wasn't tall for a woman, only four or five inches over five feet, but she used what she had well. Her breasts were perfect. Large and plump. The sight of them made my mouth water. Made me wish to have the tight peaks of her nipples in my mouth, devouring them as I pumped into her without abandon.

And there my mind went with all the naughty images again. I'd been thinking these X-rated things about the woman since I'd met her eight months ago in San Antonio.

We'd been gathering some information on Jack's wife, Winter, when Shiloh made her appearance. Sam's father had pulled his favor, declaring that Sam was now responsible for Shiloh's well-being and left without another word. Sam had been shocked that he'd even had a sister.

Eight months prior to meeting his sister for the first time, he'd met his brother, who was in the hospital on the brink of death. The brother was understandably hesitant to make any sort of connection with Sam, which was also the same case for Sam. Sam's parents had been married for eighteen years after Sam's birth. It was extremely obvious that the other children had been conceived while both were still married.

Sam being the stubborn man he was, refused to talk about anything. Which meant he was distant with his sister, refused to even speak with his father, and probably didn't have much of a relationship with the brother either. Sam was a closed off person, and in this case, he was a steel vault. I couldn't even get any goods out of my own sister about it.

Shiloh charged out the door as if the fires of hell were on her tail. Her eyes were brimming with tears, and I felt something funny happen in my chest when I realized she was upset.

Texas Tornado

Walking towards Jack, I stopped when I got close enough so he could hear me. The rain on the tin roof made it incredibly hard to hear, but I just raised my voice so he could make out my words.

"What did you do to her?" I asked.

His eyes were on Shiloh as she got into the Blazer that had definitely seen better days. "Nothing. Just told her she did good with Cat. Normally she just screams until the loud noise stops, but she sang to her and got her to calm down."

The Blazer started turning over, but the engine wouldn't catch, and I started to think that she might need a ride. However, the engine finally caught, and the Blazer rumbled to life.

"Needs a tune up. She's got an exhaust leak too." Jack mumbled.

"Hey! Where's Shiloh going? I thought she was here to get her truck fixed." Winter asked as she sidled up next to us.

"Well if she was here for a tune up, why's she leaving?" I asked Winter.

"Probably because her bastard brother didn't show like he was supposed to. You know this is his third time standing her up?" Winter fumed.

"What?" Jack and I asked at the same time.

"Yeah, she works at that diner down by that shit-hole motel off the interstate. I had to stop there the other day to pick up a passed out drunk. I was just making idle conversation while I wrote my report when I found out that the piece of junk Blazer the man had passed out next to was hers. She then started talking about it needing a tune up, and that's when she told me that she'd tried to bring it in twice before but no one was ever able to get to it."

Come to think of it, I had seen it in here twice, but never with her. "It's never been on the board. I didn't know it hadn't been worked on."

"Me neither. I just thought it was another project of Sam's." Jack concurred.

Winter just gave us both looks. "It gets better. She had to walk to drop it off, and then walk to pick it back up. Twice."

"What?" I asked, anger starting to roil in my gut.

"That's over six miles." Jack asked confused. "Why didn't she ask for a ride?"

"From what I understand, she had to drop it off early before her shift that starts at six in the morning. She usually doesn't get off until later." Winter explained. "And to do that, she'd have to get up really early to walk here, and then be able to get back home. If she got off at five, she'd still have to walk all the way here, and that'd put her at six getting here and we're closed by five every day."

"What the fuck?" I asked.

What the fuck was Sam thinking? Walking alone in the bad parts of town wasn't safe for any woman, but definitely not a woman as pretty and petite as Shiloh.

"My sentiments exactly." She said.

I couldn't just believe that Sam would do that on purpose though. Sam just wasn't built like that. Women were his weakness. "Where is Sam?" I asked finally, not knowing what else to say.

"He hasn't been in yet." Jack answered.

Walking into the down room so I could hear a little better, I pulled my phone out of my pocket and called him. It rang four times before Cheyenne picked up.

"Hello?" Cheyenne answered.

"Where's Sam?" I asked curtly.

"He was picking me up from work. We're on our way home. Why?" She asked suspiciously.

"Did he happen to remember that he had an appointment?" I asked.

I heard her asking Sam, and then his rumbled reply. "He says he doesn't have an appointment. Shiloh was supposed to come by later though."

"She's already been here and gone. She waited a little over an hour before she left. I saw the Blazer as soon as I opened the bay doors this morning, and it's only seven thirty."

"James says that you missed your sister." Cheyenne told Sam.

More mumbling, and then Cheyenne said, "We'll be there in a few."

And hung up.

Jack poured himself a cup of coffee and then took a seat at the bar. "He hasn't really had much to do with her, has he?"

"I'd just assumed he was hanging out with her without us. It's understandable, but I haven't seen her at anything, come to think about it." Winter said sadly.

"Didn't she come to the baby shower?" I asked Winter.

She shook her head. "Nope. She dropped a present at the station though."

"Why'd she come to the station?" I asked.

"She said because she didn't know where else to take it."

"What about your wedding?" I asked.

They thought about it, and I did too. "No, now that I think about it, she didn't come to that either."

"Who didn't come to what?" Cheyenne asked as she shook the water off her shirt.

Sam followed closely behind, his face closed off completely.

"We were just saying how Shiloh hasn't been to any of our functions. Sam, you know you can invite her, right? Bennett comes anytime he can. Stormy's even been here a time or two, and she lives in BFE." Winter asked.

Bennett was Payton's brother who was currently in the Navy. He didn't come to many functions now that he was deployed, but he came to as many as he could.

Sam didn't answer, just ignored her question entirely.

"Sam?" Cheyenne asked sounding confused. "What's going on?"

I definitely wanted to know the answer to that question as well. Shiloh wasn't a bad person. She was actually funny and nice. In the few times she'd actually been around me, I'd enjoyed her company greatly. I'd definitely have pursued something more with her if my life wasn't a big mess as it was. Shiloh didn't deserve to be dragged into my mess.

"I guess I forgot about her." Sam said by way of excuse.

"Three times?" Winter asked.

Sam's gaze locked onto Winter's stubborn one and held. "What are you talking about?"

Winter then went on to explain what she'd learned from Shiloh while at her call.

"Sam?" Cheyenne gasped.

"What?" He snapped.

"You've stood her up three times? What the hell are you thinking? And what the fuck, you told me she was working in a restaurant, not a rat infested hell hole." She fumed.

My sister had one hell of a temper on her. Which made me love her all the more in this instance. I was extremely confused as to why Sam would've forgotten anything, especially when it came to his own sister.

The office phone to Free rang. I stepped up to the wall and answered it just after the second ring. "Free. James speaking."

"Uhh, hi. This is Shiloh."

"Hey, Shiloh. Looking for Sam?"

"N-no. My t-truck broke down about a mile from my apartment. I was w-wondering if you knew a tow service I could c-call." She said stammered.

"Duncan's. The number is..."

"Wait! I need a pen. Hold on." She said hurriedly.

Glancing at Sam, I thought to help by offering a different solution. "I can have Sam text it to you."

"Uhh, I don't have a cell phone. But I have the name, I'll just look it up. Thanks." She rushed out before hanging up.

***

Two hours later and still there was no sign of Shiloh's Blazer.

"Duncan's." Don answered.

"This is James down at Free. We've been waiting for a tow to come in, but it's not here yet. Any ideas when you'll get to it?" I asked.

"We've only had three tows today. None in waiting." He answered.

"Did you get a call about a Blazer yet?" I asked.

"Yeah, already done it. Why?"

"Where'd you drop it off at?" I asked sharply.

Jack looked up from his computer, and Elliott looked up from his paperwork. Each gave me their full attention when they noted the anger in my voice.

"Some local diner off the interstate. Thought it was weird myself, but the lady said she lived there."

"Okay, thanks." I said and hung up.

"She didn't have it towed here. Don said he towed it to the diner where she works. Although he said that she said she lived there, too."

"Why wouldn't she have it brought down here?" Elliott asked.

"Apparently, Sam's not been a very nice big brother. Why would she bother?" I asked and then took the phone out of my pocket and dialed Cheyenne's number.

Texas Tornado

She answered with the fist ring. "Hey, Jamie. Can I call you back?"

"Ahh, no. I need to go check on Shiloh. Get Janie off the bus for me?" I requested.

"Sure, but why does she need help?"

The twins were fighting in the background, so I made it quick, explaining what I'd learned from Don.

"I think Sam needs to do this."

"I don't want to wait. Thanks. Love you."

Not giving her the chance to argue, I hung up and went out to the truck. It was still raining, and I decided to take the truck seeing as getting wet would only slow me down.

I couldn't explain why I was so mad. Mostly it was directed toward Sam. He'd been acting strange ever since he'd met his brother last year. I realize it was a shock and all, but it didn't give him a 'get out of jail free' card for being a douchebag.

Fifteen minutes later, I pulled up beside Shiloh's Blazer and killed the engine.

The soft ticking of the heated engine filled the air as rain continued to pound down in torrents.

I surveyed the area, seeing that there was, indeed, an apartment attached to the diner. It was also unsafe as hell. There was no fire escape. Only one-way in and one-way out. The door looked like it would fall with one kick of my booted foot, and to make matter's worse, there was a strip club directly behind the diner.

Not a good one either.

Bailing out of the truck and running towards the diner, I ducked inside and stopped on the carpet so I didn't track water throughout the place. The young hostess, who was all of fifteen at best, smiled brightly at me.

"Can I help you, sir?" She asked.

"I'm looking for Shiloh. She here today?" I asked.

Her smile left her face, and a look of concern replaced it. "She got hurt on the way to work today. She called in, which is why I'm here."

My heart started to beat a little harder in my chest. "Where is she?"

She raised her hand and pointed at the ceiling. "Her place."

I gave her a nod of thanks and left. Rain poured down harder now than before. I tried to stay close to the building and let the edges of the roof shield me, but still ended up getting my whole right side drenched.

Once I got to the stairs, my anger was being replaced with concern.

Her stairs were a fucking joke. At least every other one was broken in some way, if not missing completely. Gingerly, I made my way up the stairs and stopped at her door.

I knocked four times before I tried the door handle.

Locked.

Getting out a credit card from my wallet, I shimmied it in between the lock and the door jam, popping it open with hilarious ease. I made a mental note to get her a deadbolt and a reinforced steel door as soon as possible.

Texas Tornado

A woman as beautiful as Shiloh shouldn't be living in an area of town such as this. However, since she did, she needed to be prepared and safe.

In fact, now that I thought about it, I planned to get her an alarm system as well.

Stepping over the threshold, I sidestepped numerous pots that were catching the leaking water from the roof, and came to a halt in the main part of the apartment.

The area was an open floor plan, minus the bathroom that was off to the side with the door open. The kitchen was off to the far right corner, and in the closest left corner was a bed with cloud sheets. The place itself was spotless as could be.

From the outside, you wouldn't even be able to tell that it would actually be nice inside; but, surprisingly, it was.

Scanning the room, I frowned when I didn't see her. Which left only one other place she could be.

"Shiloh, its James." I called out.

No answer.

"Shiloh." I called out a little louder.

Still no answer.

Walking cautiously towards the bathroom door, I peeked inside and my heart nearly stopped. Shiloh was on her side, curled into a tight ball on the floor in front of the toilet, shivering. Her hand was cradled close to her chest, and her face and usually vibrant hair were wet with tears that were still leaking out of her closed eyes. She was wearing the same clothes as earlier, except now the dress was torn and scuffed in many places.

Two long steps later, I dropped down on my knees beside her. Placing my palm on her neck, I felt for her pulse. It was beating rapidly. Her face was flushed, and as I placed my palm over her cheeks, I could feel the heat emanating off her face from a fever.

Running my hands down her cheek, I called her name. "Shiloh."

Her eyes opened, and the fever was apparent there too. Her eyes were glassy and distant. She blinked multiple times before giving me a small smile.

"Hi James."

"Hey sweetheart. What happened?"

"Fell."

"Fell where?" I asked gently, stroking her long, wet mahogany hair.

Her eyes opened wider, and I was treated to a smile that reached all the way up to her caramel colored eyes. "A fox scared the crap out of me and I dove into the ditch."

I held my smile in check. "What hurts?"

"I think I broke my hand or arm."

"Why didn't you go to the ER?" I asked quietly, sitting her up to where she rested against the bathroom wall.

"My truck broke." She said as tears welled into her eyes.

"I remember, honey. I kept waiting for the tow truck to bring it in and it never showed, so I decided to come to you."

"That's sweet of you." She said and tried to stand.

Texas Tornado

Her breath hissed as I helped her to her feet, and the arm that was cradled to her chest was now clearly visible. And very clearly deformed.

"I think we should take you to the hospital." I explained carefully.

"I don't have any insurance."

"That's okay, honey. We'll figure something out. Let's go. Do you have a jacket?" I asked.

"No. I don't have any winter clothes. I just got a blanket last week." She explained.

"What happened to all your clothes that you came here with?" I asked as I helped her out her door and down her stairs.

There was a lull in the rain, which I was severely grateful for. I didn't want her catching a cold on top of the broken arm.

"It got stolen when I went out to eat at the diner."

"What?" I barked, and immediately regretted it when she jumped.

"Yeah, that place over there is a shit hole. They said they would send me a reimbursement check, yet I haven't seen hide nor hair of it. I go over there once a month to check." She shrugged.

I was glad her fever was making her tongue loose. I didn't think I'd get the information any other way.

"That one?" I asked incredulously, pointing at the piece of shit motel across the street.

"Yeah," She said dejectedly.

"Why'd you go to that one?" I asked as I opened the truck door for her.

She looked up, and then started to climb in. Not thinking that was the best idea for her hand, I grabbed her by the waist and hoisted her in, and then buckling her seatbelt once I got her settled.

"That's the one Sam dropped me off at. I didn't want to go there, but it's kind of hard to tell anyone no when you don't know the area. Nor do you have any money."

As I continued to speak to her about mundane things, my blood started boiling at the treatment Sam was giving his little sister. How could he do this to her? And fuck, why the hell would he drop her off at the shittiest motel in Kilgore? Goddammit. This was the one where hookers and drug dealers set up shop.

Four hours later, I bundled up Shiloh in my truck with a bright pink cast covering her arm, and enough antibiotics and painkillers in her blood stream to make her a very happy girl.

"I don't think my brother likes me very much."

"Which one?" I asked.

"Either. Sam more so than Sebastian though." She explained.

I kept my attention on the road, but peered at her out of the corner of my eye. "What makes you say that?"

"He doesn't talk to me. He doesn't allow me around his kids. Cheyenne never talks to me. He ignores my calls. He left me at a hotel in the shittiest part of town without money, food, or a way to contact him. I had to look y'all up in a freakin phone book to call him the first time."

I was speechless.

Utterly speechless.

Texas Tornado

With what she just described to me, I would think he hated her, too. Still, I knew him better and I didn't think that was the case. At least I hoped not.

"I don't know honey, but we'll find out."

She didn't reply, and I glanced over to find her head resting against the glass, asleep.

I pulled into the space in front of my place and turned the engine off. The truck's engine ticked as it cooled, and I wondered if she would have a problem staying at my place. I had a spare bedroom, so it wouldn't be that big of a deal to just put her in there. It's not as if she'd be inconveniencing me in anyway.

I also knew she wouldn't want to go over to Sam's, especially after what she'd just told me.

Decision made, I unlocked the front door, threw it open, and then went back for Shiloh. She'd shifted to lean against the console, so it was easy to open the door and scoop her up into my arms. Her body curled into mine, and she sighed in pleasure.

I walked inside, leaving the door open, and walked back to the guest bedroom. Once there, I set her down gently on the bed, and then covered her up with the quilt that was turned down at the foot of the bed.

Taking the extra pillow from the other side of the bed, I propped her hand up on it before turning to leave. Just as I was closing the door, I heard her call out quietly. "James."

Stopping the motion, I swung the door back open and went to the side of the bed. "Yeah?" I asked just as quietly.

"Did you close my door? I don't want my cat to get out." She slurred.

"Yeah, sweetheart. I locked the door. Go to sleep." I said and smoothed her hair away from her face.

I needn't have bothered saying the last part. She was already asleep.

Then my brain started turning. I hadn't been looking for a cat when I went into the apartment, and I worried that when I left the door open when I went searching for Shiloh that I'd inadvertently let him out.

Which meant I was going to have to go searching for him tonight.

Wonderful.

Chapter 3

If you're hungry, eat anyway....just in case.

-Life lesson

James

"There isn't a fucking cat in this fucking house. It must've gotten out." I growled.

I'd looked everywhere. Under the bed, in the closets, in the bathroom and kitchen cabinets. Dammit to hell, I was going to have to look outside in the fucking rain. Hell, even Cheyenne had followed behind me and looked, so the cat must be gone.

"She, literally, has one bag of clothes." Cheyenne said in surprise, holding up a suitcase in her hands.

"Yeah, she said it was stolen from the hotel the day after Sam dropped her off." I said making one more pass through the apartment looking for the stupid cat.

"What the hell? I thought her father was giving her money. Why's she living here?" Cheyenne asked with a confused look on her face.

"From what I've gathered, which isn't much, she's here because she stirred up some bullshit asking questions that involve Sam, Sebastian, her father, and her. Something their father fucked up and didn't keep a lid on. Now she's here hiding out, I guess."

Picking up the pillow off the bed, I threw it in the general direction of the wall in a fit of anger.

A cat's low-pitched snarl of outrage had me turning and looking into the corner. Following the sound, I hunkered down on my hands and knees, moving the pillow aside to find a hole in between the floorboards.

A piece of the wood that would normally cover the hole was laying off to the side, not easily seen since the wood floors were dark, concealing the hole and the extra piece of wood perfectly.

I reached into my back pocket and took out the small flashlight I kept there for convenience, and shined it down into the hole. Glowing eyes, one green, and one yellow greeted me. Followed by brown fur with black dots interspersed throughout its coat.

Reaching my hand down slowly, my hand made contact with the cat's long silky fur. Since I wasn't missing a finger, I made a move to remove the cat from the hole. He came willingly enough. The problem wasn't his refusal to come out of the hole, it was the fact that his body just plain didn't fit.

After some maneuvering, I pulled him all the way free and was just plain stunned at the amount of cat that came out of the tiny hole. "Jesus."

"Oh, my. He's a big boy, isn't he?" Cheyenne said peering over my shoulder.

Big didn't even begin to cover it. Massive. Gargantuan. Colossal. Those words were barely even fitting. The beast wasn't fat either, just big boned.

Texas Tornado

"That looks like a wild cat. Are you sure you want to take that home?" She asked worriedly.

I looked down at the cat who was no flipped backwards, limp like a rag-doll in my arms and laughed. "Cheyenne, this cat couldn't be further from ferocious. Looks like a pussy-cat to me."

My eyes moved down to the open board in the floor and my brow wrinkled in confusion. "Hold this."

The cat didn't protest in the slightest at the transfer of beds. Cheyenne grimaced and I laughed. She wasn't a cat person in the least. She was a dog person through and through.

Going back to my knees again, I shined the light into the hollow space and was surprised to see a safe as well as a sheath of papers illuminated in the dark.

I fished the papers out cautiously, and then carefully sifted through them.

You could've blown me over with what I read.

"Holy shit."

***

I didn't delay in confronting Sam. If my head could explode in anger, it'd have done that over twenty minutes ago as I left Shiloh's apartment. How could he have been so fucking thoughtless? She'd been in that shithole for well over seven months now. By herself. Scared to fucking death.

The cat hissed in my hand when Chewy met me at the front door, deterring Chewy's advance in his tracks. He stopped and eyed the cat, but didn't make a move forward to check the newcomer out.

Good for him. At least one of the males that lived in this house had some fucking brains.

Sam stood as I rounded the corner into the kitchen, eyeing the cat with a raised brow. "Whose cat?"

"That would be your sister's. Not that you care." I growled.

Sam's eyebrows rose. "What makes you think I don't care?"

"Oh, maybe the fact that your sister is scared fucking shitless to live by herself. Or maybe the fact that she recovered from cancer seven months ago. Or how about the fact that she was abducted and tortured when she was a young girl rendering her practically phobic against absolutely everything; so scared that she has to take medication, which, I might add, she can't afford right now, to help her sleep without having nightmares. And not once. Not even one goddamned time in the last eight months have you made any effort, whatsoever, to get to know her!" My voice rose with each word that came out of my mouth, but by the time I was finished I was all but bellowing.

Sam look flabbergasted. His eyes went from mine to Cheyenne when she cleared her throat behind me. "You told me she was living somewhere else."

"My father," he hissed. "Sends her money every month. I've been forwarding it to her on the second of each month like clockwork."

"Oh?" I asked. "And what makes you think that she's getting it? Because if I was getting money every month, I wouldn't be living in some shithole apartment behind a goddamned strip club."

"What's your fucking problem?" Sam asked sharply.

"My problem?" I asked in surprise. "Oh, that's just fucking rich. Did you know that your sister had to walk home today? In the rain? Because her truck broke down on the way home from *your* shop? Too bad you weren't there to help her fix it. Then, maybe, she wouldn't have a broken arm for her troubles. What exactly would you do if I treated Cheyenne the way you're treating Shiloh?"

His jaw clenched in anger, but he didn't answer. I was hitting every hot button he had, and right now, he wanted to beat the absolute shit out of me. He might've swung at me if I didn't have Cheyenne at my back.

"How about you run a check on her address. You do know where she lives, right?" I asked in a facetious tone.

"I send her the fucking checks every month, I know where she lives." He spat.

"You know she lives above the diner?" Cheyenne asked in surprise.

"Yeah," He said, regret starting to make an appearance in his voice.

"Sam?" Cheyenne asked. "What's going on with you? You wouldn't let any woman you know live over there, why would you let your own sister?"

"I went over there and did a drive by. Seemed okay to me."

The excuse was pitiful, and we both knew it.

"What?" She hissed.

Here's a little tip for all you young men out there. When a woman says "*What*," it's not because she didn't hear you, it's because she's giving you a chance to amend your answer.

I didn't stay for the rest of the fight. I knew it was inevitable and about to get heated. Cheyenne had that tone in her voice that said she was about to lose control of her temper, and I had better things to do right now than listen to them go at it.

I stopped first and looked in on Janie who was sleeping on the top half of the bunk bed in Phoebe's room. She was sound asleep with her tiny body curled up into a little ball in the middle of the bed. Her hair was in a mess covering most of her face, as well as the pillow.

Smoothing the hair away from her face, I gave her nose a soft kiss then checked on Phoebe who was asleep in her crib.

Phoebe slept as Cheyenne used to with her butt in the air and a stuffed animal clutched tightly to her chest. The sight made my chest tighten when I thought about Janie at that age. What I'd missed when I'd been deployed or on missions. I missed her first steps, her first words, her first everything when she was a small baby.

I placed my palm on Phoebe's back feeling the rise and fall of her chest before leaving, closing the door behind me.

I could hear Sam and Cheyenne hissing back and forth at each other, and I was supremely grateful that they were keeping their lover's spat quiet, seeing as I didn't want Janie to wake up. Shiloh needed my attention tonight.

Texas Tornado

The cat, still sprawled limply in my arms, shifted when I entered the door to my house. Setting the cat down, I watched him explore the area with a bored air to him. I didn't own any animals, I was lucky enough to get Janie fed and watered every day. Another living being wouldn't be beneficial to me right now, much to Janie's disappointment.

The cat must've picked up Shiloh's scent, because as soon as the cat hit the hallway, he was off like a shot in the direction of the guest room.

I followed slowly behind, laughing at the site of the humongous cat laying protectively on the pillow Shiloh's head rested on. The cat had his paws resting on Shiloh's face as if in claim of the sleeping woman.

I walked into the room and right up to her bedside. She sure was a beautiful woman, even with her face puffy from crying and a cat lying on top of her head.

Her casted arm now laid on the side of the pillow I'd originally rested it on. As careful as I could, I repositioned it on the pillow again, and then moved my hand up to rest on her brow.

Her silky hair was splayed much the same Janie's was, only there was a lot more of it. The cat was laying on a quarter of it. Some of it was tucked underneath her body, while others were splayed across her face.

"Jesus, honey. Where'd you get all that hair?" I whispered as I pushed it off her face with one blunt finger.

She shifted, inadvertently moving her arm, and then whimpered.

Glancing at my Luminox, I realized that it'd been nearly four hours since her last dose of pain medication. I'd also forgotten to fill her prescription.

"Fuck." I groaned and turned towards the door while fishing the phone out of my pocket.

I dialed Jack's number and waited.

"Hello?" Winter answered.

"Hey, sweet stuff. I was wondering if you had any extra Vicodin or something that matched that in strength." I asked without preamble.

"Sure, I have some left over from my C-section. Do you need me to bring it over?" She asked.

"If you don't mind. Jack around?" I asked.

"He's burping Cat. Well, he was before she puked on him. Now he's changing his shirt." She snickered.

I remembered those first few months before I deployed. How hard it'd been. I'd been stubborn and refused any help from my mother and sister, until one day I just couldn't do it anymore. I envied Jack and Winter being able to raise their child together.

My relationship with Anna, Janie's mother, started innocently enough. We met at a rodeo. Her sister was a barrel racer and she was there to watch her compete. I was there with my sister a week before I went into basic training. I was eighteen years old and about to become a man.

Anna and I had fun, but when I left for boot camp, I hadn't given her a second thought. Then I was deployed my first time. When I got back nine months later, I just happened to bump into her again and we'd hooked up. Only there was a consequence to my decision, and it changed my life forever.

Janie was born nine months later. I was scheduled for another deployment when Janie was two months old, and at three months, I left her for six more months. Then again when she was two months shy of two years old for another seven months.

I missed nearly half of my daughter's life, and it finally hit home when Sam and Cheyenne started seeing each other. I was missing everything, and I didn't want my daughter to grow up without her father. It was only when one of my best friend's in the world died, while on a mission, that I really understood the repercussions of my career.

Dougie was the life of the party, and when I watched a bullet tear him apart, I just knew that I couldn't do it any longer. The benefit wasn't outweighing the cost anymore. His daughter would grow up without a father, and that could've very easily have been me.

"Alright, James. I'm on my way." Winter said before hanging up the phone.

I paced the living room floor and waited.

I had no clue why I'd called Winter, and not, for instance, my sister, the nurse. Well, quite frankly, I did know. I was somewhat pissed at her, too. She had to have known that the situation with Sam was weird. That he wasn't acting right.

Didn't she ever wonder why Sam wasn't making an effort with his sister? Hell, I would've known way sooner if I didn't have so much bull crap from Anna swirling around me like an Afghanistan sand storm.

Hell, I was doing good just to get to sleep at night.

The knock at the door interrupted what was sure to be a horrible place for my mind to go at that instant.

Walking to the door, I swung it open and smiled at Winter.

She was still wearing her medic uniform, which meant that she must've just gotten home from work. She smiled brightly at me, but I missed the full effect because my eyes were drawn down to the newest addition on the Free family.

Cat was nestled in a tight swaddle in the crook of Winter's arm. Cat was also one pissed off girl, too. Of course, it'd been raining and thundering every other day here since she was born, and it was a common occurrence around the compound.

"Hey," Winter said as she slid past me inside.

"Hey," I said and closed the door behind her. "Shiloh broke her arm today, and I forgot to get her prescription filled. Can she have one of yours until tomorrow?"

"What?" Winter practically screeched, then passed the now awake Cat to me before disappearing in the dark of the hallway.

"What the fuck is that-" I heard before Cat's cry of outrage drowned out the rest of Winter's question.

The rumbling of the thunder shook the house with its fierceness, and then the sound of pouring rain followed it its wake.

Expertly cradling the tiny girl to my shoulder, I bounced and shushed right against Cat's ear, which calmed her instantly.

Texas Tornado

I smiled as I thought about how Janie used to be much the same way. I'd just about pulled out all my hair when I'd discovered a book at the super market. Figuring that I had nothing else to lose, I'd purchased it, read it, and then implemented the actions on a colicky Janie that very same night.

Much to my surprise it'd worked, and I'd been a believer of the method ever since. Cat passed out in my arms after a few more whimpers, and I tucked her in close to my chest, then followed Winter to the guest room.

I found Winter sitting on the bed next to Shiloh, cradling the massive 'cat' in her arms, snuggling him close. "This is the most awesome cat I've ever seen. Even better than Ember's!"

I was thinking that much myself. "I thought so, too. Did she take the pill?"

"Yeah. Got her to drink a glass of water, too. What'd you do to get my girl to quiet down?" She asked skeptically.

I smiled. "It's my magic touch. You just wouldn't understand."

"Well, how about you and your magic touch watch the girl this weekend. If the storms keep up, I'm gonna have to build her a soundproof room." She griped.

"Well, at least she's not colicky. Janie was the most awful baby. No matter what I did, she would cry. Feed her, she cried. Change her, she cried. Look at her, she cried. And you'd better not even think about putting her down." I said wistfully.

In all honesty, I missed every single minute of when Janie was a baby. She was five, going on forty-two, and I'd give just about anything to freeze time to ensure she didn't grow up anymore. She'd stay my little princess forever.

"We'll see how Shiloh feels. She's not going home until I get her place wired." I growled getting upset all over again about the state of her apartment.

It was completely unfit for such a young beautiful woman to live in. If I had my wish, she'd be somewhere more secure, pronto.

"Yeah, Cheyenne said something just a couple of minutes ago as I passed her place on the way to yours. She looked kind of pissed off, too."

I imagined she was. I just wondered what Sam had been telling her all these months as to why Shiloh wasn't coming around.

"Yeah, Sam has some explaining to do." I answered, and then recapped what I'd learned in the past couple of hours.

"Did it say what type of cancer?" Winter asked with alarm.

I thought back to what I'd read on the paper. "Basal something."

"Basal Cell Carcinoma?" She asked.

I nodded my head. "Yeah, that sounds about right."

Her breath left in a whoosh. "Whew! If you're going to have one, that seems to be the best type to have. It rarely spreads to other parts of the body, and it's the slowest growing. Did it say where it was at?"

"I didn't get that far. I didn't want to keep reading her personal documents. All I read was that she was 'Negative for basal cell carcinoma' and that she needs to follow up with her new doctor within six months as a precaution."

"Are you going to tell her you found it?" Winter asked.

Texas Tornado

I nodded once. "I can't *not* tell her. That just doesn't sit right with me not to tell her. And more, she'll ask where I found the cat, and that was in the hidey hole she had."

"You're a good man, James. You're also a miracle worker." She said, smiling sweetly at Cat.

Winter sat the cat back down on her perch above Winter's head, and we left the room silently. I walked to the door, grabbed the umbrella that was the size of a small spacecraft, and opened it on the front porch with a flick of my wrist.

"Well, it's just because I'm that awesome." I grinned cheekily at her.

She snorted, and stepped out under the umbrella I was holding up. We walked quickly, and Jack opened the front door before we were even half way there, stepping out on his own porch and waited as I walked his life back to him.

"Yeah, your awesomeness knows no bounds." She said dryly, taking a step onto the porch so she was under the awning before she held her hands out for Cat.

I transferred her gently to Winter's arms, and stepped back. "Look up Happiest Baby on the Block on YouTube. You're welcome."

Winter's laughter followed me home, and even though it was warm, I still felt a chill deep down in my bones. As if I was on the precipice of something big. Life altering, and huge.

Chapter 4

Don't take life so seriously. It's not like you're going to get out alive anyway.

-Louise Smith

Shiloh

My eyes peeled open, and my stomach rolled as the pain in my arm intensified tenfold as I took in my surroundings. I looked down searching for the cause of my pain, and found my hand covered in a cast. Well that explained it. I'd broken the same bone I'd broken when I was fourteen. Yay for me.

At least the color was cute. I loved bright pink and bright green. Really, anything that was neon colored was my favorite. The cast would at least match my New Balance shoes I'd bought as a splurge a couple of days ago.

Normally, I wouldn't risk spending any money due to my lack of well-paying job, but I'd gotten the call from social services a few days ago asking me to come in for an interview, and I had a good feeling that I'd get it.

I graduated with my degree in social services from Texas A&M at Galveston, and then immediately started working for the State of Texas as a social worker within weeks of graduating.

My interview!

Texas Tornado

"Mother fucking son of a cockblocker." I yelled and then jumped out of bed, purposefully blocking out the pain that radiated through my abused limb.

I'd deal with that later. I had an interview today at eleven, and if I didn't, I'd lose my chance. Broken bone or not, I was going to that interview. It wasn't the first broken bone, and wouldn't be the last. I was a clumsy person, and I'd broken five bones in my life, that is if you didn't count the four ribs, left foot, and collarbone that Zander, my ex-boyfriend, had given me the last time I'd left him.

My sluggish brain finally started to work, and I realized I was in a spare bedroom of sorts. My foggy mind clued me in that it must be James', but I didn't have time to do anything. If I didn't hurry, I'd be late.

I could tell by the sun peeking into the blinds that it must be early morning, and I still had a good two hours before I had to be there. However, I still had to get home, and then start getting ready.

Sneaking to the bedroom door, I opened it silently and peeked my head out. The hall was still and the house beyond sounded silent as well. Cautiously, I tiptoed out until I hit the bathroom, and rushed inside, closing it silently behind me.

I made quick work of the facilities, and then started searching for shoes.

I didn't find any, but I also didn't see James, so it was a partial win. I ascertained that he wasn't in the house, and stopped tiptoeing around, and started to curse when I still couldn't find any shoes.

Finally breaking down, I walked cautiously into James' room, and froze. The area itself was pretty awesome. The bed, dresser and nightstands were made of rustic pine, and had a homey feel to it. The bedspread was dark gray, and bunched down at the bottom of the bed, as if he'd gotten up just moments ago, and planned to come back shortly.

I resisted the urge to make the bed, and walked to his closet, opening the door cautiously.

The closet itself was ordered, even if everything he owned was all black, minus the stack of dirty stained jeans that were folded neatly on the top shelf. There was another stack of cleaner jeans next to the other stack, and I couldn't help but laugh.

"Organized man." I said as I dropped down to my knees and started to poke around the piles of boots at the bottom of the closet.

Instead of leaving them in a disorganized pile, my OCD took over, and I started to straighten and align the boots in order of size against the back wall. My efforts uncovered a safe that you had to have a handprint to get into, and I was proud of James for having that with a young child in the house.

A lot of parents didn't think about that detail, and it took an awful act of a child being curious to make them realize that just having guns laying around wasn't safe. It also didn't matter what income level, ethnicity, or party affiliate the gun owner was, it happened to everybody, gun safety or not.

I hit pay dirt once I reached the bottom of the shoe pile by finding a pair of Nike sandals that would tighten at the top of the foot.

Texas Tornado

"Yes," I hissed as I sat on my butt and slipped my feet into the sandals.

Yes, it'd be a clumsy walk, but I'd make it in no time with my determination. That, and it wasn't raining anymore.

Getting to my feet, I shuffled out the bedroom door and walked up to the living room window. Seeing no sign of movement, I used my ninja skills, and slunk out the back door and made my way around the side of the duplex, being careful to stay in the shadows that the morning sun casted.

Once I made it to the side of the garage, I looked to make sure that no one was in the lot, before walking sedately to the open front gate. I'd gotten to the road before my name was shouted.

Whom it was shouted by, I didn't know, but I didn't stop. In fact, I turned on the turbo blast, and took off like a shot. My adrenaline was pumping, and only pushed me faster. I so did not want to talk to anyone right now, and least of all my prick of a brother.

It'd been in my first hour on the floor of the bathroom that I decided just to say, 'fuck it' and ignore him from now on. I was tired of putting forth all the effort with my family and getting nothing in return. My dad. My brother. Brothers. Mother. No more, I was done. Finished.

"Fuck," a man grunted from a good distance behind me.

I let the first smile break over my face in weeks. Did I mention that I was a sprinter, as well as a long distance runner? Yeah, I kicked ass in high school. I broke state records in the 100-meter dash and the 400 meters.

Although my distance running was lacking compared to my sprinting, I still did good when I put my mind to it. Cross-country kept me in shape during the off-season, and I made myself stick with cross-country even though I hated it with every fiber of my being. Sprinters weren't made to go the distance.

Another curse sounded from behind me, and I let out a laugh this time. Spying my shortcut, which I rarely used lately due to the mud, I took it despite my reservations. I lost my sandals in the first mud puddle, and had to stop to go back for them, although, I didn't put them back on. I was in the forest now, and it was very unlikely there would be anything but twigs on the ground.

Yelling sounded somewhere behind me, but I kept going. My lungs had that good burn going, and I felt exhilarated.

Running was my therapy. Although I sucked balls at the distance, I kept doing it even though I hated it.

"I'm gonna beat your ass when I catch you, you little shit." Sam yelled.

I cackled. My ass he was going to catch me. I knew these woods like the back of my hand. I'd met with the owner, a lovely woman in her late seventies, and asked her if it would be all right. She'd readily agreed, saying I was a sweet 'child' and so I spent my days off exploring.

That, and hidden stashes of things in the woods, planned an escape route, and made maps of the woods for just in case.

"Mother fucking son of a bitch. Goddammit." Sam growled.

Brother bear has a potty mouth.

Texas Tornado

Ten minutes passed before I found my opening in the woods that would lead me beside the old shitty hotel grounds. I'd just stepped foot on the compact gravel when an arm, attached to a beefy torso, snuck its way around my torso and stopped me in my tracks.

The breath I'd just taken in gushed out of me, and I doubled over the arm as my feet left the ground.

I knew instantly who it was. James, with his tight ass covered in tight greasy blue jeans, tossed me over his shoulder just as I'd managed to get another breath.

"Put me down, you big bastard." I growled and started kicking.

"Not a chance, Speedy Gonzales." James laughed and headed to his big mother of a bike.

"No, really. Put me down. I have," I started, and then stopped abruptly. "What time is it?"

"Nine fifteen." He answered but didn't stop walking.

"An hour and forty five minutes before I have to be at my job interview. Not to mention that I have to walk because my truck broke down." I ground out.

Pushing up so my good arm rested on his back, I looked around for a possible escape route.

"And you didn't just ask one of us to drive you home because...why?" He asked.

I did notice that he'd veered from the direction of his bike and started to cross the street to the diner, and my apartment.

"Because I didn't want to see that big bonehead right there." I emphasized the insult with a finger pointed in my brother's direction as he finally made it out of the woods.

He glared at me as James laughed when he saw whom I was pointing at. "Yeah, I don't blame you. Let's get you dressed, and I'll take you to your interview. Where's it at?"

I didn't know. I meant to look it up when I was at the library a few days ago, but I'd forgotten. "The social services building."

"Okay, I know where that's at." He said as he started to climb the stairs.

"Thank you for taking care of me." I said to James' ass.

"You're welcome, Speedy." He said and set me down on my feet in the living room of my apartment.

I glared at him.

When I found that my glare didn't affect him at all, I went to the dresser that I'd scored off the side of the road, grabbed the outfit I'd set out on top of it days ago, and searched through my closet for my secondhand knee high boots.

Sam entered shortly after I made my way to the bathroom with my clothes, and I wanted to beat my head against the wall when a thrill of happiness shot through me at the idea of my brother actually paying attention to me.

I knew the first time I saw him that I'd totally forget every single thing I'd been telling myself for the past seven months. I was so starved for a connection that I would take anything I could get.

Surveying myself in the mirror, I grimaced at what I saw.

Texas Tornado

My eyes had dark bags underneath my eyes, my palm that I could see was scraped up and raw from my fall, and I had other scratches and bruises covering my arms. Grimacing at the sight, I walked to the shower and turned it on full blast.

I stepped in without waiting for it to get warm, because, let's face it, I'm not paying enough in rent to get a hot shower. I washed my hair as best as I could with one hand, soaped up my body, skipped shaving my legs, and hopped back out within five minutes.

I blow dried my hair, thanking God that I had great hair that blow dried straight and not frizzy, making it possible not to worry about a flat iron.

My makeup was minimal at best. Each movement of my arm caused pain to shoot through me, and I was gritting my teeth and saying that the makeup was done with just mascara and a little concealer.

I was dressed all the way up to the part where I had to zip, and then cursed myself. "Fuck, what the hell am I supposed to do now?"

Doing the only thing I could, I opened the door a crack and peered out at the apartment. James was reclining in my recliner with a dirty bathroom towel underneath him to keep the grease from transferring to the fabric.

Sam was propped up against the wall, just as silent as James, glowering at the wall in front of him.

Both men's eyes transferred to the door as it cracked open more and waited.

"I need someone to zip and button my pants." I said through the crack.

Sam's eyes went towards the ceiling, and James chuckled as he got up and made his way to the bathroom. He pushed it open without waiting, and his hands found their way to the zipper.

I sucked in the slight pudge of my belly, and silently cursed myself for the fries I'd snacked on the day before yesterday. I'd never be skinny. I've always had a slight 'chunkiness' to my build, no matter the amount of exercise I got in.

I thanked the good Lord above that the pants zipped and buttoned without popping a seam, and sighed as he took a step away from me.

The man was sex personified. He was so damn sexy that I wanted to throw myself at him. However, I'd learned better from my ex-boyfriend, Zander. The man had royally fucked me over when it came to men that I would forever hesitate to involve myself in another relationship.

I'd always think twice before making myself vulnerable again. Not to mention that James' hands were nearly twice the size of Zander's, which only meant that he'd hit twice as hard.

No thank you.

It didn't matter that I knew James would never hurt me. Push a man far enough and he'd retaliate. At least that's what I'd learned from past relationships.

I'd had two abusive boyfriends in my life that I'd managed to get out of before anything bad had happened. Then Sebastian had been hurt in his motorcycle wreck, and I'd lost my objectiveness. My head

Texas Tornado

was so worried about Sebastian and his son Johnny's well-being that I'd failed to watch over my own self.

By the time I'd figured it out, it was too late. I was already too deeply ensconced to get out, and Sebastian was too busy to be messed with. Who the hell knows where my father was, and who the hell cared.

James snapped his fingers in front of my face, and I ripped myself from my thoughts, blushing as I realized that I'd been staring at his dick for the last who the heck knows how long.

"Sorry." I muttered.

"No problem, Speedy. Anything else?" He asked.

I held my foot up in answer, and he bent down to zip the side of my boots up. "Make sure you get the pants tucked into the boots fairly well, or it'll look weird."

"I've been dressing a little girl for five years now. I think I can handle tucking your pants into your boots. At least you're not asking me to pull your wedgie out."

I snickered. "That girl of yours is a hoot."

His smile lit up the room. "Yeah, she is. I love the shit out of her. Now, I could do with a little less 'Daddy I've got snot in my hair' and a little more 'Daddy can we go watch a movie.' The girl sure has me wrapped around her little finger, though."

I smiled wistfully. I'd always wanted children. In fact, I wanted a house full. However, after the disaster that was Zander, I knew I probably would never have any. At twenty-six and three quarters, I still had a lot of time to have them, yet I wasn't so sure of my judgment at this point. I never wanted put an innocent child's life at risk, which equaled no kids for me.

I smiled at him and patted his hair. "So, you'd rather her grow up and start dating horny boys? Because that's what comes with the aging process."

His scowl would've made some women cringe back in fear, but not me. I may have been beaten, but I never stopped fighting. I wouldn't back down to anyone ever again, and I'd fight until my last breath.

Not to mention that his anger didn't seem to be directed at me, but at the thought of his little girl growing up. "It's okay. I know for a fact that daughters will always need their daddies."

His scowl morphed into a cool professional facade, which didn't surprise me much. My father was a taboo subject around them. Not that I could tell you why. From what little I knew of my father, he wasn't a bad man. Only a free spirit who wouldn't settle down.

"Whatever." I said as I turned on my heel and exited the bathroom.

"About time. How long does it take to zip up a pair of pants?" Sam said in exasperation.

"Well, first he had to help me put on a pair of panties and hook my bra. Then he had to help me get my wide hips into the pants. *Then* he zipped them." I smiled at him sweetly.

His eyes narrowed, and I could've sworn he looked pissed. Then I thought better of it. What did he have to be pissed about? According to him, I was nothing. An inconsequential person in his life that wasn't worth his time.

Sam's eyes went from my face to James' face as he exited the bathroom behind me. His hands went up in a 'don't shoot me' gesture, and he returned to his perch on my recliner.

Walking to the kitchen, I studied the clock for a few moments. It was fifteen passed ten, which meant I should leave shortly if I wanted to get there a little early.

"I have to go. Can either one of you tell me what's the best way to go?" I asked, turning to face the two men again, edging as inconspicuously towards the door as I could.

James didn't look like he noticed, but Sam came off the wall as soon as I made my first move in the direction of the door. "What the hell is your problem, and why are you running from us?"

I froze, and then my temper exploded. "What the fuck do you care, boyo? I don't owe you any explanation what so ever! Now, if you'll please see yourself out." I said as I stomped towards the door, opened it, and stomped down the stairs.

My broken arm throbbed, but I pushed it away, and kept with my forward motion.

"Smooth, Sam. Is that how you picked my sister up? Do you use those skills on all the ladies?" James chirped.

I contained my smile, heading back towards town.

I didn't make it far before the roar of a motorcycle growled to life, and James pulled up next to me on the street. "You know, it's really not safe for you to be walking out here like this. Some man could snatch you off the road, and we'd never know."

"They could try." I muttered, stopped, and turned towards him.

He smiled as he placed his giant clodhoppers onto the ground and waited for me to jump on. Handing me his helmet, I situated it over my head awkwardly, and then climbed on. It'd been a while, but I managed to mount the bike with a fair amount of ease, and scooted close to James, but not close enough that anything good was touching.

"You're gonna have to move closer to me if you don't want to fall off." He chuckled.

Reluctantly, I moved forward until my crotch was snug to his backside, and then wrapped my good hand around his chest, resting my casted hand on his thigh.

"Good girl." He said right before he patted my thigh with his large hand, and then took off like a rocket.

I squealed.

His laughter didn't bother me. I was a real girl when it came to bikes. I don't know a thing about them, only that they go fast, they're big, and they're chick magnets. I'd only ridden on them with my brother and Zander, but you could see the long lingering looks that women gave them.

The wind whipped my hair every which way, and I wondered why I even bothered to blow dry it. It would've saved me time if I'd just done it this way to begin with. I wouldn't have had to force myself to do it, which, in turn, wouldn't have made my arm hurt worse.

Texas Tornado

The ride was fairly short, I knew from my many explorations through town that we were in the historical district, but it wasn't near the courthouse as I'd assumed.

He stopped in front of a plain brick building with only a tinted glass door that had "Child Services of Rusk County" stamped on it with plain white letters. I reluctantly let my body slide from the bike, and barely held back the moan. My face was a different story, because James must've read something on it if the smirk that tilted up his lips was any indication.

"Thanks for the ride, James. I'll see you later." I said as I handed the helmet to him and turned my back on him.

"I'll be waiting." He yelled just as I reached the front door.

I turned to look over my shoulder. "Who says I'll need a ride?"

Obviously the opening I'd inadvertently given him was too good to pass up, because he smiled widely and said, "Oh, baby. You're more in need of a ride then anybody I know. Although, I'm not sure it has anything to do with a motorcycle."

I'd barely contained the palm/forehead slap I wanted to do after that line. Barely. However, I managed it as I opened the door to my possible future.

My last thought was that I'd absolutely kill for a ride from him. In a heartbeat.

Chapter 5

If his lips are gonna be on something I made, I'd rather it be a duck call.

-Jase-Duck Dynasty

James

Cursing as the phone in my pocket stopped ringing before I could answer it, I glanced at the screen and groaned.

Twenty seconds later, it started up again. "Hello?"

"Mr. Allen? This is Lillian McBride, with Child Protective Services. Is this a good time to speak with you?" No nonsense Lillian asked.

Gritting my teeth against the irony of being outside her very building while she was calling me, I managed a stark, "Yes."

"We've had another report filed against you. We would like to come out sometime in the next week to evaluate the allegation." She said formally.

No bullshitting with this one. The woman was a hardened shell of a woman. Although, I guess she would be. She'd seen it all in her fifty something years, and then some. The sad thing was, was that most of those 'things' she'd seen were all about children. Poorly treated, abused children.

"What is the report this time?" I asked with a frustrated sigh.

Texas Tornado

I'd had social services, as well as police, called on me at least once a month over Janie. My ex, Anna, decided that she wanted to be a part of Janie's life after all, and was using everything in her power to get it. What I hadn't figured out yet was why.

A little over a year ago, Anna had tried to say that Janie wasn't mine. Luckily, after a DNA test, it was proven that I was Janie's father, no longer giving her a leg to stand on. Then the stupid woman tried to sue for custody of Janie. Which didn't go well for me at all.

The judge that presided over the case was a man hating woman activist who hated me on principle. She didn't care that Anna had signed over her rights to Janie. All she cared about was doing what was best for women.

The bile still burns when I think about the court hearing that day.

***

Six months ago
Stevens v. Allen
Family Court of Rusk County

"Ms. Allen, can you tell me why you signed away your rights?" Anna's douche of a lawyer asked.

Anna struck a sad face and forced a lone tear to trail down her cheek. "James, I mean, Mr. Allen, told me he would force me to, and it would be best if I did it the easy way."

What a load of bullshit. I'd never done any such thing. I'd given her two months to come back before having my lawyer contact her.

She'd signed away her rights in front of a fucking judge for Christ's sake. I didn't force her to do anything.

Fucking bitch.

I heard Cheyenne and my mother's sharp inhalation behind me after Anna made her explanation, and I prayed that they both held it together. This shit wasn't easy for me either, but I was good at waiting.

A sniper had to be.

"No further questions." Mr. Douche smirked.

Chairs creaked as the occupants of their seats shifted while waiting to see what happened next.

My lawyer, Todd Masterson, stood and made his way to the box where Anna sat. She shifted uncomfortably at the power emanating from him, and I inwardly grinned.

The man was fucking awesome. Six feet four inches of hard muscle wrapped up in a sleek lawyer's suit. He'd been a marine for twelve years, and a lawyer for seventeen. He knew his shit, and I had every faith in him. After 9/11, he'd enlisted, and hadn't looked back since. He'd handled my affairs for the past six years, and my mother's before that.

"Ms. Steven's," Todd boomed, then flexed his hands. "Have you pursued any contact with Janie since you signed away your rights?"

Anna shifted again. "Well, three years ago I tried to see her, but that man," She pointed in Sam's direction. "Wouldn't let me, so I left."

Texas Tornado

Sam didn't shift when the scrutiny turned his way. In fact, his presence only seemed to multiply. The man was a fucking robot when he wanted to be. Not one thing could shake our captain. Oh, he could be angered, or upset, but you'd never be able to tell. He'd just kill you first. He'd slit your throat, facial expression never changing.

"Well, from what I understand from my records, that was four years ago. What exactly have you been doing since then?"

She didn't have an answer right off hand, so she took a few seconds to think about it. "Well, he told me that if I returned, that I wouldn't like it. I felt my life was in danger, so I stayed away." She finally answered.

"What did he say that made you feel threatened?"

"Objection." Mr. Douche yelled.

"Sustained. Mr. Masterson, please stay on topic."

I was confused as to why that wasn't on topic, but with the way that the judge kept glaring at me and Todd, I wasn't sure there was a reason. She was just that bad of a bitch. The woman was going to cost me custody of my daughter. I knew it.

Twenty minutes later, my fears were confirmed. At least partially.

"Ms. Stevens, I am granting you supervised visitation, with a chance of partial custody after five months if the third party supervisor confirms that you are worthy. Dismissed." The woman snapped, then clanged the gavel.

My stomach was at my feet. Janie didn't know her mother at all. That wouldn't stop her though. At six, she was very intelligent. I'd told her about her mother, about why she wasn't with her any longer.

Janie knew, on some level, that her mother wasn't there because her mother didn't want her. Therefore, Janie seeing her, even in a supervised setting, didn't sit well with me.

Unfortunately, there was nothing I could do about it just yet. Only figure out what Anna's ulterior motive was before she hurt my little girl.

***

The sigh that slipped out of Lillian's mouth surprised me. She was normally careful to be completely partial, but I had a feeling that Anna's false claims were wearing on her patience.

"The anonymous tip that was obtained says that you are bringing unconscious women that you've drugged home and then copulating with them. Where then you make them walk home." She finally said.

"Ummm, okay. I guess I'll see you soon. Mrs. Lillian." I said tightly, hanging up at her proper Goodbye.

What. The. Fuck.

I haven't had a woman in my house in five fucking years. That didn't mean I'd been celibate since then, but I sure haven't fucked any of them in front of my daughter.

Then what she'd said hit me, and I wanted to fucking kill someone.

An unconscious woman could very well be Shiloh. Although unconscious, I hadn't fucked her. I most certainly would've remembered that. The woman had been the star of my jerk off fantasies for seven and a half months now.

And if they had seen Shiloh being carried in by me last night, then that meant that they had eyes on me. "Motherfucker." I growled.

Yanking the phone out of my pocket and all but spit my words out to Sam on the other line. "Find him."

***

Shiloh

"Hello, Ms. Mackenzie," The woman who'd be doing my interview, Lillian, said before gesturing to a seat. "Please, have a seat. I'm sorry I was delayed. I had to make a quick phone call to someone about a case."

"That's okay, Mrs. McBride, I understand." I said once I was situated in my seat.

She sighed loudly, and I was startled. Lillian looked like a woman that would die before sighing, so I assumed the case was a bad one.

"Once you're hired on, I would love to go over this case with you. I've heard such good things about you. Captain Brady didn't have anything but nice things to say. He said you've helped a lot of children in your short time as a social worker." She explained.

Captain Brady was like a second father to me. He knew my dad, and was always there when I needed something. He'd also helped me sign on with the Galveston PD when I was nothing more than eighteen newbie. I'd been a police dispatcher while I went to school for my Social Services degree.

"Yeah, Captain Brady is a great man." I agreed.

I had to force myself not to say hell of a great man. I'm not sure how that worked with a job interview. After working at the police department around a bunch of men, as well as my brother, I just didn't have the vocabulary of a debutante. I swear like a sailor, and it's not often that I curb it. However, I'd do just about anything to get out of my current job, even if it meant changing my attitude for the time being.

"You have impeccable references. However, I'm a little concerned about the notice you gave with your previous employer. He did say that you left without notice." She said, her stare holding mine unflinchingly.

"Yes, ma'am. Without telling you my life story, I had some trouble with an ex-boyfriend of mine. He wouldn't take no as an answer, so I moved out of town." I explained.

I didn't tell her that I'd found out I had a brother, and then started digging into my father. I wanted to know more about Sam, and that inevitably cost me my job, my life, and my happiness. Sure, my ex was definitely not my favorite person, but I would never give a man that much of a hold over me.

Part of it was true, so we'd just go with the less descriptive explanation.

Her mouth pursed when she heard the story of my ex, and I knew I had the job.

"I'd like to start you out on a probationary period. It's customary for all new hires. I don't see you as having a problem with it. Once you've worked here for 90 days, we'll have an evaluation of your performance, you'll get a raise if we deem you worthy, and then your benefits will kick in. How does all this sounds?"

"Sounds perfect. When would you like me to start?" I asked almost giddily.

I tried really hard not to bounce in my seat like a teenager high on Edward Cullen and his glittery super awesomeness, and I was 99 percent effective. I couldn't control the bounce of my leg, however.

"Tomorrow morning. We don't come in until nine a.m. You're more than welcome to come in at eight if you need a lunch break, but most of the office just come in and eat at our desks. We work until five, most days, but there will be the off chance that you have to work late due to a case. You'll have certain cases that are assigned to you, but don't hesitate to ask me or anyone else in the office for help." She smiled.

"You'll be given your own car; feel free to use it when you need to, just don't overdo it. Umm, what else?" She asked as she tapped her pencil on the desk. "Oh! Never go in a residence if you feel unsafe. Trust your gut instinct. We have police officers that are on call for us when we need them."

I understood that completely. Many of the children that were in the system lived in a potentially dangerous environment. There was no way we could know if that same threat against the child was posed against us as well.

"I understand." I whispered.

"Well, if that's all, we will see you in the morning. You'll get your car then as well." She said standing and holding out her hand.

I shook it, and she led me out into the main office again. "Have a good rest of the day, dear. I'll see you bright and early!"

I nodded my head and smiled, then pushed the door open. I was momentarily blinded by the sunshine, and it took me a few minutes to adjust. James wasn't there, which really didn't surprise me much. Bum me, yes, it did. Surprise me? No.

I glanced up at the clouds that were moving by at what felt lie the speed of light, and looked further into the distance to see black clouds on the horizon. Then my broken arm started to throb, and I closed my eyes willing the pain away.

"Great. Just fucking great." I growled and started down the sidewalk.

"What's great?" James asked.

Screeching like a banshee and jumping four feet in the air, I whirled and turned towards the alley that I was in the process of passing. James was straddling his bike, both elbows resting on the gas tank and crossed. He was staring at me with amusement on his face, and I wanted to punch him in the nose.

"My arm hurts." I snapped.

His smile fell away instantly, and he stood, still straddling the bike, and fished out a bottle of pills from his pocket. "Here, I got these filled for you while you were in your interview."

I smiled warmly at him, feeling like a complete ass. "Thank you. I really do appreciate it."

He flipped the saddlebag on his right side open and pulled out a Coca Cola, handing it to me after I had a pill in my hand. Shoving the pill bottle in my purse, I took the drink from him, grimacing inwardly. I hated Coke, but anything was better than my throbbing arm right about now.

"You don't like Coke?" He asked as he saw me make a disgusted face after I drank.

"No." I said, handing the offending drink back to him.

"Weird." He said, taking a swig.

"When I was younger, that used to be the only thing my mother would have on hand. It didn't take long for me to attribute starvation to the taste of Coke." I said without thinking.

"You starved?" He barked.

I jumped at the bite of anger in his tone. "Yeah, I guess you could say that. The only time we ate well was when dad came for a visit. Things would get better for a while after that, but it didn't stay that way. Whether it was because she ran out of money, or just plain didn't care what my father would do is beyond me."

He didn't say anything, and I didn't want him to. I didn't want anybody's pity. Instead of allowing more questions, I started walking back down the sidewalk. James cursed behind me and started the bike up.

The alley seemed to amplify the loud rumble of the motor, and I had to smile. It sounded like a monster.

Said beast pulled up beside me on the sidewalk. "Get on. I'll take you home."

"I can't. I have to go find some appropriate work clothes. Lucky for me it's business casual."

"I'll take you wherever you would like to go. Come on."

The rest of the afternoon was spent at the Goodwill and a few consignment shops. What most people don't realize is that there is actually good stuff at these places. Even before I was forcibly moved to Kilgore, I shopped at the Goodwill. I just didn't have it ingrained in me to pay full price for something that I could get nearly twenty five times cheaper somewhere else.

"If you don't mind, I need to run home real quick to make sure I get Janie off the bus, and then I'll drop you off back at your place."

He didn't wait for my acquiescence though, just pointed the bike in the wrong direction and roared off.

We actually caught Janie's bus when we were about a mile away from Free, and James and I laughed at the googly eyes that all the children were giving us. Janie waved frantically from her seat at the front of the bus, and James played the doting father, waving back to his baby while still keeping a close watch on the road.

Once we got to the bus stop, a very excited Janie, whose feet were moving faster than her mind, tumbled off the bus. James made a move to get up and help his baby up, whom was now crying, but I gave him a pat, signaling that I would handle it. He was in an awkward position with my bags, and me all on the bike behind him, and I felt it prudent to help in any way I could.

"You okay, sweetie?" I cooed as I dropped down next to Janie on the dust.

The bus driver yelled a goodbye, and pulled away, leaving us in silence, minus the soft crying coming from Janie. "Y-yes."

Texas Tornado

"What happened, punkin' head?" I asked, smoothing her blonde wispy flyaway hairs back against her scalp.

Tear tracks ran in straight lines down her cheeks, and she looked absolutely pitiful. The wound itself was fairly basic, scraped knees that everyone dreads, but overall she was in good health.

"I fell off the fucking bus." She said in one of the sweetest voices I'd ever heard.

"You sure did punkin' head. You know that's a bad word. You really shouldn't say that." I scolded gently as I helped her to her feet.

"I know. I heard Uncle Max say it yesterday while he was working on the Dyna we have in the shop." She said with absolutely no apology anywhere in sight.

"Yes, that's a boy thing. Girls shouldn't cuss. What kind of Dyna was he working on?" Liar, liar, pants on fire. I was going to hell. My mouth could compete with a Marine's vocabulary with ease.

"It was a 2002 Dyna Super Glide. It's really pretty. Uncle Max was replacing the brakes because the dumbass who owns it doesn't know what the fuck he's doing. Says the Dyna was too much bike for a banker douche like him, but at least it wasn't one of those pocket rockets that guys with small dicks normally like to ride." She explained.

Do not laugh. Do not laugh.

My eyes raised from Janie's hazel ones to the identical ones of her father's and I saw the mirth floating around in his eyes, trying just as hard as me not to laugh his ass off, too.

"Honey, what have I told you? What goes on in the garage stays in the garage. We don't repeat bad words anywhere else but there. Got it?" He asked with a twinkle in his eye, and then stooped down to kiss her skinned knee.

"Yes, daddy. It feels all better. Can I have a beer now?" She asked with a pouty lip.

"Sure thing baby. I bet there's a few in the garage fridge. Why don't you go check?" He asked as he stood to his full height.

Janie didn't wait another second. One second she was leaning into her father, and the next she was halfway up the drive.

James turned from watching his daughter's retreat to studying my face. "I really don't give her beer."

I laughed. "Yeah, I got that. Root Beer?"

"Yep. They come in those little baby cans that don't even seem worth it. The guys make sure it's always stocked with her favorite. Otherwise they have to hear her complain." He snickered.

"I'm sure she doesn't complain in the slightest. What I think happens is that y'all spoil the shit out of her." I said as I walked up to the garage and watched as Elliott opened her baby can of root beer for her.

"Thank you, Lott. I love you." She said in her little pixie voice.

If it were possible, Elliott would've melted into a puddle of goo onto the floor. He reached his hand down and ran his knuckles on her cheek in a loving gesture, then pulled her ponytail.

"Hey!" She said with indignation.

Texas Tornado

Her shout was followed by a shot to the balls, which, luckily, Elliott had the wherewithal to block. He wasn't able to block the frog to his thigh, though. Which caused him to start jumping around crying out. It was a good act. That is if he was actually acting.

"You taught her that didn't you?" I laughed.

"Uhh, no. That would be Ember. She felt that she needed to know how to defend herself. She's got one hell of a right hook, too." He agreed, eyes watching his daughter as she walked to the bike that Sam was working on, then taking a seat next to him on her own stool.

"You want to talk to him?" He asked.

My eyes snapped to James' face and I flushed. Dammit. All it took was one freakin look at my brother and I started to wish I had him as a friend. My head kept saying 'Caution, Keep Out!' but my heart kept saying, 'That's your brother. He needs you as much as you need him.'

"No." I choked. "I would like to go home, though. I can walk. Looks like that storm passed us by."

A car pulled into the parking lot behind us, but I ignored it in favor of watching my feet.

"It didn't. It just hasn't reached us yet. Are you sure you don't want to stay another day? I don't mind. Janie and I love guests. Every once in a while it's nice to have someone to talk to that doesn't tell me how much she loves GI Joe and Iron Man." He said, placing his palm on the small of my back.

Tiny little shivers sparked from his hand, down to parts lower that hadn't seen the light of day in well over a year.

The warmth that his touch had caused took a flying leap off the proverbial cliff when an absolutely adorable woman stepped out of a silver Fusion. She was short, reminding me of Payton and Blaine. Short blonde hair that gathered around her shoulders in choppy layers brought attention to her face, which reminded me of those baby dolls that have the blush painted on in the perfect circles on their cherub cheeks.

"Hey, Jamie." The woman said, blushing even more perfectly.

She was honestly the most adorable woman I'd ever seen, and I hated her.

The loss of James' touch at my back was like a cool bucket of water being poured over my skin. His arms opened wide, and I had to step out of the way to make sure I wasn't mowed down by the little sprite.

Stupid Tinkerbelle.

You know, in Peter Pan, Tinkerbelle was a real bitch. She wasn't nice in the slightest, and I always wonder why Disney portrayed her as this cute little fairy, when in reality she was Satan's spawn.

I contemplated the horridness of that sneaky little bitch as I walked down the driveway, and down the road. When I got to the cutoff through the woods, I decided it was best to go ahead and take the shortcut seeing as James was right, and the dark clouds of black were currently straight above me.

Then I cursed myself for getting jealous and leaving when I should have just stayed and waited. But when I saw James' arms wrap

Texas Tornado

around that woman, something in my chest caught, and I felt the need to run.

I'd experienced enough of that feeling for a lifetime, and I was definitely not standing around watching a man I had a crush on macking on some woman. No sir-ree-bob.

Chapter 6

Roses are red, Foxes are clever. I like your butt, let me touch it forever.

-Redneck Love Poem

James

"Jolie, how are you?" I asked her, quite frankly surprised that she even showed up.

The last time we'd seen each other, a couple months ago, was when I was on a date. She'd acted like I was the devil incarnate. Then her friend had died in his motorcycle wreck, and she'd called to see if I could fix it.

Now that I'd seen it, I was pretty sure nothing short of scrapping it would work with it. There was just nothing salvageable to be had; it just looked like one large pile of metal that was welded together.

The wreck had to have been horrific.

"I'm doing okay, Jamie." She smiled sadly, and then the tears started falling.

I pulled her into my arms again, and she went willingly. I was a sucker for tears. Didn't matter who cried, man, woman, or child. They killed me, and I'd do just about anything to make them stop short of walking away.

I'd held her the night that her father had killed my best friend, too. I wanted her to know that no one blamed her, even though she blamed herself. She'd come to the hospital to offer her condolences. At first, I'd thought it was only to make sure her father was all right, but she never even went to the nurse's station to check on her dad. Instead, she went straight to Briggs' parents and dropped down to her knees apologizing profusely.

Jolie was a nobody. She had nobody. She needed nobody.

She'd slipped into my heart that day, and stayed there. Even now, twelve years later, I still cared for her. Although once I'd thought it was romantically, I now feel different about her, in a way that a good friend cares about another good friend.

"Daddy?" Janie asked from beside me.

I let Jolie go, and stepped away from her to crouch down so I was eye level with Janie. "Yeah, baby?"

"Where did your friend go? I wanted to show her the Dyna, but I can't find her anywhere." Janie asked.

I stood quickly, scanning the parking lot and surrounding area for Shiloh.

Shit!

How long had she been gone? I hadn't even noticed that she'd left!

"Max!" I yelled and turned to him.

"What?" He grunted, eyes moving from the tire he was trying to get off a Mustang to me.

He wasn't Jolie's biggest fan. He'd always felt that she was manipulative. I'd always thought that she was just a sweet girl needing attention. We agreed to disagree.

"Did you see where Shiloh went?" I asked, trying to keep the panic out of my voice.

"Yeah," He grunted again, one of the lug nuts finally giving way. "Walked down the driveway and North on Second. Why?"

"Fuck," I growled. "She can't get in. I have her new key since I had better locks installed."

I didn't want to leave Jolie in her upset state, but there was no way I was just leaving Shiloh out in the rain.

"Hey, man. Can you hang out with Jolie here for a few while I run these over?"

I knew his answer would be no. The man really didn't like being left with Jolie. Never had. Said she changed when I wasn't around. I'd never witnessed it, even when I'd tried to be sneaky.

"She's got a perfectly capable brother over there. Not to mention, she looked pretty pissed when she left. I'd be willing to bet she didn't even go home." He said as he worked the final lug nut free, making the tire lean to the side awkwardly.

Then the first sound of thunder boomed in the distance, making my decision for me. "Okay, Jolie. I gotta go. I'm sorry." I said as I grabbed her into another tight hug before releasing her.

"It's o-okay. I'll be f-fine." She said as she turned on her heel and practically ran to the car.

As if I didn't already feel bad enough, the girl always had a way to make me feel worse than I already did. Especially that night I'd caught her trying to fuck the worst bully in the school.

Texas Tornado

"Why do you let her do that to you? She treats you like her little lap dog." Max huffed.

Ignoring him, I grabbed Janie by the hand and walked her to the back of the garage.

"Come on, Janie. Let's go get the truck and find Shiloh."

"She can stay with me. As long as the harpy isn't here, I'm good." He said as he stood and gestured to Janie. "Come here, kemosabe. Let's see if we can get this POS working."

"I don't like that Harpy either." Janie whispered.

Although, like all kids, it was louder than her normal voice, so everyone that was eavesdropping in the garage heard what she'd said and chuckled.

Bastards.

***

Shiloh

My door had two shiny new locks on it, as well as a shiny new brass door handle. What the fuck? Did Marjorie change the locks while I was gone?

Sure, I was getting this place for a song, but that didn't mean she could just go and change the locks without telling me. Or letting me get my things out first. She never struck me as the type to be vindictive, so what reason did she have to change them while I was gone?

I planted my foot, spun on my heels, and just made it the first step down when the skies opened up. A-fucking-gain.

"Shit." I hissed trying to cover my arm with my body to reduce the chance of it getting sopping wet.

By the time I made it into the diner, the majority of my body was drenched, and I cursed Marjorie for having my locks changed without telling me. Crazy old bat.

Lizzie, a young mother of three, glanced up from the coffee she was pouring at the bar when I scrambled inside. "You look pretty awful." She mused.

"Thanks. Marjorie around?" I asked.

"She was here early this morning, but I haven't seen her since." She said putting the coffee pot on the warmer.

"I was trying to figure out why..." I was explaining when the roundness of Lizzie's eyes went to the size of saucers. "What?"

Her mouth worked like a fish, and I turned around very slowly to find a huge ass gun aimed right at my face. The barrel of the gun looked massive, and I couldn't help but wonder what the bullet that came out of the gun would do to my face when it took me out.

Fuck.

My eyes traveled from the gun's excessively large barrel to the masked man that was holding it. His stance was twitchy and unsure, but the gun never wavered. "Bring her out here!" He roared.

"W-who?" I asked. The hitch in my breath made it apparent that he was scaring the absolute shit out of me.

"Marjorie!" He roared.

I flinched at the vehemence in his voice. God, but I just couldn't freakin' win. My life was one huge clusterfuck to the tenth degree.

Texas Tornado

Here I was, twenty-six, going on twenty-seven, and I was about to die. Alone. Unloved.

Hooray.

Fuck it. If I was going to be shot, I damn sure won't be going out without trying to fight.

***

James

"Okay, where the fuck are you?" I growled as I came back down the stairs of Shiloh's apartment.

I rounded the corner to the diner and my heart nearly stopped.

Shiloh had her hands hanging down limply at her sides standing next to the bar. A young woman, twenty two at most, was behind the bar, mouth slack jawed and her hands up by her ears, and a man in his late sixties who resembled a grizzly bear with his wild brown hair and large round body stood in front of them both with a .357 revolver pointed straight at Shiloh's face.

My basic survival instincts, the ones that were honed to a razor sharp point in the deserts of Iraq and Afghanistan, the ones that kept me and most of my brothers alive during the most brutal of times, took over. My vision sharpened, my hearing fine-tuned, my adrenaline coursed thickly through my veins. The rapid beat of my heart thumped an erratic tattoo against the wall of my chest.

When my eyes stayed locked on the man with the gun, even when Shiloh's scream ripped down my spine and settled deep in my gut. My hand tightened minutely on the gun that I had in my hand, even though I had no knowledge of pulling it. Nor did I have knowledge of aiming it.

However, I found myself with one eye closed, staring down the length of the barrel. Tritium sights framing the large man's center mass, ready to pull the trigger. With one breath, I found my calm. The next, I pulled the trigger.

***

"Mr. Allen, can you please repeat what happened again one more time?" Detective Pierson Howell asked with condescension dripping like acid from his every word.

"Are you arresting me?" I finally asked.

"No. I'm just trying to procure what happened here. Some things don't line up." He ground out.

"I've already explained the encounter in its entirety. I've explained what I saw happen. I explained that I couldn't afford to wait, that I felt like the situation would deteriorate very fast. Therefore, if I'm not under arrest, then I'll be leaving. I have a young daughter at home, as well as an inconsolable woman to take care of. If you'll excuse me, *Detective*." I snapped and turned.

Detective Pierson didn't like the way I said detective, and I saw his hackles rise as soon as I said it. "Oh, yes. I've heard about the allegations that are being filed against you. Tell me, is it true? Do you rape your daughter?" He droned from directly behind me.

I froze. My hands clenched, and my body tensed in anticipation.

Texas Tornado

My eyes rose and my mouth opened, but Shiloh, who was standing to my right, erupted. I say erupted, because there were no other words for what happened next. She simply exploded.

"You have got to be kidding me!" She screeched.

The men and women loitering, as well as the crime scene techs, male and female officers, and brothers, froze and watched the explosion unfold.

"This man," Shiloh gestured to me with her pointer finger. "This man saved my mother fucking life! That man was about to blow my head off. He had a fucking .357 pointed at my face. Do you know what a .357 does to a watermelon? It fucking explodes. Every fucking inch. There is no way you would ever be able to fit those pieces together again."

She got closer as her temper raged. The next thing I knew, she was in Pierson's face, finger millimeters from his chest. She knew better than to touch him, but that didn't stop her from rising on the tips of her toes and getting in his face.

"And the nerve. The guts it takes to imply that this man," Another finger pointed in my direction. "to say that this man *rapes* his child."

"You don't know their relationship. You don't see how he dotes on her. Gives her everything she needs and wants. Adores her. He would never, ever, do anything so vile as to rape his daughter. To even imply that is so beyond the element of reason that it's practically hilarious. That man would castrate anyone that even thought about harming his daughter. He'd chop off their balls, open a gash in their belly, and make them bleed. You are a pathetic use for human flesh, and I will see your superior officer about this. You will be taken off this case so fast your fucking head will spin."

Snickers were the only thing that could be heard through the crowd.

Shiloh stepped back from Pierson, but as she did, her foot hit an uneven spot in the ground, and she pitched forward into the detective. He took that opening as an attack on his person, and moved.

Shiloh went down hard onto the pavement. Her face smashed into the wet grass that lined the side of the parking lot. Her face narrowly missed hitting the curb by mere millimeters. The pink cast that encased her arm didn't. It smashed into the unforgiving concrete with a thud, and she cried out in agony.

"Get off her!" I snarled.

I knew better than to touch him, but it took everything I possessed to stop me.

"You are under arrest, anything you say or do..." Pierson snarled, pushing Shiloh into the grass even harder, yanking her hands behind her back so hard and tight that her back bowed with the effort to keep her shoulders from pulling out of the socket.

I was mere milliseconds from going for Pierson's beady little eyes when a black wall of muscle plowed into Pierson, having him face first in the asphalt of the diner's parking lot in the next heartbeat.

Ignoring Sam's attempt to rein in his temper and not beat the ever-loving shit out of Pierson for daring to lay his hands on his baby sister, I went to Shiloh and helped her sit up. Her hand went to her casted one and she cradled it close to her chest, but her face was set in grim determination.

"You okay, Shiloh?" I said, dropping to my knees and pulling her into the wall of my chest.

"Pissed, but okay." She said.

"Get off me!" Pierson screeched.

My eyes followed the screeching sounds, and I very nearly laughed. Sam had Pierson detained with a knee in the small of Pierson's back, and one hand keeping his hands behind his back, much the same way he'd done to Shiloh.

"Oh, does this not feel good, you prick? Do you not like it when you get treated the same way you just treated an innocent woman? I don't give a goddamn if you're the fucking queen of England. You will never touch my fucking sister again, do you hear me?" He shouted in Pierson's ear.

Pierson cowered away from him, his head turning, pleading practically for help from his fellow officers. None of it came.

"Do you see what is being done to me, you imbecile?" He sneered at the closest officer.

The man, one I'd seen from time to time around town, was a good man. He had a wife and new kid at home, and loved to show off pictures of his little boy. That same man who loved his kid so much turned his back on a fellow officer and walked further away from the scene.

Pierson tried it three more times with three other officers, all ranging from rookies to the most seasoned officers, all walked away and left him on his own.

"Now, I'm gonna let you go, but I better not find you even thinking about my sister again. James is off limits, too. You have an airtight story from him and eight other witnesses. Stop being a little prick and do your job." He hissed as he shoved off him and stood.

We'd had our first run-in with Detective Pierson last year when Winter shot an intruder in her bedroom. Ever since then, we'd had the displeasure to be on his 'list.' He made it a habit to make sure we were on the up and up. Every once in a while he'd drop by on the pretense of having a 'talk' while subtly taking stock of everything that we said or did for the half hour he managed to weasel out of us.

"She attacked me!" He whined nasally.

Luke, a good friend and police officer, chose that moment to finally make his presence known. "Peterson, you're fucking nuts if you thought she was attacking you. She's about half your size and you easily have a hundred pounds on her. Knock it the fuck off before they try to charge you with something you can't weasel or bribe your way out of."

Shiloh started to rise. I helped her stand, and wrapped my arm around her waist for support. Luke turned and studied Shiloh before sighing and turning to Sam.

"Since this is a crime scene, she's going to need to find a place to stay. I can't let her up to her apartment until tomorrow evening at the earliest." Luke sighed as he turned and surveyed the area.

"She's right here. You don't have to talk to her brother. It's not the seventeenth century, douchebag." Shiloh scolded.

I smiled despite my horrible mood, and then outright laughed when I saw the surprise overtake Luke's face. "Ahh, Luke. You should know better."

"She's going to come home with me." Sam growled.

"Like fuck." Shiloh laughed.

Sam's scowl turned ferocious as he pinned Shiloh with it. "What?"

"Just because you decided to be a brother for once in your miserable existence doesn't mean I'm going to fall head over heels in love with the idea that you actually want something to do with me now. It's going to take a lot more than that. Plus, I might annoy you in the middle of the night. I think I'll take my chances with the hookers over there." She pointed at the fleabag motel across the street.

Sam winced. "Look, Shiloh…"

"Don't 'look Shiloh' me. I don't care. I. Don't. Care. You're a shithead, and I'm not ready to talk to you yet. I'm still nursing my snit. Maybe after a few times of you proving that you can be more than a giant douchebag, I'll actually spend some time with you."

Sam seemed to deflate at her words. Guilt and disappointment flashed in his eyes before he covered them with a blank expression. He nodded once, and then turned to Luke to speak about what had happened.

"You'll stay with me." I told her.

"Okay." She agreed.

Knowing that was too easy, I turned to her with raised brows.

She looked guilty for a moment before smiling wide. "My clothes are already at your house, along with my cat. There's no reason not to stay with you. In fact, it makes more sense to stay with you. But, keep your hands to yourself. Also, try to keep the fucking with your girlfriend at a minimum. I need silence to sleep at night."

"Girlfriend?" I asked flabbergasted.

"Yeah, that girl who you had your arms wrapped around today. That girlfriend."

"I don't have a girlfriend. That was just a friend."

"Right." She scoffed.

"She was." I snapped.

"Whatever you say."

"Not to mention the fact that I have a six year old at home. There won't ever be any loud fucking there." I said somewhat wistfully.

In truth, I wanted more from Shiloh than just to have her under my roof. I wanted her under me. I wanted her sweet delicious, curvy body underneath mine, writhing and straining while I thrust wildly inside her. I wanted to fuck her so hard that she screamed. Yet that would never happen, now or later, no matter if Janie was there or not.

I couldn't let it. My heart wouldn't be able to withstand Shiloh, the Texas Tornado. I'd been gutted and burned before, and I wasn't sure I could handle it from Shiloh. She was a force to be reckoned with.

Chapter 7

Teach your girl to shoot, because a restraining order is just a piece of paper.

-Life Lesson

Shiloh

"Hey there, Boris." I said to my cat, who'd made himself at home in James' kitchen sink.

"You know, that's an industrial sized sink." James supplied with a smile evident in his voice.

He stepped to the side of the counter and watched as Boris caught a drop of water that'd leaked out of the faucet. Which was normal for him. I never bother to leave him a bowl. I just turn the faucet on to where it'd drip every few minutes.

"He's a big boy. I found him on the side of the road on one of my many walks home." I explained. "He startled me, and I fell."

He laughed, like I'd intended. "Why does that not surprise me?"

"It shouldn't. I'm a very clumsy person. Although the only accident I've ever been in was when I backed into my first boyfriend's car when I was sixteen. He smacked me, but then my brother kicked his ass and beat the shit out of his car with a sledge hammer." I smiled wistfully.

James had a scowl the size of the Grand Canyon on his face. "I'd have done the same."

"Yeah? Well, Cheyenne is a pretty wonderful woman. I sure wish I'd have gotten a chance to get to know her." I agreed.

"Cheyenne wasn't who I was talking about, but I do agree with you, she's a pretty good sister. Why does it sound like you're leaving?" He asked with another frown on his face.

I ignored that question. I'd taken the job with social services, but it was a temporary position, pending availability for a job opening, while a woman took medical leave after she'd given birth.

"I didn't thank you yet, and I should. That was a pretty complicated shot." I observed.

He nodded his head, a saddened look entering his eyes. "I was a sniper in the army. It was an easy shot. Try over three quarters of a mile away, and then get back to me. What time do you have to be at work in the morning?"

Guess he didn't want to speak about blowing a guy's head up like a watermelon dropping on to concrete. At least he wasn't wearing the man's brain like I was. Speaking of which, I needed a damn shower in the worst way.

"Nine. Can I use the shower?" I asked, then headed in the direction of the bathroom I'd glanced at earlier.

"What would you do if I'd have said no?" He asked drolly from behind me.

"Showered anyway, of course," I smiled and flipped the light on in the bathroom before coming to a standstill, mouth open in fascination. "Wow!"

Texas Tornado

That's all that came to mind when I saw the bathroom. In a way, it was fucking awesome, but it was a little much to handle at first.

"Yeah, Janie got to choose the decorations," he laughed.

"Well, I have to say, that it is definitely interesting. She's a little obsessed, though." I laughed with him.

I couldn't say that at six I was any better. However, where I was obsessed with My Little Pony, Janie was obsessed with motorcycles; which I guess was to be expected.

The bathroom was a plethora of Harley Davidson. Orange walls with black stripes. Motorcycle Fatheads adorned the wall behind the bathroom door. Motorcycle toothbrush holder and soap pump. The hand towels were black. Everything matched perfectly, that is until you got to one thing.

"Why the white curtain and rug? It seems a little out of place." I said with a raised brow.

He bellowed with laughter now.

"Oh, you'll see...." He said cryptically. "Towels are in the closet. Just shove all the toys to the side. I'll go take a shower, too. Then we can figure out something for dinner."

With that comment, he left, shutting the door quietly behind him.

The shower felt glorious. I scrubbed my skin until it turned a bright pink with a bar of soap that smelled like bubble gum. I washed my hair with Johnson's baby shampoo, secretly enjoying the baby fresh scent.

Turning the shower off, I stepped out onto the white bath mat, and then closed the shower curtain behind me. Then I burst out laughing.

"Oh, my God!"

Janie's only two things that didn't match were the shower curtain and the rug. However, I could see why she'd bought them. I hadn't noticed in the shower, but now that I'd turned around and got a good look at the curtain, I couldn't miss the bloody handprint that showed up. Whether it was from the heat or the wetness, I didn't know.

The bath mat was more of the same. Each drop of water showed up red, and you could clearly see two perfect prints of my feet from where I'd stepped on it when I got out of the shower. Each drip of water off my body only added to the effects.

How cool!

It wasn't until I was done admiring Janie's decorating skills, however, that I comprehended that I didn't have anything to wear other than blood-splattered clothes. Sneaking out into the hallway with a towel wrapped securely around my chest, I tiptoed into James' room in hopes of getting a t-shirt before he got out of his own bath.

His bathroom door was cracked slightly, and I could hear the pound of water hitting tile, and the sound of James moving around. It wasn't until I got to James' dresser that I realized that I could see through the crack in his door.

What I saw made me gasp. Whether in appreciation or apprehension, I didn't know.

Texas Tornado

At first, I didn't notice the man standing under the spray. I noticed the difference between his bathroom and Janie's bathroom. White walls, black towels, and practically boring décor that managed to draw the eye, rather than bore it. There was no shower curtain in his, only a clear glass that went from ceiling just about waist level, and from there the glass became frosted.

James was standing there, water streaming from the faucet above his head, falling down his body in rivulets. Head hung. His muscular arms were up high above his head, holding on to the top of the glass with both hands. His chest was clear of any tattoos except for a lone crosshairs tattoo centered over a skull right over his heart. I could also clearly see the peak of something black sneaking up over his shoulder from his back.

He was wearing a pair of dog tags that fell to about pec level, drawing attention to his muscular chest, and rock hard abs. I followed the ridges of his stomach lower until my gaze was interrupted by the different colored glass. Disappointment settled in my gut as I wished that the stupid frosted glass wasn't there. Then maybe I could see the other half of his body. Specifically the cock I'd felt through his clothes earlier when he was holding me.

While I was trying to will away the glass covering his lower half, one of his hands came down, rubbing down his chest, abs, and then lower. My eyes flew to his face, and I watched as his face went from blank, to a picture of pleasure in the next second.

He growled low in his throat, and I let my eyes devour his body. The motion of his hand behind the frosted glass could only be one thing. His hand was moving slow at first, and I watched as the muscles in his arms, chest, and abs tensed and relaxed with each movement. Slowly, he picked up speed until his whole body was tensing in anticipation of his release.

Arm pumping fast, I could now hear the 'slap, slap' of skin against skin.

Unconsciously, I let my own hand sneak down until I was touching myself as well. My middle finger working my clit at the same speed that James' hand was moving on his cock. Somewhere in the back of my mind, I realized that what I was doing was so very wrong, but what would it hurt to watch?

I found that out a few seconds later when he came with a grunt. His eyes snapped open, and then his lust-filled eyes locked to mine. My own orgasm coursed through me, but there was nothing I could do but let it flow through me.

I told myself to run. To move my feet. To get out of there.

Yet my feet stayed locked in place as the shower door opened, and I got my first good look at James' massive appendage. With a freaking piercing. In his freaking penis.

"Mother fucker," I breathed.

His smirk pointed out that my comment didn't go unnoticed by him. He grabbed the closest towel off the towel rack and started drying himself off with practical motions. First his shoulders and chest, then down to his legs. His hair, and finally his package.

All the while I watched, willing myself to move.

Texas Tornado

The door opened all the way, and he walked up to me slowly, as if he was scared I'd run if he moved too fast. "Like what you saw?"

All I could do was nod. "I-I came for a t-t-shirt. My clothes are dirty." I stuttered.

Grabbing a t-shirt off the end of the bed as he passed, he stopped in front of me, feet inches away from my own. Reaching down, he slowly pulled my hand, and my face flamed when I realized that my hand was still buried in between my legs.

What he did next floored me.

Bringing my hand up, he pulled the two fingers I'd been using to stroke my clit, and sucked them into his mouth. Running the length of his tongue along each finger, sucking and licking the juices from them.

My face flamed for a different reason this time. Desire.

"Maybe next time you can join..." James started to say, but then was interrupted by the front door banging open, and then slamming shut.

"Daddy! I'm hungry! Cheyenne sent me home. She said I needed a bath, and to ask you for dinner. They were eating broccoli rice shit. I didn't want to eat with her ass anyway." Janie griped.

Nothing could've been more effective.

The desire I'd been feeling was instantly replaced with shock, then my flight instinct kicked in and I ran to his bathroom, slamming the door behind me.

My God. What have I just done?

***

I emerged from the confines of the bathroom fifteen minutes later. When the cool air of his bedroom hit my face, I was relieved to see James nowhere in sight. I could hear James low deep voice speaking with the high-pitched one of his daughter's, and laughed when I heard the conversation.

"Daddy, can we color tonight?" Janie asked.

"As long as it's on paper."

A muttered curse had James' stifling a snort, but then he scolded her. "Janie, sometime this week you're going to have someone else come visit you. Don't say any bad words in front of them, okay?"

That brought up another question I'd meant to ask him. What did that cop mean by being investigated? Would my new job ask me to do that? I'd have to tell them no, and then they'd want to know why.

It'd be a good idea to at least find out why before I'm brought into the middle of it.

Slipping on the sweat pants that were so nicely laid out for me on the end of the bed, I walked out of the room, and steeled myself for the embarrassment of seeing James again.

I wasn't disappointed. The man looked at me as if I was sex on a stick, and his eyes devoured everything. From the way I wasn't wearing a bra, to the t-shirt that still smelled of him, all the way down to the sweat pants that hung low on my hips, and only stayed on because of the drawstring.

"Shiloh!" Janie cheered. "Daddy's ordering pizza. What kind do you like?"

Texas Tornado

"Sausage and pepperoni." I answered immediately.

"Hey," Janie smiled wide. "That's daddy's favorite, too!"

Perfect.

By the time the pizza was devoured, I was in a much better mood. I'd let my guard down some, allowing Janie to entertain me with her cunning personality and wit. James was a good father. He didn't let Janie's constant need to question and badger him affect him in the slightest.

I knew that whatever allegations against him were most definitely false, and I knew I'd be saying something to my supervisor, regardless of whether she brought it up or not. There were so many people in the world that deserved to have their children taken away for the way they treated them.

James, however, was not one of them. He was patient and kind. He interacted with her. She obviously adored her father. It was the type of relationship I'd secretly wished that I had with my own father. The type where you knew that he'd do absolutely anything for you, and would protect you always.

I'd almost began to think that I'd made too big of a deal of our sexual encounter earlier, that maybe the attraction was just one-sided, when Janie made an innocent statement about Boris, and then James went and ruined my lazy contentedness.

"I love your cat, Shiloh." Janie said as she petted Boris, who was sprawled out indelicately in her lap. "Daddy, don't you love Shiloh's cat?"

"Oh, yeah. I love Shiloh's cat." He said with a slight smile on his face.

For some strange reason, I didn't think he was talking about Boris.

Chapter 8

Our flag does not fly because the wind moves it. It flies with the last breath of each soldier who died protecting it.

-T-shirt

James

"Come in." I said to the straight-laced woman at my door.

"My name is Lillian McBride, and I'll be conducting the interview today. May I sit?" She inquired.

"Absolutely," I gestured towards the couch.

I winced when I saw her have to shove one of Janie's many GI Joe dolls to the side.

"I only show that you have Janie, who do these belong to?" She laughed, then pulled an army out from beneath her as she sat.

"Sorry about that. Those are Janie's toys. She has a thing against pink and anything girl related." I quipped.

She smiled. "How funny. How are you doing today, Mr. Allen?"

Bile was slowly rising in my throat, but I played her game. I wasn't sure if she even knew how nerve-wracking it was to be investigated by CPS, let alone be accused of something so nauseatingly horrific. "I'm well, thank you. And you?"

"Well, also. Now, I've already conducted the interview with Janie. She was quite adamant that you were the 'best father in the world' and she was 'tired of seeing me.'" She laughed.

My jaw dropped open, speechless.

"Oh, don't worry about it. It's nice to see a girl know what she wants. She was very vocal, and told me exactly what she thought. I have no doubts that the claims against you were made under false pretenses. However, we still have to follow up in a few months. Do you have any questions?"

"No, ma'am." I rasped.

The interview went as expected. She asked me about my home life, about my job. What I did in my spare time. What I did to punish Janie. What happened when I left? Who watched her while I was working? Overall, I felt that I'd answered the numerous questions efficiently.

"My daughter is the most important thing in my life. I'd never do anything to harm her." I finally said, totally beside myself with worry by that point.

She smiled warmly at me, and then stood. "Now, don't think that these false reports aren't being investigated. They are. I give you my word that we aren't letting false allegations pass. If you have any questions, please don't hesitate to give me a call. Although, from what I understand, you've got a fine young lady staying with you that already knows quite a bit about what's going on."

Her wink took me by surprise, and I walked behind her as she headed for the door. "Have a good day, Mr. Allen. Don't worry. This'll all be resolved shortly." She proclaimed, before dropping into her red Honda Civic, and pulling out.

Texas Tornado

Just as she was moving towards the front of the building, my phone rang in my pocket. Digging it out, I put it to my ear and answered with a terse, "Hello?"

"James," Shiloh said in her husky voice. "They released me to move back into my apartment. Can you meet me there with the keys when you get a chance?"

All the woman had to do was speak to me now, and I was instantly erect.

"Sure," I answered, even though that was the last thing I wanted to do.

In fact, I wanted her to stay, but I knew she wouldn't like that. The woman was determined to make it on her own, and damn anyone who got in her way.

"Thanks," she breathed, and my dick hardened even further.

I decided to accidentally forget that we had her cat, as well. If I didn't bring Boris, she'd have to come see me again. I'd decided that after the other night, I wouldn't stop until she was mine. I'd make it to where she wanted me back, but I'd do it slow, because I didn't want her to take off without telling me.

I'd repeated the sight of seeing her barely covered and fingering herself repeatedly in my mind numerous times since it'd played out. It'd been three days, and I've been semi-hard since.

The hard part wouldn't actually be in convincing her, though. It would be in convincing her brother.

"I'll come meet you there in half an hour. Does your truck run good?" I asked.

Sam had finished her truck in less than a day and a half, putting new spark plugs, headers, exhaust, and tires on the truck. Then he'd proceeded to tune up everything that he could. As well as changing all the fluids and running a performance test on it. To say he felt bad would've been exaggerating.

"It ran great," she agreed. "I'll have to remember to thank Sam for getting it done so quickly."

I snorted. That was what the man was hoping. He'd about killed himself getting her truck running perfectly, and refused anyone's help when it was offered.

"Alrighty, see you in a few." I said and hung up.

"What's that look for?" My sister asked from beside me.

My eyes turned towards her, and I groaned. "Why are you so worried about it?"

She turned her nose up at me, and started walking towards her truck. She was dressed in scrubs, about to head to work for the night. Seeing her dressed in those clothes reminded me of how proud of her I was. She'd overcome a lot, sacrificed so much to take care of Janie while I was deployed and following my career, that I would be forever grateful.

"Janie's being picked up by mom tonight, don't forget." She said, opening the door to her Silverado.

"Sam know you're driving your truck?" I snickered, goading her.

She lifted her lip in a mock growl. "Careful, James. I have a new sticker to put on your truck."

Texas Tornado

"Don't you dare! I'm tired of having to keep a razor blade in my pocket." I commanded.

She smiled cryptically, and then laughed. "Hey, make sure you ask Shiloh if she wants to go camping next weekend. We're going to Caddo Lake. Mom's watching the kids. No excuses."

"Yes, ma'am. I'd planned on asking her tonight. Although, I thought that your husband might grow a pair and ask her." I joked.

She rolled her eyes. "Got another dinner and movie night going on?" She asked as she threw her nursing bag into the floorboard.

"No, not tonight. Shiloh's house was released as a crime scene and she's going home." I answered, trying my best not to sound bummed.

"You're gonna be my brother in law." She snickered.

"What?" Sam barked from behind us both, causing us both to whirl around, guilty looks on our faces.

"I didn't do it!" She screeched.

Sam's scowl turned on her, and she jumped into her truck, slammed the door, started it with a roar, and took off in a spray of gravel.

I tried to sneak away while his attention was otherwise occupied, but he sensed the movement and returned his attention to me. "What did she say before she left?"

"To ask my brother in law if he wanted to go for a beer tomorrow." I said, covering for Cheyenne's big mouth.

His eyes narrowed, but he didn't call me on it. "Okay, sounds good. How'd Shiloh's truck run?"

"Good from what she told me. But she only drove it about three miles to work, so I'm sure she hasn't figured out that you put a chip in it yet." I laughed.

"It gets better gas mileage." Sam grumbled.

"Yeah, I'm sure that's why you did it." I laughed. "Sam, why don't you just try to talk to her? Make an effort. She's a kind person. She wouldn't have stuck around this long and kept trying if she wasn't."

"I fucked up. I was so hurt that I didn't realize what I was doing. Keeping her at a distance was to protect me, and I regret it with my every breath. I could've lost her the other day, and I never even knew her. What kind of a brother does that?" Sam sighed and hung his head.

"A brother that was confused and overwhelmed. I think you'll find a companion in her. She didn't have the best of childhoods either. Seems to me like y'all could compare notes." I explained before heading for my bike.

Sam stood with his head down, and didn't look up to me as I passed on my bike. I wasn't worried though. Sam wasn't the type of man to let things fester. He was a fixer and a doer. He'd get this ironed out with Shiloh, and they'd have a relationship. Which just added one more hold that kept her firmly ensconced in my own life in return.

I felt my phone vibrate in my pocket as I pulled onto Shiloh's street. However, it wasn't until I ignored it for the third time, and pulled into Shiloh's apartment lot that I was able to get to it.

"Hello?" I greeted my lawyer cautiously.

Texas Tornado

Normally he just left a message if I didn't answer, and it alerted me of something wrong when he kept calling.

"James," He greeted tersely. No bullshitting for him, which I liked. "I just received notice that Janie's visitation with Anna will start this weekend. She'll have four hours of supervised time starting at ten in the morning Saturday."

My breath hissed in between my teeth, and I squeezed my eyes shut tight. I heard Shiloh's truck pull into the spot next to me, but I didn't acknowledge her presence. Instead, staring at the speedometer on my bike, eyes locked to it like it was my lifeline.

"Do I get to approve the supervisor that stays with my child?" I asked, pinching the bridge of my nose hard.

"Actually, yes, you can. You have a few options in that department." He explained them to me.

"So, you're telling me if the person I choose is a certified social worker, I could have them supervise the visit?" I asked once he explained the options to me.

Looking up, I caught Shiloh's curious eyes on me, wondering where I was going with that line of conversation, and what I was talking about in general.

She was wearing blue jeans and a black polo shirt that was tucked into her pants. Her beautiful hair was down, pinned up half way with a contraption that looked like a claw of some sort. Her jeans were molded to her body perfectly, and I quickly looked back down at my gauges to keep my mind in line.

"Yes, we can speak with a few. Make sure we find someone that will keep Janie's best interest at heart." Todd confirmed.

"Actually, I have the perfect person in mind. She's also fiercely protective. I think she'll be perfect." I said as my eyes locked with Shiloh's.

Clarity slowly took root in her eyes as I ironed out specifics, and she nodded her head in understanding and agreement before I'd even finished explaining the situation to her shortly after I'd hung up.

"I feel like a weight has been removed from my chest, and I can breathe again. I've been dreading this day, going on six months now. They'd told her she needed to finish some sort of therapy session, and then the visitation would start. I'd hoped that she would flunk out or something, but of course not. She was always so determined to do something when someone told her she couldn't. Now I know she'll be safe, and I can count on you to watch over her and protect her."

"I'll make sure that everything stays in Janie's best interest, James. Always."

***

"That movie was shitty." I declared as soon as the credits started to roll.

"It's the best movie ever! How could you say that? They died together. They'll never live without each other again." Shiloh cried.

"She also didn't remember him. How torturous is that? I would never wish that on the person that I loved." I grumbled, upset that the fucking movie upset me so much.

Texas Tornado

"If that person was truly in love with you, then it wouldn't matter. You'd remember and that woman would be there, waiting. That's what love is about. Sickness and health." She explained, wiping her eyes with the edge of the blanket that was covering her lap.

We'd just finished watching The Notebook, and she'd cried for the last twenty minutes of it. I'd reluctantly agreed to watch yet another romance, and she'd given me this shit. At least the other two we'd watched were somewhat uplifting.

"I liked How to Lose a Guy in 10 Days better." I grumbled.

She laughed at me. "You would. Sweet Home Alabama was my favorite in high school. The other was a close second. This one always made me sad, so I didn't watch it much."

"Then why the hell did we watch it now?" I asked.

"I wanted to see if you'd watch it. Tomorrow's Twilight."

"Fuck no. I'm not watching that shit."

She turned on the couch and surveyed my expression. "Please?"

Fuck me. Just like Janie. If she added a droopy lip, I was a goner. "Jesus."

"Come on, what will it hurt?" She asked, practically bouncing in her seat.

"My pride." I muttered.

She leaned closer to me, putting her face inches away from my own. I could smell the sweet smell of her skin. Something that smelled like tangerines. I could see the mirth shining in her dark melted caramel look of her eyes that were boring into mine.

Then she did the one thing that always got me. Curled her lip down in a pout. My eyes zeroed in, begging me to taste her; but before I could make the move, she retreated to her side of the couch. Although, I noticed that she left the pout firmly in place.

"One condition." I demanded.

"What?" She asked cautiously.

"You have to go on a date with me. Sunday. All day." I declared.

She looked at me wearily, but nodded her decision. "Deal. As long as you let me choose what we do."

"Deal."

Chapter 9

Never do a Texas girl wrong. Even if she doesn't have a gun, her daddy will.

-Tips on living in Texas

Shiloh

"I love you, baby. I'll see you in just a few short hours, and then we'll go watch your movie. Okay?" James said, crouched down in front of Janie, holding both of her hands.

"Okay, daddy." She said and stepped back from him, grabbing my hand in the next instant.

James watched warily as I made my way up to the house that Janie's mother, Anna, was currently occupying. His sharp gaze was practically burning a hole in my back. We'd discussed it, yet I knew he still had a hard time letting me watch over Janie, even though I knew he trusted me.

Even with all the trust in the world, I knew he would be sitting in the exact same spot across the street when we were done in four hours. I also wasn't surprised when I heard the sound of two more motorcycles coming down the road, and coming to a halt beside James. All the men I'd met that somehow belonged to my brother were great men, and Janie had each one of them firmly wrapped around her little finger.

Anna's home wasn't a bad place, and the smell of cut grass showed me that it'd just been mowed, making me wonder if it was just for our benefit. Then I got to wondering how she afforded a place like this. It was in a nicer area of Longview, a city just thirty minutes away from Kilgore.

Janie and I drove to Longview in my new company car, after getting permission from my boss, Lillian, of course. James followed at a safe distance behind, never letting us out of his sight.

This wasn't the first time I'd done the 'supervised visit' thing, but it was the first time I had such a vested interest in the child that I was charged with watching over. That's not to say that I didn't watch over them the same as I would any child, though. It just meant that I knew this child personally, as well as Janie's father.

"I don't want to go, 'Loh." Janie exhaled on a sigh.

'Loh was a new name that Janie was calling me. She's said that my name was too long, and then went about shortening it.

"I know, pumpkin. We'll get done fast, and then we'll go to Dairy Queen and get a blizzard. What-"

"Janie!" A woman squealed and practically shot out of the house in our direction.

Janie hid behind me at the woman's screech, and the woman came to a stop kneeling directly in front of me. Face to crotch.

Janie's boney arms were wrapped around me from behind. Her face was buried in the small of my back, averting her face from the woman's excited squeals.

Texas Tornado

"Oh, Janie! I've missed you so much!" She said with a saccharine sweet voice.

Although not obvious to most, it was obvious to me that the woman was lying through her teeth about how much she missed Janie. After six years of working with parents and children, I knew when one was lying. If you didn't, then a child could potentially get hurt, and that wasn't happening on my watch.

"Ms. Stevens. It's nice to meet you. Could we go inside, please?" I asked Anna.

Rather her head because she was still talking to Janie through my crotch.

"Of course! Janie, would you like to see all the toys that you have?" Anna cooed, still crouched down.

Taking Janie's arm, I led her to the side and curled my arm around her shoulders. Anna's eyes followed the movement, and she pivoted, staring at Janie intently.

"Would you like something to drink? I have a bottle for you when you get thirsty." She smiled as if she'd accomplished some great feat.

"Bottles are for babies." Janie snapped.

She was right. Janie was drinking out of adult cups now. What the hell was this woman thinking?

"Oh, well, I guess we can go find a sippy cup at the store for next time." She said with confusion.

She snapped out of the confusion moments later by jumping up and clapping her hands, then barreling back inside, expecting us to follow.

"It'll be okay, pumpkin. I have a water bottle you can drink from, as well as a pb&j in my pack for your lunch that your dad made."

"Good," she muttered.

She followed me inside reluctantly, turning around every few moments as if to check that her father hadn't abandoned her while she wasn't looking.

I chanced a look back, too. What I saw was Gabe and Jack placing a comforting hand on each of James' shoulders lending him support. Turning my back, I took a deep breath before breaching the door to Anna's home, and closing it quietly behind me.

I knew the next few hours would be trying, but I had no idea how much.

***

Teeth gritted tightly, I held Janie's limp form in my arms, and walked quickly to the car.

One look at my face had James stepping off the sidewalk, but I shook my head no, indicating that now was not the time. Which it wasn't. I wanted to get the fuck out of there before I ripped someone's goddamned head off.

I strapped Janie into her booster seat, and then drove back to Kilgore, head pounding with each bump in the road. Occasionally, I'd glance back at the three bikes that were following closely behind me, and gave a sigh of relief.

Pulling into the parking area in front of James' house, I closed the car door quietly, and then stormed off in the direction of the woods that lined the back patio area. Once I found a tree, I turned my back to it, and then slowly sunk down until my knees were in tight against my chest. Then I put my head on my knees and willed myself not to cry.

I felt James' body crouch down before me, and it took me a good fifteen minutes before I had enough control over my temper before I looked up at him.

His hazel eyes bore into mine, and I let out a breath before I started to explain.

"That woman is not fit to be a mother. She tried to feed Janie strawberries, which I know damn well and good you'd told her last night that she was allergic to when you were on the phone with her. As well as the court telling her. Then she had a fucking bottle, *a baby bottle*, of milk that she practically tried to force Janie to drink. When she refused, Anna stormed off, and then brought it back in a margarita glass. Which, apparently, was the only type of glass that she had. Not to mention the fact that I could smell the rancidness of the milk from where it was placed across the table from me. Then she tried to change Janie's diaper. The next four hours were spent with Anna on the phone with someone, whom I'm guessing owns the house, because she told him she'd be done with her meeting around one, and to come home as soon 'the little girl' left, while we sat on the couch and played on my phone. She kept saying how she was sorry that he wasn't allowed home, and that maybe she could just sneak him in next time."

As I offered my explanation, James' body became more and more like stone. By the end of my diatribe, the only thing moving was the breath in his chest. His pulse was pounding. Veins stood out all over his hands and forearms from the tightness of his clenched fists. His breathing was rapid, and I knew he was about to explode.

Not taking the time to think of why, I made the only decision I could, and threw myself into his arms. I wrapped my arms tightly around his chest, holding him down when he went to stand. To do what, I don't know; but I knew if I let him leave right now, he'd be beating the shit out of something or someone.

"Let me go." He said through clenched teeth.

"No." I said, hanging on as he stood anyway.

"Let me go, now."

I ignored his request, and continued to hold on to him. My arms were around his waist now, one hand locked around the other wrist, holding on for dear life.

He proved that my strength was no match for his in the next moment, effectively freeing himself from my grasp, and marching towards his bike.

I caught up with him seconds later, jumping on his back and curling my legs around his waist. "James!"

From the corner of my eye, I saw Cheyenne carrying a sleeping Janie into her house, and closing the door behind her. Sam watched the spectacle I was making, but didn't comment.

Neither did Gabe, Elliott, Jack, or Max.

"Get off." He demanded.

"No." I snapped.

"Get. Off."

Texas Tornado

"No."

"Fine." He snapped, and then mounted his bike.

Me being on his back, I had no choice but to follow.

Which is how I ended up riding like that on James' bike, going excessively fast, and enjoying the absolute shit out of it. Once I realized he wasn't going to stop, I let my feet relax from around his waist, placed them on the pegs, and held onto James as he accelerated out Free and onto the main road.

Four hours of riding, and one state later, James parked in front of a warehouse with what had to be fifty other bikes, as well as numerous cars parked in front of it. We'd passed the Louisiana border over two hours ago, and I had no clue where we were.

He swung his legs over the side, and then stalked off into the direction of the front door. When I realized he wasn't even going to look back, I scrambled off the back of the bike and stumbled towards the door he'd disappeared into moments earlier. I stumbled because my ass was asleep from riding on the back of the bike for four hours, and don't even get me started on the state of my bladder.

The door banged shut loudly behind me as I stepped through the door. Immediately my senses were assaulted. Smoke hung heavily in the air, and the sounds of fists meeting flesh drew my eyes to the middle of the room where a clearing that a crowd was gathered around.

Cheers went up as the sound of a heavy body hit the ground with a sickening thud.

I couldn't see James in the mass of people, so I crept closer to the makeshift ring. All the while, my mind kept repeating, 'The first rule is that you do not talk about fight club,' which had me snickering.

My mind reeled. Was this place legal? What the hell would happen if there were a fire in here? Where would the massive amount of people go? Would I be trampled to death? Oh, my God, are those two people having sex?

Sure enough, they were. The woman looked a tad bit slutty with her blue jean skirt hiked up over her ass, and her red thong pushed to the side as she rode a leather bound bearded grizzly bear of a man's tattooed cock.

The man saw me watching, and leered at me. "You can have a ride next."

James showed up at my side after that comment and glared at the man. The man's cock withered inside the woman at James' psycho stare, and it took everything in me not to laugh at the woman's growl of frustration.

James took me by the hand and led me over to some metal bleachers. "Sit." He growled, and then left me again.

A man's booming voice came over the loud speaker as I continued to survey my surroundings. "We've got a special treat for everyone tonight. Guess who's here? No guesses? Well, then I'm proud to say that it's the one and only Scope is in the house! He'll be fighting Jumper!"

The crowd of three hundred roared. Which made me wonder who this Scope character was, and if Jumper was a regular.

Texas Tornado

I wasn't in suspense long when out of the corner of the room, a man who could easily resemble a goddamn Mack Truck entered the ring. Followed shortly by a now shirtless James, with all his rippling, lickable muscles.

Then they started beating the absolute crap out of each other. Round after round. Punch after punch. For Jumper having at least a hundred pounds on James "The Scope" Allen, he sure didn't act like it.

My eyes were glued to James as his muscles rippled and contorted with each punch, jab, and dodge. I noticed that they didn't use their feet, which I thought was probably a good thing, much to the disappointment of the crowd.

I was sickly fascinated with the entire thing. Surprised, too.

Never would I have thought that James was into a thing like this. He seemed like such a 'nice guy' that it astonished me that he had all this bad underneath his good 'ol boy exterior.

"Alright, boys. Two minutes left. If you don't have a KO, then it's a tie!" The announcer bellowed.

It did, indeed, end in a tie. Both men were pouring sweat, and billowing air like freight trains. James' jeans were now soaked to at least mid-butt, all the way around, with sweat. Bruises were forming on his cheek, and he had a split lip that was seeping blood. He touched the cut with the tip of his tongue and winced.

Then the girls surrounded the two men as they shook hands as if they didn't just try to beat the living crap out of each other. Which, in turn, signaled my desire to leave seeing as I didn't want to have to scalp the bitch who was pawing the man I wanted with my next breath.

Thinking now would be a good time to find a bathroom, I got up from the hard metal bleachers to search. I found it down a dimly lit hallway back beside the bar. When I went to the bathroom, I failed to notice the cracked door I had to pass on the way. It wasn't until I was done and walking back towards the bar that I heard a distinctly familiar voice that had my temper rising to the forefront.

Stepping just outside the door, I stopped and listened.

"Who's the bitch?"

"Fuck you."

"Why's she got your boy?"

"She volunteered to watch over him for a few, while I got my business taken care of."

"Seems to me like she's more than that."

"If she was more than that, she'd be getting more of me. Mainly consisting of my dick. Which she isn't."

"Who do we have here?" A man said from behind me, and then slammed me into the room and onto the floor, following me down shortly with his body straddling my back.

Reacting on instinct, I twisted and turned, but found myself unable to release the hold the man had on me. He held me down effortlessly. Heart pounding and opening my mouth to scream one second, the next the man was ripped off my back and thrown across the room and toward the familiar voice.

Texas Tornado

James' arms came around me, and scooped me off the floor, pulling me back into his sweaty chest, and I nearly collapsed in relief. Then came the anger.

Swinging my head towards the man sitting in the office chair behind a large desk, I stomped toward him, picking up the closest thing I could find, an unopened bottle of Jack Daniel's Whiskey, and threw it at him.

He dodged it easily, and it hit the wall with a thud, shattering on impact. Glass tinkled to the ground along with the sound of sloshing liquid. Coming to a stop directly in front of the desk, I vaulted it and catapulted myself over the edge, hitting the man with the full force of my body, and proceeded to beat the shit out of him.

Or tried to.

"Knock it off, you crazy shithead." Sebastian bellowed while dodging a blow to the groin.

"You fuckhead! That man was on top of me and all you're gonna do is stare at me?" I kept wind milling my fists at his face.

He held me off with a hand planted in my chest. "Chill the fuck out. You surprised me! I didn't even know it was you!"

"Yeah? Well fuck you." I said, finally landing a kick to Sebastian's groin.

Then I was pulled off by James, and held in a firm grip. Not that it stopped me from trying to go for Sebastian's face still.

"What the fuck are you even doing here?" Sebastian roared.

"She's with Scope, boss." The man that 'Scope' tossed across the room gritted out as he made a move to stand.

"Stay. Down." James snarled.

The man stopped trying to get up instantly, and went down, holding his hands up in a placating gesture.

"What the fuck are you doing with Scope?" Sebastian, my evil brother who hadn't called me in weeks, snarled right back.

My arm started throbbing, and I was near tears when I replied. "What the fuck do you care?"

Sebastian's demeanor changed in a flash, and he was up and leaning over the desk in concern when he noticed me cradling the cast to my chest.

"Why are you in a cast?" He asked.

I ignored him to turn around and bury my face against James' bare chest. Sweat slicked against my cheek, but I figured it didn't really matter since my tears were now mingling with his sweat. My shoulders shook with each sob that was released from my body, making James gather me closer to him, and start whispering into my hair.

"Stop crying, you're breaking my heart." He murmured.

"My arm hurts." I groaned.

"You got any Tylenol?" James rumbled.

I assumed someone handed him something, because he moved his arm from around my shoulders, making the muscles in his chest bunch and relax. The sound of pills being tapped out of a bottle had me turning and raising my hand to take the medication.

Dropping them into my hand, I threw them into my mouth and swallowed them dry, gagging only once.

Texas Tornado

Disgusting.

"I'm waiting." Sebastian grated.

My eyes turned to him, and my eyes went down his body, cataloging what I was seeing. His hair was the normal black that I was used to, but now it was a bit longer, not the usual military shortness he was so anal about. His t-shirt was the usual black, jeans the usual faded, and boots the usual motorcycle ones. The only thing different?

That would be the leather vest he was wearing. *A cut.* Although he'd worn it before, it was never with me, and never in eyesight. I'd seen him and dad wearing theirs, but never when they could help it. When I did see it, it was because I was snooping, or peeking, or sneaking around somewhere I wasn't supposed to be.

Nine months ago when I'd found out about Sam from Sebastian, I'd started to really pay more attention. Things that had only been a passing thought, now turned into more than nagging curiosity. The one and only time I'd been able to get an up close and personal look at his vest, no cut, was when Sebastian had gone skinny-dipping with Lilly Rose Tanner two years ago.

I'd been at my mother's house, taking care of her while she had the flu, and had just come over to Sebastian's to see if I could borrow a humidifier that I'd left at his place. Seeing that he was otherwise occupied, I'd pawed through his clothes that were laying on the picnic table, and saw it laying there.

Curiosity being the bane of my existence, I picked it up, studying it and trying to figure out why he never let me see it. I knew he had it on. Most of the time he'd cover it up with a sweatshirt, or a flannel long sleeved shirt.

"What are you staring at?" Sebastian growled.

James' body tensed at the tone Sebastian had just used, and I reacted quickly, trying to diffuse the situation before my brother got his ass kicked. "What do you care what I look at?"

Sebastian's scowl went from who I now realized was James, to me. "I wasn't talking to you. Why the attitude, June?"

I gritted my teeth at the use of my middle name. My dad and him were the only ones who ever called me that, and it drove me fucking nuts. "Well, if I have to tell you, then it obviously won't matter to you what I have to say, because it's apparent to me you don't really care."

If that wasn't a "woman answer," I didn't know what was. However, I couldn't help it, that's the way I felt. He hadn't answered any of my calls, texts, emails, or even my mail I'd sent the snail mail route. I was hurt, and sad. I'd needed him, and he wasn't there.

"You know I love you, June. Don't act like that." He sighed.

"Act like what? That I'm hurt? I haven't heard from you. I haven't seen my nephew in over eight months. You just drop me like a hot potato when dad dropped me off. I've needed you, and you weren't there. You've always been there, and then suddenly you're just gone. No explanations, no nothing." I hadn't realized I was crying until James wiped the tears from my eyes with the palm of his hand, and wrapped me up tighter.

The door to the room closed quietly behind us, and I noticed that we were alone now, the three of us. Sebastian had stood, but wasn't coming any closer. Although, that might have had something to do with the glare James was throwing him.

"Fuck," James growled. "You Mackenzie brothers sure know how to hurt your sister."

"What?" Sebastian barked.

"What, what?" James asked with a raised brow.

"What are you talking about? What did Cash do to hurt June?" Sebastian asked, tension radiating from his pores.

"Cash is Sam, in case you're wondering. June is me. They call everyone by their middle names. Except for Sebastian. He won't go by his middle name." I said, smiling with glee.

"Why?" James asked, obviously intrigued by the smile that had erased the tears from my eyes.

"Don't you dare, June." Sebastian growled.

I eyed him and thought about how hurt I was. Still was.

I knew he wouldn't be happy with me, and probably wouldn't speak to me for weeks. However, I figured, so what? The man hasn't spoken to me in seven months, what were three weeks?

"Do what?" I asked, fluttering my eyes at my big brother. "Tell James that your middle name is Sue?"

Sebastian reached out for me in the next instant, but James suddenly thrust his body in between Sebastian's and my own, barricading Sebastian from me by using his own body.

"What the hell? Your parents in love with Johnny Cash or something?" James asked after Sebastian backed off, and returned to the other side of the desk.

I watched the calculation in Sebastian's eyes. How his eyes flicked from me to James, wondering what the connection was and why he was protecting me. Honestly, I'd like to know the last one myself.

"My father is, what you could say, a fan." Sebastian explained reluctantly.

"Daddy goes by his middle name, too." I supplied.

James eyes focused on mine, and a smile turned up the corner of his lips, before it disappeared when he focused on something towards the side of my face. His hand rose, and the pad of his thumb traced the apple of my cheek, and I winced.

"Fuck! What the hell?" I asked, raising my hand up to cup my cheek.

"Bruised." He explained, and then his glare turned from the swelling on my cheek to Sebastian. "What the fuck were you thinking letting that happen to your sister?"

Sebastian held his hands up. "I didn't know my sister was here. Nor did I know what was happening until it'd already happened. My man was just watching over my back." He explained.

He hated explaining. The tick in his jaw highlighted that fact, and I had a feeling that James somehow knew it.

"Well maybe if you paid attention to your sister a little more instead of going out of your way to ignore her, you'd know more. That, or pick better people to watch you're back. She was a defenseless woman. You don't treat women like that. She could've been anyone; been there for anything. Look, I have one more fight tonight. Y'all take that time to figure your shit out. And if you hurt her, I'll kill you. You'll never see it coming."

With that succinctly put statement, he left.

"Well, the man is sure hot for you. Did he fuck you yet?" Sebastian snapped.

My eyes went from the empty doorway to Sebastian's hate filled face.

He had some massive chip on his shoulder, and I sure wasn't going to stand here and let him berate me for something I'd never even done. I didn't even know why he was mad. Hell, I never said one single word about the trashy women he saw. Not one single word about the hoe bag of a woman he got pregnant.

Then I berated myself, because that hoe bag, Lindsey, was dead. She couldn't defend her actions anymore, and I had no room to talk. I didn't have the best track record when it came to men, and I'm sure it bothered Sebastian that I was seeing someone, and he didn't even get to run a background check on the man.

"Well?" Sebastian hissed when I took too long to answer.

"Go fuck yourself." I said before turning and following the sounds of cheering.

James was fighting again, except this time it was the bear-man I'd seen fucking that woman earlier. He was easily twice the size of James length and width wise. His hair was a wild mass of snarls around his head, and his beard was tamed by a ponytail holder. It reached down to his chest, and I couldn't help but think that was a bad idea to give someone a 'handhold' when it came to a fight, but who was I to say anything?

I'd been taken down earlier by some man, and I had no ability to fight back. Hell, I didn't even know how to fight back, other than throwing a punch when they were distracted. I'd always had my brother there to do it for me. Now, I wasn't sure what I had.

Chapter 10

Are you going to do something, or just stand there and bleed?

-Tombstone

James

Peter's (Portal to the crowd) fist flew past my head like a fucking wrecking ball, and I pivoted, narrowly dodging his other fist by millimeters. Motherfucker, he was quick. Even quicker than the last time we'd fought. The kid was really learning how to fight. Not that he'd win. I'd been doing this since I was fifteen.

When I was a kid, I had a lot of pent up aggression. With no father to tell me how to channel it, I started punching an old punching bag that Max's father had in his tool shed. Not one to be outdone, Max had started, too. Then the fights started happening.

Briggs, my other best friend, discovered an underground fight club of sorts one weekend when he'd gone to Shreveport, Louisiana to visit his grandparents. It wasn't until after Briggs' death, however, that I finally worked up the courage to start fighting.

Briggs, Max, and I met in middle school during JV football tryouts. We bonded so well because all of us fucking sucked at playing football. We never saw the point of it. We all had a problem with authority, and having football coaches screaming at you because you dropped the football wasn't something that had interested us at the time.

So, we became fast friends, doing anything and everything together. That all ended one night when Briggs was in a drunk driving accident.

On our way home from mudding in the Tally Bottoms, Briggs had just pulled onto Highway 31 when a drunk driver hit him head on. The man had been driving in the wrong direction. Being that Highway 31 was a large highway, Briggs never thought to look the other way as he merged into traffic. That was the biggest mistake of his life.

Max and I had watched in horror as the two cars collided. The drunk went from eighty miles an hour to nothing in just a few short horror-filled seconds. Briggs' car folded like a motherfucking accordion. Much the way my face was about to, if I didn't start paying attention to the fight.

Shaking off any residual wraiths, I faked a right jab and swung my left in an uppercut. My fist met Peter's jaw on a brutal upward swing, and he dropped to the floor like a stone.

Not even panting, I backed away from the fallen man, and stopped just to the edge of the ring, waiting. The unofficial referee dropped to his knee beside Peter and did the count, declaring me the winner by a knock out.

My rage somewhat appeased by the two fights, I turned my head to check on Shiloh. Much the same as earlier, I couldn't find her. However, this time I wasn't scared shitless. I knew her brother wouldn't let anything happen to her now that he knew she was there.

I hadn't realized that ownership of Fields of Punishment had transferred hands. Which was very sloppy of me. Sloppy got people killed, and I had a girl that depended on me to live. I would never let her down.

"Who's ready for *Shiva*!" The Announcer roared, snapping me out of my mental assault of my dumbness.

The announcer reached his desired effect, and the crowd roared at the name. A small snort came from my opposite side, and I turned, and looked down to see Shiloh sitting on a folding metal chair just behind where I was standing.

"What?" I semi-yelled at her.

Before she could reply, I finally heard the whispers.

'*Oh, my God! Shiva's fighting?*'

'*Holy crap, Shiva never fights.*'

"*Shiva's fucking hot. I can't believe the VP of The Dixie Wardens MC is fighting. Scope's gonna get his ass kicked.*'

The whispers continued, and I finally looked to Shiloh.

"Who the fuck is Shiva?" I asked.

"*That*," she laughed. "Would be my big brother."

I started to sing 'Joy to the world' in my head. Why? I don't know. I sing Christmas songs when I'm happy, and right then, I was over the fucking moon. I've wanted to kick that little fucker's ass for over two weeks now. Sam wasn't the only brother she'd been upset with, and anyone that made a woman like Shiloh cry was 'cruisin' for a brusin'' like my lovely sister always says.

Rubbing my hands together in glee, I stepped back into the ring.

Sebastian made his appearance moments later, in jeans only, just like me.

"No lower body." Sebastian declared.

"Okay." I agreed outwardly. However, inwardly I said, 'Yeah, right.'

"You fucked her yet?" Sebastian growled.

I didn't reply, nor did I move. Which would've been what he wanted. For some reason, I'd pissed him off, and what better way to retaliate than a fight in his own establishment. Fuck me up, get his revenge against something I'd done, and make himself look good in front of his club. Win-win for everybody.

But me, however.

"Not yet. Soon, though. Maybe tonight."

He didn't react either, but the telltale twitch at the corner of his left eye gave away his irritation.

"My sister sucks at picking out men. She has a track record a mile long of assholes that I had to take care of. Figure I'll just get rid of you now, and save myself the trouble later."

"That right?" I asked him. "Where have you been for the last seven months if you protect her so much?"

"Busy." He snarled.

Oopsey, must've hit a nerve with that one.

We started circling each other, neither one willing to make the first move. The crowd was chanting 'Shiva's' name, urging him to 'kill that motherfucker!' and "Don't hurt the pretty boy's face.'

"Is that so?" I laughed. "You and your brother have a lot in common. Sam decided that he didn't want to have anything to do with her either."

Texas Tornado

Sebastian came to a stunned stop, and I took advantage of his temporary lack of attention and struck. My fist met his face with a satisfying crunch, and his nose sprayed an arc of blood over the concrete floor.

Not one to be outdone, Sebastian struck out moments later with a right hook to my face, but I deflected it enough that it only grazed my jaw.

We traded punches like that for ten more minutes, and finally, the rage that had been present since finding out that Anna would be seeing my daughter started to fade. With each punch, hook, jab, and block, I started to think beyond my rage. That's when the real fight began.

***

"You have a baby. In a bar." I joked.

Shiloh's eyes regarded me with annoyance before she turned and did another circuit in front of the bar in her brother's office. The boy sleeping in her arms was much larger than the tiny little infant that we'd seen two years ago.

"Don't use Sweet Home Alabama quotes on me. They won't work." She growled.

I was in a good mood for the first time in what felt like two weeks. I'd needed that fight more than anything, and I appreciated Sebastian for giving it to me, even if it wasn't for the same reasons as I'd had.

"Where'd Terry go?" Sebastian asked as he shrugged his cut back on as he entered the room.

Shiloh mumbled something derogatory, but the only thing I'd made out was 'crazy bitch.'

"Your lovely sister sent Terry home." Jordan, the man who'd nearly lost his life earlier when I'd seen him on top of Shiloh, said.

Jordan was a prospect, and although I know he was doing his job and protecting Sebastian, I didn't give a fuck. It would take me a long fucking time to think of him in any other way other than hatred.

Sebastian's glare returned to his sister, and I barely contained the chuckle that was forming in my chest. I know how that felt. My sister did 'things for my own good' all the time, whether I wanted them or not.

"If you need someone to watch my nephew from now on, please call me. I don't think it's good to have the sitter giving a blowjob to some burly man drunk on God knows what, while my nephew is in the same room. Especially when the man is saying, 'yeah, baby. Suck my fat cock. Get up here and sheathe that hot cunt over my throbbing pork meat.' I think not."

Sebastian's face turned hard as stone, and then he turned and left the room abruptly. Seconds of silence followed, and then the sound of a large bodied person being dragged kicking and screaming could be heard. Then said man was unceremoniously dumped inside the office.

"You're telling me you fucked the help while my kid was in the goddamned room?" Sebastian bellowed.

Texas Tornado

My eyes went to Shiloh, and the young toddler in her arms, wondering if the sound of his father's bellow would wake him, but it didn't. Which made me wonder what the boy had witnessed, in his young life, to not even to flinch at such a commotion.

"Awww, man. Johnny was sound asleep." The man sporting a broken nose, and most likely a broken rib or two, whined.

"Johnny's my goddamned kid, not yours. I decide what is and isn't good for him. If he's fucking sleeping, then you leave him the fuck alone. Go find someone else to fuck, and make sure it's not the fucking babysitter, either. I trusted you to watch over him. What the fuck would've happened if someone had come in while you were fucking the help. What could you have done with your dick in someone, Torren?"

Torren's face went red with embarrassment at his lack of attention.

"Oh, he found that out first hand when your sister yanked Terry off his cock and threw her out the back door naked. Then came back for Johnny, all the while giving poor Torren the lecture of his life."

"Get out of my sight." Sebastian growled.

Shiloh started for the exit when Sebastian sighed, superbly exasperated. "Not you, June. Torren, get the fuck out and don't show yourself for a couple of days."

"Yes, sir." Torren nodded and left.

"Take a seat James. Shiloh." Sebastian gestured to the couches across the room.

I sat down on the loveseat, leaving Shiloh the recliner, but she surprised me by taking a seat next to me, scooting close. Leaving me no choice, I raised my arm and she cuddled into my side before laying her head down, and quite literally, falling asleep.

Sebastian sat down across from us with a disgusted look on his face. "Do you have to get that close to my sister?"

"Hey," I said, shrugging. "This is all her."

He nodded, watching his sister and son sleep for a few minutes before looking up at me. "Tell me what's been going on."

I decided to ignore the demand in his voice, and gave him a recap of the last eight months.

"Goddammit. I told my father this wouldn't work."

"What?" I asked, trying to sit forward and forgetting that Shiloh was using me as a bed.

Leaning back against the couch, I waited patiently while Sebastian debated what he shouldn't and should divulge.

When he finally started speaking, I quite literally had no words.

Nothing in my life could've surprised me more than what he said.

***

Shiloh

"Holy shit." My mind screamed.

It's amazing what you hear when you pretend you're sleeping.

Mind blown.

Chapter 11

Ladies- if your men don't know how to fire a weapon, you have a girlfriend.

-Earl Dibbles, Jr.

Shiloh

"Where're we going?" James asked again, for the fifth time.

"You'll see." I said cryptically.

We were on the 'date' that I'd promised, and I wanted to see him in his element, and the only way I could think of doing that was taking him somewhere I knew he would love.

When we'd gotten home from Louisiana, I'd decided to sleep over at James' place since it was so late, and I would've been over early for our 'date' in the morning anyway. As I was coming outside this morning, I ran into Sam. He'd apologized, for the seventeenth time, and I took pity on him by trying to make conversation.

I'd asked Sam about the girls, and eventually it'd turned into what James loved doing, and that was how James and I ended up going to the shooting range.

Of course, him having the Y chromosome automatically made him have to drive. So I'd given him directions on how to get where we were going. Once we'd gotten on the last road, his demeanor had changed, and he knew exactly where we were going before we pulled up to the gates.

"Sam told me you'd have a code to get in." I explained when he just looked at me.

"Yeah, I do." He agreed.

Lifting his right butt cheek, he fished out his wallet from his back pocket, dug through it, and the produced a card that had *National Rifle Association Member* on it. Once he had it swiped and the gate swung open, he pulled his Bronco in through the gates and waited for it to close behind him before starting down the long drive.

"Where are we going, exactly?" He asked carefully.

"Well, I have two reasons for coming here. One," I said holding up a finger. "Is that I want to practice with my .38. I have a concealed handgun class next weekend, and I don't want to make a fool of myself. The other, is that Sam said you'd enjoy coming here. He even sent me with a rifle."

His eyes shifted to take in the backseat, but looked at me in confusion when he didn't see anything.

"I had Cheyenne hide it in the back for me. I didn't want you to tell me no." I said cheekily.

"I would've never told you no. It's just that..." He started to say before trailing off.

"What?" I asked confused at the emotion I saw in his eyes.

"I had a friend who died while on a mission with me. He was my spotter. Ever since his death, well, let's just say I haven't found incentive to get out here." He said gruffly.

Sam had told me that might be the case, and I didn't tell him that I had his rifle in the back of the truck. Sam had been holding it ever

Texas Tornado

since his mission failed, and Dougie had died. I'd also gotten the story on Dougie, and I was truly heartbroken to hear of it.

According to Sam, Dougie was James' spotter. While on a fact-finding mission, they'd been made, and when they were going to the extraction point, Dougie and James had both been hurt. Only Dougie had died, while James had lived. Sam said that ever since, James hasn't been acting the same.

I wasn't sure if James would shoot his rifle, but I figured I would let the option be available if he decided to face his fear.

"When was the last time you shot your rifle?" I asked curiously, as he came to a stop outside the handgun range.

I hopped out and went to the back of the truck, waiting patiently for him to take in his surroundings, and then finally open the back hatch with his key.

"A few years." He hesitated. "Four to be exact."

Four years ago was when Dougie had died. And that broke my heart a little bit.

"Well, don't laugh at my target shooting skills." I said lightly, very aware that his mood was taking him down a dark path that I very much didn't want him down.

"I'll help you, honey." He laughed lightly.

Five boxes of ammo, and a thirty-minute search of the immediate surrounding area for the copper casings later, James and I were standing beside his truck staring at the rifle range.

"We don't have to do this." I explained hesitantly.

"It's okay, I've put this off long enough."

With that bold statement, he grabbed the case to his rifle and walked up to the area where he could set up his rifle. He did so with swift adept movements. First came removing the rifle from the case. Then he checked the chamber, the safety, the scopes mount, and finally set up the bipod to where the rifle rested on the table.

Ejecting the magazine, he loaded the shells that Sam had handed me earlier with a hopeful smile, and replaced the magazine into the bottom of the gun. Gesturing to his earphones with his eyes, I reached forward and placed his pair he'd produced from under the seat in his truck over my ears, and stepped back to sit on the concrete bench that was directly behind him.

Since no one was in the rifle target area, he didn't have to tell anyone that he was walking down range. Using a fancy handheld device, he took his staple gun and a target, and walked downrange. It took him what seemed like forever to walk, and walk until he was at his desired distance.

Once there, he pinned the target to the metal wire that was hanging across the range, and then walked back to me, licking his finger, and holding it in the air as he came back towards me. Seeing that he was in his zone, I stayed quiet, not asking the questions that were barely being held in, practically burning a hole to escape the confines of my mouth.

He took his time setting up, reading the handheld device, and then producing a pen and post-it from his pants. He wrote something down, looked at his scope, and adjusted it in some way that I couldn't really see from my vantage point.

Texas Tornado

I was utterly flabbergasted by all that went into the process. The man was stunning when he was in his element.

Today, he was wearing dark washed jeans, brown mud-caked boots, and a fitted gray t-shirt that hugged his muscled torso to perfection. He had on a pair of blue Oakley's that covered his expressive hazel eyes, and his beard, that just yesterday resembled a five o'clock shadow, now covered the lower half of his face with a scruffiness that only added to his sexiness.

Now, with his cheek snug against the stock of the rifle, his eye close to the scope, and his muscled shoulder cradling the butt of the massive gun expertly, I was sure I'd never seen anything sexier in this world. The man was the picture perfect example of a man.

His hand flicked up in a gesture of ready, and I held my breath, waiting for him to finally break through the barrier that he'd put up four long years ago.

Crack.

The sound of the rifle shot echoed through the tall Pine trees, and I let out the breath I'd been holding.

"That's some damn fine shooting there, son."

My heart leapt in my chest, and I turned sharply to find my father standing behind us. Although muffled, James' curse didn't escape my awareness.

"Hi, daddy." I smiled.

***

James

"Mr. Mackenzie." I nodded my head warily after switching the safety on my M21.

Silas Mackenzie was an intimidating figure. He was wearing jeans that had holes in the knees, a black t-shirt, and a flannel shirt that was hanging open. A small amount of leather peeked out every time the wind gusted. Which made me notice that he was covering the leather cut that was probably exactly the same as his sons had been last night.

I could make out a shoulder rig over his big burly shoulders as well, most likely hiding the same hand cannon I'd seen him sporting the last time I'd seen him. His hair was buzzed close to his scalp, but it did nothing to hide the silver lines of his hair. His beard was cropped close to his jaw, giving him a rugged appearance.

His arms were crossed closely across his chest, and he was looking at Shiloh with no short amount of love in his eyes. That look changed once his eyes turned from her to me at my greeting.

"I see you finally got back out here, boy. It's good to know you haven't lost the touch." He said, nodding towards the range.

How he knew that I'd gotten a good shot, I didn't know. From my naked eye, I could barely make out the bullet hole that ripped through the middle of the target. Directly in the center of the 0 at center mass. I could most certainly tell when I had my eye at the scope, but he didn't have anything but his eyes. Although they were cold and calculating.

"Yeah," I answered when I could think of nothing else to say.

"May I speak to you in private for a moment, James?" Silas asked.

I nodded in affirmation, and Silas' sharp gaze turned pointedly in Shiloh's direction.

"What, you want me to leave?" She asked in mock outrage.

"No, we'll go." Silas said with exasperation before turning to leave.

I gave Shiloh a raised eyebrow as I passed.

Once I'd passed her, I followed Silas in the direction of his bike that was parked at the end of the rifle-designated area.

"Hey, can I shoot your rifle?" Shiloh yelled towards my back.

"No!"

Both Silas and I yelled back in unison.

"That girl is curious, so we better make this quick or she'll shoot it anyway." Silas laughed.

I didn't say anything, just waited for him to tell me what he needed.

After years of being friends with Sam, of hearing all the stories of how he'd suffered when he was younger, I didn't know how to handle what I'd learned last night. Didn't know how to proceed. Whether I should tell Sam what I'd learned. Whether I should tell Shiloh.

"Sebastian told me he informed you last night. I need to make sure you keep that shit quiet, or a lot more than just my life will be at stake."

"I understand. Although, I'm not sure it's conducive with having a life with your children." I said carefully.

"You don't think I don't know that? Why do you think I've alienated myself from them? I've made sure that they're not in my life for their safety, not mine. Do you think it doesn't kill me? Fuck." He hissed.

I winced at the despair I heard in his voice. "As an outsider to this, I can tell you that they're grown adults, and they deserve to know."

Silas' fingers crossed and linked behind his head as he paced back and forth.

"They already hate me. There's no reason to make it known to them. Them understanding the truth won't change the fact that I ignored them their entire lives. Protected them, yes, but been there for them when they needed me? No. It's too late."

"It's not too late for your grandchildren. Pru, Piper, and Phoebe are young. They don't have a grandfather. They could really benefit from having one." I explained.

"Yeah, I don't think Sam is going let me get near them, even after he hears why I've done the things that I have."

"He may not at first, but, eventually, he'll understand. He may not like it, but he'll know that at that moment in time, that he wouldn't have done anything differently."

"Maybe," he hesitated. "I have one last assignment that I'm working on, and then we'll see."

"I'm not keeping anything from them if they ask. I won't just outright tell them. However, when they ask, and I know that they will, I'll tell them everything I know." I said carefully.

He nodded in understanding, and swung his leg over his ride. Starting it up, he was about to put it into gear when Shiloh cried out for him to wait.

He turned off the engine, and turned just in time to catch Shiloh as she threw herself into Silas' arms.

Silas' muffled, "Oomph." Made me want to smile, but I held it in check when I caught the look of adoration that crossed over Silas' face.

"I love you, daddy." Shiloh whispered to him before leaving back the way she came.

"She knows." He said with a disgusted sigh.

"Yep."

"Watch over her. She's going to open a big ass can of fucking worms if she doesn't keep her nose out of my business. I can't afford the distraction right now." He growled.

I looked at him pointedly, and he sighed. "Yeah, yeah. I know. Just try your best."

"Always."

***

"When are you going to tell Sam?" She asked quietly.

"I'm not. Well, not yet. We'll see if that changes in the future." I sighed.

"Alright." She agreed.

She agreed so nicely, that I knew Sam would know before the week was out. It just wasn't sitting well with her. Her conscience wouldn't let her keep this from him. Which I guess was for the best, because I was having doubts about telling him myself. Maybe it'd be better to come from his own sister, rather than his brother in law.

"Just wait till I'm not there to do it. I'd rather not have my ass kicked, if it's all the same to you." I said.

"Yes, sir." She said, saluting me.

"What movie are we watching tonight?" I asked instead of confronting the sarcasm.

"Frozen." She explained.

I grimaced. That was Janie's favorite movie, and I watched it no less than twice a day.

"What if I don't want to watch that?" I asked.

She laughed. "Well, I guess you'd have to take that up with your daughter. I promised her ice cream and Frozen yesterday if she'd give it a try at her mom's. Since she did so well, I figure we owe it to her."

Fuck. She was right. "Okay," I relented. "There just better be beer."

She snorted. "Yeah, well I'm gonna need something to drink, too. There's only so many times I can tolerate it as well."

Chapter 12

Ladies, wearing heels is not sexy if you walk like a newborn calf.

-Life Lesson

Shiloh

"Where do babies come from?" Janie asked the group as a whole.

We were eating dinner at McAlister's Deli with all of the women. Cheyenne had her three kids and Janie, Payton had her daughter, Blaine had her son, Winter with her daughter, and Ember had her two as well. Cheyenne had called a meeting of the minds, and since this was the most kid friendly, we decided it was as good of a place as any.

"Uhhh, why do you ask, sweetie?" I asked into the shocked silence.

"Daddy was talking about missing his baby this morning when he was holding Cat. He kept rubbing his beard along her hair and telling Jack how much he missed his baby." Janie said around a mouthful of macaroni.

My mind went down the dark road, and I kept thinking about what he could do with that beard. How it would feel with his bearded mouth running along the sensitive insides of my thighs. How it would feel to have his mouth on me... down there.

"Beards, sweetheart. Amazing beards." I said wistfully.

It wasn't until I heard the women all out laughing that I realized I'd said it aloud. "Whoops. Didn't mean to tell you that."

"Aunt Chey, Uncle Sam doesn't have a beard. How do you have three babies with no beard?" Janie demanded.

"Well, honey," she choked. "Uncle Sam has a beard every morning before he shaves it. Trust me on this."

Conversation flowed, and I allowed myself to let it sink in that I was actually a part of this. Over the past two months, I've gotten to know these women fairly well, and I was honored to be a part of their tight-knit group.

I've also become very close to James and Janie. They are a huge part of my life, and each movie we watch, and night out we spend together, the happier I seem to be. It made me realize how a real family should feel like, and I envied James' relationship with his little girl.

The more I thought about what I'd learned from James and my father, the more I've come to understand that I need to talk to Sam. Only, I don't know what or how to go about doing so. I know he'll be hurt, and we've just begun building a relationship of a sister and brother. I didn't want to chance telling him and losing that building closeness. Although, I knew I didn't really have a choice. It would have to be done, and I'd just have to hope that it didn't hurt him.

"Cheyenne, would it be possible for me to speak with Sam later tonight? Without the kids?" I asked softly.

"Of course. All you ever have to do is come over and I'll take the hellions on a walk or something." She agreed quickly.

Texas Tornado

"Motherfucker!" Ember yelled, bringing the attention of not only our immediate table, but every table in the fucking restaurant to her face.

"What?" We asked in unison.

She threw her phone into the middle of the table, refusing to answer.

Since it was closest to me, I brought the phone closer and scanned the screen, anger simmering in my body at what I'd read.

Reading the anger on my face, Cheyenne slipped the phone from my grasp before reading it over herself.

My mind was racing. What could I do? Then I had an idea.

"Where are you going?" Cheyenne asked as I started hustling towards the door.

"To bail your brother out of jail."

***

Although I hadn't made many connections with the police department, I still had to deal with quite a few of them on a daily basis. It would take time for them to come to trust me, but one thing was for sure, 99.8 percent of the department did trust James.

However, they'd seen me being picked up by him, taken out on dates by him, and generally around town with him a lot over this past month. More than once, I'd been asked about James or Janie by a passing police officer. So when I showed up at the police department a little over twenty minutes after he'd been arrested, most of them were more than aware of who I was to him.

"Ms. Mackenzie." A young officer nodded in greeting as I approached the front desk.

It took me a few moments, but finally I remembered. "Howard! How're you doing today?"

He grinned. "Doing good. That woman we picked up last week was picked up on another warrant yesterday."

A smile overtook my face. "That's fantastic news!"

It was, too. That woman was a menace, and didn't deserve to have the two beautiful children she had. Luckily, after a neighbor heard the mother yelling at her daughters at three A.M. the police were called. I was called shortly after that, and we made the decision to have the children placed into the temporary care of the girls' paternal grandparents.

They'd found drugs and other paraphernalia in the home, as well as a half assed porn shoot going on in the back of the house, all the while the girls were cordoned off to a small laundry room. One of the girls, the two year old, had wandered out of her cubbyhole and walked into the middle of the amateur porn film that was being filmed.

After enduring tons of yelling, the neighbor had finally called the cops, fed up with the horrible language. The cops had been flabbergasted at what they'd seen, and Howard, in particular, had helped me straighten out the fiasco.

"Are you here to bail James out?" His disgust at the mere thought was very apparent.

"Yes," I said hesitantly.

Texas Tornado

"I think that's the biggest crock of bull I've ever heard. I can't believe he was arrested on those charges." He growled.

"Can you tell me what they were?" I asked cautiously.

He looked into my eyes for a few moments, searching them with cool cop eyes. Then, as if coming to a decision, he leaned forward over the desk and spoke.

"Detective Howell brought James in this afternoon. I'm not even sure how you heard about it yet, seeing as we've not released the information. Anyway, supposedly he caught him attempting to assault his ex-girlfriend. The girlfriend pressed charges saying that James tried to rape her last night."

That. Fucking. Bitch.

"Take me to him. Is his lawyer in there with him?"

"Umm, apparently he asked not to have his lawyer."

I looked at him pointedly. "Seriously, you really think he's that stupid?"

"No. I thought..." He started to explain, but I interrupted him with a wave of my hand.

"You need to go in there and stop that interrogation. I'm going to make a call, and then you can take me in there."

I made three phone calls. One to James' lawyer, one to Sam, and one to my father. I just hoped they got here in time to stop the impending blowup that was a result from one officer's careless actions.

***

"What's going on here?" Todd bellowed so loud I could have sworn the flimsy old pains of the police station's windows shook with the force.

Todd Masterson was an intimidating man. From what I've learned of him from James, he was a Hard Ass, with a capital H, and a capital A. A marine during the first year after 9/11, he'd taken his fair share of shit, and it looked like he was plain out of patience. Even now, in jeans and a t-shirt, the man oozed authority. When he stormed past me as I sat in the old rickety chairs in the front office, I just smiled, and waited.

This should be fun.

"You've had him here for well over four hours. He's repeatedly asked for a lawyer, I'm sure. He's told you that he was with someone all night last night. Instead of verifying his whereabouts, you've decided to continue questioning him? Tell me something, did you even read him his rights yet? Please tell me you at least did something right." Todd growled.

He did sound like he was growling, too. I'd probably start hyperventilating if he even looked at me like he was doing to the other men in the room.

"We haven't been able to find Ms. Mackenzie to verify anything." Detective Howell bit back.

"Well, if you'd only left this interrogation room, you'd see that she's sitting in the front office chairs. She has been for well over twenty minutes now. She called me from the phone number that I'm sure Mr. Allen gave to you. Please, keep telling me how you couldn't get ahold of her." Todd hissed.

Oh, man. It took everything I had to keep the smile off my face. Howard wasn't doing so well. He had his face buried in the crook of his elbow where it rested on his desk. His shoulders were shaking with contained laughter.

The front doors banging open with a harsh staccato against the station's brick siding brought my attention to the door, and I lost my humor immediately.

The girl, who I later learned was named Jolie, stormed in, a worried expression on her face. Instead of going to Howard, she went to the woman that was in the corner of the room answering the phone. I heard her speaking in urgent tones, and I knew I wasn't going to like what she had to say as soon as she was pointed in the direction of Howard.

Once she reached the desk, my fears were confirmed when her frantic voice asked for James. Over. And over.

Tears were spilling down her face, and I wanted to slap her. She didn't have that ugliness that you get when you're truly upset. These tears were more of what I would call fake. Her nose didn't run, her face didn't flush. Her hands were wrapped around her purse instead of frantically wringing her hands together in nervousness like I was doing.

I wondered what type of relationship she and James had shared. He'd only told me of them being friends in high school, and it never progressed beyond that. Which I was eternally grateful for.

After two months, I was really sure that I wanted to move to the next level with James. Although he'd been a gentleman since that first night he'd caught me watching him masturbate in the shower, I longed for him to just pick me up, throw me on the bed, and fuck the living daylights out of me.

However, he'd told me he was giving me time, and if I was truthful, I needed that time. I'd always jumped feet first into all my relationships, and even though I've only dated three people seriously, I complicated the relationship by getting physical too early on. I didn't wait to build the relationship first as I was doing now with James.

Now, I was extremely sure of what type of man James was, and I knew he would never hurt me. At least not intentionally.

I needed for him to prove to me that he wouldn't hurt me and that he could be different from everyone else. However, there was still a small part of me that felt like if I let him in all the way, he'd leave me alone and hurting just like everyone else I loved in my life did.

And there was no question of loving him. I'd fallen into lust with him when I'd first laid eyes on him, and slowly, over the past few months, I've come to realize that what I'd originally felt for him had burrowed deeper, and I was well and truly on the road to love.

Jolie the manipulator managed the get a more comfortable computer chair to sit in, and I had to tamp down my irritation. She'd placed herself smack dab in the middle of the doorway's view, so when James came out, he'd see her first.

Which is what happened.

Texas Tornado

A tense hour later, James was striding purposefully out of the back room where I guessed the interrogation rooms were located. Todd towered behind him. An upset grim line graced the thin lips of his mouth.

Across the room, Jolie shot up out of her chair like her asshole was on fire, and practically launched herself at James. He caught her, whether out of reflex, or desire to do so, I didn't know. However, my mind was seeing red. I wanted to pull that bitch back by her fucked up hair and yank enough of it out to make it all one length.

Since I was across the room seated in a chair nearest the door, I could see when James' eyes closed and he sighed. Desire to be there completely gone, I got up as quietly as I could, and slipped out the door. I didn't even make the stupid little cowbell that signaled the door-opening clang.

I walked purposefully to my truck.

I ignored Gabe, Max and Jack who were both lounging on their motorcycles. I ignored the shout of my name. I ignored everything except the steady staccato of my flip-flop covered feet making the slick-slack sound against the paved sidewalk.

Once I reached my truck, I opened it with the key, slammed the door behind myself, and left the parking lot as sedately as I could.

One thing I knew for sure as I drove out of the parking lot. I wasn't going to deal with that shit every time Jolie showed up. It was either her or me, because I knew damn well that James would expect the same of me if the situation were reversed. I'd been put last too many times in my life. I could see if it were his child, because children needed that from a parent. However, Jolie was no child. Not even close.

Chapter 13

I'm wearing black until they make something darker.

-T-shirt

James

"You fucked up." Max said from behind me.

I turned from watching Jolie drive away to Max, who was still leaning against his bike casually. His legs were crossed at the ankle, and his arms were crossed tightly against his chest. Jack and Gabe were in similar positions, both watching me with the same frown of disapproval.

"What?" I asked, completely and utterly exhausted.

All I wanted to do was see my kid, and take a seat on the couch with my two girls and watch another stupid movie. As long as it wasn't Frozen.

"Going to that bitch over Shiloh." Gabe drawled.

My brows drew together in confusion. "What are you talking about?"

"We're talking about that woman rushing to your rescue, calling your goddamn lawyer, pulling some of her only connections with the few cops she's made friends with in her short time here to get you out. Yet, you let her leave with a beaten look dominating her pretty little face."

My stomach dropped, and I remembered in that instant that I thought I smelled the soft scent of her perfume in the police station's lobby. Yet, when I'd turned around, I'd only seen the door closing softly, and I'd put it out of my mind as Jolie rambled on and on about how awful it was that I'd been arrested.

Setting her away from me as quickly as I could, she'd then started rambling on and on about how someone had been stalking her. Which was how she'd learned I was arrested in the first place. She'd come down to the station to file a report, and had overheard it from the desk clerk.

I'd practically had to drag her to her car. Although I was sympathetic with her plight, I'd had a rough day myself, and I wasn't up to listening to her incessant whining today. However, she'd showed up more and more over the past two months, and I was at the point where I didn't want to put up with her at all. I'd thought I'd been lucky that Shiloh didn't see Jolie launch herself into my arms. Now I knew I wasn't lucky.

"Fuck," I growled, eyes pointed at the bright blue sky.

The clouds were moving quickly, which inevitably meant that we were on the verge of another thunderstorm.

"You could say that again." Max agreed.

"I didn't want her to touch me. She keeps bugging the absolute shit out of me. But I can't tell her to stop. It's like kicking a fucking puppy. She looks up at you with those big brown eyes and really pours it on until you cave. She's relentless." I said, exasperated at the situation.

Texas Tornado

"Well, you're going to have to do something about it. Shiloh said something to Winter the other day about her. I only walked in on the end of their conversation before they both stopped talking, but from what I heard, she really dislikes the woman."

"Amen." Max growled, looking away.

Thinking she needed some time to calm down, I decided to go check on my girl, and then I'd go searching for Shiloh.

"Were you able to get my bike?" I asked my friends that were currently avoiding eye contact.

"No, you're more than welcome to ride bitch though." Jack rasped.

I eyed him for a few moments, but decided it wasn't worth it. Fuck it. It was only about a two and a half miles from the gym. I was still in my gym clothes anyhow. Talk about embarrassing. I was in the process of benching two fifty when three cops poured into the weight area.

I'd known immediately that I wasn't going to like what they'd have to say. So, I'd re-racked the weights, and then followed the cops out of the building where they'd proceeded to cuff me and stuff me into the back of the unmarked police car.

Without realizing I'd done so, I started jogging. It wasn't until the gym, and my bike, came into view that I realized I'd made the ten minute jog to my bike without even saying goodbye to the friends that always had my back.

I knew they'd understand, and I didn't dwell on the fact that they were probably concerned about me.

Straddling my bike, I pulled the key from around my neck and started the bike up. The low throaty roar soothed some of the frustration that was coursing through my veins as it usually did. When I'd gotten back from Iraq, the only thing that had calmed the nightmares enough was the roar of the bike, and the feel of the wind in my face.

I rode home, relishing the sun soaking into my skin, and the smell of the pine trees as they whizzed past me. Dark clouds gathered in the distance as I rode. My mind wasn't the riot of emotions that it had been when I'd left the police station, but I kept feeling a sense of unease. As if something was about to happen that I wasn't ready for.

***

"Hello?" I answered my phone.

I'd been on the line trying to find Shiloh for the last two hours, yet I couldn't find her. The women didn't know where she was. Her boss didn't know where she was, and her house was empty. I'd even called her brother. Well, the brother that doesn't live two doors down from me. Sebastian had said that he didn't know where she was, and if he did know where she was, he wouldn't tell me because I'd obviously fucked up if I couldn't find her.

After a frustrating five-minute conversation with the man, I hung up the phone and watched Frozen with Janie. Again.

It wasn't until I was carrying Janie over to Cheyenne's house that I heard the high feminine cackling coming from the direction of Jack's place that was all the way across the compound's grounds.

Texas Tornado

Repositioning Janie's sleeping form on my shoulder, I carried her forward until I could see what was going on.

What I saw made my jaw clench tightly.

Every single one of the mother fuckers were there. They knew I'd been looking for her. I knew for certain that at least Gabe and Elliott knew, since I'd reached them first in the attempt to speak with their wives.

"Ember, truth or dare?" Shiloh half yelled/slurred.

"Truth." Ember slurred.

"If you were home alone at night and you heard a fart, would you laugh or be scared?"

Snorts from the men, and piercing laughter from the women followed that statement.

"Honestly, I'm pretty sure I'd laugh. Then I'd probably freak." Ember groaned.

Barely reining in my temper, and most definitely not in a laughing mood, I turned and left the gathering. After two hours of being worried sick, I just didn't have it in me anymore. I was tired. Exhausted. And ready for all of this bullshit to be over.

Once I got to my place, I laid Janie down in her bed before locking all the doors, windows, and arming the alarm. I brushed my teeth, and then fell into bed with an exhaustion that seeped deep into my bones. I rubbed my eyes with my fists, and contemplated shutting off my AM alarm when the knocking started.

I almost ignored the thumping at the door, but thought better of it when it started to pick up decibel levels. Really needing Janie to stay asleep, I rose out of bed. My bones cracked as I made my way to the door.

I stabbed the keypad's buttons with the blunt tip of my finger with brutal force. Then I started snapping the locks out of place, and then yanked the door open. I wasn't surprised to see Sam at the door, and I also wasn't in the fucking mood. Which I told him.

"What the fuck do you want?" I demanded.

His eyebrows rose at the tone of my voice, but I couldn't help it. I was mad. And if I wanted to be truthful with myself, a little hurt.

"Got a problem?" He asked with a calmness that made me want to punch the fucker in the face.

"No. I'm fucking tired. You made me get out of bed, and I wanted to sleep." I answered.

All truthful answers. However, not the total truth.

He knew I was purposefully not telling him everything, but the fucker wasn't my captain anymore. He could suck my dick.

"Gabe said he saw you walking back to your place. Must not have been that tired."

I pinched the bridge of my nose in between two fingers, and promised to donate my porn collection to a local youth shelter if God could make my headache go away.

"I've got a fucking headache. My body aches from sitting in a straight backed metal chair for four hours, and I'm tired. What. Do. You. Want?"

Texas Tornado

He studied my face for a few moments before uncrossing his arms from his chest and taking a casual pose against the side of the stucco wall that lined the outside of my house.

"I'm not sure I want my sister mixed up in your shit."

"My shit?" I asked, completely amazed that he'd brought that up to me.

"Yeah, your shit. I don't want her hurt. You've got all this shit swirling around your life right now, and I really don't want that to affect my sister." He confirmed.

I wanted to hurl his own shit back at him. What about all the shit he'd brought on my sister? What about his old man who was more of a goddamn danger than anything that I could bring to his sister's life?

I stared at him for a few more moments before making the hardest decision of my life.

"Okay." I nodded, and then stepped back, closed the door, and re-armed the system.

It wasn't until I was in bed and listening to the storm that'd been threatening the entire day pound at the glass of my window that I finally let the pain of his words roll through me.

Pushing the rioting emotions back down, I contemplated what my next step would be. I knew for sure I couldn't leave the county. The court, for one, wouldn't allow me to. I also wasn't so sure I wanted to leave the place I'd grown up in. To take Janie out of school in the middle of the school year.

That didn't mean that I had to stay here, where Shiloh would be a constant reminder of what I wasn't allowed to have. I also didn't have to stay working at Free. I'd had dozens of job offers since I'd been discharged from the army. I could take the one with the police department easily.

Which if I was being honest, I'd been contemplating more and more lately.

Decision made, I fell into a fitful sleep. Only to awake a little over two hours later with my heart damn near pounding in my chest, and the still warm sensation of my good friend's blood running hot over my skin.

"Goddammit Dougie. Goddamn you." I said into the darkness.

***

"What's going on, daddy?" Janie asked me as I carted a few duffel bags into my mother's house.

Janie was used to staying here whenever my mother wasn't working. What was not normal was having me moving my shit in, taking over Cheyenne's old room.

"We're going to stay here for a little while, pickle-lilly." I answered.

She beamed at me, completely unaware of the sadness that waivered my voice for a split seconds before I masked it.

"That's awesome, daddy! Grammy got me a trampoline!" She squealed.

That didn't surprise me either. The woman couldn't say 'no' when it came to her grandchildren. Especially Janie. What had my

Texas Tornado

brows rising was the fact that I hadn't put the trampoline together, and I damn well knew those fuckers didn't come fully assembled.

"Who put it together?" I asked her.

"Granddad Todd." She said before running towards the back yard and scrambling through the net that surrounded the trampoline. As if she didn't just drop a fucking bomb and take off.

'Granddad Todd' and Grammy have some 'splainin to do.

Chapter 14

If you can still hear your fears, shift a gear.

-Biker Truth

James

Two weeks later

I saw her as soon as she walked through the door. Of course I did. It's like my body was fine tuned to hers, because in the next instant, her gaze met mine across the expanse of the room.

I was sitting in a meeting with the rest of the SWAT team, listening to the captain harp on and on about teamwork. We were having the 'monthly' meeting at The Back Porch. We'd rented the back half of the restaurant for the next four hours. I was told that we'd go over our weekly schedules, hand out updates on anything and everything that had changed over the past month.

Luke also told me he'd introduce the new guy, which was me.

I'd contacted Luke the day after I moved back to my mom's place. He'd laughed and told me to come fill out the employment forms, and I could start work the next day. Therefore, while Janie was off at school, I was filling out form after form of paperwork. Handing in my living will. Setting up a retirement account and all that other fun first day on the job stuff.

Texas Tornado

    Shiloh stopped short of crossing the invisible barrier that seemed to cordon off the part we'd rented out and the rest of the restaurant. She watched me, and I watched her right back.

    My heart ached heavily in my chest, and I cursed Sam for the thousandth time since he'd left me that night with his parting words. *Stay away from my sister.*

    Finally coming to some sort of decision, she turned on her heel and walked to the front of the restaurant. Speaking with the cashier, she handed over her money. Moments later the cashier handed her a small to-go bag and a receipt. When the cashier tried to hand her another smaller bag, Shiloh shook her head and said something else.

    Both sets of their eyes turned and locked on me, and I had to wonder what was going on. The answer came shortly after Shiloh's departure when the same cashier brought the small bag over to me and set it down quietly before turning to leave.

    Luke and Downy gave me raised brows, but I ignored them and opened the bag. My heart warmed at the piece of chocolate cake dominating the bottom of the bag. I grinned and pulled it out, picked up my fork, and dug in. Downy and Luke watched in annoyance since the Captain had just said we didn't need any dessert a few minutes before Shiloh walked inside the door.

    Ignoring their pleading looks and the droning voice of the captain, I thought about how miserable I'd been in the last two weeks. Sitting in front of the TV made me feel like I was betraying Shiloh, but I felt like I'd betray Sam if I went against his wishes.

It was getting increasingly harder by the minute not to call or text her though. I wondered what Sam had told her, which then made my mind drift off into darker places that my ex was firmly implanted, and I forcibly ripped my mind of that particular train of thought.

There was one thing I was sure of right now, and that was that I hoped I continued to have the strength to stay away from her. Although, it wasn't looking too good from at present.

***

Shiloh

Three weeks later

My eyes wandered over to the empty house at the end of the lot, and I had to stop the despair that started to course through my bruised heart.

I hadn't seen James in twenty-two days, fourteen hours, and five minutes.

The night of the police station incident, I'd driven around for two hours before deciding that I needed a woman's perspective. What it turned out to be was an impromptu wine fest, and I was drunker than I'd ever been three hours later.

The next morning, I'd woken up to a pounding headache, but a much clearer head in Sam and Cheyenne's guest bedroom. After speaking with my brother for a few minutes about nothing of consequence, I'd then tried to go see James. However, after searching for him at his place, and then the garage, I was told that he hadn't shown up for work that morning.

It wouldn't be for another four days that I became aware of the silent tension that was going on at the garage. I'd shown up another time to see if James was available to talk, and was told, yet again, that he wasn't there and hadn't shown up. 'Hadn't been there in well over four days now.'

Although Jack had said it with a light tone, I'd been able to read the worry that had crossed over his features before he'd managed to mask them. It continued ever since. No one's seen hide nor hair of him. He wasn't answering the phone, and pretty much cut himself off from his friends and loved ones.

Cheyenne was being quiet about it all, making it a point to change the subject when her big brother was asked about. Which broke my heart, because most of the time it was me asking her about him. She acted as if I'd done something wrong, and I really wished I knew what the heck it was.

Sighing, I forced myself to walk to Free's office.

I came to a sudden halt when I entered, startled that the entirety of the Free family, minus James and Janie, were all crowded around a small flat screen TV that hung on the wall. It was a little after one in the afternoon on a Tuesday, and my only day off this week. It for sure wasn't all of these people's day off.

"...want to reiterate that no news has been released on the police officer that was shot. The SWAT team was getting into position when a shot rang out from the building across the street. Another one followed shortly after the first. A man fell two floors from the top of the old Coca Cola plant as a result of that shot. He was pronounced dead on arrival at GSMC. The chief of Kilgore Police has yet to issue a statement..." The announcer on the TV was explaining what looked like a shooter that was picking off people that passed through downtown.

"What's going on?" I asked.

Everyone startled and looked at me, even the men. Sam looked guilty. Cheyenne looked terrified. Yet not one person said anything, which made the fear for those people take on a different tone. One that was fear for someone I loved.

"What is it?"

When no answer came, I turned to my brother, imploring him with my eyes to tell me.

He'd just opened his mouth to say something when a police car pulled into the lot, stopping Sam's explanation in its tracks. We all watched as a man, who I now knew as Luke, stepped out of the car.

He was in what had to be the standard SWAT gear. Black cargo pants, black shirt with SWAT spelled out on the chest, and a black Kevlar vest. His hair was a mess, as if he'd been running his fingers through it in agitation.

Which if what I'd just seen on the news was even half as bad as it sounded, was enough to make anyone's hair crazy. He walked with purposeful strides up to the office door and walked in. Directly to Cheyenne.

Texas Tornado

He glanced around the room and hesitated as he saw everyone gathered there, but seemed to come to some decision before turning back to Cheyenne and addressing her.

"Your brother was shot. He's completely fine, being seen at GSMC, but he wanted me to come here and tell you that he couldn't make the dinner date the two of you had planned, and asked that you pick Janie up from school." Luke said softly.

Sam stiffened, and Cheyenne nearly collapsed into his arms.

Not thinking twice, I turned and ran to my car. The drive to the hospital took fifteen minutes. Partially because there was no traffic, but mostly because I was driving a hundred and ten down the highway.

When I pulled into the hospital parking lot, I took a few minutes to compose myself before I bullied my way into the ER. One look at my face had my hospital contact, Marty Sims, turning and walking away, purposefully ignoring me as I stomped my way into the Major ER.

James' tattooed back brought my attention to the far side of the room. A nurse in her twenties with perky boobs and painted on eyebrows tried to stop me from cutting across the room, but I ignored her. James' head popped up and turned to the commotion, and his sharp eyes locked on to me as I barreled towards him.

James was sitting with his legs hanging over the side of a hospital bed. His bare back was facing away from me, black cargo pants covered him from the waist down. He was also wearing a black

SWAT hat facing backwards that was perilously close to making my mouth water.

Once I ascertained that he didn't have any major trauma that I could see, I threw myself at him. He caught me with a small grunt, and wrapped his arms around me, pulling me in tight to his chest. I trembled in his arms, and it wasn't until James' deep gravelly voice said, "Don't cry," that I realized that I was doing just that.

And it was nasty crying at that.

My tears were running down the expanse of his bare chest, and when I leveraged myself up with my hands, placing them on his legs, he grunted in pain. Immediately I extracted myself from his arms carefully, and gasped when I saw that my hand was resting on a white gauze bandage.

"What happened?" I asked softly, gently removing my hand from the tender wound.

"Fucker shot me before I could get my shot off. Dammit."

My brows puckered in confusion. "Why would you be shooting somebody anyway?"

He looked at me as if I was crazy. "Because I'm part of the SWAT team, and they're the ones that take down suspects that are picking off innocent people with .22's?"

"Since when are you on the SWAT team?" I asked in confusion.

"Since when I accepted their offer. Didn't Sam tell you?" He asked.

"No," I said, heartbroken that my brother had kept that from me.

Texas Tornado

Even when he knew I wanted to speak to him. To see him again. I'd thought with the peace offering of chocolate cake would've broken the ice but I never heard from him. Why would my brother keep this from me when he knew I loved him?

I started to rethink letting my brother back into my life after he'd fucked up so royally in the past year. I'd spent every goddamn night with that lying sack of dog crap. I'd asked at least once a day if he'd heard from James, and each time his response had been, 'nothing yet.' I'd told the shithead that I was falling in love with James.

"That," I said, shaking my head, not knowing what the hell to say. "I-I called him every day to see if he knew where you were. I thought maybe you were on vacation or something. I went over there every night, hoping that you'd be home, and you never were."

James' jaw tightened as he listened to me babble.

"Mr. Allen?" A man asked from behind me.

James looked up, and I turned in the circle of his arms and stared at the man with silver hair. Obviously a doctor, he had a warm smile and a smooth voice.

"Yeah?" James nodded.

"My name's Dr. Stone. Are you ready to be stitched up?" Dr. Stone asked as he set his clipboard down and took a seat on the rolling stool.

It was during the fourth stitch in James' thigh that Cheyenne and company showed up.

James didn't acknowledge Sam's presence at all, and neither did I. Cheyenne gave a raised eyebrow to James as she looked from our linked hands to our faces and back. I made a move to remove my hand from James', but he held on tighter so I couldn't get it away from him unless I wanted to make a big deal of it.

"That looks nasty." Cheyenne said in way of greeting.

"Feels nasty too." James agreed.

"It'll leave a pretty wicked scar. Luckily, it only grazed him. Could've been a fuck of a lot worse." The doctor muttered, and then apologized. "Sorry. I was a combat doctor in the army for twenty years. I don't have control of my mouth at times."

"That's okay," I laughed as the doctor did another stitch. "James would be swearing right along with you right now if it wasn't for me."

James squeezed my hand tight before slapping his sister's hands off the side of his face. "Fuck, I said I was fine! Get off me!" He snapped.

His sister slinked away into Sam's arms, which made me finally look at Sam's face. He did not look pleased. My back straightened at the audacity of his anger that was not only palpable, but every bit of it was directed at me.

I gave him my best stink eye, and then turned back towards the doctor that was just finishing the final stitches in James leg.

"You know the routine, I'm sure. Ice. Keep it clean. Take the stitches out in a week. Antibiotics need to be taken twice a day for ten days. I'm assuming you don't want pain meds?" Dr. Stone asked.

"No." James confirmed.

Texas Tornado

"Alright, I'll send Jennifer in with your discharge papers. Hope you feel better soon. It was a good thing you did." Dr. Stone said as he left the curtained off area.

Silence commenced as we waited for Nurse Jennifer to come discharge James.

Sam's face was hard and closed off, emotions wrapped tightly so I couldn't read him at all. With a look of disapproval at me, he started speaking to James, completely ignoring me in the process.

He asked him about his job on the SWAT team, whether he was happy or not, what happened today when he got shot, how often they trained. The shop talk persisted through Jennifer handing over James' discharge papers, and then continued on until we reached Sam's bike.

Both men stopped and turned to study me. I felt the need to get the heck out of there, but I wasn't leaving until I could talk to James. Make him see that we would be good together. To let him know that Jolie didn't bother me anymore.

Well, not that much anyway.

Sam opened his mouth to say something. What, I didn't know, because I interrupted him before he could get the first word out.

"Can I take you home?" I asked James, completely ignoring my brother.

"Yeah, I'd like that," he agreed. "Where're you parked?"

"I parked at the back of the lot and ran in." I gestured towards where my car was parked and started to walk forward.

Sam's voice sounded from behind me. "Shiloh," he started.

I turned like a whirlwind and was in his face in the next second. "You know, right now I'm very upset. I'm mad that I gave you so much of my trust only for you to break it. I'm mad that you knew I was aching to see him and you didn't tell me what was going on. He could've died today, and where would that have left me? You want to know where? I'd be devastated. Over the past month, I've thought of little else than seeing him again. He makes me happy, and I deserve that."

I was crying again, and the heartache on Sam's face gave me a moment of doubt, but I pushed it viciously away. Starting to turn back to James, Cheyenne's voice stopped me.

"That decision was all me. I didn't think he needed to have the distraction in his life right now. He's so caught up with trying to get custody of his daughter, having that piece of trash lying about anything and everything she can think of. I just didn't want him to be used right now. I asked Sam to not tell you anything, and then I had him play the sister card with James. I never meant for it to hurt...." Cheyenne explained.

"That wasn't your choice to make. Did I step in when you jumped in the sack that first night you met Sam? No. Did I say anything at *all* about how fast you moved? No. I didn't interfere in your life choices, even though it went against everything that was ingrained in me to do so. Have the same courtesy for me." James snapped, taking my hand and leading me away.

We didn't speak while we walked to my truck. I handed James the keys like I'd done so many other times before. He opened the passenger door for me and helped me inside. Then he grabbed the seatbelt, leaned over my lap and snapped it into place. Slamming the door, he walked stiffly to the driver's side, and hopped inside like the movement didn't pain him, even though I knew it did.

We sat quietly in the parking lot for a few tense minutes. I could tell there was something that James wanted to say, but something was stopping him from doing it. After about four minutes of just sitting there, I broke.

"For the love of all that's holy. Spit it out!" I boomed.

I hadn't meant to yell quite so loud, but with the cab of the truck, it echoed off all the corners and made it much louder than I'd intended.

James' head turned, and my breath started coming in pants when I saw the raw emotion and heat in his eyes. "Five fucking weeks. It's been fucking torture. The only good thing about all of this was the job I got with the PD. I didn't realize how much I missed being a useful person. That doesn't mean that it didn't hurt every fucking second to ignore your calls. Your emails. Your texts. The only thing making it bearable was Janie. Then Janie would tell me how much she missed you, and I'd be thinking about you all over again."

I pursed my lips because I was unsure of what he wanted me to say. I'd done those things, and he hadn't called me back once. Although, if I'd known he was staying at his mother's place, I would've just bombarded him there instead of stewing for five weeks.

With my non-response hanging in the thick air, he started my truck and drove it out of the hospital parking lot.

He didn't acknowledge Sam's wrist flick, and neither did I.

His mother's place was in a very nice neighborhood that I hadn't seen yet. Although I've passed it many times. Its location was perfect. About three minutes from the local schools, five minutes from the police station, and two minutes from Free. The house was immaculate. I was willing to bet my entire life savings that James was the reason it looked so beautiful.

"The house is beautiful." I said in awe.

"This is the historical district. All these houses were from the beginning of the Oil Boom we had in the 1930s. Solid in structure. The inside looks even better than the outside. My father bought it when it was a piece of junk, and fixed it up during his leave from the Army. When he died, it started to deteriorate. Old houses need constant upkeep. Shit breaks, and you have to replace it. Then something else breaks the next week. My mom wasn't much of a handyman, and couldn't afford much in the way of extra fees. When I started working, I used my money for the upkeep on the house. I learned a lot of shit just from having to fix everything myself." James explained.

He sounded a tad nervous, and he was speaking much more than he usually did. Which I found quite cute. "Can I see the inside?"

"Of course." He nodded and opened the door.

When I went to open my own, his voice froze me in my tracks. "Wait for me. I'll get it."

I waited. Because it wasn't often when you found a man that would open the car door for you. James was that old-fashioned type of man that did it without thought. Never once had I managed to open my own door, and I loved it.

I probably resembled the biggest bitch on the planet when I watched him hobble around the truck to my door instead of just getting out myself. I could see the grimace of pain on his face no matter how much he tried to hide it. However, I knew that he wouldn't appreciate the fact that I was trying to help him out.

I knew from experience that men didn't like their defaults on display. Men like James and my brothers didn't show pain, didn't acknowledge it, and didn't speak of it. If you knew what was good for you, you just didn't bring up the obvious. Instead of ignoring the fact that he was probably in a lot more pain than he was letting on. I'd grown up with Sebastian. I knew better.

I slid down from the truck before he could actually lift me, and I got a growl at my impertinence. I ignored it. There was no way I was letting him lift me as he usually did.

"How long does it take to mow this place?" I asked, aghast at the vast amount of green grass that covered the corner lot.

"A while. It needs to be done again, but seeing as we only have a push mower, it'll be a good week or so before I can get it done. It'll feel worse tomorrow." He said gesturing towards his ripped pants and the bandage that poked through from underneath.

"I can do..." I trailed off at the sharp look of *Hell No* on his face.

I smiled and started walking towards the front door, stepping over the bike that lay down across the walk, but then turning back to move it out of the way so James didn't have to do the same. He gave me a mock glare, but the smile that curved up his lips let me know he wasn't really irritated with me.

I kicked the kickstand out on the bike and had to laugh when I remembered how Janie had reacted last week when her mother tried to give her a bike with training wheels.

"You should have seen how Janie reacted when her mother pulled out this pink sparkly bike with streamers on the handles. Oh, my God. I thought she was going to explode."

"I saw. It didn't make me happy. Janie's been riding a bike without training wheels for two years now. It was too small and she hates pink." James said with exasperation.

"You were there?" I gasped.

I'd continued to take Janie over to see her mother one day a month. I should've known he wouldn't be far behind on those days. He didn't trust Anna in the slightest. Hell, each subsequent visit we had with her made my status of her as an unfit parent even more and more concrete.

James grin was blinding when he turned around from opening the front door. "Oh, I was there. I watched as you held Janie when that bitch went to put her arms around her. I watched when Janie left two hours later attached to your back. I watched you drop her off at Cheyenne's. I watched you walk inside your apartment and forget to set your alarm."

The last part was growled. Come to think of it, I did remember not arming it. I also remember my brother calling to tell me that it wasn't armed, and wondering how he even knew that little tid-bit of information.

I gave him an accusing look, but he looked unrepentant. "So that's how Sam knew. His only explanation was *'Do you think I'm stupid.'*"

"Yeah, I should've known something was up then when he wasn't upset that I'd followed you home and knew that you didn't arm your alarm. He was happy that I'd called, and that I was watching out for you. My fucking sister." He snarled.

After I closed the door, I put my hand on his shoulder. "Hey, this wasn't your fault. I'm sure Cheyenne had a really good reason."

"You know, she probably didn't have a good reason at all, but I'll let her explain it to me in a few days. Maybe then I won't be so pissed off. This five weeks has really been sheer hell."

I watched him lift his fingers and scratch his beard like he was contemplating saying something else, and when it continued on for another minute or so, I decided to give him some time and explore.

The first room I came to was a formal dining room. However, there was a Lego wonderland dominating the eight-foot glass table that gave it a 'lived in' feel instead of a 'don't spill a goddamn thing' feel. Hell, the chandelier over the table had a string of army men hanging from the crystals.

"Yeah, my mom would have a fucking cow if she saw this right now. However, she informed me last week that the house was mine, and that she planned on moving in with Todd Masterson when she got home from her next assignment."

I gasped and spun around. "Your mom is fucking your lawyer?"

His eyes squeezed shut as if he was in pain. "Yeah, from what I can tell. They got close during my first trial for custody of Janie ten months ago. They've taken it slow since they lost their significant others, whom they loved like crazy.

"Awww," I cooed. "How sweet!"

He glared at me, took my hand, and showed me the rest of the house. You could definitely tell that it was a family home. Kid's toys were laying everywhere. James' socks and boots in the kitchen under the table. Dirty dishes in the sink. Cereal boxes out on the counters. Toothpaste cap of the tubes. They needed a housecleaner. Although, every bit of it is what you would expect in a home. What I didn't expect was to walk into a dream room when I came to the door in the kitchen.

"Most houses in the South don't have basements due to flooding and the Texas Red Clay making it nearly impossible to dig. I'm not sure why this house has it. All I know is I'm glad it does. I've made this into a hell of a down room. I hadn't realized how much I missed it until I moved back here."

When I walked down the stainless steel steps, I stepped out into the ultimate man cave. There was a bar in the far corner made to look like a traditional Irish pub. The ground was concrete. However, it was unique in that it was painted a deep black. The walls matched the Irish theme of the bar, and had a wooden look to them. A massive sectional sofa sat against the far wall and faced an even more massive TV.

Texas Tornado

Neon beer signs and metal stars lined the walls. The front wall behind the bar held a map of the United States made out of license plates. Pictures of the Free 'crew' were interspersed here and there. I was even more surprised to see one of me. Everything fit what ultimately defines 'man cave' except one thing.

"Is that a hammock?" I asked walking towards it.

"Yeah," James answered from directly behind me.

It was connected directly to the ceiling by chains. "Why?"

He laughed. "I get asked that a lot. Normally I say it's a sex swing because it annoys Cheyenne, but since she's not here to enjoy my taunting, I'll tell you the truth."

"And?" I asked with raised eyebrows as I sat back carefully into the hammock.

"I just wanted it. It gets fucking hot in the summer, and when we were in Iraq and Afghanistan, we slept on them. Sometimes when I can't sleep, I come down here. I can find it instantly on a hammock."

"Oh," I said somewhat disappointed that there wasn't a better reason. "I like the sex swing explanation. It sounds better."

His eyes darkened as he watched me throw my hands up above my head, which in turn exposed some of my belly. Goosebumps trailed over my body at the look in his eyes. Liquid heat pooled in my nether regions, but I didn't rub them together. That would only bring more attention to my plight.

He leaned down and placed his hand at the top edge. "Scoot over so I can lay down."

With a little maneuvering, I scooted over to the edge, and he rolled into place beside me. His leg seemed to buckle, though, because instead of easing down onto the hammock, he collapsed. The momentum of the shift in weight had me rolling so I was all but lying on top of him. My chest in his face. My left leg straddling his firm stomach, and my arms grabbing onto the ropes above his head.

His hands gripped my waist tightly, and it was all I could do not to rub my nipples against his face.

"Fuck," I hissed and looked down into his eyes.

His mouth was level with my right nipple that was only shielded by a thin camisole. His eyes were dark and focused intently on my cleavage that was practically spilling out of my shirt.

From there, I'm not sure what happened first. It could've been me leaning down, or it might have been James leaning forward, but my nipple somehow ended up in James' mouth. The fabric of my knit skirt slithered up my backside as James' hand made its way up my thigh.

His hot mouth transferred to the other nipple, and my hands found their way into his hair, giving it a good yank when his seeking hand found my cotton covered core. Scratch that. They were no longer cotton covered anything when James' hand fisted the flimsy fabric, and wrenched them from my body.

I jolted at the surprise, and reared up. My nipple escaped his mouth, and I looked down at him in astonishment. "You just tore my favorite pair of panties!"

Texas Tornado

His smile was definitely non-repentant. "I'll buy you another pair." He said just before fisting my hair, looping the ends around his fist, and pulling me carefully forward.

"My first boyfriend got me those panties! They have sentimental value!" I said in mock outrage.

I wasn't really. I'd gotten them at the dollar store the first week I was in Kilgore. He didn't need to know that though.

"Good riddance." James murmured right before his mouth settled on mine.

I've had three sexual encounters in my life. Once with my high school boyfriend of five months. Once with a one night stand. And then there was Zander, who was the most selfish person on the face of the planet, so I never counted his sex. He was *a stick it in and come* kind of guy.

James was definitely not. Just from one simple kiss, I was so very close to tipping over the edge into an orgasm that I pulled away. My hips, however, did not stop their grinding, and I saw stars.

"Jesus, that's all it took? Just your pretty little pussy rubbing up against my dick?" James asked, breathless from our kiss.

My hands went to the bottom of my camisole, and yanked it over my head. My breasts sprang free, and with no obstacle in his way, James latched onto them again with a voraciousness that surprised me.

"We can't do this on here." James said in between breasts.

"Watch me."

Although it took some doing, I finally maneuvered myself to where my feet were planted firmly on the floor on either side of James body. Lifting up, I started fiddling with his belt to get it off. After three failed attempts to get the belt free, I finally glared at James. He tried to wipe the smile off his face, but didn't quite manage it in time.

When I started to get off him, he reared up and wrapped his hands around my hips again. "Relax. It's a police belt. It's not meant to come off easily."

With deft movements, he used his one free hand to work the belt loose of the loop. The clinging signaled he'd worked it free, then his hips lifted as he ripped the belt out from under his body. It hit the floor with a dull thud, and he lifted his arms so his fingers were gripping the wooden slat at the very top.

"Be gentle with me." He rasped.

"Oh, this won't hurt your leg in the least. Now that dick of yours...." I trailed off as I saw the 'dick' under question.

"Jesus," I exclaimed. "I'm not really sure how this works."

"How what works? You've never had sex before?" James asked, looking quite alarmed.

"Of course I've had sex!" I practically yelled. "What I haven't had sex with, though, is a man with a piece of metal in his junk."

"It's the same concept, sweetheart. Just ease onto my cock. The piercing does its own work. It'd help if you got it nice and wet with your mouth first, however."

I looked into his eyes to see if he was joking, but only need shined through. Shuffling back on my feet, I bent down and gave his cock head an experimental lick before fisting his hard length in my hand. My fingers encountered the piercing that had a starring role in my fantasies over the past few months, and I ran one finger around the top bead of the piercing.

The metal, warmed by his skin, was smooth. "Doesn't this affect how you pee?" I asked just as I let my mouth sink down on his fat cock.

His strangled reply amused me. "Not unless I'm hard."

Running my free hand down the length of his cock, I let my other wander down to cup his ball sack, and tug it lightly. He involuntary forced himself into my mouth, and I withdrew to take a breath.

"What kind of piercing is this?" I asked on my next lick that went down the length of his shaft.

"Reverse Prince Albert." He gasped as I took his cock back into my mouth. The head of his cock met the back of my throat, the metal ball making the feeling incredibly weird.

James' strangled cry made me laugh. "Can you fucking ride me already? I'm dying here."

I let his dick slip from my mouth and stood. The knit skirt I was wearing fell, concealing my lady bits from his viewing pleasure. His response was to jackknife out of the hammock, place his own feet down onto the floor, and yank the skirt up until it was just under my breasts.

I'm sure he'd have taken it all the way off if he could've done it without standing and putting pressure on his leg. "Impatient are we?" I asked.

"I've been fucking coming in my sleep again like a damn teenager to dreams of you and how you taste. You have no goddamn clue how embarrassing that is. I can't get the taste of you out of my mind. I torture myself all day long wondering if you taste the same as you did that day." He groaned as he fell back to the hammock.

"Maybe we can do that later. Right now, I want to fuck your brains out." I said softly before taking my abandoned position back up.

The head of his cock kissed my entrance, and just as I was about to sink down, he stopped me with a firm grip on my hips.

"Fuck," James said trying to sit up again. "I need to go get a condom."

"Only if you really want to. I'm clean. I had to have some tests run before I came here. I didn't have any diseases, and I've been on birth control for a really long time." I said, hoping beyond hope he didn't ask me why I needed testing before I came here.

I'm pretty sure that'd be a mood killer to know the girl you were about to fuck into outer space had cancer less than a year ago.

"I'm clean, too. I had to have a physical to get hired on at at the PD. I also had a vasectomy when I had Janie." He explained as he helped me line up his cock with my wet entrance.

Dropping my weight down once I had an inch or so inside me, I about burst out of orbit. That fucking piece of jewelry, combined with the size of his dick, stretched me and hit all the right places at once. Not one single iota of space was available for him to add more. I felt so full to bursting that I was already teetering on that razor wire that separated me from my orgasmic state.

"Jesus you're tight." James gritted out between clenched teeth.

"It's been a while," I explained.

"It feels like it's been never. Ride me already." He said, trying to move my hips to the motion he wanted.

I let him move me the way he wanted, totally feeling the way his cock's piercing dragged against the spot inside of me that had never been stimulated by anything but me before.

"Oh, God." I panted as I moved myself up with the rhythm of his hands on my hips.

I sank down only for him to lift me back up again. The slap-slap of our bodies meeting was the only thing besides our mingled breathing that could be heard in the room.

A glorious feeling of euphoria started to come over me, and I knew if he could keep it up just a few moments longer, I'd be falling over that cliff.

"I'm close." I exhaled.

His response was one of his hands leaving my hip, and sliding down to collide with my clit. With deft flicks of his fingers, he worked me closer and closer to the pinnacle.

With his growled demand of, "Come," I burst.

My channel clamped down hard on his cock. My pulsing vaginal muscles worked his cock, and shortly after I started to slow down, he sped up. Over and over he pounded into me, only extending my own orgasm.

"Fuck me!" He growled.

Doing just that, I started to slam myself down on his shaft. The slapping of our bodies meeting only got louder. However, the new sound of our mingling juices could be heard as well. His abdominal muscles tensed, and with one last thrust, he planted himself inside me as far as he could go.

Pulsating heat splashed against my cervix, sending me into another smaller orgasm that the one before it, but no less intense.

Falling forward, I lay against his chest. Both of us breathing hard and fast.

"That was..." I said, at a loss for words.

"Perfection?" He laughed.

"Yeah, perfection. I think any more sex like that'll likely kill me. You'll have to do all the work next time. I'm in no shape to keep that up as much as I want it." I quipped.

"I think I can handle that. Just give me a few to recoup some of my breath."

Quiet moments followed that announcement as we both caught our breath.

A board creaked above us, and we both turned our head until we had the basement door in our sights.

"Is that door locked?" I asked sitting up.

"Nope. The only other person it could be is my mom, who is out of state, or my sister." He said, sitting up as well.

We didn't rise, because to be honest, this would block more of our bodies from whomever it was than us standing and trying to scramble across the room and behind something to get dressed. That is if I could even find anything to dress into.

Texas Tornado

The creak of the basement door announced someone's arrival. "James?" Cheyenne called.

"If you don't want to see the swing in use, don't come any further down." James growled.

The descending feet stopped in their tracks, then turned and quickly ran back up the stairs. "Ohhhh, yuuuck!"

James' chuckle, combined with my own, made him slip from the snug depths of my body in a wet rush.

"We've made a bit of a mess." I stated the obvious.

"Sometimes a mess is a good thing."

Chapter 15

The most dangerous place on earth is between a biker and his bike.

-Biker Truth

James

Once I was changed, I glanced at my watch and saw that I had a little over fifteen minutes before Janie got off the bus for the day. She'd be happy to see me instead of Mrs. Kowalsky. Nothing against the old broad, but she tried to treat Janie as if she were still a two year old kid instead of a six year old. Janie liked the woman, but I'd win out every single time.

Washing my hands quickly, I walked down the hallway, wincing with every other step as my leg throbbed. Hell, it wasn't even that bad, but the feeling of the top layer of skin being gone was almost worse than any other injury I'd had before.

My eyes scanned all the photos that lined the hallway as I walked past. Every stage of Janie's life was featured in that hallway. Most of the newest ones were Janie's school photos and Christmas pictures. Cheyenne and mom used to take her to get her portraits made in a studio when she was a baby so I'd see how big she was getting.

Soft voices made me slow in my progression towards the living room. I stopped as I got to the mouth of the hallway, listening to my sister explain.

Texas Tornado

"I never meant to hurt you both. I was just trying to get James to make a move. He seemed so unhappy working at the garage. I'd known that he was getting offers from Luke to join the SWAT team, and I wanted him to pursue it. The only way he'd make that decision was for him to have a reason to leave Free." Cheyenne explained hesitantly.

"Well, you definitely accomplished that." Shiloh said dryly. "Next time, maybe you can try to not use our relationship as a diving board. These last five weeks have sucked balls."

Cheyenne made a miserable sound in her throat before continuing. "I never intended for him to leave. Hell, he wouldn't even speak to Max. Which is saying something because it's not often that those two don't speak. They're the type of friends that end up sitting on their porch when their ninety-five and yell at the neighborhood kids to get off their lawn."

"It was me. I'd pissed him off, and he needed a break." Shiloh sighed.

"What are you talking about?" Cheyenne asked.

"I told him in a voicemail that he'd have to choose Jolie or me. I left it in a note on the kitchen table before y'all got me drunk that night after James' was arrested."

Coming further into the room, I watched Cheyenne's lips purse. "They have an extremely weird relationship. When Max and James were younger, they had another friend, Briggs, who'd died. Everyone used to call them the Three Musketeers. One night, while on his way home from a party, Briggs was hit by a drunk driver, and killed. That drunk driver was Jolie's father. James hated how the school treated Jolie, and he befriended her. I'd always thought that Max felt the same until recently. Max doesn't like her at all either. He says she's manipulative, and uses James any way she can."

"I can definitely see that. The only times I've seen her are when she's needed something from him." Shiloh concurred.

Feeling that it was time to set their illusions straight, I came into the room and stopped behind the back of one of the couch. I placed my arms down on the back and leaned in to take the pressure off my leg.

"Let me tell you girls something about Jolie. I don't love her, nor have I ever loved her. I feel bad for how she was treated after Briggs' death, and I try to help her out any way I can. I am aware of how she tries to manipulate me to get what she wants. However, when I look at Jolie, I see a stray beaten dog who hasn't been treated nicely in a long fucking time. She's manipulative because she doesn't know any other way to be. If she's not that way, she's treated like a stray dog again. I have never been, nor will ever be, in love with her. I'm in love with you, Shiloh. There's a large difference between the way I am with her, and the way I am with you." My eyes were on Shiloh as I said the last few statements, and I watched as her eyes lit with happiness.

"James..." Shiloh started to say before I interrupted her.

"As for you," I said turning my gaze to Cheyenne. "I am your older brother. I have four years on you. I am thirty-one damn years old. I do not need you interfering with my love life. You could've cost me something great. Something that meant the world to me. How easy is it to find someone that fits well in your life when you have a kid to think about? To add on to the fact that you brought one of my greatest friends into it is even worse. I've trusted Sam's judgment for many years. If I wouldn't have, I'd have been dead. I think next time you need to think about the consequences of your actions before implementing those actions. You put a strain on a relationship that was nearly twelve years in the making. I've always trusted him to be straight with me, and it really hurt to know that he didn't approve of me and Shiloh being together. It's killed me the last month not to be around her, but I only did so out of respect of the man I trust most in the world."

The sound of Janie's bus stopping outside of the house stopped me from any further explanation, so I hobbled to the door and opened it with a wide smile on my face. I waved to Mrs. Kowalsky who was watering her petunias. Again.

I forced myself not to limp so I didn't alarm Janie, and I waited with my arms crossed against my chest for her to notice I was home. It didn't take long.

She'd just gotten to the bottom step of the school bus when she spotted me standing next to her bike. "Daddy!" She shrieked and launched herself off the bus and sprinted across the yard. Only she didn't come to me, she veered off at the last possible second and shrieked, "Shiloh!"

I could only laugh. I was happy she liked Shiloh because she was going to be seeing a lot of her. Shiloh started to head inside with Janie wrapped up in her arms when we heard the distinct sound of pipes pulling on to our street. Shiloh froze, as did I, as we watched Silas pull into our driveway and shut off the bike.

When he stood up, you could tell he was hurt by the grimace of pain on his face as he swung his leg over the bike. His face was a shadow of pain as he took the painful steps toward us.

I knew it was bad just by the grim expression on his face. Something was seriously wrong.

"I need you to call Sam over here now. I've already called Sebastian. He'll be here in less than an hour. Got any beer?" Silas asked.

"What is he doing here?" Cheyenne snarled.

"Daddy, are you okay?" Shiloh asked as she inched closer to him.

"Not now, baby. I need to sit down or I'll fall down. Show me where, 'cause once I sit I won't be getting back up again." He said with strain evident in his voice.

"You can lay down on the couch. Daddy sleeps there all the time. Sometimes he lets me color on him while he does." Janie supplied.

"That sounds perfect, Caroline. I appreciate it." Silas said as he walked stiffly to the couch.

"Nobody calls me Caroline. I only get called Caroline when I'm in trouble." Janie snapped.

The distaste for the name was beyond anything I've ever known a kid to show for something like a name. Normally it's reserved for broccoli, or scorpions. Not a name though.

Texas Tornado

"Yes, I know. I just don't understand why you're going by Janie when your name is Caroline Jeanine. Caroline is a good strong name." Silas winced as he sat down carefully.

"Cause my daddy wanted to call me Janie, that's why." Janie said stubbornly, but still gave him a pillow to prop up on so he would be more comfortable.

"My apologies, Janie." Silas whispered solemnly.

"Can someone tell me why the hell he's in our house? Better yet, someone get him the hell out." Cheyenne fumed in the corner of the room with her arms crossed across her chest.

Silas gave Cheyenne a long thorough look before coming to some sort of decision. "My boy picked a good woman. What would you do for him, Cheyenne? Would you fight for him? Kill for him? Leave him? Let him go if that's what he wanted?" Silas volleyed the questions at her one after the other, and with each question, Cheyenne's ire became more confusion than not.

"If that's what it took. I'd do absolutely anything." She agreed.

"That's what I thought. Maybe you and my boy need to take a step back and think of it from my side of things. Do you not think I had reasons for doing the things I did? Do you think it was easy to do anything to my boy? Kids are supposed to have what Janie here has; not what my babies had. I did my best though, and I think I've finally met my match." He was whispering gruffly by the time he finished. Pain was etched on his face, but this time, it wasn't because of physical pain, but emotional.

The sound of Sam's Suburban pulled up outside, and I saw on Cheyenne's face that she was torn. She didn't want to hurt Sam, but she knew what Silas had to say might potentially change his whole outlook on his childhood, and maybe even his entire life. Just like I did as soon as Sebastian told us a little of it the other morning. Only, not once in the past few weeks had I told Sam what I'd learned, and I didn't know how the outcome would turn out by the end of this meeting.

One thing was for sure, and that was that lives would most assuredly be irrevocably changed.

***

Sam sat on the recliner. His head was in his hands, and he looked fucking defeated.

It was hard to see.

Sam has always been bigger than life to me. When I was a green-nosed, hot-shot sniper all of twenty two, Max and I were selected to join a covert-ops team. We'd thought we were bad asses, and Sam was the first one to prove us wrong. He pushed us so hard that we wanted to quit, but only the knowing smile on Sam's face that showed he knew we wouldn't cut it kept us going.

It was only later that we found out Sam had the upmost respect for us. He'd told us that he'd never seen two people work harder to become someone that was needed. He'd told us that he was proud of us, would always trust us at his back, and would be honored if we'd protect his for him as well.

Texas Tornado

Never in my ten years of knowing the man had I seen him quite so defeated. Even when we'd been in impossible situations and staring down the gun of a M-14 did he look like this.

"Tell me one more time." Sam demanded of his father.

"I don't know what's going to change in between the third time and the fourth, Samuel Cash." Silas rasped.

"Please..." Sam left the request hanging, and he was rewarded when Silas continued. A-fucking-gain.

"The summer I met your mother was my first infiltration into a MC that was known for chain-raping women, filming it, and then selling the videos. They also had a lucrative stable, as well as some coke running on the side. The first time I saw your mother was the day that they normally did the grabs. She'd been in the cross hares of one of my 'brothers' when I claimed her. I didn't know what else to do. Goddamn mission and all that shit didn't care about a few casualties. They were looking at the bigger picture. So, I did what I had to do, only they wanted to film me taking her the first time as my initiation into the club. That was my test. I passed with flying colors." He snarled.

Sam's fists went tight at his forehead, but he didn't interrupt as he'd done the previous three times. Instead, he stayed seated. Oh, don't get me wrong, he was pissed, but he wasn't going to interrupt this time.

"That's the day you were conceived. I kept your mother separate from the club. I fell in love with your mother, head over heels. However, the club didn't do monogamy, and I wasn't expected to either. Not wanting them to hurt my 'citizen wife' as they called her, I found Lettie. That's where your brother and sister came in. I had an 'ol lady, that was aware of what went down in the club to an extent, and then I had your mother, my real wife in the eyes of God and the government."

Sebastian smothered an oath from the recliner beside Sam, but he still looked calm and collected. He'd heard the explanation before, but I'm sure he was still just as affected now as he was then.

"So then what?" Sam asked.

His voice was tight and controlled. No emotion was leaked from it whatsoever.

"I stayed in the CIA. They felt it'd be paramount for me to stay in the club. Make a name for myself. By the time you were three, I'd made so many enemies, and it wasn't safe for me to leave The Agency, nor the club, which was well on the road to being completely legal. The club became my home. After routing out the shit, making the businesses legit, what was left became mine. By then your mother already hated me. She knew about the club. Knew she wasn't welcome there, even though by that point it was safe for her if she'd been interested in becoming a part of it. Knew I had a woman on the side. Then there was my so called 'second in command.'"

"Shovel." Sam nodded.

"Yeah, after he fucked your eye up." Silas shook his head.

The eye in question must've been when Sam was pushed by Silas' second in command when he was just a young boy. The man had pushed him so hard that he'd fallen and cut his eye open on a motorcycle's chrome wheels, barely missing his eye by a matter of millimeters.

"I was done following orders that were sent from The Agency. Those men were mine, and I'd do with them what I damn well pleased. The club was very important to me, but you more so. Shovel was the last boy left over that wanted everything to go back to the old ways. We weren't making the same money, but it was also nothing to sneeze at either. He was pissed at everything I represented. It was the worst mistake of his life taking his anger out for me on you. Your mom left the last time, and I decided it was probably for the best that she stay gone. Maybe she'd get a better life without my fucked-up-ness leaking over onto her. Lettie didn't last much longer either. I didn't have to keep up appearances any longer, and she didn't like the new me." Silas told him, eyes closed.

"You still love her." Sam stated the obvious.

"Burns everyday." Silas answered simply.

"You beat her." Sam accused.

Silas' eyes snapped open and he was off the couch before anyone could even blink. The man was quick. Even hurt he had the speed of a striking snake. Sam stayed seated, but barely, when Silas' crowded his space. Which was hard for Sam to do, but he managed it.

"Never," Silas emphasized that with a pointed finger in Sam's face. "Never, did I beat that woman."

"She used to have bruises. Rope burns. Marks. *Someone* did something to her." Sam hissed.

"I haven't a clue what you're talking about, son." Silas said, shaking his head.

He didn't either. The confusion on his face was evident. Either he didn't do it, or he didn't *remember* doing it.

"It only happened on the times you brought her back home after she ran with me. You'd punish her, and the next day she'd be fucked up again. Planning on the next time for us to leave."

A small smile came over Silas' face before he covered it with the blank mask.

"I don't know that I need to get into logistics with you about your mother, but answer me this. Tell me it's never crossed your mind to tie your woman to your bed. To spank her. To let her know she's yours and nobody else's? To let everybody else know, too. You may not have expressed it, but I bet it's crossed your mind before, hasn't it?"

I, for one, knew that feeling. It'd been growing a lot over the past few months, but ever since this afternoon with Shiloh, I had this raw need inside of me to make sure she knew she was mine. To make sure that everyone else knew it too. It was a burning need that I'd never experienced before.

Cheyenne snickered from the corner before she smothered it with her hand over her mouth. Her eyes were wide and filled with mirth. I just knew that if Ember were to have been here, they'd be going at it like little girls. Giggling and carrying on.

Sam's eyebrows pinched together in thought, and then spread wide as realization dawned. "That's...that's just fucking sick."

Texas Tornado

"Well, it was all consensual. I loved that woman with everything I possessed."

"You could've shown it better." Sam muttered.

"If I'd have shown you better...or her better... you'd be fucking dead. I gave up everything I loved so everyone could have a better home. I don't know a single fucking one of my kids as I should. Have you ever tried treating someone you love with every single cell in your body, as if they meant nothing to you? To see the betrayal? To know that you'll never know your goddamn grandchildren. It eats my guts every day to know I let you slip through my fingers. To know that the man you became, one I am proud of more than anything, wasn't that way because of me. Not that the anonymity did your sister any good."

The lasts words out of Silas' mouth were muttered under his breath. Obviously he hadn't meant for us to hear him, but we did.

"What do you mean?" Sam thundered.

Silas' lips thinned, and he didn't say anything.

"Was this the abduction James said something about? What happened?" Sam demanded.

"Quiet." Silas hissed. The threat was more than evident, which was enough to snap Sam's mouth shut with an audible snap.

Silence followed his command. So much of it that you could hear the movie playing in the family room. Shiloh and Janie talking about what they were doing for dinner. Obviously, that was enough to make Silas sure that Shiloh wouldn't overhear what he was about to impart.

"I was sloppy. I loved that little girl more than anything. I made the mistake of taking her out for ice cream on her sixth birthday, and it cost that girl everything. I was jumped by a man that recognized me. How, I don't know. I wasn't wearing my cut. I was in a brand new truck. I didn't even go to town. It was just a fucking fluke to have a member from a rival club at the Tobacco Junction across from the Dairy Queen. They knocked me out when I was getting the goddamn ice cream and she was playing on the playground. When I woke up, she was gone. I didn't find her again for two more days. She wasn't the same, and never has been since. From there, I just distanced myself, and never gave anyone any attention, too scared that something like that would happen again if I did."

"That's why she has nightmares and night terrors?" Sam asked brokenly.

"Yeah," he said nodding his head. "She doesn't remember much from those two days, and I thank God that she doesn't. She wasn't in good shape. No bones were broken, and she wasn't violated, but I have a feeling that they tortured her in other ways. Although, I'll never know for sure. There was no one left alive when I was done."

Shiloh would've been Janie's age when she was taken. Even thinking about the same thing happening to Janie made me understand where Silas was coming from. Since he couldn't leave the life he'd made, he did the only thing he could. And that was cut the people he loved the most off from his life, at the expense of his own happiness.

Knowing that a change of topic was needed for now, I asked the question that had been on the tip of my tongue since he'd arrived.

Texas Tornado

"How about you tell us what's wrong with you, and why you're here right now?"

"Amen." Sebastian muttered.

The preliminaries needed to be covered for Sam and Cheyenne's benefit. Otherwise, they wouldn't have listened.

"Frozen, 'Loh!" It was repeated twelve thousand times before I could hear the sounds of Frozen coming from the family room again. "Okay, okay. Fuck." I heard Shiloh mutter under her breath.

She was with the kids. Although she wanted to hear about what was going on, someone needed to keep the kids occupied, and since she'd heard half the story before, not to mention being somewhat a part of Silas' life, unlike Sam, she volunteered to go watch a movie with the kids while the grownups could talk.

Silas sighed. "This doesn't leave this room. I've worked my entire fucking career to get this piece of shit, and I'm so close I can fucking taste it."

Reaching into his vest pocket, he pulled out a folded up file folder. With careful precise movements, he started to extract each sheet, laying them down carefully and neatly so everyone could see.

"Who's..." Cheyenne started to say when her voice strangled as the last picture was set out.

"Yes, that is what you think it is."

My inner fury skyrocketed as I took in what was laid out before me. Little girls, all under the age of what had to be thirteen, dead. All of them were Caucasian. Not as precise on hair color though. Some were blondes, others brunettes. One curly redhead.

"As you can see, they have a thing for little girls. I won't go into detail on what's been done to them. Y'all can read that information for yourself. I don't want to read it again. Needless to say, they don't have it easy after they're taken. The foreign trade for Caucasian American girls is through the roof. The man who's the ringleader of this has a thing for pre-school aged blondes. He also has the entire South Eastern side of The Cerberus Legion at his back seeing as he's the president of that region."

Silence. Utter goddamn silence.

"What..." Sebastian said shaking his head. "What..."

Sebastian was a badass in every way. From what I'd learned from Shiloh, he was a marine for five years. After Shiloh had left us alone while she put her nephew down to bed, I'd learned some more about him that he wouldn't have divulged if she were to have been in the room.

After his second tour of duty in Afghanistan had commenced, he'd done some thinking about things before deciding not to re-up his commitment. He'd prospected for a year before he'd been patched in with The Dixie Wardens MC. He worked tooth and nail for the next eight years to become vice president. His dad didn't give it to him; it was earned.

From what I'd come to understand about The Dixie Wardens Motorcycle Club from my contacts and a few favors from Jack and Winter, I'd learned that the majority of The Dixie Wardens MC were all law abiding citizens. Sebastian was a member of the local fire department, as were quite a few others. There were also a few police officers in the mix.

However, just because they had regular jobs didn't mean they didn't take care of a problem with lethal force if need be. Didn't protect their territory and club with their lives. They were nothing to sneeze at. A solid four state spread with three separate charters, they demanded respect. They dominated Louisiana, Arkansas, and Alabama. In those three states, they were the ones you thought about when you heard someone talking about a 'motorcycle club.' However, they were also in Texas and Oklahoma as well.

They were a solid 1000 plus members strong and still growing. For Sebastian to have a reaction such as the one he was having now, he had to believe that it was bad.

I'd only heard about The Cerberus Legion from the media and paper. Since they weren't in the area, I had no reason to be concerned before. However, now it was different. Something was happening here, and it was big.

"The agency isn't sure where to go from here. My cover was blown two nights ago when we had a meeting. They'd contacted me for alliances in my states. They wanted a way into the Southern portions of the US so they could find a way to smuggle their cargo into Mexico. Which is how it was supposed to go since we'd been feeding them the information on us for nearly a year. I'd done pretty good just coming off as a president of a MC. Then your fucking shithead of a sister started asking questions about you, and everything went to shit. I'd told him I didn't have any children. No wife. No 'ol lady. Then your sister went and did background checks, and started hunting for birth certificates, asking questions. Found your mother's name. The birth certificate has me listed as your father. I was selfish. I needed that connection to you, although I thought I'd done a good job in hiding it from my enemies. Left no ties or connections. Not from my own goddamn daughter though. It was sloppy of me, but the man had a thing for princesses, and I didn't want him to think he could have my daughter so our alliance would be more solid. It all just added up, things worked against me. His man found Sebastian first, and the other two later." Silas explained with his face in his hands.

"The club doesn't know that Sebastian's yours?" I asked, bewildered.

"No. I didn't want them treating me differently if they knew I was his kid. Never came up again. They knew we were close, but they probably only contributed it to the fact that I was VP." Sebastian explained.

"You didn't bring him around when he was a kid?" Sam asked with surprise.

"He was there some when he was a baby, but from then on, only sparingly, and never after the age of nine. Lettie moved two towns over and took them with her, refusing to bring them back. I went to them when I wanted to see them." Silas explained.

Footsteps from the hallway had me turning my head. The others didn't hear it, didn't know the house like I did. Didn't know the creeks each step on the old hardwood floor made. I did, which is why I was able to see Shiloh's devastated face as she came into the room.

Texas Tornado

***

Shiloh

"Hello?" I answered my ringing phone.

"Hi, Shiloh. How are you doing?" Melissa asked.

Melissa was the team leader for our division of CPS. She was a hard woman, but with over twenty-eight years in the child protective services, who wouldn't be?

I liked her, and respected her. Not once in my four months of working there had she had anything but hardness in her voice. That changed with this phone call. She sounded utterly defeated.

"I'm okay," I answered hesitantly. "What's going on?"

She sounded very close to tears. "Lyle Jennings and his mother's house burned to the ground last night. The mother perished in the fire. Lyle is in the butterfly room in Dallas."

My stomach sank. Lyle and his mother were a special case. Lyle's mother, Nadia, a seventeen-year-old rape victim, was on our watch list. She found out six weeks later that she was pregnant by the man who'd raped her, and from there it just went downhill from what I'd heard. When she was six months pregnant, she overdosed on anxiety medicine, and was hospitalized for three weeks.

Although she was released, she was still put on the 'watch list,' as it was called around the office. She was given random visits every week at all different times to ensure the safety of the child.

After almost killing herself and her child, she'd straightened up. No more depressing moods. She was in school and held down a job as well. I entered the picture when she was kicked out of her parent's house. Apparently they were Christian, god-fearing people, and didn't think that anyone could have a baby out of wedlock.

However, seeing as they were members of the church and didn't want to look bad when they kicked their pregnant daughter out, they allowed her to live in the house with them until the baby was born. Then kicked her out since she decided to forgo adoption like she'd originally planned.

I'd helped her find an apartment just two weeks ago. She'd been living in a women's shelter for four months. It'd been frowned upon by the boss woman, but I'd done it anyway. That girl deserved a fighting chance, and if I had to put myself in a position of warning with my superiors so she and her child could have a better life, then so be it.

Except now, it didn't matter. She was gone.

"What's Lyle's prognosis?" I choked.

"It's not good, sweetie. They don't think he'll make it. When they got to him, he'd inhaled a large amount of smoke. They say his lungs are most likely beyond repair. They moved him to the butterfly room so his family and friends could say goodbye. Nadia's parents didn't sound like they would make it. I'm sorry, Shiloh. I know this family meant a lot to you."

"I'm going to need the next few days off so I can be with him. He shouldn't be alone." I told her.

"Take it. I'll let Lillian know." Melissa said softly.

Texas Tornado

We hung up shortly after. I sat on the edge of the couch watching Frozen with Cheyenne's girls asleep on various pieces of furniture, and Janie leaned up against the base of the couch on the floor. She was staring at me with a concerned stare.

I smiled sadly at her. "I've got to talk to your father for a few minutes. Can you watch the girls for a little while?"

"Yes, I can." She agreed softly.

I got up and moved to the living room where the meeting was being held. I heard my father speaking. Heard him blame me for starting everything into motion. Didn't care.

Shuffling into the room, I went to the one person that I knew would never put me second. Would always make sure I was okay. Wouldn't let me hurt if it could be helped.

His eyes tracked my progress across the room. He'd spotted me even before I made it into the room. His eyes were trained on me as soon as I'd crossed the threshold.

When I got close enough, he extended his hand up to me and I placed my palm in his.

"Could I speak with you for a minute?" I pleaded with my eyes for him just to come. Even though I knew he was in the middle of an important conversation. I needed him now, or I just might fall apart.

He stood, but Sam's voice stopped his progress. "Where're you going? We still have a lot to hash out."

Sebastian's voice uttered agreement. "Go back to the other room."

"It'll just take a minute." I pleaded.

"This is your life we're discussing, princess. It won't take much longer, promise."

Well, I guess my petty problems didn't amount as important to them. James looked torn. I knew he wouldn't want to choose, so I made the decision for him. I'd also realized that I was leaving whether he was with me or not. He'd just have to catch up later. I wasn't letting that boy die alone.

"It's okay. I'll talk to you in a bit." I said, tapping his chest, and turning to leave.

"Well at least she listens sometimes..." Sam muttered under his breath.

I whipped around so fast I started to lose my balance. Waving off James steadying hand, I turned to Sam and glared.

"Fuck you." I said pointing at him.

Then I turned to Sebastian. I was mad at him, too. That, and my bitch button was pushed.

Pointing my finger at him as well, I said, "Fuck you, too."

Cheyenne's laugh made me turn to her. "Fuck you, too."

Her smile slipped off her face, and she looked hurt that I'd said it to her as well.

I didn't say 'fuck you' to my daddy. That'd be against every southern bone in my body. That didn't mean that I wasn't mad at him, as well. It just meant that I wouldn't verbally express the 'fuck you' - it was mentally implied.

I left the room in the silence, and turned back towards the family room where the girls were still sleeping, minus Janie who was now watching Brave instead of Frozen. She looked up as I entered the room.

With that one look, I fell in love with her, just as much as I was in love with James. She looked like her father. Not even a hint of her mother showed in her. Her attitude was James to the T. Her face also showed extreme concern, which, for a six year old, was impressive. She was very aware of what was going on around her, and intelligent on top of that. It was a good quality to have.

I sat down on the floor next to her and explained what was going on, and told her not to tell her father until everyone else wasn't in the room. She agreed, and I told her as soon as the girls woke up, to make sure their parents were told.

She agreed.

Giving her a kiss and a hug, I left the room. Then the house through the backdoor. I walked through the yard, made a mental note to jump on the trampoline when I came back next, and walked to my truck. I was lucky that the truck was so far from the house. Hopefully they wouldn't notice I was leaving.

Not that I was really trying to avoid them. I just didn't want to get into a fight about my safety when that little boy was dying in the hospital without anyone to hold his little hand.

I made it out of the neighborhood without incident, and then drove straight to Dallas, not stopping once. Luckily, I'd just filled up the tank the day before, so I didn't have to stop along the way.

The hospital was easy enough to find. The only problem I had was parking. Since it was such a large hospital, they made the parking garage nearly a mile away from the hospital itself. They offered a shuttle, but I didn't have time to wait the fifteen minutes they estimated for it to be back. Instead, I started running. Luckily, I was wearing comfortable clothes. I made it there in under five minutes, and was on the floor that Lyle was on in less than two.

The nurse's station was empty, but a nurse showed quickly, and I gave her my credentials, and told her I was there for Lyle.

"Do you know about the butterfly room, dear?" She asked sadly.

"No," I shook my head.

"This is the room that was created for family to say their goodbyes to the children. It is a happy place painted in bright, cheerful colors. There are Disney characters smiling on the walls. It's made to be a place of comfort and peace. With one as small as Lyle, he doesn't really realize what's going on. He's woken a few times, but never for long. I'll show you in there. Are you ready?" She smiled warmly.

As we walked down the hall towards the butterfly room, I tried to prepare myself for what I was going to see. Unfortunately, nothing ever could.

The little bubbly, happy boy, all of seven months old, looked so very tiny in the hospital crib. He was hooked up to multiple wires and lines. He had a breathing tube down his throat, which made his mouth hang unnaturally to accommodate it. His tiny little hands were lifeless on the mattress beside his body. His hair, filled with blonde ringlets, was matted to his face and head.

Tears started leaking out of my eyes to see that normally vivacious personality gone. None of it was there anymore. Nothing showed of the happy baby who always had a hearty smile on his face every time I saw him. He looked utterly broken.

"He's in no pain, honey. I promise. Now, I'm going to explain to you what will happen from here." She explained as she checked a bag that was running to a tube that was inserted into his tiny little hand. "This is going to be a painless process. As you can see, he's on oxygen. The doctor doesn't think he'll make it much longer, despite the oxygen. He's barely holding on. Don't be alarmed if the machines start blaring their alarms. It won't be very long now. Do you have any questions?"

"No," I shook my head.

"Do you need me to bring you anything?" She asked softly.

"No," I choked. "No."

"Okay, honey. Press this button right here if you change your mind."

With that, she left, and I held Lyle's hand, and waited for him to be brought home.

Chapter 16

I'm scared of walking out of this room, and never feeling the rest of my whole life, the way I feel when I'm with you.

-Dirty Dancing

Shiloh

"From what I've been told, Lyle was a gentle soul. He loved life, and lived it to the fullest. Now he's home, where nothing will ever hurt him again. He'll forever be remembered, and loved." Reverend Justice preached solemnly.

My heart felt lighter today. It'd been a week since Lyle had passed. Originally, the state was going to bury Lyle and his mother together, side by side, in the plot awarded by the state in a cemetery on the outskirts of Jefferson, where they'd lived. Sadly, Nadia's parents decided to bury her in their family plot, sans Lyle, and didn't tell anyone of the service until after it was finished.

Throughout the entire process, James remained a rock. He held me through my crying jags. Offered help, suggestions, and his ear for me to rant about the injustices of it all. What he didn't offer was judgment. He wasn't mad that I'd taken off without him. Concerned for my safety, yes. Upset? No.

He'd shown up at the hospital an hour after me. I smiled at the Root Beer he'd offered me, and took it with silent thanks. He'd sat with me for around seventeen hours, only leaving for bathroom breaks

Texas Tornado

and phone calls to Janie. At two in the afternoon the next day, Lyle took his final breath.

The nurse had been correct. The alarms all shrieked their warnings, scaring me half to death. Sadly, they weren't able to bring him back, even after multiple measures to do so, as per state regulations.

Then commenced the drama, which led us to now. Lyle being buried in the tiny little coffin, in the tiny little hole. Alone.

He wasn't sent away from this earth alone, however. The entirety of Sam's Free Family, my coworkers who'd been on the case, my father, my brother, and the entire damn Dixie Wardens Motorcycle Club showed. Which surprised and shocked me. I'd never been a part of The Dixie Wardens Motorcycle Club. Although they were aware of me, they didn't know my relation to my father and Sebastian. Well...they didn't used to be.

They did now.

They also treated me like gold. Like I was someone precious to them, even though I'd met them all of three times before this last week.

My father had given me a little more insight on the why's and how's of his life. I'd had so many of the questions answered that have always lurked in the back of my mind, that it made me admire him all the more for doing what he'd done. After seeing child abuse at its finest, I respected a man that could forgo a relationship with his children in deference to their safety. Many parents I've come to see in my years on the job hadn't, and those children had suffered all the more for it.

Lillian walked up to me as the last shovelful of dirt was placed in the whole. She was dressed in a black calf length dress, with pearls in her ears and around her neck. Her hair was in a beautiful up do that showed she'd really put some effort into looking her best.

For Lyle.

Which made me unbelievably happy to know that people cared.

"He had quite a gathering show to send him off. I'm pleased." She said with a fond smile sent my way.

No condemnation about the sixty bikers dressed in leather vests. Each vest had a wraith like woman dominating the back of each with flaming eyes. Which, quite frankly, surprised the crap out of me. The woman came off as a proper, prim older woman. Never would I have thought she'd be accepting. However, she'd been gracious and kind to each and every one of them.

She laughed when she saw the confusion on my face at that comment. "I could give you a lesson in biker culture if you'd like. I was married to the love of my life, Jeffery, for thirty years before he died. And, each one of those years, he belonged to a motorcycle club very much similar to your own. I loved every minute of it, too."

The only intelligent thing that came out of my mouth was, "Wow."

She smiled, and then turned to examine the grave. There was no headstone yet, but the office had started a fund, and would be providing one for Lyle soon.

"Try to have a good rest of the weekend, dear. We'll be seeing you soon. James." She smiled warmly at the man who'd just wrapped an arm around my stomach before turning on her heel and walking to her Buick.

"Did you hear what she just said?" I asked.

"About the motorcycle club?" James queried.

"Yeah," I nodded.

"I've come across quite a few bikers in my life. The ones that belong to clubs are all normal people. I know that they come in all shapes and sizes. All walks of life. Even ones that drive Buicks when they're seventy, and help kids get out of dangerous situations." He supplied.

"Let's go. Janie's with my dad, and I don't want her to learn any new bad language." I admonished.

"Hey," he said holding up his hands. "I don't mean for her to learn those words. She doesn't hear them from me. I know better."

***

"But," I said trying to change James, my dad, Sam, and Sebastian's mind. "I don't need to be babysat. I want to sleep in my own bed. Not on the couch."

My father was currently residing at the Allen homestead, as was Sebastian and Johnny. The only room that was open was James' mother's room, and I sure as hell wasn't sleeping in there. That's just weird.

"Shiloh June Mackenzie, stop arguing. There are some fucked up men in this world, and I sure as fuck don't want them getting their sick, sadistic hands on you. It'd kill me. Please stop arguing and sleep on the couch." My father, the traitorous bastard, pleaded.

He knew I'd listen to him. In my twenty-seven years of life, I can count on two hands the number of times I'd been told what to do from my dad. Each one of those times, my life was in danger. This last time was with Zander. He'd told me to stop seeing him, that he wasn't a good man, and I hadn't listened. Having experienced my father's intuition, I knew he wasn't just telling me this for no reason. Which was why he was the one to tell me to stop arguing. If Sebastian had done it, he knew what I would've said. It begins with a 'fuck,' and ends with an 'off.'

"Fine. Don't expect me to be happy about it, though."

"When have you ever done something you didn't like in twenty six years?" Sebastian muttered under his breath.

"Twenty seven." I stomped my foot for emphasis.

Sebastian looked startled, and then remorseful. Yeah, that's right. Sebastian, the one person who never forgets anything, forgot my birthday.

He looked incredibly remorseful. "I'm sorry, 'Loh. I can't believe I forgot."

"That's okay," I shrugged.

Everyone else in the room wore a guilty expression as well. James, Cheyenne, and Sam all sat on the couch watching the show.

Texas Tornado

Waiting for the inevitable to happen. Which it did, and now I was on that couch for a fourth night in a row. Hooray.

I was currently standing in the middle of the room while everybody else had seats. Sebastian and I'd been arguing about bodyguards. Then it'd degraded down to 'You're not staying in that piece of shit place by yourself.' Not to mention that they still weren't happy that I'd left when someone was trying to kill my father, and would use anyone and anything to make that happen.

"Have a seat, Shiloh. We need to go over some things before you start work on Monday." My father asked.

Left with no other choice, because if I tried to run, they'd probably tackle me to the ground before I even cleared the landing, I did as ordered. Turning on my heels, I stalked towards James side of the couch, and plopped down in the gap between him and Sam.

Both men grunted at the force of my body hitting them, but I wiggled until I was snugly between each of them. "Please, let me move over." Sam said dryly.

"Thanks." I smiled at him.

James' arm went around my shoulder and pulled me closer into his body. Sam's eyes went hard for a few seconds, but it was gone quickly. I looked away from Sam's face to my father and raised my eyebrows.

"Zander," I tensed at the mention of his name. "What did you tell him when you were together?"

My lips thinned, and I pinned them between my upper and lower teeth to keep in the expletive that wanted to pour out of my mouth about him. I would've sounded like I had Tourette's if I'd let it slip. However, I composed myself before asking him to clarify the question.

"I told him a lot of things. How about you give me an example of what you think I told him?" I asked.

What I was hoping was that they didn't ask me about *that* night. I'd managed to keep the details from everyone, even Sebastian, the almighty know-it-all. They already thought I was a fucked up mess, there was no reason to confirm it.

"Anything significant. Anything about your brothers, or me." My father explained.

"I'm not sure what you wanted me to tell them. I didn't even know about Sam. But Zander was my boyfriend, and I did tell him things. Like the fact that I could possibly have another brother. I would never intentionally share anything that would put anyone in danger if I could help it, though." I said completely confused.

Why would what I told him matter? I couldn't explain the relationship I had with my father. My brother was a soldier. That's what I always told everyone, because there wasn't anything else *to* tell. There wasn't anything to tell about Sam because I'd never even met him before in my life at that moment in time.

"Just tell her!" Cheyenne exclaimed from the other side of Sam.

My father sighed. "Around the time you started digging about Sam, I was in the middle of a deal with one of the largest motorcycle clubs in the country. Glen Larson, the president, mentioned a brother, but it wasn't until last night at a meeting of the minds that it finally clicked on who the brother was."

"Well, who the hell was it?" I sighed exasperatingly.

"Zander." James rumbled.

His chest vibrated with that deep rumbling sound he did when he was unhappy. My eyes closed, and a wave of embarrassment washed through me. God, I am such a fuck-up.

"I'm sorry." I whispered, devastated.

"He went by all our defenses." Sebastian said soothingly.

His attempt to exonerate me from my mistakes only upset me more.

"Yeah, but did you let him into your life? Into your bed?" I snapped.

"No. But you also aren't the one involved in dangerous shit like dad and I am. It's not your job to worry about whether someone will use you to get back at us. That's our job, since we're the reasons they're doing it in the first fucking place." Sebastian snapped back.

James' breath had stopped moving rhythmically at my mention of letting Zander in my bed, and it was then I noticed the clenched fist above his knee, and then the placement of my elbow. Digging in deep where he'd been shot not even a week ago.

"Shit!" I exclaimed and moved myself further away from him.

He hauled me back until I was practically sitting in his lap. "You weren't hurting me."

"Well something was!"

I didn't have time to think when the next moment I found his mouth against mine. His tongue in my mouth, teasing me with short shallow strokes. His large hands holding my head still.

The couch rising from displaced weight made me disentangle my mouth from James', and then my face flamed when I saw everyone watching the show, and Sam standing on the opposite side of the room from where he was only moments before.

"It's like nails against a chalkboard to hear about you being with another man. It rubs me the wrong way, and I don't want to talk about this anymore. However, if you value your privacy, you won't bring it up in public again. Next time I won't stop at just a kiss." James said against my lips again before giving me a quick kiss, and moving me back to the couch next to him.

Clearing my throat, I felt the heat rise in my cheeks, but I told them everything I knew about him. Well, almost everything. My pulsed raced a little when I thought about what I was holding back, but outwardly, I was a rock.

"You're not telling us something." James whispered into my ear.

Shock poured through me. How the hell would he know I didn't tell everything? I wasn't fidgeting. Nor was I sweating. How could he possibly know? Then he ringed my wrist tighter, and I realized that two of his large, blunt fingers ran over the beat of my pulse at the base of my wrist.

Busted.

Sam's eyes followed James' movement, and then read the look of surprise on my face. "What else?"

Texas Tornado

The man's body language reading abilities were just uncanny.

"It doesn't have anything to do with what you're asking." I clipped.

"Shiloh," Sam sighed.

"It won't do you any good. She wouldn't tell me anything either." Sebastian muttered and then took a sip of his beer.

"Alright. We'll talk about this more in the morning. It's fifteen until midnight. Let's sleep on it." My father said as he stood up gingerly and made his way to the back of the house where he was staying.

We all watched him go. None of us moved.

"Does anyone else think it's weird to have him around?" I finally broke the silence.

"Fuckin' nuts." Sebastian and Sam agreed at the same time.

"Well aren't y'all cute." I said sarcastically.

Cheyenne snickered from across the couch, but quickly covered up the lapse in judgment with the palm of her hand.

"Sebastian," Cheyenne asked as Sam handed her her sweatshirt and pulled it over her head.

"Yeah?" Sebastian raised his eyebrows.

I took a sip of James' coke that was on the floor between our feet, and promptly spewed it everywhere with Cheyenne's question.

She pursed her lips. "What's your middle name?"

Sebastian's head whipped around and glared at me.

"What?" I asked innocently.

I might have mentioned to Cheyenne that we all had matching themes for middle names, but that was only because I was emotionally compromised with Lyle's death, and I needed something happy to lift my spirits.

I did *not* tell her what his middle name was, though. I wouldn't go that far. Sebastian may not kick my ass, or harm me in any way, but the man knew how to hold a mean grudge.

Sebastian turned his head slowly until he regarded the sincerity in Cheyenne's question. I think she truly wanted to know. It was important for her to know more of her husband, and that meant getting to know his family.

Finally coming to a decision, he told her. "Sue."

"That's fucking awesome!" She said in awe.

"Glad daddy dearest decided to bestow that name on you and not me." Sam muttered as he grabbed his wife's hand and led her to the door.

In the next instant, they were gone, closing the door quietly behind them.

James followed them to the door and locked the dead bolt, chain, and armed the alarm. Sam's bike roared to life, and pulled out of the driveway moments after. The sound of the Harley's pipes disappeared, and Sebastian cleared his throat behind me.

"You love him, don't you?" Sebastian asked as we watched James disappear into the kitchen.

Texas Tornado

Startled, I turned from staring at James walk around the house, checking the windows and locks. When he disappeared into the kitchen, I replied. "I'm fucking screwed."

He chuckled at my less than succulent comment, wrapped his arm around my neck, pulled me into him, and kissed my forehead. "You deserve someone to love. Tell him about what happened with Zoolander. He may've hurt you, and he may have brought you down for a while, but he no more broke you anymore than I was able to get you to stop following me around when you were a kid. He deserves to know what happened."

"Zander." I corrected automatically.

The man was notorious for saying Zander's name incorrectly. Sebastian had hated Zander with a passion. So much so, that every time they were within the same air space, Sebastian referred to him by anything but his actual name. Then what he'd just said finally sunk in with me, and I gasped.

"You know?" I asked incredulously.

"I know everything." He said cryptically before leaving the room silently.

"What does he know everything about?" James asked as he came up to me, pulling me into a hug.

I wrapped my hands around his torso, and buried my head into his chest. "I'll tell you. I promise; just not right now."

He tightened his hold for a few moments, and then loosened it. "I wish you could stay in my room with me. I just don't want your dad to hear and feed my nuts to me when I'm sleeping."

I laughed. "You'd wake up before he got too far with it."

"That I would." He agreed with a laugh of his own.

Our kiss goodnight was anything but chaste, and by the time I was lying on the couch with my borrowed pillow and blanket off James' bed, I was feeling anything but tired. In fact, I was downright horny.

After an hour of zero sleep, I decided that just maybe, I needed some ice cream.

Getting up, forgoing the pants, I tiptoed to the kitchen in James' newest SWAT t-shirt, a pair of panties, and rainbow knee socks. I got the spoon, the half-gallon of chocolate banana Blue Bell Ice Cream, and took a seat at the table. Boris, my cat, leapt up beside me and took his spot, waiting for his turn to lick the spoon.

I ate a quarter of the ice cream, which had done wonders at cooling my body heat down, but not the heat still pooling in my core. Getting one more spoonful, I set it down on the table, and Boris started licking away, purring so hard that it vibrated the table, and the chair. Hell, it might have even been vibrating the floor.

Feeling the chill in the air, because, hey, it's normal for a man to leave the thermostat set on off when it's forty degrees out, I grabbed my blanket, and made my way downstairs. TV was better than nothing. Even if I had to settle for infomercials.

Only I didn't have to, because the first thing I saw when I turned on the large flat screen TV in the basement was a soft-core porn on HBO. Which I immediately turned back off. Or tried to.

Texas Tornado

Somehow I hit a button that turned the surround sound on, because suddenly, the soft moans and grunts of the couple having sex on the screen assaulted me at all angles.

"Oh, yes, just like that. Do it to me baby. Uh huh. Uh huh." The woman's fake orgasm reverberated off the basement walls.

"Oh, my God. Turn off you stupid piece of shit!" I squealed, randomly pressing buttons now.

Blessedly, after pressing everything under the sun on the biggest fucking remote in the world, peaceful silence ensconced the room. Heart pounding, I collapsed into the hammock.

The only light on was the Red Dog neon beer sign hanging above the TV. Which was why when James leaned over my face from behind me, I shrieked like a wiener and fell out of the hammock.

"Mother of pearl!" I said as my body hit the ground with a heavy thud.

"Were you just watching porn?" James asked, making no attempt to help me up. "With the surround sound on?"

"Yes, but I got off, and didn't see a reason to watch it anymore." I quipped breathlessly.

He laughed quietly, leaned over, and gathered me into his arms. I did notice he was very careful not to put any added weight on his leg that'd been grazed by a bullet. Which then led me to notice the tight black boxer briefs he was in with white dots on them.

"I like your underwear," I laughed, as he laid me down gently in the middle of the hammock width wise.

"I like 'em." He acknowledged, spreading my legs wide and stepping between them.

I decided to play off the intense arousal that I was feeling, and asked, "Do you have any other pair of polka dotted underwear?"

His hands spanned my hips, squeezing. "They're not polka dots. Look closer."

Oh, I'd look closer all right. Leaning forward, I sat up until my face was directly in line with the hard column of his cock. The dots were now skulls up close, and then I noticed the waistband.

"Does your underwear say 'The Punisher' on them?" I snickered.

Lifting my hand, I ran a lone finger along the elastic around his waistband. His stomach tensed, and I smiled.

Good.

If I had to be horny, so did he.

His hands went to the bun in my hair, pulling me until my mouth was a millimeters from the hard ridge of his dick. If I stuck my tongue out, I could lick him. Easily.

"Yeah. Now, are you going to suck my cock? Or do I need to just get down to business?" He asked gruffly.

My panting breath fanned his rock hard cock, and I knew he could feel the heat of my mouth. I also knew he was anticipating it.

I wished the lights were on so I could see what I was doing somewhat better, but I just used my sense of touch.

"Are you sure you can handle standing? Do you want to lay down instead?" I asked just before I ran my tongue along the waistband of his briefs.

Texas Tornado

I'd intended to go from hip to hip, only my mouth found the head of his cock peeking out the top of his briefs, and I got distracted. His inhale of surprise tore through the silent room like a rocket launching. Pulling the waistband down only slightly, I zeroed in on my target with precise accuracy.

I licked the tip almost delicately, tasting the salty cream that wept from his tip. A growl sounded above me, drawing my eyes. I looked up at him, and then took the head into my mouth, sucking strongly.

Although it was hard to see him clearly, I could tell his eyes were glued to the action of my mouth taking him in, hollowing with the force of my suction.

"Take more." He commanded.

I obliged, pulling his underwear down until the waistband was underneath his ball sack. However, now both balls were now on display as well, drawing not only my eyes, but my mouth to the delicious feast.

Forgetting that he wanted me to take more of his cock inside my mouth, I started to lick, nip, and suck on the twin globes. Pulling one, and then the other into my mouth delicately.

The grip of his fist in my hair tightened, and I found myself being pulled away from my feast, and being fed his cock instead. I wasn't upset. That was just as good, if not better.

He worked his cock in and out of my mouth like he was a mad man, yet not once did I choke on his length. He had an uncanny ability to judge when he was getting too far in, and pulled back before my gag reflex kicked in.

"Suck me harder." James demanded.

I sucked.

Hard.

"Oh, yeah. That feels fucking awesome. God, I could come right now." He gasped.

I felt empowered, only sucking all the harder.

With a roughness I'd never experienced before, he lost control.

He ripped his length from my mouth, pulling back on my hair as he did so to free himself with a loud pop.

"Turn over on your knees. Be careful." He growled.

I did so carefully.

He helped by holding the hammock steady as I rolled, and then gingerly pulled first one, and then the other knee underneath me. His callused hands moved from my hips to the edges of my panties and yanked, making them pool at the bend in my knees.

The position felt incredibly awkward, making me grasp the netting with clutching fingers.

However, in the next second, I didn't feel awkward in the least. With one rough thrust, he was inside me.

The pound of his hips against mine jolted me forward, pulling me off him. Then he repeated the process by pulling back on the netting as well as thrusting forward.

The added thrust of his hips, and the pull back on the hammock, rammed his cock into me so hard that caused a twinge of pain. The jolt of bliss overshadowed that twinge of pain exponentially, successfully throwing me higher and higher until I burst into a thousand shards. Lights exploded behind my closed eyes as my pussy clamped down hard on his cock.

His groan of completion followed on the heels of mine; his big body shook with the force of it. I looked over my shoulder and only saw the silhouette of his large form still coaxing the last dregs of his release from his cock. With that one glance, a smaller, but no less significant orgasm pulsed through me, making my body shutter.

"Fuck," he hissed.

"Yeah," I panted.

He pulled away from me carefully, and I thrust my arm down in between my legs to catch his come before it leaked out all over the hammock, and then the carpet. Warm liquid filled my hands, and I resisted the urge to grind the heel of my hand into my engorged clit while rubbing his leavings into my overheated skin.

He returned momentarily and lifted me up carefully.

I kept my hand covering myself, and he produced a towel, cleaning up my core first, and then my hand. Once finished, he tossed the towel into a hamper that was sitting in the corner of the room, and then helped me pull up my panties.

Once we were both settled in the hammock, I finally figured out what was niggling in the corner of my brain throughout the entire encounter. "What happened to your piercing?"

"I don't wear it all the time. I was young when I got it. My friend, Dougie, bet me three hundred bucks that I wouldn't do it. I proved him wrong, and woke up with a pierced dick and couldn't have sex for months while it healed. I pop it in from time to time, but mostly I don't wear it anymore. I have a phobia of it getting caught on something and ripping my cock in half." He explained.

I snickered and then cringed at the though.

"Normally you wouldn't be hanging around with your dick out for it to snag on things." I replied dryly.

I felt his chest rise as he huffed out a laugh. "Yeah, that's true. It doesn't stop me from having the thoughts though."

"Tell me about Dougie." I requested, letting my fingers dance on the ridges of his abdomen.

Tensing beneath me at the question, he quivered like a bow, strung and ready to be released. "He was the friend that I was telling you about. He died four years ago while we were on a mission. He has...had a daughter Janie's age. Kayla. He was always so upbeat and happy. When he died, we lost something that was an integral part of us. I still get the urge to call him every time I think of a stupid fucking joke. He was notorious for one liners. But then, when the time came, he'd ruthlessly fuck up a tango and not even blink an eye."

The sadness in his voice tore a hole through my heart. "I'm sorry. He sounds like an unbelievable man."

"He was." He said softly.

"Will you tell me what you refused to earlier?" He asked after the silence continued for a few more minutes.

I tensed, but then relaxed, remembering my brother's words from earlier.

"It's not pretty." I explained.

Texas Tornado

"There are very few things that would keep you silent about something you felt passionate about. I don't think that it's pretty. In fact, I bet it's something horrible, and I'll have to restrain myself from walking out of this house afterwards and tracking that piece of shit down."

"Sebastian had always told me that Zander was no good. I should've listened." I said, swallowing on a suddenly dry throat. "It started out small. Cruel words here, a slap upside the head there. Then, before I could really do anything about it, Sebastian was hurt in that motorcycle accident. I don't know if I was just oblivious, or what, but the slaps upside the head turned into slaps across the face. A punch in the stomach. It wasn't until I walked in on him fucking another woman in his apartment that I realized what a fool I'd become. And so, I left him that night, only for him to follow me down the hallway of his apartment and beat the ever loving shit out of me, while he was naked and his dick was swinging. Then he dragged me back into the room and fucked the woman while I watched with a broken leg, arm, and a few cracked ribs."

James' arm tightened with each declaration, and by the end of it, I could feel him shaking in rage. "What the hell did the woman do while this was going on?"

"She was drunk, I guess. When Zander was done fucking her, he tossed me outside the door of his apartment, and I crawled down the stairs and to the street before I was found and taken to the hospital. I filed charges on him, but he got that woman to corroborate that he didn't do anything." I said with disgust.

"Do you know what the bullet of a fifty caliber does to a man's head at a mile away?" He asked casually.

I had a feeling I knew where this was going, and stood.

He grunted when I used his stomach to push myself up, and asked, "Where you going?"

"To bed, stud. You've got an early doctor appointment, and I have to do some laundry." I answered as I made my way to the stairs. He grunted, but followed me up the stairs and to the living room where I laid down.

He covered me with the blanket he'd remembered to grab from the basement floor, and covered me. "Night, Shiloh June."

"Night, James Jonathan Allen." I sighed.

Sleep came swiftly after that. Sated and sleepy, I slept until the next morning when the smell of bacon wafted through the house and woke me from a dead sleep.

Chapter 17

It's good to have beardless friends when you go out. People will assume you're their leader.

-Bearded fact

Shiloh

When I walked into the kitchen, stumbling and rubbing my eyes, I was surprised to see an older woman standing at the stove. She was dressed in distressed jeans and a stylish t-shirt. Her feet, however, were covered in tennis shoes that reminded me of kid's high tops, but who was I to judge? I still wore my Doc Martin's from back in high school.

I said a silent prayer of thanks that I'd remembered to slip on pants before coming into the kitchen. If what I guessed was true, this was James' mother.

I was proven right in the next moment when she turned. Staring at me was an older version of Cheyenne. She had the exact same features that Cheyenne had. Only her hair had streaks of silver streaked in with the golden blonde.

Her smile lit up the room, and she held out her hand to me. Moving forward, I placed my hand in hers, and she yanked me into a hug every bit as exuberant as the ones I received from Janie.

"You must be the infamous 'Loh I keep hearing about." She smiled.

I laughed. "You must be Daina. Yeah, that's me. My brother used to call me that when we were younger. When Janie started calling me that, that was the first time I'd heard it in nearly ten years; a blast from the past for sure."

"Yeah, that's my girl. At least you're not called Big Grandma like I am." She laughed, and then cursed when the smoke alarm started going off.

I grabbed a magazine off the kitchen table, and then walked to the shrieking alarm and started fanning it. "I'm an old pro at this. I cook, but I'm also forgetful. It's hit or miss with me."

"You've got me pegged as well." She laughed. "I'm afraid you're the last one up. Janie's visiting with Kayla. James' went off to his doctor's appointment. Your father and brother disappeared around a half our ago and didn't enlighten me on where they were going." She explained.

She reminded me of a peppy blonde cheerleader, only about thirty years older. She was very beautiful. I could see how the powerful and magnetic Todd Masterson had snagged her up. She was everything I could hope to look like thirty years down the road.

"They do that." I said as I walked towards the refrigerator and grabbed the milk. "They also do this secret crap, and whisper like little girls. Only now, James and Sam do it, too. So it's like the boys club. No girls allowed."

"Yeah, Max and James have always done that. Then the other boys came, and I haven't been able to walk into a room without it silencing like a whore just entered a catholic church since." She agreed.

I smiled at her comparison. "James mentioned something about needing to hire someone to mow the lawn. I was wondering if you had a lawn mower. If you do, I'll do it myself."

She set a plate of eggs and bacon down in front of me. Then grabbed me the ketchup, a fork, a napkin, and the pepper. "James told you what I liked before he left, didn't he?"

She laughed. "That boy of mine is very efficient."

"Thank you." I said before digging in, just managing to ignore the little remembrance of last night, and his very thorough efficiency.

She sat down with her own breakfast. When I glanced at it, I understood how she was able to look fucking awesome. It was a half of a grapefruit, two pieces of whole wheat toast, and a cup of coffee.

She must've seen me eyeing her food with a disgusted look on my face, because she explained. "This isn't my ideal breakfast. But once I hit forty, my metabolism took a nose dive. I've learned to eat healthy to make up for it. As for the lawn mower, it's in the shed out back. Although, I want to warn you. It's a long job. It took me over two hours to mow it when I was still doing it. I haven't done it in four years, but the yard hasn't gotten any smaller."

"That's okay. I've been needing exercise anyway. I haven't been able to run for a while. I got my cast off two weeks ago, and haven't worked up the courage to get back to the gym. Although, it looks like your son won't let that one slip much longer. He wants me to learn some self-defense." I said.

She nodded. "Gas is in the back of the shed. Careful of all my fabric. It's a bit of a mess in there."

The next twenty minutes was spent talking about Daina's newest embroidery machine, and how expensive of an endeavor it was to pursue. She'd contemplated doing her crafts full time now that she was eligible for retirement, but was waiting until her next three contracts were up before she made any permanent moves.

Once breakfast was finished, she laughed happily when I gave my plate to Boris. "You've got a mini dishwasher."

"Yeah, he's just like a dog, I swear. He'll even fetch."

"I haven't had any pets here since Cheyenne's dog moved out. I can't tell you how hard it is to have to scrub food off of dishes when you've had your own pre-washer to take care of that little chore for you for the last five years."

After a few more minutes of gabbing about my fat cat, I went to James' room to get dressed.

I stripped off my clothes that I'd worn to sleep, and tossed them on the foot of the bed. James bed wasn't made, so I did that quickly before digging through the bag at the bottom of the closet for a thong and sports bra.

Once I was clothed in some tight fitting short shorts and a yellow racer back tank top, I made my way out to the back yard shed. The mower was easy to find, and even easier to start up. It was obviously well taken care of and rumbled to life after only the second pull. It put my own lawn mower to shame.

Texas Tornado

It was an hour into mowing the front yard that James' bike pulled up, and he surged off it in a huff. I had to let the engine die before I heard what he was yelling over the loud mower.

"What the fuck are you doing?" He roared.

I raised my eyebrows at his foul mood, cocked my hip, and stared at him. I noticed, as he shot toward me that he was trying to hide his limp, but wasn't quite successful. Which irritated me even more.

"What I'm doing?" I asked. "Well, it looks obvious to me..."

My gesture towards the lawn mower and the grass only served to darken his mood even further. His eyes blazed. When he finally made it to within a few feet of me, he grasped me by the waist, tossed me over his shoulder, and stomped towards the side of the house.

"Hey!" I barked. "I wasn't done!"

He ignored my verbal protest.

I would've twisted and tried to get out of his ironclad grasp, but I didn't want to hurt him or me. We rounded the corner of the house, and I was dumped unceremoniously into the chase lounge that overlooked the koi pond I'd only glanced at earlier.

James had his hands on the top of his head, turned towards the pond, contemplating it. "What's the big deal?" I asked.

He stayed facing the fishpond, but his voice carried over the gentle sound of the waterfall. "Your dad's got the worst goddamn motorcycle club in the country trying to fuck him in the ass. They'd do anything to do it too. Even use his own daughter against him. Is that what you want to be? Bait? Cause they'll use you. They won't leave you whole afterwards, either."

The venom of his anger startled me. I'd known he would be annoyed that I was mowing. However, it'd never occurred to me that it would be unsafe. If I'd known, I would've never done it. I wasn't a bad ass. I was a fucking social worker. How was I supposed to know that I couldn't mow the fucking lawn?

My anger took a fever pitch, and I stood up, locking my knees and getting right up against his back. I used my pointer finger to poke him sharply in the back.

"Listen here, you big hairy bastard." I said poking him again. "I know how to take direction. All you need to do is tell me the things I can or can't do, and I'll be sure to follow those directions to the letter. Do. You. Understand. Me?" Each word was emphasized with another poke.

With the last poke, his own temper seemed to give way. Whirling around, he towered over me, the finger of his own hand poking me between my breasts. I could see the emotion rolling across his face, and I backed up. He followed me, stalking me like a panther. "I did fucking tell you! Last. Fucking. Night."

I didn't remember any such conversation, but I decided it was in my best interest to agree to disagree. That is until he got in my face. I noted that the beard covering the lower half of his face was shaggier than normal. As if he hadn't had time keep it trimmed as he usually did. Over the past week, it'd only gotten longer, and it looked hot. The look suited him. The patch that covered his chin started to shine shimmery silver, as if it was prematurely going gray.

Texas Tornado

On some men, a scruffy beard just didn't look good. On James, it only seemed to accentuate his hotness factor. The alpha male in him somehow was magnetized. Nothing said I'm no one's bitch like a badass beard.

I longed to feel his bristly chin chafing against my cheeks, my sensitive nipples, and the tender flesh of my thigh.

Then his condescending comment plowed through my perusal like a hot knife through butter. "Maybe if you pulled that pretty little head out of that tight little ass, you would've known that you shouldn't be out strutting that hot fucking ass in public."

My spine went taught, and I stood up until our bodies touched. My breasts were rubbing along his chest. His cock, which might I add was harder than a steel pole, hit me at tummy level, and my eyes were level with his chin.

Tilting my head up, I ran my sweaty palm up the side of his arm, passing over the distended veins, past the bulging muscles of his biceps, over the soft cotton of his t-shirt, up his neck, until my fingers came to rest on the scruffy hair that covered his chin. Then I fisted what little I could, and yanked his face down to mine.

There wasn't much hair, but there was enough. His face came down close to mine, until I could feel the hot, panting breath against my overheated skin. "My fucking pretty little head is not up my *tight* ass. In fact, my ass has never had *anything* up it. Not that you'll ever fucking know. You're officially cut off."

Letting go of his face, I started to slide to the side, only to find my ass against the cushion of the lounger, and James' body following me down. James' mouth crashed down against mine, and after a short amount of protest, I gave in to the assault.

Twining my arms around his broad shoulders, I thrust my tongue into his mouth. Our tongues rubbed sensually against each other, and my back arched unintentionally, rubbing my distended nipples against his rock hard chest. James pushed hard with his hips, and my legs spread wider to make room for his.

"God, you look so fucking hot. Your ass jiggles when you walk, and your boobs bounce. I watched you for five minutes before I finally came back to reality. I can't believe you mowed the lawn in this. You probably gave the neighbors across the street heart attacks. Mr. Winfrey's probably dying a happy man right now." He never stopped nipping, sucking, and rubbing his scruffy beard against my sensitive skin.

I was doing my best just to stay conscious during his sensuous assault. Each brush of his bearded face against my sensitive skin, and the grinding of his hips against my pulsating clit, had me hurdling towards an orgasm that was sure to send me into oblivion.

Needing to feel more, I ripped my tank top down until my breasts spilled over the top of it, exposing the turgid points of my nipples to the midday sun. "Suck them."

I didn't have to ask though, because his mouth was already pulling one of the tips into the slick heat of his mouth. He sucked hard, pulling back roughly until my nipple burst free of his mouth with a loud pop. He wasted no time in giving my other nipple the same treatment, and I ground myself into the rigid length of him even harder.

A loud barking from the neighbor's dog next-door, and the hiss of a cat brought me out of my ecstasy-induced fog, but then James mouth descended, and I found myself divested of shorts and panties, even though my tennis shoes remained firmly in place.

The tip of James' tongue ran down my rib cage, past my belly button, and down into the thatch of hair that covered my sex. "You smell like sex."

"J-J..." I tried to tell him something, really, I did, but as soon as his tongue found the hard bud of my clit, I couldn't even remember my own fucking name, let alone tell him what I wanted.

"J's good. You can call me J from now on. Nobody else calls me that." He said, and then went to town on my pussy.

He devoured me. There was no other word for what he was doing to me. He sucked the juices that were leaking from my core, swallowing them down as fast as I produced them. The thumb on his right hand thrummed my clit with expert precision, and the thumb of his other hand massaged my perineum.

It wasn't long before I was so caught up in the feeling of his hands and tongue, that an orgasm blindsided me. Completely off balance, I found myself pulling on his beard again, holding him in place so he wouldn't stop doing what he was doing.

Somewhere in the back of my mind, I remembered that we were outside, in broad damn daylight, fucking. Fucking loudly.

But I didn't care. I was so far gone, that he could have been doing me in front of the whole damn town and I wouldn't care.

Just as I started to come down from my mind-blowing orgasm, I found myself impaled on his cock. Then he was rutting. In and out of me, over and over. His cock slammed into me so hard that now I wasn't laying on the flat part of the lounger. I was moving up the incline, and he was pressing me down.

The angle was absolutely delicious. The head of his fat cock worked me perfectly. He hit that spot. The one I'd only read about in magazines. His gaze held mine prisoner, and he watched my eyes as he fucked me into the chair.

Frustration started to become apparent on his face, because within moments, I found myself nearly folded in two as he brought my legs up to his shoulders, and he leaned in. "Oh, yeah. That's what I wanted."

This position allowed him to go deeper, and there was nothing I could do about it. Not that I would want to or anything. The tip of his leaking cock kissed the entrance to my womb, and with each thrust of his length into me, I took him deeper and deeper.

His gaze left mine as he bent his head. He watched my breasts jiggle up and down with each of his thrusts.

Leaning down, he took the tip of one aching nipple into his mouth, and sucked hard.

With the two sensations, I went wild. My hips tilted into each of his thrusts, allowing him to go impossibly deeper. His teeth bit into

Texas Tornado

my nipple, causing me to buck wildly. Then his free hand that was resting on my ass moved.

The pad of his thumb brushed my anus.

The move was startling, but he didn't stay at the puckered hole for long. Shortly, he moved to the pad of tissue that lay in between, and massaged it with his thumb. He switched breasts, sucking hard once more, and I exploded.

I gritted my teeth against the urge to scream, and squeezed my eyes so tightly shut that I could have sworn they would bruise.

His thick cock continued to pound into my over sensitive tissues, but it wasn't long before he couldn't stop his own climax. His deep growl against the side of my breast warned me of his impending orgasm, and I squeezed my vaginal muscles tight, and worked his pulsating dick with my inner tissues.

After a few more short, jerky strokes, he froze. My eyes opened to see his own on mine, and I couldn't help but laugh. "Jesus, you've got me folded like an accordion."

He looked down at the position of my body, and laughed, pulling out carefully.

There was no stopping the flow of come that leaked from me, and I made a mental note to clean it up as soon as I got my clothes. Oh, and found the ability to support my own weight.

"Yeah, I guess I do. You make me crazy." He laughed as he pushed his semi hard cock back into his jeans, adjusted himself accordingly, zipped up his jeans, and righted his shirt.

I found my legs able to move, and pulled my bike shorts back up my legs, forgoing the panties seeing as they were ripped in four places. How he'd managed to do that, I don't know, but I was nowhere near complaining.

"Your mom probably saw us naked." I grimaced.

He disagreed with a shake of his head. "She went to bed nearly an hour ago. That's why I'm here instead of at Free working. I didn't want you left alone."

I smiled. "Why would you be working at Free if you have a job with SWAT?"

"I still work there three days a week." He said with a raised eyebrow.

"When?" I demanded. "How come I never saw you?"

"I didn't want you to." He explained.

Once I situated myself, I walked with him in through the back door. He sat down at the table, and I went to my bag, grabbed a new pair of panties and clean shorts, and then changed. He was still sitting in the same spot, however now, he was scowling at something he was reading in the newspaper.

"What?" I asked as the scowl on his face turned deadly.

Not saying a word, he handed the paper over, and then tapped his finger at the article that was part of the front page. My own mood plummeted, and I swore savagely. Then I turned around, slammed into the bedroom, grabbed my laptop, plunked down on the bed, and wrote the best letter I've ever written in my life.

Texas Tornado

I'd even managed to be professional, withholding every single curse word and bad name I had in my vocabulary. I could feel James eyes on me as I typed, but I was so furious, that if I didn't get it all out and write it all down, that I just might tear someone a new one.

Twenty minutes, and a five page letter to the editor later, I was exhausted, and near tears. How could someone write something so awful?

"You okay?" James rumbled from across the room.

I looked up, and lost it.

I was enfolded into his arms shortly after, and he held me while I cried. "H-how could someone say something so awful?"

He didn't answer.

"S-she didn't ask for that. She had such a hard life, and she really turned herself around. She would've never purposefully set fire to her apartment and killed herself." I sobbed.

He still didn't say anything, and I didn't expect him to. He knew Lyle and Nadia's story. He knew just as well as I did what had happened to her, how traumatized she was. And to think that some reporter thought that just because she'd lived in a halfway house, and was out in a dark alley the night she was raped, that she was asking for it, sickened me.

Steeling myself, I stiffened my spine, pulled away from James' safe arms, and dashed the remnants of my tears away from my face. "I'm going to get that reporter fired. She'll be lucky to work as a freakin' janitor by the time I get through with her."

James smile was quick and hard. "I like the way you think."

"God I could kill her with my own bare hands." I fumed as I stood and paced, contemplating the way my Doc Martin boots would look against the woman's face.

"How about we head to Free? Work off some of that pissed off energy?" James offered.

"I like how you think, J." I smiled brightly at him.

His answering smile warmed me to the tip of my toes.

Chapter 18

How to tell a woman is mad at you: 1. She's silent. 2. She's yelling. 3. She said 'whatever' 4. She acts the same. 5. She acts different. 6. She murdered you.

-Men's guide to women

James

I winced as Sam dropped Shiloh back to the ground. For the fourth time.

"You're not listening. I told you not to drop your shoulder. When you drop it, you lose that extra push that will let you throw your elbow back. Go out, not down." Sam explained patiently.

I'd tried to tell her that myself, more than once, but she was stubborn. Even worse than my sister, in fact. I'd given up the instructing to Sam's impeccable patience, and waited for the fireworks to start.

"If you weren't so god forsaken big, I wouldn't have to worry about dropping my shoulder. You'd be lying at my feet, crying about the loss of your future children. Instead, my elbow just hits a granite slab you call abs, and hurts me instead of you." Shiloh stomped her foot for emphasis.

"You think that they'll go easy on you? Let me tell you a secret. They won't." Sam snapped.

Shiloh's face darkened, and she made a 'come on' gesture with her hands. Sam's eyes narrowed, and the tick in his cheek gave away his annoyance with his baby sister.

I, however, found it hilarious. It was nice to see the big man off his game. It wasn't all the time that you got to see the almighty captain lose it in front of everyone.

"Again." Sam snapped.

Shiloh did as instructed, and even managed to initiate the original move, but Sam's bulk overpowered her once again.

"What's the damn point of this move again?" Shiloh growled from the ground lying flat on her back.

The door to the room clicked open, and my eyes drew from the blue mats towards the seats in the corner of the room. Everyone was there, watching the show.

"You're being a baby. You're lucky I'm such a good man. I'm going easy on you." Sam said as he offered her his hand.

Taking a sip of my Gatorade, I promptly spewed the contents onto the ground in front of me.

"Shut up. You'll never be the man your mother is."

The bellow of laughter that threatened to burst free from me was smothered when Sam threw Shiloh to the mat, yet again. She hit the hard floor with a thump, and she groaned.

Once Sam helped her up, she shuffled over to me and snatched the drink out of my hand. She gulped down the contents of the drink, and then thrust the empty bottle back into my hands before turning and staring at her brother with her hands on her hips.

Texas Tornado

Sidling up to Shiloh, I gave her a sharp smack on the ass, and then walked towards Sam. "She's pretty good if she could get over the anger."

He nodded in agreement, checked his watch, and then grimaced. "I have to go get Cheyenne from work. I'll see you at your place for dinner."

With that he left, and Shiloh glared at him the entire way.

"Let's go, Speedy." I called to her and gestured with my finger to where I wanted her.

She came slowly, only wincing every other step.

I'd used her hard right before we came here, and I felt sorry that I made her do this now. "If you're too sore, we can leave." I offered.

Her eyes narrowed. "Did I say I was too sore?"

I shook my head. "No."

"Then show me how to defend myself." She harrumphed.

Thirty exhausting minutes later, we were still in the same place we were earlier, only I was the one losing my patience. Shiloh was sitting on her ass, glaring at me. We'd long ago lost our audience since Shiloh's attitude only went from bad to horrid. After the third snicker from the peanut gallery, I'd kicked them out.

"What's the problem, Shiloh?" I asked, exasperated.

She pursed her lips, but at my pointed look, she finally explained. "I don't want to hurt you."

I rolled my eyes. "You couldn't hurt me even if you tried."

"What?" She half yelled.

"You heard me." I said, laughing at the absurd thought. "That's why you've been only giving me half ass moves?"

"Yeah," She said, trying to keep the exasperation out of her voice. "I really could hurt you, you know."

"You could try."

"What, you don't think that a woman could bring you down?" She asked.

"I think that you have a chance to get away, not to completely subdue me. You sure would try, but no matter what, a man is always going to be stronger and faster than any woman." I said carefully.

"So let me get this straight," she said. "You don't think I can take you down. In fact, you don't think that any woman could take you down."

"Right." I agreed.

"What do you want to bet?" She asked.

I could see the wheels turning in her head, thinking carefully.

"Anything. You could bet anything. I know for certain you couldn't incapacitate me for more than a few seconds."

I should've known. I mean, I knew there were ways that she could take me down. I just didn't think she knew any yet. I hadn't gotten that far with her as to teach her those. She wasn't even learning the most basic form of self-defense. However, in the next instant she proved me wrong.

"Deal." She said, and then I watched, as if in slow motion, when her hand snapped out, palm rigid, as she brought it down into a hard, sharp strike against the carotid artery on the side of my neck.

Texas Tornado

I came to, seconds later, to find myself staring at the ceiling. I blinked once. Twice, a third time, and then sat up.

My head was pounding, my back ached, and I turned my head and found Shiloh all the way across the room, a sheepish expression on her face.

"Does that count?" She asked.

"Yes," I said, embarrassed, but also proud as hell that she was able to do that.

"Where did you learn that move?" I rasped.

"YouTube." She supplied instantly.

I shook my head and muttered. "YouTube."

"So what do I have to do?"

I was sorry that I asked.

Chapter 19

There's not crying in baseball.

-A League Of Their Own.

Shiloh

Tapping the button on the side of my blue tooth headset, I replaced my hands on the wheel, and tilted my head forward so my hair covered the blue tooth device once again.

"Hello?" I answered.

"Ms. Mackenzie?" A strange male's voice asked from the other end of the line.

"Yes," I said hesitantly.

Looking left, then right, I pulled out into traffic, and headed West to Fourth Street. I was heading to a case's house, and I was in a hurry. Normally I wouldn't have even answered the strange number, but James said he'd be calling me from work right about now, and I thought it was him.

"This is Albert Buchanan with the Longview News. Do you have a few spare moments to speak with me?" He asked.

"Yes." I clipped.

He sighed. "I understand your position on the matter of the article that was printed in our paper on Sunday morning. We've retracted it, and had the reporter issue a public apology. I wanted to call and get your permission to print the letter that you sent the editor." Albert explained.

"Uhh," I hesitated.

I didn't see anything wrong with it, and if I was being truthful, I wanted the world to know how upset I was that an article like that was written that completely overshadowed the real issue at hand- that a very young woman and her son died in a very horrible way.

"Yes," I said firmly. "I'd like that."

"Excellent. We'll be running it in tomorrow's paper. Please be on the lookout for it." Albert explained.

After a few more pleasantries, we hung up, and I pulled into the Newman's driveway. I sighed when I looked at the clock and realized I was still fifteen minutes earlier than our scheduled appointment.

The Newman's were a new case. The case itself was fairly routine. Child abuse wasn't abnormal in today's society. What was abnormal was for it to be grandparents accused of doing the abuse. Normally, it was the parents being accused and then the children would be relocated with their maternal or paternal grandparents if able.

The Newman's case was of two children, ages seven months, and five, reportedly showing up to daycare with unexplained bruises. The daycare official was the one to contact child protective services, and I was called out to the Newman's house to do an unscheduled well check.

Forgetting that I was waiting for James' call, I got out of the car, grabbing my briefcase on the way, and walked swiftly to the front walk. After several knocks, the door was cracked open, and a grizzly voice emerged.

"What you want?" The man asked.

"Hello," I said to the door. "I'm Shiloh Mackenzie with child protective services. May I come in?" I asked authoritatively.

"No." He snapped, and then slammed the door in my face.

I sighed.

Normally, right about now, I would call the police to ask for assistance, but for some reason, my inner warning meter had taken a detour, and I didn't use the opportunity to call for assistance like I should have. Instead, I knocked again.

When the door opened this time, I got a face full of shotgun.

"Get inside. Now." The old man demanded as he flung the door open wide.

Not knowing what else to do, I woodenly followed his instructions. When I crossed the threshold, the first thing I saw was the massive amount of firearms spaced sporadically throughout the house. In Texas, it's normal for people to have firearms.

What's not normal is for them to have that many. I counted over sixty guns in crevices, on the couch, hanging on the walls, propped up in corners, laying over every available surface, and stuffed in between couch cushions.

And those were just the ones I could see.

Then there were the bullets. And shot gun shells. All shapes, sizes, and colors. I wasn't a gun expert by any means, but I knew that this wasn't normal. For someone with this type of collection, I would think that they would have them in a safe, or up high, out of the reach of small children.

Then horror struck me as I saw the baby in the corner. She was sleeping curled up in a ball, chained to the goddamn wall like an animal.

My brain raced as I came up with, then immediately omitted ways of how to extract myself from this situation alive. I knew one thing for sure- there was no way in hell I was leaving the children here on their own. They were coming with me. No matter what.

"Sit down in the corner by the baby." Mr. Newman, I assumed, ordered.

I followed his directions, and maneuvered myself to where the baby was behind my body, just in case.

"Frank!" An older woman's voice screeched from the room beyond this one. "Who was at the door?"

"CPS bitch!" He yelled back.

"What?" She screeched again.

"CPS bitch!" He yelled back again.

"What'd she want?" She continued.

"Nothing." He answered.

"Okay." She confirmed. "What'ja want for supper?"

"Got any of that sausage shit?"

"Yeah."

"That."

"Okay."

The yelling finally stopped when a child's voice yelled from the same direction. "Gram, I gotta pee. Let me out."

"Frank!"

The name was a demand, and the old man looked studied me, before yelling back. "I'm busy. Get off ya' fat ass and open the closet yourself."

Oh, my God. The five year old was in a closet? What kind of fucked up place was this?

My mind circled around scenario after scenario, and not one single idea came to mind. That is until the phone in my pocket started pulsating like a heartbeat, indicating that James was calling.

Discreetly lifting my hand up to the hands free device on my ear, I pressed the button and let my hands fall back into my lap. Frank didn't move, nor show any suspiciousness, so I continued to stay still, and listened.

"Shiloh?" James asked.

Waiting a few beats, he tried again.

"Hello? Shiloh? Are you there?" He asked, anxiousness becoming quite apparent in his voice.

With still no answer, he withdrew the phone away from him, if the sound of static and fumbling sounds were anything to go by.

"She not there?" A man asked on the other end.

It took me a few moments, but I finally placed the owner of the voice. Downy. James must be at work. Good.

"It says I'm connected. Hang on." He requested.

Texas Tornado

"Mr. Newman, what are you going to do to me?" I asked, trying my hardest to hide the quiver of fear in my voice.

***

James

"Who're you calling?" Downy asked from the desk next to mine.

It was my first day back at work in two weeks, and it showed. My eyes were heavy from what little sleep I managed to catch before being called out for a SWAT run at 3 AM. My leg throbbed when I moved quickly, but I was happy to be back. In the short time I'd worked with Luke and Downy, I realized how much I missed the team camaraderie.

Sure, I had the same team aspect while working at Free, but I didn't get that adrenaline rush when working on a bike that I got when I was running a call. When my body was behind that scope. When my finger pulled the trigger. Free would forever be my home, but I had another team now that I trusted almost as much as my old team.

"Shiloh. I need her to go pick up Janie for her doctor's appointment this afternoon." I said while punching in the numbers on my desk phone.

The phone rang once before she picked up, but she never said hello.

"Hello?" I said into the phone.

No answer.

"Hello? Shiloh? Are you there?" I tried again.

Still no answer.

"She not there?" Downy asked.

Moving the phone away from my face, I looked at the handset to make sure I was connected. I was. Putting the headset back up to my face.

"It says it's connected." I said, apprehension, and a lifetime of training, started to make me aware of the odd nuances. Like the fact that if I listened really close, I could just make out the sound of a clock ticking in the background of the phone. The ding ding of a game show on a television.

"It says I'm connected. Hang on." I said, holding up my finger.

That was when I heard Shiloh speak.

"Mr. Newman, what are you going to do to me?" Her voice quivered in fear.

"Anything I want to, girl. Now shut up and let me think. Don't even think about moving either, or I'll blow that pretty little face of yours off." A man growled.

My hands were moving before I even contemplated my actions. Downy watched as I signaled to him that there was an unknown hostage situation. He confirmed he understood with a nod, and started making the appropriate calls.

The next ten minutes sailed by in a flurry of action. In less than four minutes, the entire SWAT team was in my office. Gear on. Guns loaded. The phone was now on speakerphone, and we listened as Shiloh gave everything she could think of to us.

"Mr. Newman, isn't there a homeowner's agreement for the mobile home park of Shady Lane that says all firearms have to be stored properly in a fireproof container?" Shiloh asked, sounding bored.

"Sure. Not that I really give a shit about any homeowner's association. They already make me mow my freakin' lawn, and keep it at a regulation one-inch height. They can suck my hairy ball sack if they think they can control what I do with my guns."

With that information, we were on the move. I left the speakerphone where it was, and our information specialist, John Atoms, took over where I left off.

Downy handed me my rifle case as we walked out of the room and to the truck. The truck was a ton and a half pound beast that could carry nine men and their gear safely. It was an armored vehicle on steroids that could hold its own. Even against a fucking tank. It had the motor of a Mack truck, and ran up to speeds near one hundred and fifty miles an hour, without even red lining it.

Terror started to course through my veins. She'd said guns. Not that one wasn't enough to accomplish the act of killing, but multiple meant he could potentially hold a siege, and never stop until he ran out of ammo. That could take weeks. Shiloh didn't have weeks. She was living on borrowed time already.

Then the terror was accompanied by white hot rage. What kind of man would hold a woman hostage? For Shiloh to be there in the first place, it also meant that there were children involved. Which only added to the complications that were already arising.

"Someone needs to contact Shiloh's boss, Lillian McBride. See if they can drag up any information..." I started to say before Luke interrupted. "I already did that."

I nodded. My mind was flying in a dozen different directions. What kind of structure were we looking at? How many guns did he have? What were the access points? How many children were in the building? Every single aspect of how it could go wrong. What do if a certain situation arose and how to get Shiloh out with her life still intact.

"We're here." Luke's voice jarred me out of my head, and I focused.

A calm settled over me, and I no longer felt the emotions. They were buried deep, pushed inside a tiny closet in my mind, where they would stay for the duration of the altercation. If they didn't, I couldn't perform my job. And that was not acceptable.

I wasn't surprised in the least to find one of Silas' MC members at the end of the street. He was surprised to see the armored truck, though. Which meant he'd been following Shiloh, watching the surroundings, but was completely unaware of what was going on inside the house itself.

Which was sloppy.

I fully expected the man to be chastised within the next few minutes, but I wouldn't be sparing him the time. He'd figure out that he fucked up here shortly. Then I'd have Sam and Sebastian here within the next ten minutes. Not that I minded in the least. Especially

Texas Tornado

Sam. I trusted him with my life, and felt the same way with Shiloh's life as well.

When we pulled up about four houses down from the suspect's house, we were met with two other police officers. None other than Detective Pierson Howell, and his junior detective that couldn't kiss anymore ass even if he tried, were lead on the scene. Oh, joy!

They were both standing, leaning against their unmarked, dressed in wrinkled button down shirts, wrinkled khaki slacks, and ugly ties that had long since been loosened from their necks. They could've been twins if you didn't count the age difference between the two. Both had short, stylish brown hair. The same scrawny build, and dark brown eyes.

As we pulled up alongside them, they straightened, and scowled.

"Guess we get tweetle dee and tweetle dumb for first on's. Joy to the world." Luke drawled sarcastically.

First on's were known as first to arrive on scene. How they managed to finagle that, I didn't know. Normally they were trying to ruin innocent people lives who worked hard for a living. Why they were here, when any other uniform in a police car would've sufficed was beyond me.

We all made our way out of the armored truck, and stood to the side, surveying the scene. Luke, who was now head of the SWAT department, stopped to speak with Detective Howell.

"Anybody come in or out since you arrived?" Luke asked Howell.

I ignored the conversation, and scoured the nearby area for the best place to set up my rifle. Normally, when choosing spot to use your sniper rifle, you'd choose a place that was high up, with a basic amount of cover.

There was nothing of the sort here. Only rows and rows of mobile homes. Not even a damn tree in sight.

"Looks like you'll be on a roof." Downy said from my left.

I nodded, but didn't say anything else, still surveying. My eyes caught on Shiloh's company vehicle. The door that was slammed shut on my emotions threatened to burst open, but my strength won out, and I was able to keep it firmly closed. Good thing, too. I didn't want to be responsible for the death of my girlfriend, that's why I wasn't taking any lead on this op. My emotions were too close to the surface. I would never be able to make a hard decision that could potentially harm Shiloh, and I wouldn't.

"Luke!" Michael, another member of the SWAT team called from the side of the truck. "Lillian McBride is on the phone. She says there are two children in the household. Ten months and five years. Both boys." Michaels said.

"Who has the blueprints?" Luke called back.

"I do." Detective Howell said mildly, as if he had all the time in the world to just relax and wait.

My eyes turned hard when Luke held out his hand for them, and the detective shook his head. "No. I think you better tell me what you're doing here first, then I'll show you the blue prints."

"Detective," Luke growled. "I can't tell you a goddamn thing if I don't know the layout of the house. It has a lot to do with what's chosen, and how we go about doing our job."

Texas Tornado

Knowing that he had it under control, I made my way across the street, climbed up the closest tree to the house on the corner lot, and stepped gingerly onto the roof of the mobile home. From there, I laid out my rifle case, popped the sides loose, and started to assemble my rifle.

Even if it was department issued, it was one hell of a rifle. I'd sighted the bolt action M24 the day I'd been issued it. It's checked for precision twice a week, and cleaned after each use. Although it didn't have the same specs as my own rifle, it suited the job that it was designed for, and was an incredibly reliable weapon.

Laying down flat on the roof, I brought the scope up to my face, and reviewed the area with a practiced hand.

"Wind speed is ten miles an hour to the Southeast. Distance is 54.86 meters. Temperature is seventy eight degrees." Michael said from beside me.

Making the necessary adjustments on my scope, I continued to watch. The blinds were drawn, but I could just make out a man crossing back and forth from one side of the living room to the other through a part in the pulled blinds.

"Subject one in the living room. I can tell it's a man, but that's it." I called into my mic.

"Clear shot?" Luke rasped.

"Affirmative." I confirmed.

"Stand by."

Downy's voice came over the line. "Movement in the backyard."

"It's the boy." Diablo, another member of the team confirmed.

"Can you get him?" Luke asked.

"Affirmative, stand by." Diablo acquiesced.

Moments turned into a minute. A minute turned into minutes, and just as we all started to get anxious, Diablo came back on the line.

"Got him."

I let out a breath. One down, two to go.

The distant sound of loud pipes coming closer and closer confirmed that Sam did, indeed, get appraised of the situation. And by the sound of it, there was the rest of the team with him as well.

Once the sound died about half a mile away, I waited, eyes never wavering, for the next set of instructions.

"The negotiator is twenty five out." Luke said.

Fuck.

My thought was seconded by nearly the entire team, minus Luke. Which wasn't surprising. We depended on the nearest town, Longview's, hostage negotiator. Our town was just too small to warrant such an expense. When Luke had come on four years ago, he'd started working on the captain to start a SWAT team of his own instead of relying on Longview's SWAT team as well. He'd agreed, but some things, such as a negotiator of our own, just cost too much for such a small city.

"Guess we're in for a wait, boys." Luke commanded.

***

Shiloh

"I've got her here, sir." Frank said into the telephone at his ear.

Texas Tornado

The baby behind me was still just as silent as he'd been when I was secreted to the corner over thirty minutes before. I could tell by placing my hand on the child's chest that he was breathing, and I wondered if he'd been given something to make him sleep. It wasn't normal for a child to sleep this much in the middle of the day. Nor was it normal for the child not to stir when I'd purposefully tried to wake him when Frank had left the room only moments before.

"No, sir. She's alone." Frank said, nodding his head.

He drew up to the window, and drew one of the blinds down. Not being able to get a good view, he pulled on the cord, and raised the blinds up to their highest height. Once he looked around, he withdrew from the window, leaving the blinds open as he went.

"Frank! The boy went outside." Mrs. Newman rasped from the front room.

My nose was itching, and I could smell the distinct smell of pot wafting from the direction of the voice. Just wonderful. That's exactly what I needed. A stoned old woman in the back room, and a psychotic old man in the front. What the fuck?

"Leave him. He's feeding that mutt in the backyard like he was told to do on his next shitter break." Frank bellowed back before returning to his phone conversation.

Good. I knew that meant that the boy would be in safe hands. I knew that James was out there. The man that was now on the other end of the line was relaying what was going on to me. Talking to me, reassuring me. Which meant a whole lot. I'd be a nervous wreck right now without him. When I got out of here, I'd give him a kiss smack on the lips.

Well, maybe not on the lips, but he'd for sure be getting a hug.

"She's five ten, one hundred and fifteen pounds. Brown hair. Wavy. Good boobs. Nice hand full. Pasty white skin. Her legs look a little chunky. Ass is nice and round." Franks said from across the room.

What a dick. I was five foot seven inches. He was definitely off on my weight by more than thirty pounds, but who was I to complain? My hair was a nice shade of auburn. My boobs were more than a handful to most men, but when it came to James, they fit perfectly in the palm of his hands. My ass had been getting bigger, but I didn't think it was that big. As for the pasty white skin, it was November, what did he expect to happen when it wasn't summer?

Anyway, who would he be talking to? It was like he was expecting me, even though the visit itself was unannounced. That was the whole point of an unannounced visit, so they wouldn't be expecting you.

"I don't see any cops. Her phone hasn't vibrated or rang. I don't think anyone is any of the wiser." He explained to the person on the other end.

Hah. That's what he thought. I couldn't wait to see his face when he saw the SWAT team storm his house. I hope he accidentally got shot, too.

"The missus's got bingo at the Elk Club at seven. You'll be able to get in by yourself?" Frank asked.

Texas Tornado

His face turned into a frown, and you could tell he was upset about what he was hearing. "If I take the kids with me, then it'll be a shit night. You can't play bingo with those little shits. They'll be awful."

He listened to the other end, his scowl becoming more and more fierce as he listened.

"Fine." He snapped and slammed shut the phone, tossing it against the couch cushions.

He looked at me, and pointed his finger. "Look what you've done. That bonehead biker had to push his beat up nose into my business, and now I've got to deal with the frickin' CPS and take them to Bingo night. Can't wait to listen to this for the next week. Great."

He walked out of the room, and I shot to my feet like my ass was on fire. I knew that they were out there, even though I couldn't see them. James was probably up on top of one of the roofs.

I scanned and scanned, still not seeing him. Finally, I decided that maybe he'd be able to see me, and it was my best hope.

Using my hands instead of speaking it aloud, just in case he was close enough to hear me, I held up two fingers, then signed the letters a-d-u-l-t as slowly as I could, and then held up one finger, and spelled out b-a-b-y. I wasn't sure if whoever was out there would know what I was spelling, but I figured it was worth a try in any case.

However, that was all I was able to get out, because the rear door slammed open, Frank called out for the boy who went outside over ten minutes earlier, and then he growled a frustrated curse when the boy never came.

Frank called to his wife, who started shuffling herself into the family room, not sparing me a single glance, and then made her way outside, closing the front door as she went.

Minutes ticked by as Frank bellowed for the 'boy' to return. It was only after ten such minutes of this continuing, that he finally called out for his wife again, only for her to not respond either. Secretly, I was giggling inside. Outwardly, I was as cool as a clam as I sat with my back against the sleeping child and waited.

It didn't take long for Frank to come barreling back in the room, waving his shotgun around. "Where'd she go?"

I looked at him and pointed towards the front door, staying silent.

"She never came back in?" He asked, eyes frantically searching the living room.

I shook my head. More than likely, the woman was now in police custody. Not that I'd be telling him that.

He figured it out though. "You got buddies out there? You call the cops bitch?"

I shook my head. I wasn't technically lying.

"You bitch!" He said, and then raised his shotgun.

I closed my eyes, almost serenely, and waited. I knew it was going to happen. James would shoot the fucker, and I really hated seeing heads explode. Like bad. So, to block it out, I plugged my fingers into my ear, crowded the baby back behind me, and squeezed my eyes tightly shut.

Texas Tornado

    I felt the boom, even though I didn't see or hear it. Something heavy thumped hard onto the floor somewhere across the room from me, but I stayed where I was. I didn't even open my eyes.

    It wasn't until I felt the distinct impact of the door hitting the wall that my body was leaning against before I opened my eyes. Then I quickly shut them again, my mind refusing to acknowledge what had once been Mr. Newman's head.

    Something touched my shoulder, and I opened them to find a black helmeted head in my face. I resisted the urge to slap it away, instead waiting patiently for the man to speak.

    "You okay?" Helmet head asked.

    I nodded.

    "The baby?" Helmet head probed.

    I scooted over carefully, revealing the sleeping form huddled in the corner.

    "I think they gave the baby something. He hasn't moved an inch since I got here. Pulse is strong though." I explained.

    "Medic." Helmet head bellowed.

    Just then, a commotion at the door had my eyes travelling to it, and I was relieved to know that James was finally there. True, it wasn't as if I could see the man, per say. However, I knew that body almost as well as I knew my own. Regardless of whether I could see his skin and face or not.

    "Shiloh!" James yelled as he barreled towards me.

    I made to stand, and helmet head helped me up.

In the next moment, I was engulfed in James' arms. Although it was anything but comfortable to be pressed up against his hard, unforgiving helmet, with his sniper rifle slung over his front, and the million and one tactical thingie mabobbers hanging off his belt, I hugged him back for all I was worth. Not caring in the slightest that I'd most likely be sporting bruises tomorrow.

"I'm so glad you're okay." James groaned.

I held him even tighter before I said what I really wanted to say. "What took you so long?"

Texas Tornado

Chapter 20

Never argue with a woman holding a torque wrench.

-Life Lesson

Shiloh

Weeks passed, and within no time at all, Christmas was around the corner.

After the hostage situation at the Shady Lane Mobile Home Park and the Newman's, James made it a point to drill home the idea of safety. Lillian herself had now mandated that for each unscheduled visit, we have the presence of a uniformed police officer to accompany us.

Now here I was, with eight days until Christmas, and I was bored.

James, Sebastian, Sam, and my dad had all made it a point to spend some time with me, but I always ended up being so freaking alone. I'd started doing Insanity in a vain effort to stay in shape, since everyone refused to let me go outside to run. Which didn't really upset me so much as make me feel claustrophobic. I was so freaking tired of being caged up in this God forsaken house that I would go nuts.

The ringing of my phone pulled me out of my contemplations, and I answered it on the second ring. "Hello?"

"Hey, Shiloh. Want to come over to Free? We're going to play some games. Have margaritas, and then decorate the Christmas tree." Blaine said giddily into my ear.

I pulled the phone away from my face, and readily agreed. "I love you, Blaine. Will you have my babies?"

"Yes, you just have to come over first!" She laughed. "I'll send Elliott over in the truck. He'll be there in fifteen minutes, okay?"

"Yes, thank you." I said before hanging up the phone.

Looking down at myself, I decided that the bright green leggings with purple jingle bells would be festive, and decided against changing them. I covered up my black tank top with James' old high school baseball sweatshirt and slipped my feet into my Ugg boots.

Yes, they were ugly, but they were soft and warm. The eighty-degree weather had finally decided to act like winter, and had dipped into the low twenties overnight, making it colder than a witch's tit. Especially since James refused to turn the heater on anything above sixty five degrees.

I folded the blanket I'd been using moments before, and then grabbed my purse, and waited by the front door patiently, like a good girl.

The knock at the door came a few minutes later, and Elliott's voice projected through the door. "You can come out, Shiloh."

I grinned as I yanked open the door. "You can have my babies, too. Thanks for saving me."

He laughed. "I think that's anatomically impossible, but you're welcome."

"I'm so flipping bored. James got called in, and I'm dying here all by myself." I sighed as I walked to his truck and hoisted myself inside before he could even open his own door.

Texas Tornado

"Yeah, so bored that you told one of the local church people off." Elliott laughed.

"I didn't tell them off!" I said indigently.

"That's not what James tells me." Elliott snickered as he backed out of the driveway and headed towards the main road.

"It was honestly not that big of a deal. I don't understand what the big fuss is about."

"So, when the pastor of the church down the street from you asked you where you were going when you died, you didn't mean to say Rader Funeral Home?" Elliott gave me a teasing look.

"Well, yeah, I did mean to say that." I finally agreed.

I mean really. What did the man expect when he dropped that bombshell in my lap? Yes, I did believe in God, but I didn't want it thrown in my face that I was a sinner. Nor did I want him to tell me I was going to hell because I didn't make church every other Sunday.

"Everyone got a real kick out of that at the shop when James told us." He explained as he pulled onto the street that Free was located on.

Up ahead of us, a log truck pulled onto the road, and I gave an involuntary shudder.

"I hate those things. Ever since I saw Final Destination, every time I see one of those, I think about the chains breaking and the logs skewering me through the front glass." I explained to Elliott who sported a wary look.

He laughed. "Yeah, I can see that. I feel the same way when I see them on the interstate."

Pulling into Free, he parked his vehicle around the back, and walked with me to the side door that led to the activity room in the back of the garage.

All the women were gathered there, margaritas already in hand.

"Hey, y'all started without me?" I yelled as I made my way into the room.

"Of course not. We just heard you pull in, and we picked up our glasses." Ember said guiltily.

Liars. Ember's was nearly half-gone. Blaine was on the verge of empty, another empty glass was next to my full one that Ember had just gestured to.

"Liars." I laughed and went to my drink, taking a large swallow before turning to take a seat at the table.

"Later, ladies." Elliott said as he walked towards the outer shop area.

"Wait!" I called to him, stopping him before he could leave.

"Yeah?" He asked, turning around.

"Thanks for the ride. And will you send Janie in here for some food?" I asked sweetly.

"Sure thing, sweetheart." He agreed and left.

The next hour was spent playing Apples to Apples, but was interrupted when Janie came storming into the room. Her eyes were flaring hot, and she turned her head, scanned the room, found my eyes, and the stomped towards me with deliberate steps. She reminded me of her father when she had that determination etched on her face, and I couldn't withhold the smile that took over.

Texas Tornado

"What is the reason I can't be out in the shop with Max and Sam?" She demanded.

I managed to catch the laughter that threatened to spill from my throat, but only just barely. "Well, I was wondering if tomorrow you wanted to go shopping for Christmas presents before we go visit your mother."

She grimaced. "I'll go shopping with you, but only if you take me to the Harley shop."

I pursed my lips. "Well, that'll work for your dad, Sam, and the rest of the guys, but what about your grandmother and Cheyenne?" I asked.

She thought about that for a moment, but then came up with the perfect solution. "We'll go to Lowe's, too. They're right across the street from each other."

The laughter bubbled out of my throat, and I smiled at her, pulling her in tightly and giving her a big hug. Her wiry arms wrapped around me surprisingly tight, and I luxuriated in the warmth she exuded.

Never once had I seen her mother get a hug like this, and I was more than a little smug about it.

"What? You've gotten to hear Max sing?" Blaine blurted from across the room.

"Yeah, hasn't everybody?" Payton asked.

"What're y'all bellyaching about?" Gabe asked as he came into the room.

Grease covered him from head to toe, and he looked like he'd been letting oil drip all over him instead of letting it drip into the drain pan like it was supposed to.

"Yick. What've you been doing?" Ember eyed Gabe from across the room.

Gabe's smile lit the room. "What, do I look that bad?"

"Yeah." Ember wasted no time in telling it how it was.

He laughed, went to the fridge, and grabbed a beer. "What's the big deal about hearing Max sing?"

"You've heard him sing?" Blaine breathed, hanging on Gabe's every word.

"Well, yeah. But he was drunk, so I'm not sure it counted. So have you, now that I'm thinking about it." He laughed and left the room, beer in hand.

"Payton, go ask him to sing so we can hear."

I rolled my eyes. Yeah, right. Even I knew that wouldn't work. The man was very private. Although quick to lend a hand and laugh, he never volunteered any information about himself. In the year or so that I'd known him, I could count on one hand the number of things that I'd learned about him from his own mouth.

"He wouldn't do it." Payton sighed wistfully. "He doesn't do it very often, and when he does, it's only 'cause he thinks he's alone."

"I thought you'd all heard him sing before." I questioned.

"So Max says. I was drunk. I don't remember a thing that happened that night." Blaine pouted.

"I bet I could get him to do it." Janie said from beside me.

Texas Tornado

Every eye turned toward her.

"You know, that'd probably work. The girl's got every man here wrapped around her little finger." Cheyenne teased.

Which was why, five minutes later, all five of us were pressed to the side of an old El Camino, watching as Janie pleaded with Max to sing to her.

"Janie," he whined.

"Please, Uncle Max. Come on, please?" She said, giving the pouty lip for extra incentive.

Sighing, he turned towards the motorcycle he was replacing the exhaust on, and started singing, tightening bolts as he did.

We were all dying by the time he'd finished the last verse. *Cowboys and Angels* definitely would be a must buy song for me in the very near future. Max could've easily made a career out of singing. It just showed the type of man he was that he'd decided to protect our country instead.

"That good, pumpkin head?" Max asked Janie.

"Will you sing Frozen?" Janie tried the lip pout again.

"I draw the line at country. I'll sing anytime you want, but it's gotta be country. Give me some George Strait, or Garth Brooks anytime over that Disney crap."

Janie contemplated what Max had just said, absently leaned over and grabbed the next bolt to hand it over to Max, and finally arrived at what she'd been thinking. "Daddy says that Johnny Cash and George Jones are the best. I'm inclined to agree with him."

"Well, not that your daddy is wrong, but there are other people that sing country that are worth listening to." Max laughed.

"Daddy says that country music is about life. That no other music can even compete." Janie continued.

"That's true." Max agreed.

"Daddy told me I couldn't sing 'I'm in Love With a Stripper' anymore. That's how I know. He said that country was the way of life, and I had to live in the North before I could sing anything else." Janie told him solemnly.

The girl could talk a mile a minute, but the things that came out of her mouth were just amazing.

"That's not a good song for a girl like you to sing." Max nodded, his hands deep inside the belly of the bike.

Then, out of the deep blue seas of Janie's head, she rocked our worlds. "My mommy makes me sad."

Max froze and turned to Janie. His hands were covered in grease, but he gathered Janie up to him and gave her a hug. She didn't care about the grease in the slightest.

"Why does she make you sad, pumpkin?"

"She makes me talk to some man when Shiloh has to go to the bathroom. She measures me for dresses and never gives them to me. She told me last week that she had a surprise for me in a couple more weeks, but she won't give that to me either."

Time seemed to freeze.

Although we'd thought we were being inconspicuous, we were proven wrong when Max called to Payton.

"Payton, baby. Will you bring me a beer?" He called, concern etched tightly over his handsome face.

Payton stayed frozen, just as I had. We both, as well as Blaine, Ember, and Cheyenne, knew something more was going on. We just didn't know what.

"What're y'all doing?" James asked from behind me.

I jumped six and a half feet in the air, and spun around, hand clutching at my heart. "Jesus, did you have to do that?" I gasped.

Texas Tornado

"What are y'all doing with my kid?" He asked suspiciously.

Max, having heard James' question, stood up to his full height, Janie in hand, and came straight towards us. Reaching my hands out, I took Janie from him, and left Max and James to talk in private.

Hours passed.

Sebastian arrived to take us back to James' house, sans James. Janie and I spent a few hours coloring, making dinner, and getting ready for bed. Not once in those few hours did she mention to me what she'd said to Max. Which made me aware of the bond those two had, and how I'd need to work harder to get in there.

Sebastian hadn't stayed, which didn't surprise me. The two of them stayed over every night, but were gone until after I went to bed most nights and before I woke most mornings.

Daina was with Todd, according to the note on the table, and I stifled a laugh at the reaction that would raise out of James. Although they weren't officially moved in together, they still stayed together most nights. Daina only returning to grab even more clean clothes. It wouldn't take long until everything was at Todd's place if she kept it up.

As I tucked Janie into bed, and kissed her lightly on the forehead, she looked me straight into the eyes and rocked my world for a second time that day. "I love you, Shiloh."

Tears blurred my vision. "I love you too, sweetheart." I said as I brushed her hair away from her eyes.

"Will you tell daddy to come give me a kiss when he gets home?" She asked as her eyes closed.

"You know I don't have to tell him. He comes to see you every time he gets home, no matter what time it is." I laughed.

"Yeah, but there may be a time when he forgets, and that's your job. To remind him." She said sleepily.

Kissing her cheeks one last time, I stood, and backed out of the room, my eyes staying locked on her, closing the door quietly.

My sleep that night was fitful at best. I'd woken twice to find no James, no dad, and no Sebastian. It was going on four in the morning, and I was starting to really worry.

Which is how I found myself in the basement, watching Top Gun, wishing that I knew how to fly like Goose and Maverick. The movie ended, and I decided that James definitely chose the wrong branch of the military. Navy dress whites were way cuter than the Army's dress uniform.

Getting up to go check to see if anyone had arrived home, I came to a sudden halt with one foot on the first step when James' voice halted me.

"I love you. You know?" James' deep voice said from above me, making me jump yet again.

James was sitting at the very top. Back against the door.

I'd been longing to hear those words from him for months. Except I'd expected them to be sweet, not harsh. He looked haggard. His hair, what little of it there was, was in disarray. His eyes were blood shot, with half circles making his eyes look bruised. His skin was flushed. His knuckles were bloody and raw.

"I love you, too." I told him.

"I know. You've shown it." His voice sounded dead.

He'd been fighting again. He also smelled like a brewery. Which also explained where my dad and Sebastian were. If James was at their place, then they wouldn't have left him there. At least not while he'd been drinking.

I climbed the steps slowly. His head was level with my stomach when I finally came to a stop two steps below him. "What's wrong, J?"

"Fucking everything." He sighed, letting his head drop.

Texas Tornado

My hands raised to touch him, but his harsh voice stopped me in my tracks. "Don't touch me."

Freezing in place, I asked, "Why not?"

He'd never told me I couldn't touch him. In fact, he'd gone out of his way to do little things like bring my hand to his cheek. Run his fingers through my hair. Touching was a large part of how he communicated.

"What's going on?" He laughed darkly. "My daughter's sick fuck of a mother's been letting strange guys talk to her, while I've sat around with my thumb up my ass. I knew she was acting strange. Not once, in four years, had she tried to get Janie, and then all of a fucking sudden, she wants to be a part of her life again. Where's she getting the money to fight for custody? How's she able to live in the richest goddamn neighborhood in Longview. Those houses cost a mint. All these questions have been rolling around in my brain, but I let it slide. Tried to fight her with the letter of the law on my side. Well fuck that. Not anymore. I'm not above blackmail and manipulation."

"What'd you do?" I asked hesitantly.

"What I had to do. She won't be seeing my girl again. Ever."

The sadness in his voice made my heart feel heavy. "That's okay. As long as it doesn't take you away from her."

His face hardened into a deep slash. "We'll see."

The no touching thing wasn't working for me anymore. "What do you mean, we'll see?" I snapped as I yanked his head up by his hair.

His eyes were hard and dark. "Not in the mood to deal with your shit right now, Shiloh."

"Yeah?" I taunted, holding his hair a little tighter.

"Yeah," he seethed.

"What're you going to do? Spank me?" I goaded.

"I'm warning you, Shiloh. I'm not in the fucking mood. I'm more than a little drunk, I'm pissed, and I've been fighting all night. I'm on edge, and I don't want to hurt you." He said between clenched teeth.

His body was vibrating, but not with anger like he'd like. No, it was need. Desire. He needed some sort of release.

He'd tried to fight. That hadn't worked, so he'd turned to drinking. And when that still hadn't gotten him where he needed to be, he'd come to me. I had what he needed, and I wanted to give it to him just as much as he wanted to take it.

"Stop being a titty baby, and take me." I snapped.

Something in him tore loose at my statement, and he launched himself off the steps, scooping me up in his arms as he went, tossing me over his shoulder like a sack of grain.

The door to the basement slammed open, and he marched with deliberate steps to his bedroom, closing the door with care, which completely contradicted his haste to get me in his room.

A wave of weightlessness overcame me as he tossed me from his shoulder. My back hit the mattress with a bounce. My abdominal muscles tightened, and I placed my hands down at my sides, watching as he ripped the clothes from his body.

"Get naked. On your knees." He snapped.

The harsh overhead light snapped on, enabling me to see the perfect line of his body. In all the time we'd been together, we'd never actually been with each other like this in the light. Everything we'd done always happened late at night, with the lights minimal at best.

His body was luscious.

Although scars of all sorts were evident on his body, not in any way did it detract from the perfectness. His arms were large and defined. His

Texas Tornado

pectorals sculpted and firm, dog tags nestled in between the valley of his chest, leading down to his ridged abdomen.

His pants were the last to go, and as he slid the pants down, his cock bobbed out from its confinement, angry and throbbing. The veins on his length were numerous, drawing my eye as they throbbed, pulsing harder and harder with each frantic beat of his heart.

His balls hung low between two muscled thighs, and swung as he took a step towards me.

"Guess since you can't listen, we'll do this the hard way." He said, stooping down, grabbing something, and then coming towards me.

The gleam of metal in my periphery tore my eyes from his pulsating erection, making me turn. In his left hand, he'd grabbed a pocketknife.

"Wh-what are you doing?" I asked hesitantly.

"Well, figured this would be the fastest way to get those clothes off you."

I wasted no time after that to shed off my t-shirt and yoga pants. Then turning over and waiting for him.

The clatter of the knife hitting the nightstand, and then falling off the side didn't deter him from his goal. No, not James. He had his plan in mind, and he wouldn't be deviating from it.

The hot lash of his tongue startled me, momentarily making me pull away. The sharp sting of his hand slapping my ass surprised me, and he pulled me back towards him with his hands on my hips.

"Don't move." He growled against the soft, sensitive skin of my thigh.

Then I couldn't speak. I had no words for what he did next. He didn't either, which is why he showed me.

His tongue parted my folds, licking from the tip of my clit to the top of my ass. He got me nice and slick, my juices mixed with his saliva, creating a hot, slippery mess. His face had to be covered as he assaulted my clit, flicking it back and forth, and thrust his hot tongue into my pulsing sheath.

Each deft movement of his tongue brought me closer and closer to the pinnacle, but just as I was about to roll over, he abruptly stopped and pulled himself up until he was kneeling directly behind me.

The hot hardness of his cock slid up my inner thigh, and the head knocked against my clit, nearly sending me over as well, before he pulled back and lined his cock up with my weeping core.

Both of his hands found my hips, and he slammed himself inside of me, allowing his hard cock to tunnel inside, finding a home deep within my body. What was different this time was that he didn't control his movements. Normally, he'd stop, not willing to go too far into me because of his size. This time, he didn't.

"I've been dying to go this deep." James rasped, before sliding back out, and slamming back inside.

I couldn't say this was a bad feeling, just something totally new. Entirely foreign. Each snap of his hips had him bottoming out, running the engorged head of his cock horribly deep. Deliciously deep.

"Lean down and put your face flat against the bed." He commanded.

I went down to my elbows and put my face against the soft comforter. And not once did he stop pounding into me with deep, steady strokes. Still not in the desired position, he put his hand in the middle of my back, applying pressure until I dropped down flat, with my shoulders on the mattress.

His hand wiggled in between my body and the mattress, thumb grazing the pebbled bead of my nipple. Somehow, my nipple found a home between the two knuckles of his middle and pointer finger. Once in the desired position, he pulled out, keeping his fisted hand on the mattress, allowing a sharp pinching sensation to radiate through my beaded nipple, shooting a hot burst of pleasure straight to my core.

He repeated the process on the other side, until both of my nipples were held tightly in his grasp. Then he started fucking me. Hard. Much harder than he'd ever done before. Each push of his hips had my knees rising off the bed, which in turn tugged deliciously on my nipples that were still held in his unyielding grip.

To stifle my cries of pleasure, I buried my face into James' pillow. Breathing in his scent, while he tunneled inside of me, it somehow loosened what little control he had left.

Everything happened at once. My cry of release burst free of my lips, he yanked the pillow away from my grasp, and left with no other way to stifle my screams. I turned my head and bit down on his forearm, staunching my cries of pleasure.

At my own loss of control, he pulled free of me abruptly. My convulsing core cried out at the loss of his thick length. My eyes squeezed tight as I thrust my hands down between the bed and my body, thrusting my fingers into my body to relieve the emptiness he'd left me with.

However, I understood why he'd done it moments later when I felt the hot jet of his semen burst free of his cock and land in wet splashes against my ass, dripping down until it reached my fingers that were still working inside of me with furious pushes.

Once his semen hit my fingers, and our juices combined, another orgasm burst free of me, launching me to the place that I only ever accomplished when I was with James. His cock returned to me, pushing past the two fingers that were still buried deep, and stopped when he hit the end of me.

Leveling himself up, he turned us until we were both on our sides, him still buried inside of me.

When I started to pull my fingers free, he stopped me with his hand, and held us together until his cock softened and slipped free. He removed my fingers, tangling them with his own, and curled them in tight to my body, pulling me closer until no space was left between us.

It was close to five minutes later before my body and mind finally reconnected. "I need to shower." I said finally.

"In the morning." He said in a sleep tinged voice.

"It is the morning." I argued.

"Shiloh." He sighed.

"But..."

He tightened his arm, effectually stifling my protests.

"Tomorrow. Go to sleep." He demanded.

"Fine." I huffed.

Sleep came easily after that. My body was exhausted, and with the one glance at the clock before I nodded off, it didn't really surprise me. It was going on five in the morning. Tomorrow should be fun.

Chapter 21

You had me at, "I hate that bitch, too."

-T-shirt

James

I looked across the room one more time at Shiloh's sleeping form before closing the door softly, and heading into the kitchen. The sound of my mother's and Janie's voices woke me around four hours after I'd fallen asleep, and I felt like I'd been run over by a freight train.

My head pounded, my eyes burned, but one thing I couldn't complain about was my satiety. I was so goddamned sated that I could fucking breath again. Oh, the anger was still there, but the furious recklessness wasn't. I still would go forward with my plan, but I wouldn't be stupid about making the plan become reality. Something huge was happening right under my nose. I planned to find out exactly what it was. Today.

"Hi, daddy. I can't find Shiloh." Janie said as she saw me.

I smiled. "She's asleep in daddy's bed. Mom, could you give me and Janie a minute?"

She smiled her mother's smile at me, and patted me on the head before leaving the room.

"Janie, I need to talk to you about something." I started.

"Are you going to marry 'Loh?" She questioned.

No bullshitting with my girl. She had too much of me in her to deal with shit she didn't need to. Straightforward was how I liked to deal with everything, and my girl was the same way.

"Yes, baby. I'm going to ask her. I just wanted to make sure you understood what that meant." I replied.

She looked at me. Those big eyes staring at me. Her blonde hair was in a sideways ponytail and braided. She was wearing tight skinny jeans, her black cowboy boots with the lime green fringe, and a black tank top that said heart breaker on it.

She was nothing like her mother. Didn't even look like her. For which I was very thankful for. One day Janie might decide that she wanted to know more about her mother, and when that day came, I didn't want her to have a reminder that a part of her life would forever be missing. Something that was so integral in how she came to be.

"Can I call her mommy?" She finally asked.

My heart stalled, and started galloping full force. "Well, I don't mind. But I think that's something you need to make sure is alright with Shiloh first. Okay?" I asked.

"Yeah, daddy. Where were you last night?" She raised her brow. That move was so much like Cheyenne that I wanted to laugh.

"Mom!" I called, knowing she wouldn't be far away.

My mother entered a few moments later. I was surprised to see that Todd was with her. Even though I'd known that they were together, I still hadn't been faced with the fact that my mother was now intimately involved with someone. However, one look at Todd's

Texas Tornado

possessive hand at the small of my mother's back made me hyperaware.

My father died when I was really young, and not once had I seen my mother with someone in all those years. I was happy that she was moving on after all this time. She deserved to be happy.

I stood and walked over to Todd, holding out my hand. He shook it, nodding his head at me in acknowledgement. Yes, he knew I was okay with him and my mom being together. The flash of relief in his eyes showed that he wasn't sure how I'd react, which made me smile.

"So, Todd. I was about to tell my mother that I was marrying Shiloh. When will you be making an honest woman of my mama?" I joked.

His eyes narrowed. "Well, we haven't really gotten that far. She told me I have to ask permission before we discuss dates."

No bullshitting. Just what I liked.

"You have it. Now, what's for breakfast?" I said, raising my eyebrows at my mom in question.

Silence echoed through the room at my abrupt change in subject. Then my mom finally came unglued, and disentangled herself from Todd's arms. Then proceeded to make breakfast.

"I'll be back. I'm going to wake Shiloh before we get started." I said, heading out of the kitchen and walking towards my room.

No, strike that. Our room. She wouldn't be leaving.

The shower was running when I crossed the threshold, and I stopped, took a breath, willing my cock to get under control, and stepped into the bathroom. The shower turned off just as I was opening the door, and my breath halted in my chest as I saw Shiloh step out of the shower, dripping wet.

I swallowed convulsively, letting my eyes wander down her body, but forced myself to remain still. I didn't have time. There were people waiting downstairs. I had to go meet with Sam and Max. I had to go Christmas shopping. Ring shopping.

My eyes followed Shiloh's gaze to my forearm where a perfect set of teeth were outlined prominently on the meaty part of my arm. Then my eyes found the tips of her nipples, slightly reddened from last night's activities, and all the excuses abruptly flew out the fucking window.

Twenty minutes later, Shiloh proceeded me into the kitchen, and then promptly flushed bright red when my mother's disapproving eyes, and Todd's humor filled ones, landed on us. Pancakes were half eaten, as well as eggs, sausage, and slightly cold coffee.

I pulled Shiloh's chair out for her, and she sat, placing a napkin in her lap. I took the chair at the head of the table with Janie on my right and Shiloh on the left.

It was after we finished breakfast, and Shiloh loaded the dishes in the washer that I dropped the bomb. "Shiloh, you won't be taking Janie to see Anna any longer. I filed a suit for full custody, and I'm getting Anna's visitation revoked. We're going to beat her at her own game."

Texas Tornado

***

"Did you find anything else?" I asked Jack as he typed away at the computer.

"Not much. What I did find was enough for now. It'll get the custody suit dropped on her end. Ever heard of a Sloan Lerng? That's the name that keeps popping up every time you trace Anna's calls on the days she has Janie. He's got no history, and I mean none. He doesn't exist. Which means it's an alias." Jack recapped to the group.

Well that much was obvious. I could've told you that before I even looked it up. Although, my guess was that it was a burner phone, not that it was actually registered to someone. Which begged me to wonder....why?

Let's say that he did, indeed, use a burner. That would mean that the burner wouldn't be registered to anyone in specific. That would mean, if Janie had told the truth, which she did, that it would be the word of a child's against an adult's word. And that adult, Anna, could pretty much say she didn't know what on earth Janie was talking about.

However, by having the phone actually registered to someone meant that he *wanted* to be found. Which, even if we found out who it was an alias for, didn't mean we could pin it on that individual.

Whoever it was thought he was smart. Too smart to be caught. What he didn't know was that he'd already made a mistake. He'd messed with the wrong little girl. That little girl not only had a very protective father with an extensive military background, but also the love of five other men, who also had extensive military backgrounds.

Not to mention the love of every single member of the SWAT team, who also had extensive military backgrounds.

Whoever this person was, had already signed his own death warrant. He was already standing with one foot in the grave. He just didn't know it yet.

I watched Jack's fingers as they typed away at the computer, never looking back at us while he spoke of what he'd found. I watched for the reaction I knew was coming as soon as the words fell from my mouth. I knew he wouldn't want to do it, and hell, under any other circumstance, I would've never even thought to ask this of him. I knew how much they'd suffered, yet I couldn't *not* do it. This was my baby. My Janie, and I would use ever resource I had at my exposal.

"Jack," I started. "Can you ask Winter to help?"

Jack's body froze, and the door behind me opened. I didn't turn. I watched Jack as the muscles in his shoulders, forearms, and back flexed and then relaxed, as if he was fighting an inner demon.

"Oh, Jamie." Winter's voice said from behind me. "The man loves you. Of course, he would ask his beautiful, intelligent wife to help. He loves Janie, as do we all."

Winter's tone was light and breezy, but I could tell that she'd meant every word by the sincerity that was very much evident in her voice.

Turning, I found Winter standing just inside the office door, Cat cocooned in a soft-looking blanket in the crook of her arm. She smiled

Texas Tornado

warmly as she walked up to me, went up to her tippy toes, and kissed my chin.

"Now, you take Cat," she said gently placing the sleeping little girl into my arms. "While Jack shows me what he's got."

I looked down at the bundle in my arms and smiled. A little pang of sadness went through me as I stared at her sleeping face. Hair jet-black like her father, with the same porcelain skin as her mother, she looked like a sleeping doll. I'd never even contemplated having another child. Until recently.

I loved Janie with everything I had. When a man had a child, there was nothing to explain it. The entire focus of your life shifts. You live your life, but you live it for a different reason.

Where before, you worked a job so you could have nice things, after a child, you work a job so your child can have nice shoes. Or toys. Or My Little fucking Ponies.

The entire earth shifted the first time I laid eyes on my girl. No longer was I confident in the world around me. Which helped make the decision for me to pursue a career as an Army Ranger. To protect my child the best way I knew how. By making sure the country she lived in was safe and protected.

The only bad thing about that decision was not being able to see her. To smell her. To hear her whisper in my ear about pink spiders crawling over me as she tickled me with her little hand, and the invisible bug I needed to kill before she could go to sleep.

I was here now, though. Janie had me now. And what had caused me to be absent with Janie wouldn't be an issue with any future children.

Anna and Shiloh couldn't have been any more different from each other.

Where Shiloh was warm and caring, Anna was hard and indifferent. Where Anna didn't have direction, Shiloh had become a social worker in three years instead of the usual four. Becoming a licensed professional at the young age of twenty-one.

Shiloh would be an exceptional mother. Hell, for all intents and purposes, she already was. To Janie.

"Deep thoughts?" Sam's voice pulled me out of my Hallmark Moment.

My eyes raised to his. "Yeah, just thinking about having another kid."

"You can borrow the girls. They'll clear that up right quick." Sam quipped.

I laughed, as he'd intended.

"Anagram." Jack mumbled.

Sam and I turned to him to see Winter hunched over her keyboard, typing faster than a cyclone. Her curly red hair was in a curly mass falling over her shoulders, and obstructing her face from view. Jack was leaning over the back of her chair, watching over her shoulder as she typed.

Texas Tornado

"Goddammit. Why didn't I think to do that?" Jack asked standing and running his rough hands through his hair, making it stick up on end.

"Because you're hot shit wife is just *that* good." Winter teased as she kept typing.

The phone in my pocket rang, so I walked towards Jack and handed the baby off. He took her gratefully, pulling the baby close to his chest before turning back to watch the computer monitor. Shoving my hand into my pocket, I finally got it loose just as the phone stopped ringing. It started ringing immediately after, making my heart start beating triple time when I saw it was Shiloh.

"Hello?" I answered urgently.

"Uhhh," Shiloh hesitated. "You've gotten two calls from the dish company. Normally I wouldn't pry, but they left a message. Twice. Anyway, they say you've been ordering, ugh, a lot of porn in the last hour, and they want to make sure the charges aren't happening by accident. I've been here all morning, and Janie's playing with Kayla outside on the trampoline. No one's in the house to order porn."

When you think of things people are calling to tell you, not even once had the thought of someone illegally ordering porn through my account registered. Hell, it hadn't even been on the fucking radar.

"Uhhh," I said, perplexed. "I haven't been ordering porn either."

Winter's head snapped in my direction, and she stood quickly, walking over to me with her hand extended.

"Hey June Bug, Winter wants to talk to you. Hold on a minute, okay?" I asked.

When she affirmed, I handed the phone over to Winter, who'd immediately hit speaker phone and sat back down. "Alright, chicka. Tell me the details."

Shiloh went over what she'd heard on the messages, and then waited while Winter went to work.

In the meantime, I pulled up my mobile banking and, sure enough, I'd had over nineteen charges for pay-per-view charged to my account. What the heck?

After a few minutes of speed clicking and typing, Winter hooted, jumped to her feet, and fist pumped her arm in the air. "Score one for Team Stoker!"

"Jesus, you're mother's a fucking nut. Poor girl. You're going to have the nutty gene, too." Jack murmured to his now awake daughter.

"Hey!" She said indignantly.

"What'd you find?" Sam asked to try to stem the fight he could see brewing.

"Well, this crazy girl finally figured it out." She said sticking out her tongue towards Jack.

He chuckled. "Figured what out?"

The sound of a commotion coming from the phone stopped Winter before she could explain, and my blood ran cold at the voice that I heard above the sound of breaking glass and furniture.

"Give me my fucking kid!" Anna screeched.

"Go fuck yourself." Shiloh hissed.

Go to the safe room, Janie. Go to the goddamn safe room.

Texas Tornado

I hadn't realized I'd been yelling it aloud until Shiloh repeated my plea, screaming it to the girls in the background. The girls' cries faded, until I could hear nothing else, but the struggles of Shiloh, and the screams of Anna.

"Call Sebastian. Find out who he has on Shiloh, and get him fucking in there." I shouted as I made my way out the door.

Sam was already on his feet, as was Jack, and they were following close on my heels. Winter stayed with my phone, and was on her phone with someone, too. I just hoped it wasn't the police. I had shit to say to Anna, and that wasn't conducive with her being in police custody.

As soon as I made it to the parking lot and on my bike, I started it, throttled it up so loud that my ears popped, and plunged out of the parking lot and onto the street.

By the time I was on Stone Road, I was doing over one hundred and thirty miles an hour and taking corners as if I was on rails. I didn't have any doubt in my mind that Shiloh could handle herself. She showed me that the other day when I taught her self-defense. Or at least that's what I thought I was doing. In reality, she was just worried about hurting me, and after making a bet, she'd upheld her end and proved me the fool.

So no, I wasn't worried about Anna. Shiloh could handle Anna. I just hoped that Anna was alone.

The drive that normally took ten minutes took less than five, and I rolled up to the stop sign that connected my street to the main road, pulled over into the bushes, and hopped off. I ran through the neighbor's yards, hopping fences as I went.

When I got to the fence that separated my yard from Mrs. Kowalsky's yard, I paused and listened, straining my ears to hear everything I could. When I could hear nothing, I went to the back of the yard, and slipped in between the two loose boards that I used to use to sneak out when I was a teenager.

Although stiff, and definitely much cozier than it used to be, I managed it, and stepped into my own yard. Once through, I withdrew the Colt .45 from my ankle, and palmed it. The heavy weight was comforting in my hand, settling my nerves as I got down to my hands, and then to my knees in the grass. The large trampoline with the safety net hid me from view. I used it as cover as I made my way underneath of it to survey the scene before me.

And a scene, it was.

***

"Why don't you tell us what's going on, Ms. Stevens." Max warned. "I'm not in to hurting women, but I'll make an exception in this case."

Max's stone cold voice sent shivers down my own spine. I could only imagine what it was doing to a positively terrified Anna. Not that I gave a shit. The woman could rot in hell for all I cared. I just wanted to get some information out of her first. Which was why I'd called Max as soon as I'd made sure that there wasn't any other people involved in the earlier altercation.

Texas Tornado

She shook her head, thinning her lips tightly, and clamping her teeth over them to keep them sealed. The look of apprehension on her face intensified when Max went down on one knee in front of her. Looking over his shoulder, he addressed me. "Close the door on your way out."

Anna's sharp inhalation followed me out of the room.

Twenty minutes later, Max stepped out of garage, and walked up to the gathering with purposeful steps. He didn't waste any time with pleasantries, either.

"Sloan Lerng is an anagram for Glen Larson. Originally, Anna just wanted money. She got in a bind and needed some leverage to get it. That's why she tried to get custody. Then another opportunity, in the form of Larson, came along and she needed custody for a different reason." Max explained what he'd learned.

A commotion from the front door had Max, Sebastian, Sam and I turning to see Jack barrel through the door, car seat in hand, and Winter trailing behind him. Before I hadn't been alarmed on who was entering the house. Gabe was in front watching, just in case, and he wouldn't let anyone through without one hell of a battle. However, with one look at Jack's face, and I my stomach sank.

He'd gone back to Free once he'd been sure that the scene was secure. Winter had been on the phone with Gabe when we'd left, not the police. Which I'd figured out when he showed not even ten minutes after we'd arrived, telling me that Winter had called him. Now, they were back and they didn't look settled at all.

My stomach sank as I saw the haunted look in Jack's eyes, and I braced myself, because I knew I wasn't about to get good news.

"They want your daughter. They want to sell her. They've already got upwards to a million dollars on her head. The pictures that Anna's been sending them have been posted to some..."Jack shook his head, searching for words. "auction site, I guess. They bid on pictures. Most of the site has the kids shown in some sort of cage. Janie's pictures are the only ones that are 'free,' for lack of a better word."

My eyes closed somewhere in between his explanation, but when I opened them again, a fury that I've never felt before, never knew could exist, flooded through my veins. It seeped into my blood like a raging wildfire, and there was nothing that was going to stop it from getting revenge.

"Show me," I demanded.

"I can't. I crashed the site. I have some screen shots though. Here." She said, offering me her phone with her pictures already opened.

I scrolled through them, one by one, something in me breaking to see all these pictures of my little girl, my baby, on a website that sold children to the highest bidder. Goddammit. Her sweet smiling face was, the one that was so fucking beautiful that it made my heart ache, was in a category that signaled her as '*Virgin, Caucasian, female, six years old, and blonde.*'

"How," I swallowed thickly. Bile was creeping up my throat, and it wouldn't stay down long. "How did they find her? How'd she get on her radar?"

Texas Tornado

"I can answer that." Max said as he strolled back into the garage and slammed the door so hard it shuttered.

He came back not even thirty seconds later with a smile on his face.

"I won't be needed. Your woman is taking care of that for me." He smiled wide.

Something that felt like relief shuttled through me. I didn't condone violence to women, but I knew that if they'd given me the chance, I would've killed Anna with my own bare hands. To know that Shiloh was doing it so I didn't have to made me burn with love for her.

I looked over Sam's shoulder as he opened the door, and a small smile graced my face as I saw Anna, still strapped to the chair, getting her face slapped repeatedly by Shiloh's hand. I loved that woman, not only because she was everything to me, but that she treated my child like she was everything to *her*.

"Tell me. Now." She emphasized the word 'now' with another slap to the face.

Anna reared back as if she was about to spit, but Shiloh stepped back and to the side, completely avoiding her attempt. "Now, now. That wasn't very nice. Let's see if we can come to an agreement."

***

Shiloh

"Tell me what I want to know!" I yelled, slamming my fist into her face with the entire weight of my body.

The rocking chair rocked back, and then swung back into place where she'd been earlier.

***

An hour earlier

I'd been standing in the backyard earlier, watching Kayla and Janie play on the trampoline talking to James and Winter when I'd heard the sound of glass breaking. Going into the direction of the front door, I came to a standstill when I saw Anna's face, and her arm trying to get through the broken pane on the door to unlock it.

I was glad I had the alarm off, because otherwise, the police would've been here, and I didn't want them here. Not yet. That woman had some explaining to do, and I could seriously use her presence to my advantage.

Grabbing ahold of her hand as she searched for the lock, I pulled her forward until her face rested against the door panel, and her arm was stretched down, so the sensitive part on the inside of her upper arm was forced into the jagged glass.

When she started to struggle, I causally started a conversation with her, as if she wasn't hanging there by her fucking arm. "Did you know that you have a major artery that runs along the inside of your arm, right about where your arm is forced in through the glass right now?"

The struggling stopped, but the yelling started, which brought the attention of the girls, who immediately started screaming too. Well, shit.

Texas Tornado

"I want my freaking kid!" Anna shrieked.

I laughed sardonically. "Yeah, right. I'll get right on that."

"Go to the safe room. Go to the safe room." James was yelling from my discarded iPhone.

Janie's eyes snapped to my phone that was on the coffee table next to the couch, and then grabbed Kayla's hand and shuffled her towards the hallway, and then back into her bedroom. I was grateful that James had said to go to the safe room. It hadn't crossed my mind, although it should've.

He'd shown it to me the first day I'd stayed in his house. He'd told me that four years ago, Cheyenne and Janie had needed to hide, and she'd had to resort to the closet since there was nowhere else for her to go, and when he'd gotten home, he'd made a safe room in case the need to use it ever arose again.

"You're such a fucking bitch. You ruined everything. Do you know how hard it was to get to where I was at, only for your haughty self to show up and 'supervise?' You better believe that that girl is leaving with me today. I've got my life riding on this." She hissed, still not struggling.

The throaty roar of a motorcycle ran down from the main highway, and I knew that James was nearly there, although I became concerned when it didn't stop in front of the house, but quite a bit further away.

"I've been waiting for half the damn night for you to be alone. You're nothing, do you hear me? Nothing!" She shrieked.

"Problem here, darlin'?" A smooth velvety voice asked from behind Anna.

My eyes snapped up, and I smiled when I saw Tiago a.k.a. 'Kettle' as my father's MC referred to him as. He was, for lack of a better word, beautiful. His skin was smooth, perfect, and lightly bronzed. His face was eloquent, sharp lines, and a strong jaw. His nose was perfectly straight, and not a blemish was in sight. Other than the leather vest, the only thing that would keep him from being too perfect was the mohawk that was on top of his head, the sides shaved clean down to the scalp so the inch of brown hair left on his head stood straight up.

I'd asked my brother after I'd met Tiago what the name 'Kettle' meant, and he told me that one second, Tiago would be just fine, completely calm, and the next he would just snap, like the whistle of a teakettle. I'd shivered thinking about that man 'snapping' and having to witness his change, but the only thing I'd seen from Tiago was politeness.

"Yeah, this is James' ex-girlfriend. We're just going to talk for a few minutes, if you don't mind." I clarified.

"Okay, just yell if you need me." He said, turning and walking back down the walkway, and then across the street to lean against a tree and wait.

I snickered. "Now, where were we?"

Texas Tornado

***

When I'd heard Jack's voice, I'd made my way to the hallway from James' room after having changed into different clothes since mine happened to have a smidgen of blood on them.

Which proved to be fruitless when I heard what Jack had to say, which led me to now, when I was beating the absolute shit out of Anna after overhearing, and coming to the conclusion that Anna probably had more to say. And knowing that I had the incentive, in the form of my right and left fist.

"You know, when I was twelve my daddy showed me how to throw a punch. You see, the secret is to make sure not to tuck your thumb into your hand, and use your body's momentum" I explained, and then demonstrated.

Her head snapped back, hitting the back of the rocking chair, before she righted it to glare at me. "We know about the website. About the plan to auction Janie off. Now we need to know the details. Let's face it. You're not going to win here. In fact, you're probably going to jail for the rest of your life...if you're lucky. I'll make sure James doesn't get you a cell shared by an Amazon with a steel pole fetish, and in return, you'll tell us everything. Understand?"

Her eyes had widened at my mention of knowing about the auction, and the realization that this was the end had finally sunk in.

"I lost money, and they told me I owed them fifty grand by the end of the year, or they'd use my body as payment. I'd come here originally to ask for money from James, but when his stupid bitch of a sister refused to even let me see him, I had to use other means. Then I met some biker at the park while I was watching Janie and that other little shit play. From there I was just supposed to get Janie for him, and he'd pay off my loans."

"That's all you know?" I asked, sickened.

"Yeah, what else is there?" She snapped.

I studied her, and believed that she was telling the truth. She didn't know anything else. "Do you know what they were going to do, precisely, with your daughter?"

Her mouth tightened, but she nodded once, confirming that she knew they were selling her to some random person with the wallet to do God knows what to her.

The next few moments were filled with my questions and her answers.

How do you reach him? *Cell phone.*

What was his name? *Sloan Lerng.*

Did you ever speak to anybody else? *No.*

Where were you to deliver her to once you had her? *Off the interstate, near an abandoned hotel.*

"How do you feel about being raped?" James asked emotionlessly from behind me.

My heart stalled, and I whipped around to stare at him. What kind of question was that?

Anna's eyes widened, and she started to weep. The first time she'd done so since she got over an hour ago.

"You don't like the idea of rape? Don't worry. I'm not that type of man. But the person that you were going to sell our daughter to is.

Texas Tornado

How do you think a six year old would handle that, hmm? She'd be damaged for life, not just physically, but emotionally as well. Jesus Christ, I can't even stand to look at you." He said before turning and leaving the room.

"He's right, you know. You are a piece of shit. I hope you like closed spaces." I said before following behind James, sidestepping Jack, Winter, Sam and Sebastian as I went.

Winter gave me a reassuring smile, but I wasn't sure things were going to be all right this time. Not until that man, that horrible awful man, was ten feet under. Only then would everything be all right.

***

I woke up to find James gone, and the light rhythmic thumping of my cat playing in the living room.

Standing slowly, and stretching my arms up high over my head, I yawned, and then grabbed a pair of shorts off the floor.

It wasn't until they were halfway up my hips that I realized that they were a pair of James' running shorts, but I didn't care. They were super comfortable. Even though they fit, which was slightly depressing if I was being truthful. I didn't even have to cinch up the drawstring.

The loud thumping, and then the scrabble of claws across the hard wood floor sounded again, and I couldn't help but laugh to myself. The damn cat sounded like he was climbing the walls. He'd been to do that every once in a while when he saw a bug.

I peeked carefully around the corner of the hallway towards the commotion that Boris was making, and damn near fell over in a fit of laughter.

James was sitting in his recliner, and had his gun in his fist. He was moving it from side to side, and up and down. The laser that was attached to his gun moved with the motion, prompting Boris to attack it. Or try to, at least.

James looked up at my laughter, but didn't stop. "What?"

"Just try not to shoot him, okay?" I teased.

I knew he wouldn't shoot him. The man was a fricking genius with a gun. But still.

"What exactly are you doing?" I asked finally.

Boris wailed when James clicked the laser off his gun, and shoved it behind him, situating it into the back of his jeans. "I got a new sight in the mail, wanted to try it out and see how it fit. How it worked. Get used to it."

The matter of fact way he just explained pointing a laser sight that was attached to his gun around the room for my cat to play with surprised me, although it shouldn't have.

"I hadn't intended to play with him at first. It was only when I was sighting down the barrel and Boris jumped up trying to catch the light that I started to play with him. It isn't loaded." He shrugged.

"You're such a weirdo." I chided.

He smiled, and held out his arms to me. I went to them willingly.

Texas Tornado

His arm wrapped around my shoulder as I dropped into his lap, and his large callused palm found a home on my thigh, and I wriggled in his lap trying to get comfortable.

"Jesus, please stop rubbing your ass on my dick. There's only so much control left in me." He ground through clenched teeth.

I stilled, and laid my head on his chest. "You wanna talk about why you're not in bed?"

His erection deflated like it'd never been, and I mourned at the loss. However, this was more important than some quick romp. James was hurting and he needed me.

"Will you tell me about your cancer?" James rasped.

Out of all the things I'd been ready to hear him say, that wasn't even on the planet with it. I was so startled, so surprised, that I couldn't stem my reaction. My breath hissed into my lungs, and a sob choked me. James soothing hand worked up and down my back, soothing me as I got myself under control.

"H-how did you know?" I asked quietly.

"Your papers in your floorboard. When I went back for the cat the night you broke your arm, I found the cat in the floorboard. There were some papers there, and I read them." James said simply.

I couldn't be mad at him for that, I was the one who'd sent him to my place for my cat in the first place. I also remembered trying to get my cash stash out of the floorboard so I could go to the doctor, but the exertion had made me want to vomit, and I'd passed out in the bathroom not even moments after getting in there.

I nodded in understanding. "When I was a kid, I spent a lot of time in tanning beds. It was a vain thing to do, and I learned about a year and a half ago what the effect of all that tanning had done to my skin."

I leaned my head back against his chest, and pulled up my shirt, lowering the pants I'd borrowed from around my hips, and showing him the small scar on my hipbone. "This is where I found a weird looking mole. My OB/GYN sent me to a dermatologist, who then removed the mole and sent it off to be tested. It turned out that it was a Basal Cell Carcinoma. They removed it and I had two radiation treatments on the area, but considering the area, they weren't quite sure if I could ever have children. I haven't had one single period since then. We're assuming that I won't be able to. Although I'm still on the Depo shot every three months."

His hand ran over the area of raised skin where I'd had the mole removed, and he looked pained. "I'm sorry, Shiloh. The papers said it was negative, though."

I nodded in understanding. "It was with the second mole I found. That one was on my foot. They just removed it."

"Well, shit." He sighed.

"Yeah, it did suck pretty bad. But I get a thorough exam every four months just to make sure."

He leered at me. "I can help with those thorough exams."

Shiloh laughed at him.

Then James leer melted away, and his face was serious again.

Texas Tornado

"When Janie was a baby, Cheyenne had taken her into her eleven month baby checkup when they thought she was showing signs of Leukemia. That was the worst six weeks of my life. They ran test after test, and I'd never been so scared in my life." James told me.

The thought of Janie having cancer literally made my blood run cold. "What'd she end up having?"

"Anemia. Prescribed her to take those little Flintstone vitamins. Acted as if they didn't just fuck us for an entire six weeks. 'Oh, hey, this is Dr. Mack's office. We just wanted to tell you that Janie's fine. She needs to take a Flintstone Vitamin once a day though. Have a good day.'

"Wow" I said in surprise.

"I'm going to kill that man who put my baby up there. I'm going to rip his dick off, chop it up into tiny pieces, and feed them to him." James said suddenly.

The vehemence in his voice startled me, but didn't surprise me. I knew he was having those feelings. Hell, if I had the capability, I'd do the same damn thing. Only I'd use a plastic spork to do the dick cutting.

James work pager started bleating across the room, and he sighed. Moving me off his lap, he scanned the pager and started for the bedroom. He came back a few minutes later, dressed in his SWAT gear. Damn, I was hoping it was only a 'be ready' notice, but it looked like it was an actual call.

James ambled over to me, dropped a kiss on my forehead, and brought his hand up to grasp my chin, angling my head so he could look into my eyes. "Don't forget to call when you show up at any of your calls. I won't be home by the time you leave for work."

I nodded, and he let my face go before heading to the door. He stopped, deactivated the alarm, turned and watched me for a few seconds before saying, "I love you."

"Love you too, J."

He smiled at my use of his name and left, locking the door swiftly behind him.

Chapter 22

Get in my belly.

-Fat Bastard, Austin Powers

James

"Ready?" Max asked.

I smiled wide at him, showing him my teeth. Then made the 'come on' motion with my taped fist. Max took a step forward, and then I stopped him with a raised hand.

"Please, just for the love of God, don't hit my face. I have something with Shiloh later. Don't slip like last time, either." I instructed him.

Elliott laughed from his perch on the weight bench across the room, but shortly went back to his bench pressing, shutting us out for the next ten reps. Jack didn't bother trying to hide that he was watching the matchup. Neither did Gabe, who was coming into the room with a bottle of beer, sliding down the wall next to Jack until his feet were straight out in front of him.

"Are you drinking my beer?" I asked.

"Was it in our fridge?" He asked.

"Max's beer was in there too." I pointed out.

He sneered at me. "Max's beer is for people with pussies."

I laughed. Couldn't help it. Max's beer was for pussies.

"I saw you drinking my beer just the other day." Max said indignantly.

"Ember brought it to me. It was for pussy, so kind of the same thing." Gabe jeered.

I rolled my eyes. When Max started to take a step in Gabe's direction, I shoved him. He took that as my signal that I was now ready, and the match began. My first punch landed in his stomach, bowing him over. His leg retaliated by snapping out, kicking me in the ribs.

"You're dropping your right arm." Max panted.

I corrected the mistake, blocking a blow to my face. "I said not my face, douche bag!"

"What, have you got a beauty pageant afterwards?" Elliott hooted from the bench press.

"No, I'm stripping for your women later. I just want to look good for it." I taunted.

They didn't have to know what I was really doing....right?

Forty minutes later, I was a sweating, bleeding mess, and my fucking nose was broken. I took satisfaction to see that Max wasn't any better either. His eye had a cut that would probably require stitches, and ankle looked twice his normal size. Which was why we'd stopped in the first place.

"Quit bitching. I think you broke my nose." I whined nasally.

"At least you can just knock it back into place. I think my ankle's sprained. I have to run 10K in the morning." He groaned.

Texas Tornado

I rolled my eyes. We'd done much worse. About five times that on a good day when we were enlisted. "Don't be a pussy."

The door slammed open and Ember came stomping in on a warpath. Her strides were more of a stomp then a step, and her face looked like she'd swallowed something sour. Her mascara was running down nearly to her t-shirt, and her hands were fisted into tight balls.

Gabe was laying on the floor now, eyes closed. He couldn't see the tornado that was barreling towards him at Mach 5 speed. Fuck, but this was going to be good.

Walking in the direction of the fridge, I grabbed two beers, both man beers, and walked back towards Max. Handing him his beer, I slid down the opposite wall as Gabe, and settled in to watch the show.

"What do you think he did?" Max said gleefully, twisting the top off his beer and taking a swig.

He grimaced at the taste of the man beer, but didn't comment on me actually getting him a dark brew instead of that watered down bullshit he always drank. "I think she's pregnant again."

"No, I bet she backed into something in his truck. Twenty." Max bet.

We shook on it and waited.

When Ember finally reached Gabe, who now was blinking at Ember standing over him, I saw her pull something out of her hoodie pocket. A bag.

She then turned it upside down, and let no less than thirty sticks fell out, hitting Gabe in the chest with each of them. He watched as one by one, they hit him, and finally lifted his lip in a snarl.

"You pissed on these didn't you?" Gabe said, flicking them off his chest with the tip of his finger.

"Yeah, but I warned you not to knock me up, and look what you went and did. Knocked me up. A-fucking-gain. Do you realize that this last week was the first time since Luca was born that I've had a full nights rest?" She yelled.

Not waiting for an answer, she stomped towards the door again, but stopped before she reached it. "Oh, and I backed your truck in to the light pole at Skinners."

Max and I whooped. Gabe glared. Elliott laughed.

"Alright, I gotta get to the strip club. I'll see you guys later." I called as I headed into the bathroom.

They waved me off, dismissing my comment, and I went to the locker room to slip into my SWAT clothes. The more clothing I got to wear, the better. I just hoped no one recognized me.

***

Shiloh

"What is with that evil looking smile on your face?" Cheyenne asked me as we took our seats at the front of the stage.

I pasted on my best innocent look and batted my eyes at her. "What look?"

"That look," she said pointedly.

Texas Tornado

"I just want to warn you ahead of time that you probably aren't going to like this. Like, I really feel that maybe you should go outside and wait until one of us comes and gets you." I tried again.

I'd told her not to come, yet she'd insisted. She just didn't know how traumatized she was about to be.

"I'm staying." She said firmly.

"Don't say I didn't warn you." I said slowly, and then watched the crowd.

It was supposed to be gay night. I'd specifically chosen this night out, of all the nights, because I didn't want any of the women ogling what was mine. What I'd miscalculated was that gay men had friends that were women, and it was inevitable for them to want to come. Just as mine had done.

"What's going on anyway? I'm not sure gay night was the night to come." Payton supplied just before she took a healthy sip of her Texas sized margarita.

It really was Texas-sized, too. It was in a fucking bucket for Christ's sake. Not that she let the size stop her. She held it in her lap and had an extra-long straw (well, three normal sized straws taped together with medical tape) she was sucking with. The girl was adaptable if nothing else.

"If I tell you, it'll ruin the surprise. Let's just say, we had a bet." I replied cryptically.

The alcohol was well and truly flowing by the time the first dancer made it to the stage.

"This's nothing like Magic Mike," Ember said in awe.

Her complexion was a tad pale, but she looked excited to be there, so I didn't question her. She'd waved off the offer of a margarita, claiming her stomach was bothering her, which would certainly explain her complexion. I had a feeling it was her husband not wanting her to come, nor wanting her to get drunk. She'd compromised by coming, but not drinking. At least, that's what I would've done.

The man that was on the stage was jacked. There were no other words for it. He was just absolutely massive. Conferring with my pamphlet they'd handed us at the door of the night's events, I saw that the first dancer's name was Ronin. He was six feet six inches, and currently in school for biomechanics. In his spare time, he liked to do yoga and teach spin class.

"We should try spin class." I said absently as I scanned down the rest of the pamphlet, not finding the name I was looking for until the very bottom of the page.

At the very bottom, I found what I was looking for. In italic letters it read: *Special guest-Scope. Interests are- working on motorcycles. Shooting firearms. Spending time with his significant other. Shiloh June- will you marry me?*

I started hyperventilating.

The crowd around me roared when Ronin ripped his pants off, exposing his grenade filled banana hammock. However, I was too busy trying to get my breathing under control to truly appreciate the aesthetically pleasing sight that was being presented before me.

"Shiloh? Are you alright?" Blaine asked from across the table.

Texas Tornado

"Uhh," I answered intelligently.

Holy shit.

"Maybe you should slow down on the drinks." She supplied helpfully.

"Maybe so." I confirmed with a nod of my head, and then looked down at my own empty bucket that used to hold my margarita.

"Ladies and gentleman! We have a special treat for your eyes tonight! With a one-hit wonder type of performance, we present you with, *SCOPE!*" The DJ yelled over the roaring of the crowd.

My eyes flew to the stage, and what little breath I was able to catch was gone in an audible whoosh. *Tainted Love* started thumping through the strip club's sound system, and I finally took a breath.

The object of every single one of my fantasies made his way onstage. He looked freaking amazing. Well, what I could see of him anyway. He was wearing his KPD SWAT get-up. Black cargo pants tucked into black boots that went up to the bottom of his calf. The trademark black SWAT shirt and black Kevlar vest. The only thing different was his the helmet that covered his face from the crowd.

I didn't know if that was cheating on our bargain or not, but I decided I'd rather him remain anonymous if possible. I didn't want all these ladies (and men) knowing where to find him, because damn if the man wasn't sexy as sin.

A wolf whistle sounded from beside me, making me break my eye contact with the beautiful specimen of a man in front of me. My eyes moved to the next chair over and I saw Winter on her stool singing along with the song with two fingers in her mouth. As I watched, she took a deep breath, and let out another whistle.

A smile broke out on my face as I returned my attention to the stage, and the show started. Scope exited the doorway and stomped down to the front of the stage, and I do mean stomped. If I was a betting woman, I would bet that he was pissed he had to do this. Sadly, his pride wouldn't let him back out of our bet, he was an honest man, and a bet was a bet.

The man wasn't the type of person to ever make himself so vulnerable, and it made my heart melt to know he was doing it just for me.

Each *thump-thump* of the music's base had my heart jumping in my chest as Scope's torso thrust forward. Each of my nerve endings started to fire, making me flush with excitement.

"Holy shit!" Ember cried as the Kevlar vest was removed and dropped down to the stage.

Although I knew it would hit with a loud thump, nothing could be heard over the screaming women and roaring men. The man's body was delicious. He reminded me of a panther. His movements were all deliberate, but supremely graceful. My mouth watered as his hands went to the neck of his t-shirt, and *ripped* the fucking thing down the middle.

My jaw dropped open, and I gasped. My gasp was echoed by every single person in the room. Cheyenne's peal of laughter had me laughing when she realized it was her brother up there, and then she covered her eyes, still laughing, but refusing to watch anymore.

Texas Tornado

Although the helmet was still firmly in place, you could easily make out the tattoos that had given him away.

When I glanced over at the rest of my group, all eyes were glued to the stage, and I had to wonder if their men would be upset about this. A couple months ago, I'd have been jealous about letting them see my man like this, but now we were so secure in our relationship that I had no doubt whose bed he would end up in at the end of the night.

Scope's body undulated with the music, and I tried to keep my lustful thoughts from breaking through, but in the end, all I could think about was how it would feel if he was doing all those bump and grinds up against me.

I swear the man was a damn mind reader, because the next thing I knew, he was jumping off the stage and in my face the next. His perfect abs were in direct line of my mouth, and I was never one to resist temptation. Leaning forward, I licked from his navel down to where his pants rode low on his hips.

My hands settled on his gyrating hips, and I thought maybe I'd died and gone to heaven. The man was fucking hot. He'd rubbed some sort of baby oil on his chest or something, because it was slick and shiny. His dog tags dropped into my line of vision, and I gasped at the massive rock that hung directly beside one of his tags.

Snatching the chain and yanking him down towards me, I pulled the chain over his head and practically broke it in my quest to get the ring off. He laughed at my enthusiasm, and yanked the tags and ring away from me before I could extract the ring.

Yet, in the next moment, he slid the cool hard band with the oval cut diamond on my ring finger, replaced the tags on his neck, and turned around.

That made me gasp again when I saw the newest tattoo that was on his back. The only one in color, it drew the eye like a moth to a flame. Taking up his upper right shoulder was a beautiful mermaid. Bold colors and strong lines, and underneath the tattoo itself said *Always*.

I hadn't realized I was crying until the song ended and I was enfolded into strong arms, and James rough voice spoke softly to me.

"I take these as good tears?" He rasped close to my ear.

"The best kind of tears. I love you," I whispered into his chest.

His body locked at the sound of my words, and he hugged me tighter. "I love you, too."

"Couldn't y'all have found a better place to express your dirty love for each other, other than a strip club?" Cheyenne groaned, still covering her eyes.

"I'm not naked, Cheyenne." James laughed.

Cheyenne peaked between two fingers, and then covered them back again. "Underwear is naked, James."

I pulled myself away from him and looked down. Sure enough, he was in his underwear. How had I missed that? Did those say...

"Does your underwear say 'It won't suck itself'?" I asked with a small laugh.

He grinned and winked.

Texas Tornado

"Put your pants on, stripper boy." Cheyenne said as she tossed a piece of ice at him, and then turned her back to him.

He smiled, and then started looking around for the pants that he'd kicked off stage during his performance. He found them in the clutches of a drunk woman who was wearing 'bride' across a sash that bisected her chest.

Seeing his reluctance to go over there, I went for him, smiling at the young woman that looked like she should've stopped on the Texas Margaritas about two buckets ago. "Hi, congratulations on the pending marriage. Can I have my fiancé's pants?"

I had to chuckle at myself with that one.

"No, he warned she was have two." She slurred.

What the fuck was that supposed to mean? I mean I was a tad on the blitzed side myself, but I still formed coherent sentences. Her friends sitting next to her started cackling, and I immediately pictured a group of hyenas laughing. The sound grated on my ears, but I stayed calm.

"Please?" I smiled sweetly.

"Nuh uh." The bride said as she hugged them to her chest, knocking over her half-full margarita in the process.

"Look what you do!" She shrieked, staunching the flow with James pants.

Mother. Fucker.

"Give me the goddamn pants before I shove that pail up your ass!" I yelled, reaching forward to grab the pants before they soaked up anymore of her margarita.

She struggled for all of five seconds before letting go. I gave a triumphant grin, and turned to head back to James when a sailing dick nailed me. The two foot dildo was made of rubber, and looked like a real, honest to God, penis. It had veins, and was the color of flesh.

Staring at it, and then at the guffawing bridesmaids, I decided to be the bigger person and walk away. I did make sure to pick up the big dick off the floor, though. Those bitches weren't getting that back. It was a war prize.

James watched me approach him with a large smile on his face, shaking his head when his eyes found the huge dick in my hand. The circumference of it was massive, at least a foot around. I could only get my hand around a third of it.

Once I reached him, I handed him his soaked pants. "Sorry, they're a little wet. Not the good kind of wet, either."

He laughed. "It's alright. I can handle a margarita. Just glad it's not something worse."

"Alright everyone, hold hands so we don't lose anyone." Ember instructed as if we were all children.

"You aren't drunks enough, Embers. Why's is that?" Blaine slurred slightly, holding onto a tipsy Cheyenne for support.

"Someone had to drive you drunkards home, didn't they?" She answered quickly.

Too quickly in my opinion. She had a secret. Looking over at James smiling face, and the sweet way he looked at Ember, I had my suspicion confirmed.

Texas Tornado

"You're pregnant, aren't you? You weren't drinking when we were decorating the Christmas tree either." I shouted before my brain could stop me.

"They were virgins. You weren't supposed to notice." She mock scowled at me.

Choruses of congratulations were hurled at her, and she was enfolded into James' arms, hugging her tight against his chest before releasing her.

We made it to the parking lot, making sure a drunk Payton, and sloshed Blaine got into Gabe's truck okay before walking to our own vehicle.

It happened before I could even comprehend what happened. One second we were on our way to James' truck, and the next, I was down on the ground with a man on top of me. Not the right man, either. This man was one I remembered well, but not in a good way.

"Hello there, sweetie pie." Zander's hot breath said into my neck.

His body pressed mine against the concrete with excessive force. I could hear flesh hitting flesh, and grunts of exertion, and groans of pain coming from my side, but Zander's hands held my face steady so I couldn't look away.

I knew I should fight, but with his body pinning mine down, there wasn't much place for me to go. He'd left my hands free, though. And around the time I noticed that, he lifted up from me, grinning that sick smile at me that told me he was about to say something mean.

When he was about a foot away from my face, I thrust the dick in the air like a goddamn sword, and brought it down across his face, smacking him so hard in the face that he literally fell backwards, back hitting the ground like a ton of bricks.

I didn't waste time in staring at him though. I wielded my two-foot dick like The Rock in Walking Tall, and started beating the absolute shit out of him. I stayed with his face until I was sure he passed out, and then started on the rest of him. The sound of the dick hitting his flesh sounded about like one would think. Skin hitting skin.

Each thwack of the dildo striking his body sent a surge of exhilaration through me. A sense of justice. "Take that, mother fucker. Remember all those times you did the same thing to me? Yeah, well payback's a bitch!"

James amused voice flowed over me like a caress in the night. "You can stop now, June. The man's down. And his pride will forever be broken."

"Oh, yeah it will. I got that shit on video. We're going to send this to YouTube." Ember drawled.

I looked up to find Gabe's lifted Chevy angled sideways through the parking spots, half her body hanging out the window as she wielded her iPhone in her hand, no doubt recording it just as she'd said she'd been doing.

My mouth twisted into a smile.

"That's Zander. My ex." I said, pointing with the dick to the dick laying on the ground.

"We figured that when you started saying that you were going to show him what a thorough fucking felt like. You'd make it last more than thirty seconds though." James drawled.

Texas Tornado

My face blushed, and I suppressed a manic giggle that threatened to spill from my mouth. "I'm sorry."

"It's alright, sweet cheeks. Let's get these boys loaded into Gabe's truck, we'll take them to the shop and see what they have to say." James instructed as he walked towards the truck.

It was then that I saw the three other men, besides Zander, knocked out on the ground, looking in much worse shape than Zander was. I'd seen quite a few broken bones in my day, mostly on myself, but these men had *visibly* broken bones. Which made me cringe.

"Hand me the duct tape, my lady." James teased, as he walked to Ember's window with an extended hand.

She handed over a brand new roll, and James went back to each man, effortlessly wrapping it around each man's legs, arms, and mouth with quick expert movements. Then he tossed them like a sack of potatoes into the back of the truck, stacking them like wood, two wide.

"Alright, let me get my bike, and I'll follow directly behind you to Free." He said.

After a quick phone call to tell Sam what had happened, we pulled into Free a few minutes later to find Gabe, Max, Sam, Sebastian, my father, Elliott, and Jack waiting with their arms across their chests in front of the garage, bay doors open. When Ember pulled up, she yelled out the open window.

"Want me to back it in?" She yelled over the rumble of the motor.

"No!" Was chorused by not only everyone in front of her, but everyone in the truck with her.

That gave a sort of relief of the tension that was slowly amounting, and we all exited the trucks. Gabe backed his truck into the garage, and Sam closed the doors behind him.

The sound of the doors closing were like the sound of a closing a casket. Final.

***

Later that night

"Shiloh, do you want to try to have a baby?" James voice came to me in the dark.

He'd come into our room a few minutes ago, and promptly headed to the bathroom to shower the ingrained smell of margarita off his skin. I'd listened, half asleep, as he stripped. Clothes hitting the floor. Boots. Gun being placed on the counter. Extra magazines being placed directly next to the gun. Keys, loose change, and his phone in a bowl next to the sink.

He had a system when he dressed and undressed, and did exactly the same thing every time.

He took a shower in the dark, knowing his way around without needing the light to guide his way. I'd assumed he thought I was sleeping when he came in, that was why he didn't invite me to join him, nor turn on the lights.

Now, though, he was asking me this question knowing I was awake to hear it. Which meant that I didn't mishear him. He was honestly asking me if I wanted a baby.

"Uhhh," I answered intelligently.

Texas Tornado

"I want another baby. I didn't think I did, but I do. Not right now, but eventually." He hastily explained.

Something panged in my heart. Sadness filled me when I thought about my ability to have children. I wasn't sure if I could, and if this was something James truly wanted, he wouldn't be able to get it from me.

"James," I whispered. "I would love to have a baby with you, but you have to know that the chances of having them with me are slim. Not to mention nearly impossible with you having a vasectomy and me having issues."

His weight hit the bed, and I felt the covers shift as he maneuvered the comforter over his body, staying on his side of the bed. Which was normal. He wasn't much of a cuddler. I wasn't either so it worked out well. I wanted my own blanket. I didn't want to fight over covers half the night. Which was why we also slept with two different blankets.

Although probably weird, it worked for us. Every once in a while, I'd sneak my toes over to his side of the bed and bury them under his thigh or back, but most of the time I stayed on my side.

"I'd get it reversed. But we'd probably need to both go see a doctor afterwards to make sure it was feasible to even contemplate. Would you do that?" He asked into the darkness.

"I'd do anything for you. Anything." I answered vehemently.

He didn't respond. We stayed silent for some time. Almost so long that I thought he'd fallen asleep. His breathing was steady, as if his body was in a deep sleep. I stayed on my side of the bed, watching the numbers on the clock change from eleven thirty, to twelve.

"I want to get married. This weekend." James suddenly said.

"We can't. You're screwed. I want a big, beautiful wedding. I want a winter one. So you're going to have to wait till next year, because big weddings like that take time to plan. I want to wear a big dress that has a train that flows ten feet behind me. I want my dad to walk me down the aisle. I want tons and tons of flowers. I want it all." I described my dream wedding.

"Do I have to wear a tux?" He asked, sounding pained.

"Yes, because that would just look absolutely silly if you didn't." I told him.

"Fuck me," he growled.

I smiled, and felt myself slip into sleep.

Chapter 23

If you think 7 years of bad luck is too much for breaking a mirror, try breaking a condom.

-E-card

James

"Is it possible?" I asked my sister.

"Well, not by this weekend, that's for sure. She can't make anything easy, can she?" She grumbled as she started sending texts on her phone.

"I don't know who all she'd want to invite, but do your best. Maybe ask her brother? He'd know." I instructed her.

She glared at me. "I'm perfectly capable of this. Did she say what kind of dress she would want?"

I nodded, and explained what Shiloh had told me last night about the train. "She didn't say much else about that."

"Okay, you're free to go." She said, flicking her hand in a shooing motion.

I did just that, leaving Cheyenne's place, and following the sounds of kids playing towards the side of the garage. There, I found Gabe, Max, and Jack sitting on the benches while the kids played on the jungle gym we'd built during the summer.

Then I saw what Gabe was doing, and laughed. "Wh-what the hell are you doing?"

He smiled brightly at me, took a sip of his beer, and tugged on the length of the rope in his hand. The rope itself was about a hundred feet in length connected to a swing that had his son, Luca, sitting in it, hunched forward sleeping.

"Ember needed a nap, and Luca here wasn't cooperating. Works every time." He nodded at the swing.

"Why are you tugging on it with the rope?" I asked curiously.

"If I stop pushing him, he wakes back up. I was tired of standing." He said simply.

I nodded in understanding. We'd all been there. Who was I to judge? Hell, I remembered when Janie was a tiny baby, all of three weeks old, and she'd wake up in the middle of the night for the fortieth time, I'd prop the bottle on my chest, and snuggle her in close, falling asleep while she ate as slow as a tortoise.

Max stood when Harleigh started to scream in the baby swing behind us and popped her pacifier back in before coming and sitting back down.

"Zander was a bucket of information last night. He's currently in police custody. Luke loved the video, by the way." Max grinned.

"Oh, yeah. It was something to see all right. I was scared shitless for her, then turn around to see her beating the man to death with that huge dildo. It was the highlight of my life. Aside from having Janie, that is." I laughed.

"Where'd she get it?" Jack asked.

My eyes flicked to his, noting that he looked much more relaxed. Much more happy than I'd ever seen him. "Some chick threw it at

Texas Tornado

Shiloh when she yanked my pants away from her. I was wondering why she'd kept it, but I'm glad she did."

Silence. "So you really stripped?"

"It was a bet. You know I don't go back on my word."

"Sadly, we do. Just don't let it happen again. I don't want my wife seeing you in your tighty whities again." Max murmured.

"Where's Cat?" I asked Jack as I took a seat beside him.

I had about five minutes before I needed to leave, and I decided to take a load off. My body was exhausted. I'd had a tough two months, and it didn't look like it was going to get any better anytime soon.

"My brother has her. He took her to the fire station for a show and tell." Jack rumbled, sucking down another swallow of beer.

"What?" Was echoed by Gabe and myself.

"They got some new equipment for infants or some shit. Winter volunteered Cat to test the fit on a few of them." Jack informed us.

"Oh, well why do they need to test them out beforehand?" I wondered.

"You don't want to find out in the middle of restraining an infant after a car accident that your backboard doesn't work on a two month old, or a one week old. Nor do you want to find out that a blood pressure cuff is too big, therefore not giving you reliable readings, making you not give a needed medication en route that could've saved a kid's life." Gabe explained.

I shuddered. It was hard to think about a two month old like Cat needing any sort of medical treatment for any reason. Just to think of Janie on a backboard gave me heart palpitations.

"Yeah, that's about what Winter said." Jack agreed.

"All right. Well I have a training exercise. I'll catch you guys later." I said shaking each of their hands.

The ride to the police station had me looking over my shoulder the entire way. I knew someone was following me. When I stopped at the only stop light in between Free and the training facility, I sent a quick message to Sam, who was watching over Shiloh today.

Sam and I had decided after the last incident, that it was best to have one of our own guys on Shiloh. It wasn't that we didn't have confidence in Sebastian's MC; it was that when one of our own was in trouble, we made sure that we were the ones doing what was needed. When it came down to it, we knew each other well, and we knew that we'd protect with our lives. Each and every one of us had done nothing less for each other, time after time. We knew without a doubt that the same would be extended to our significant others and our children.

What I hadn't thought, was that I would need that protection for myself. I'd been too arrogant, too sure of myself.

I never saw the shooter. Never saw the bullet.

When the bullet from a sniper's gun slammed into my body, I was thrown from my bike. I looked down, at the hole in my t-shirt at my lower right chest, and knew I was screwed. I was going to die.

The blood welled from just a small round circle, to encapsulate the entire front of my t-shirt within moments, and I knew I was going to die. If not by the sniper that was likely to put another bullet in my head, then by the gunshot wound I'd sustained. It was becoming hard to breathe, and my vision started to go hazy at the edges.

Then, the last person on earth I'd suspected to see in the world, came up from behind me in a black sedan, and stopped with the passenger side door only inches from my prone body.

The door clicked open, and a frantic Jolie popped the door open, swinging it across my body. She reached down, with her tiny fucking hands, and unceremoniously hauled me into the car, grunting, crying, and cursing.

"Oh, God. Oh, God. Oh, God." She chanted repeatedly.

"Oh, fuck. I knew this was going to happen. Jesus." She cried.

I tried to help the best I could, but only managed to use my feet right about the time she'd done the hard part. I pushed the last few inches until I was leaning back against the seat. She leaned over, yanked the lever, and I dropped flat, the weight of my upper body slamming the seat backwards until I hit the limit of the seat, and came to a jolting halt.

"Sorry, sorry." She said frantically.

Then she leaned over me, pulled the door closed, threw it into gear, and slammed the gas down to the floorboard.

A ping in the back glass had her jumping, but not once did she slow down. She blew through stop signs and stoplights alike. Feeling my brain going fuzzy, I lifted my hand opposite my bullet wound, and plugged the hole that was steadily leaking blood. My finger sunk in, stanching the hole with one large finger. Even the jolt of pain wasn't enough to stop the hazy feeling from taking over.

After the third near collision, I passed out, knowing that one thing was true.

I'd failed.

***

Shiloh

"What kind of cookies does your daddy like best?" I asked Janie.

We were waiting for Sam to get back from the store with the flour and sugar for our cookies. I'd managed to get James to purchase all the ingredients I'd need, however, I'd misjudged the amount of sugar and flour that we had.

Sam had been reluctant to go at first, but after Janie got in on the pleading action, he'd agreed, albeit reluctantly.

I was in the process of melting chocolate in the saucepan for the peanut butter balls while Janie scoured over the recipes, deciding which ones she wanted to do next.

Sam had been gone for a little over ten minutes when the power went out.

I looked out the kitchen window. I was frowning at the bright sunshiny day when it struck me how odd it was that the power had gone out on a day like this. Sure, it was cold, and we had a chance of icing rain, but that wasn't until much later in the day. It was rare for the power to go out. James had just explained this morning when I asked if we should be worried about the rain that in this portion of the city, the power lines were buried, and it'd take a bulldozer digging down eight feet to disrupt the power.

Texas Tornado

Knowing that something was wrong, I trusted my gut and turned off the heating chocolate.

"Janie, I think we need to go to the safe..." I whispered urgently, walking up to her and taking her hand.

"Too late." A man said jovially.

Janie gasped in fear, shrinking back into my embrace, and I clutched her as well as I could to my chest, cursing myself ten kinds of stupid for thinking we *might* need more sugar and flour, and sending Sam to the store.

Dammit.

"Who are you?" I gasped.

"Oh, baby. This is gonna be fun. Cute girl." The man leered.

Emotions welled up inside of me. Ones that heated my blood, causing rage like nothing I'd ever felt before to tear through me at his audacity. I gritted my teeth. I wouldn't provoke him. Not with Janie to worry about.

Janie was shaking in my arms, and the sense of defeat tore through me. We weren't getting out of this. The man was freaking huge. Easily James' size, if not bigger. Tall, large ropey muscles, tattoos of skulls, naked women, and a grim reaper dominated his arms. His hair was dark, nearly black. The beard on his face could rival my father's, but instead of keeping it tidy like my father did, this man's was just everywhere. I swear his nose hair literally grew into the beard as well. He was hairy to say the least.

His eyes were the color of emerald jewels. Exactly like Zander's eyes.

So this must be the brother. Glen.

Damn, but I sure could pick them.

"Are you going to come on your own? Or do I need to knock you out?" He asked, taking a step towards me.

My eyes watched his feet as he got closer to me, and widened when I saw the knife that was sticking out of his boot at the base. Four inches long at least, all it would take was one kick, and I'd be dead. God.

"I'll come peacefully. I'll come. Please don't hurt us." I pleaded.

"Walk out the door. Go to the van. My men are outside, so don't think you can do anything funny and get away with it." He guided me, one hand on my lower back, to the door.

I held Janie protectively against me, but found my arms empty in the next moment. Janie was tossed on the floor like a piece of trash.

"We're leaving the girl here as an incentive. A show of good faith, if you want to call it that. Don't worry though. You're still going to come." He snickered.

Then he turned and regarded the whimpering Janie, holding on to my arm now, gripping it so tightly that I couldn't cover up the wince.

"You stay here. Tell that old man that we've got something he wants. It's us making the call now." The man, Glen, instructed Janie.

Relief poured through me at knowing that he was leaving Janie here. Thank God, he only wanted me.

The door opened and he all but shoved me out of it. The only thing keeping me upright was his rough grip on my arm. Janie's

Texas Tornado

squeal of alarm brought my attention back to her as she started to come towards me, wanting only to help.

"Janie, baby. It's okay. You stay here, talk to Silas for me. Tell him what this man told you, okay, sweetie?" I pleaded with her, hoping that she'd stop her advancement.

Luckily, she listened, and the door closed behind us, cutting off my view of her. "Get to the truck. Don't fuck around. No sudden moves or the girl's going with us, too."

When I was in the truck, Glen followed me in, shutting the doors behind him. When he turned, I was too slow to react, and found his face close to mine. I shrunk as far into the side of the van that I could, but there was just nowhere for me to go. I was stuck.

"Zander tells me you have a hot pussy. I think I'll try it out later." He jeered, running his rough hands down the side of my face, and then down lower, in between my breasts, and down my stomach.

I puked. Everywhere.

Boy did I puke, too. It wasn't one of those dainty throw ups where you bend over and it comes out. No, this one was projectile. It went from the bottom of my stomach, out my mouth, covering Glen, past Glen, and then covering the wall behind him.

I'd eaten a ton of cookie dough, bacon, eggs, and pancakes in the hours since I'd woken that day. There was a lot to throw up. Eventually, though, it stopped and silence poured through the van.

The men in the front seat looked on in horror, and I cringed back, praying his retaliation wouldn't hurt too bad. But it did.

His fist snapped out, landing along my jaw, snapping it like a piece of kindling with his massive fist.

The blow sent my head into the back of the van, hitting it so hard that the glass cracked on the window behind me. My vision swam, and I prayed that I'd wake up, and still have my clothes intact. Still be living.

I lost the fight with consciousness in the next moment, staying awake long enough to feel the next blow that landed on my chest, stealing the oxygen from my lungs before I passed out completely.

Chapter 24

Welcome to the party, pal.

-Die Hard

James

"How long is this going to take, Payton?" A muffled voice whispered.

My eyes felt heavy, like I'd been sleeping really hard. Kind of like when I took Nyquil for a cold. My eyelids didn't want to open, and it took me a long time to finally pry them apart, but everything was fuzzy.

"His eyes are opening now. Oh, Jesus, I'm going to get fired. I'm going to lose my license." Payton whispered sadly.

"Oh, shut up. You just gave him the meds. You didn't steal them from the Pixus like I did." Cheyenne groaned.

She sounded worried as well, and it was starting to make me curious. Why on earth would they be stealing drugs? Why did my head feel like it was filled with cotton? Why did my chest feel like something was sitting on it? What the hell was shoved up my dick?

"James?" Winter asked.

I blinked my eyes furiously, trying to clear the sleep from them. It took a couple of minutes, but I finally made out Winter's bright red hair, as well as Payton's pink, and Cheyenne's, Blaine's, and Ember's blonde.

"What the hell?" I croaked.

Another face leaned in and surveyed my face.

Sebastian.

He looked haggard. Bags resided under his eyes making it look like he hadn't slept in well past the normal amount of time. His beard nearly looked unkempt, which was a rarity for him. He was a neat freak Marine. They didn't allow their hair to get unruly.

Then a thought hit me. Although I saw Winter, Cheyenne, and the rest of the girls, I didn't see Janie and I didn't see Shiloh.

"Where're my girls?" I grated out.

It felt like I'd deep throated a mace. Jesus, my throat rivaled my chest.

Then little things started to click into place. The silence from my question started my brain working again, and panic hit me. I remembered riding to work, stopping at a stop sign, texting Sam, and then laying down flat against the asphalt. Then nothing.

"What's wrong? Cheyenne, please tell me. Please," I begged.

I hadn't realized that I was about to cry until my vision went blurry again. Blinking the tears away, I focused on my sister, and when she still didn't tell me, I turned my stare to Sebastian. His eyes, although haunted, were also filled with fury.

"They're dead." I finally said, horror filling my voice.

Sebastian shook his head. "Janie's fine. Shaken, but fine. Sam's got her. I know where Shiloh is, too. But...I need you to get her out. It's been two days, and if we wait much longer, they're just going to kill her." Sebastian explained.

Texas Tornado

I'd begun ripping out IVs and removing shit that was stuck to me before he'd even finished. It was when I started to stand that I realized that the stupid thing was still in my dick. "Tell me how to get this out." I demanded pointing at the offending area under my gown.

Cheyenne blushed, and left the room, as did everyone but Payton. "Want me to do it?"

"Just tell me what to do." I growled as I started to rip the gown off when I realized it'd be leaving me naked in front of my best friend's wife, and stopped.

"Okay, here's what you've got to do." She explained quickly, leaving me the tools necessary, and left the room.

With a deep breath, I stood on shaky legs, barely suppressing the desire to puke my guts up. The only thing that kept me from doing it was sheer force of will. I didn't have time, and it'd hurt like a motherfucker if I did.

Pants and a shirt were left on the end of the bed. Slipping into them as best as I could without bending at the waist, I continued to ignore the ungodly pain I was in and slid my feet into my socks, but stopped before I got the boots on. There was just no way I was going to be able to do it myself.

"Cheyenne," I called, however it didn't come out to well, so I cleared my voice, and called again, more loudly this time. "Cheyenne!"

She came in quickly, took in the situation, and dropped down to her knees. "I seem to remember the opposite of this happening when we were kids."

I smiled slightly at her attempt to lighten the mood, but didn't go much further than that.

Once my boots were on, I raised my hand to her, and she grabbed on to my arm, lifting with me as I stood to my feet. Slowly.

Once I was out in the hall, Payton shoved two pills in my hand and I swallowed them dry. "What'd I just take as we walked towards the elevator?"

"A pain pill and an antibiotic. You didn't finish it in your drip." She explained as she pressed the button on the elevator.

A woman's panicked voice from behind us made the girls turn around, trying to shield me with their bodies, but they're luck wasn't with them that day. I was a good foot taller than even the tallest one. They were shit out of luck from the get go.

However, when the elevator beeped and the doors open, I didn't stop for the woman that was running towards us, yelling that I shouldn't be out of bed. I just trudged forward, and leaned my elbow against the far wall, trying my hardest not to fall down.

"Where are we going?" I asked the wall.

"They're holding her at a cabin out by Caddo Lake. You'll have to climb a tree." Sebastian's voice sounded tired.

Easy Peasy. Climb a tree. Two days after being shot in the chest. No problem. Things could be worse, I could be missing a body part, I suppose.

"Okay," I agreed readily.

Texas Tornado

I'd do anything when it came to Shiloh. As long as Janie was safe while I did it, I didn't care what I had to do. I'd tear down entire cities to get to that woman.

I made it to the car before I passed out again.

It was when I was being physically lifted from the car like a child being lifted under his armpits that I came awake to find Sam staring me in the face. His eyes were cold and hard. Copper fucking fire.

"You awake?" He snapped.

"Yes," I croaked.

"Good. We got you to about fifteen feet of the tree we expect you to climb. We've got you some gear, and we'll help you as much as we can, but you're going to have to strap yourself to a limb, because we're leaving you there." He informed me.

I nodded in understanding, looking around and noticing that all the men were there, Luke and Downy, as well as about thirty men dressed in their Dixie Wardens MC cuts. I was happy to find the women gone. Who they were with and where they were at fluttered through my exhausted brain, but I trusted the men to take care of them. Trusted them with everything that I possessed.

"What am I looking for, exactly?" I asked as I shuffled to the tree Sam had indicated.

"Anything that moves that isn't Shiloh." Sebastian answered as he slipped a bulletproof vest over his head.

I nodded in agreement, and stepped up to the tree, laying my foot over the loop that they were going to use to hoist me up there. Elliott bent down, looped it over my boot and nodded before stepping back with the other half of the rope that was over a branch at the very top.

Lucky for me this was a weeping willow. The dangling greenery provided good cover, and the thick, fat branches would hold my weight well. They'd chosen well, which didn't surprise me. They were experts, just like me.

Jack came up behind me, slipped me into a jacket, being careful to watch my wounded side, and I laughed lightly. "Jesus, can y'all hold my dick so I can take a piss, too?"

Chuckles sounded, but I didn't move much more. I couldn't. I was so freaking tired I could barely breathe.

"Sorry man, I draw the line at putting makeup on you." Jack quipped as he started rubbing in the camouflage paint that would hide the pale complexion of my face, as well as my arms. I noted that he himself was decked out in much the same attire, but didn't put any further thought into it.

Sam handed me my rifle and an ear bud once Jack was done. I threw the strap over my shoulder, stuck the earpiece in my ear, and braced myself before giving Elliott a thumbs-up. Then I was moving.

I gritted my teeth against the jolt as I hit the trunk of the tree with my body, but never called out for a halt.

Maneuvering myself into the tree was another matter. By the time I'd managed to do so, I was clammy and nauseous, as well as seeing black spots.

A trickle of warmth leaked down my abs, and disappeared into my jeans, and I knew I was bleeding again.

Texas Tornado

Reaching into my pocket, I withdrew the pads that Cheyenne had stuffed in their as we left the room, and shoved them unceremoniously against my wound before tying it with the Ace Bandage.

"We're moving in. It'll take us about twenty minutes to get there. There're a couple of marshes we have to cross before we'll even make it on the grounds. Then there're the trip wires and motion detector devices we have to counteract. How many men are outside?" Sam's authoritative voice asked in my ear.

I brought my scope up to my shoulder and started counting. "Fifteen outside. All armed with AR-15s. I can see two in the windows." I called back quietly.

I scanned the windows of the house one by one until I came to the very last one. I don't know if it was instinct, or just basic knowledge that she would be in that room, but with everything that was in me, I knew she was behind that wall.

It took everything I had to turn away from that window, but I continued to scan the area. Listening while everyone continued to check in on where they were, and Sam gave instructions.

"All right, James. We're in position. Take the ones out on the edges. All that you can. When you've got them all down, let me know." Sam commanded.

Piece of cake.

My sniper rifle was sporting a shiny new silencer, which was also why it'd gained a good three pounds in weight. Resting my back against the trunk of the tree I was in, and the stock up against my cheek, I started taking my shots. All fifteen men, who were scattered over an acre of land, went down within ten minutes.

Not my best, time wise, but it would do. "Alright, you're green."

A wave of exhaustion seemed to pour through me after I was done, but I didn't remove my eye from the activity surrounding the small cabin. Although I scanned the area, I mostly kept my scope trained on the furthest window, praying I'd see my girl.

***

Shiloh

I'd nearly killed myself two separate times.

Although Glen had never returned to make his threat a reality, I knew it was just a matter of time. I'd tried to escape not even ten minutes after arriving at this shit hole, only to be caught as soon as I'd tripped one of the motion detectors, enabling them to find me easily.

Then I'd played possum, acting as if I was passed out, and tried to escape again, only for the same results.

Needless to say, the men were not happy campers. They didn't like that a woman had given them the slip, and were more than happy to show me their displeasure.

My escape attempts had only earned me another broken arm, the same one that had just healed only a few short months ago, a broken leg, and a broken nose. My jaw was still just as broken as it'd been in the van, and I passed out every time I tried to push even the minutest amount of bread into my mouth that they'd provided me.

Texas Tornado

Thus, I'd stopped trying to eat. Only drinking the water from the tap with a straw that they'd been nice enough to provide me.

Every time I looked at my broken arm the bile would rush up my esophagus, and I'd have to choke it back down, or risk suffocating on my own vomit since I couldn't open my mouth enough for the vomit to escape.

I hadn't seen Glen since the van incident, and prayed to all that was holy that I wouldn't. There was just no way on earth I'd be able to keep him away from me. I had no fight left in me, which was why I'd been laying in the same spot on the lumpy futon for the last half a day.

A sound, almost imperceptible, whispered through the stagnant room, and I moved my eyes, looking for the source. When I didn't see anything, I let my eyes drift closed, thinking this was surely the end if I was hallucinating, when the same sound, louder now, came from behind my closed lids.

My eyes snapped open, sure now that I'd heard the sound, and I came face to face with a green man.

Great. My fucked up mind had conjured The Hulk. Wonderful.

Then The Hulk gently picked me up in his massive arms, and carried me towards the bedroom door.

I was like a ragdoll in The Hulk's arms, limp and in pain, with no recourse but to lie there, and go wherever The Hulk wanted me to go.

"Got her." The Hulk said.

My eyes closed on their own accord, staying closed as the sway of my body being moved at a high rate of speed caused my broken bones to jolt with each pounding step. Bile rose in my throat again, and I swallowed convulsively to keep it down. Then, blessedly, I passed out again.

***

Sam

"James? Copy?" I called quietly.

No answer.

"James." I snapped.

No answer.

"Sebastian, I need whoever you left behind to check on him. Make sure he doesn't fall out of the tree." I called into my mic.

"Copy." Sebastian answered.

Shiloh was curled into my arms like a Cabbage Patch Doll. I noted that her nose and jaw were well beyond swollen, as was the arm she'd broken a couple months prior. Her hair was matted into a messy ponytail at the top of her head with blood, indicating a head wound of some type.

It'd taken a while for the thought of a sister to grow on me, but now I couldn't imagine my life without her. To know that she'd suffered at the hands of these men set me on a course that I'd never thought to be on. I'd always prided myself in making sure that I complied with the law, but over the past four years, the letter of the law hadn't done me shit. In fact, it'd only hindered me when all I wanted to do was save the woman I loved.

Texas Tornado

It took us fifteen minutes, exactly, from the time we left the cabin to get back to the tree that we'd left James in. Everyone was gathered around, looking up at James hanging from the harness we'd managed to get him in.

"What are y'all waiting for?" I snapped to the men ogling James. "Get him down."

"How?" Diablo, one of the members of the MC asked.

"Climb up there, dipshit." Sebastian said as he, too, walked up.

James was a big man, so with him being dead weight, and not being able to help at all, it was some time before they were able to get him down safely.

Although he looked a little paler than he'd been originally, he was still breathing and had a steady and strong pulse.

We loaded James and Shiloh into the back of my Suburban, and carefully drove out, leaving Sebastian and Silas to figure out what to do about Glen. Although this battle had been won, the war was far from over.

Chapter 25

Lord give me patience. Cause if you give me strength, I'm going to need bail money to go with it.

-E-card

Shiloh

My eyes narrowed on the bitchy nurse who'd, yet again, refused to let me leave my bed to go see James who was four doors down from me.

"I'm sorry, Ms. Mackenzie. Mr. Allen isn't receiving visitors. He's requested that no one bother him except for his daughter." Nurse Bitch said as she breezed out of the room, purposefully ignoring my frantic waving.

That bitch. She knew I couldn't call after her, nor could I press the little goddamn button since she'd moved said button halfway across the room.

I'd had surgery on my jaw, and then had it wired shut. Now all I was able to eat was food that came from a straw. Let me tell you, that's something that sucks. Why you ask? Because the hospital doesn't take the time to blend each individual food separately. They pile it all into one heaping pile, toss it into the mixer, and then blend it into one big pile of shit.

It tastes even worse. Therefore, I'm starving because I could only stomach a quarter of the food. Which would've been my next question had she stayed longer than the required time it took for her to replace my IV line which I'd purposefully pulled out to get someone in here.

Aside from the broken jaw, I also had a broken tibia, as well as a broken ulna in my left arm.

Therefore, getting around was not the easiest thing to do. At all.

Nevertheless, I'd have to go for it if I wanted to survive. Starving to death didn't sound like the best thing in the world to do. That and I missed James and Janie, not to mention my brothers and father like crazy.

I'd been awake for well over eight hours now, and not once had anyone come to see me. I was getting really upset.

The first obstacle was getting up. With the fucking bed remote all the way across the room. Using the IV pole for support, I lifted my body up, managing not to jar my leg too much. My jaw, on the other hand, was a different story all together. It throbbed with each movement of my body. Which probably meant that all my other various broken bones and bruises were hurting, too, but the pain in my jaw was just overshadowing it.

The dumb nurse did happen to leave the beside roller table though, and it helped me immensely when I leaned on it. Instead of rolling the IV pole with me, I just removed my IV. Then I managed to grab the bag that contained my pee, flipped it over until you couldn't see its contents, and started making my way slowly to the door.

Once there, I had a decision to make. Left, or right. I know she said he was four doors down from me, but I didn't know in which direction, and the possibility could really turn dire if I had to walk one way, and then the other if I chose poorly.

Then I heard James deep voice, slightly raised and near panic.

Hobbling along, I followed the sound of his voice like a beacon in the night. I'd just gotten to his door when I finally could make out what exactly he was saying, and what I heard nearly made my heart stop.

"When is she due? What makes you think it was mine? I only slept with her once." James snarled.

I was hyperventilating, and not from the exertion of getting to his room.

"Listen Layne, I know you think that it's mine, but you've got to know, we used protection. She said..." He trailed off as Layne, whoever he wass, started to yell.

I could hear the sound of the man's voice raised to a decibel that made you listen. His tone didn't allow for anything else. His voice held power, and you'd listen, or likely pay for it.

"Okay, listen, what happened between us was consensual. Now, what the hell is going on?" James snapped, grimacing when his shout jolted his chest, causing him pain.

"Jesus Christ, you've got to be kidding me. When'd this happen? Is she okay?" He rasped.

My heartbeat accelerated, my one good leg went weak, and I knew he was worried about this woman, whoever she was. She must be important to him. Did he love her? Was he in love with her before me? Was he even in love with me?

Texas Tornado

Just as I started to turn around, Sam rounded the corner, and his face turned from impassive to downright thunderous when he saw me leaning against the table and the wall for support.

His steps sped up until he was almost running and caught me just as my one good leg collapsed. "Oh, Shiloh. So stubborn you are. The nurse told me you weren't to be disturbed, that you didn't want to see us. Are you upset with me?"

I scowled at him as he scooped me up, piss bag and all. "No. Nurse wouldn't let me see James." I said through my teeth. I wasn't sure how coherent I sounded with my mouth wired shut, but I was guessing he'd gotten the drift.

"She's just jealous. I think her and James had a fling a few years ago." He spoke as he carried me into James room.

James eyes looked haunted and distant, but never once stopped speaking to Layne about the details of the baby mama's assault, even after he saw me enter the room. When the conversation continued with him saying yes and no, and then lowering his voice when he needed to speak more than syllables, I'd had enough. Guess the nurse was right after all.

"Room please." I instructed Sam, turning my face away from James sprawled body and into Sam's chest. The burst of pain at my jaw hitting his chest was nothing compared to the pain in my heart.

He carried me away, and I took one last glance at the perfect muscles of James' arms, the ripped sculpture of his chest, and the white bandage that bisected his midsection. "What had happened to him?"

I was in the hall before Sam answered the question that I wasn't aware I'd voiced. "He got shot on the way to work two days ago. Right about the time you were taken by Glen."

At the mention of Glen's name, I shuttered. "Is he dead?"

The hope in my voice must have registered with Sam, but his grimace shot that hope to hell. "Sorry, Shiloh."

The smooth cadence of his voice, followed by the rhythmic walking made my eyes heavy, and it was all I could do to stay awake. Sam placed me gently on the bed, adjusting all the lines and covers before he started to back away.

"Don't leave." I pleaded.

"Okay." He agreed, and then I was asleep.

My dreams were anything but happy. They were filled with a crazed Glen trying to re-break my jaw, James and another woman holding their child, as well as Janie in the peripheral, mad that I never came back again.

"What are you doing out of bed?" The nasty nurse from earlier asked.

My eyes blinked open, and I turned my head until I got a face full of chest.

It wasn't the same chest that I'd cried myself to sleep against earlier, either. No this one was the one I loved. The one that had a huge bandage across his chest.

He was on his side lying next to me. One of James' dog tags was caught haphazardly in the gauze, while the other dangled free against his pec.

Texas Tornado

His large arm was slung across my body, holding me in my sleep.

"Are you awake yet, sleepy head?" James' chest rumbled.

"No." I snapped, or tried to, anyway.

It came out more like 'non' and spit dribbled down my chin, which inevitably ran down his chest shortly after. I'd forgotten about my wired jaw for a split second, but it didn't let me forget it. His laughter startled me out of my mortification, and I looked up as he raised his arm, wiping the slobber off his chest, and then on the bed sheet before bringing his hand up to my hair.

"Where'd you go earlier?" He asked softly, ignoring the crabby nurse at our backs.

"When?" I asked.

"Shin?" He asked, pulling back, confused in my answer.

His hand went down towards the bottom of the bed, lifting the covers from my feet. His body remained in place, the cords of his neck straining with the effort to remain as still as possible

My off-white cast poked free, followed by my hospital-issued faded blue non-slip sock.

"James." I called, wanting his eyes.

"Mr. Allen, I've got a chair for you." The nurse urged tightly.

The pain was evident in his face as he moved, and I knew the movement to check on me was causing him discomfort, but he was too worried about something that was wrong with me rather than being worried about what he was doing to himself.

When he finally looked up and caught my eyes, I reached for his hand.

He gave me his hand, and I pulled it up until my head rested on our clasped hands.

His eyes went soft, and he smiled at me. "Are you okay?"

Knowing that we just needed to get the elephant out of the closet, I asked. "Baby?"

I think he purposefully misheard, because his eyes left mine, focusing on something above my head. "Janie's fine. Shaken up, and understandably so, but she's staying with Grammy and *Grampy* Todd."

"I'm going to get an orderly to help you back in bed, Mr. Allen." The nurse said quickly before leaving the room after she made her third attempt to get James off the bed and into the waiting wheelchair.

I snickered at the emphasis on Grampy, but didn't give him a chance to retreat. My hand untangled from his, and I took a hold of his beard, holding on tightly so he couldn't look away when I asked my next question.

"James...baby?" I asked again.

He sighed. "Fuck me."

I didn't let him go, and he didn't try to turn his head again. "Please?"

"You're hungry for peas?" He asked with a smile turning up the corners of his mouth.

I yanked hard on the beard and he winced, but his smile didn't wane. "Did your brother ever really tell you what we do?"

I thought about what my brother did as a mechanic and custom bike designer. "Bikes?" I asked, confused.

Texas Tornado

He shook his head.

"Alright, let me tell you, but don't interrupt me until I get it all out, okay? Please?" He asked softly.

At my nod, he continued.

"We're motorcycle mechanics, builders, and designers. Although, that's our day business. On the side, we help battered women escape dangerous and volatile situations. We've relocated thirty-five women. Teal, the woman you overheard the phone call about earlier, was one of those women. With me so far?" He asked.

I nodded.

"Teal knew she was pregnant before she was relocated. For all intents and purposes, though, that child is mine. I made that promise to her before she left that if something happened to her, I would take over custody of the child and do everything in my power to keep the child out of the hands of her ex-husband, and I'll stick by it. I know the situation isn't ideal, but there isn't one single thing I can do about it. Nor would I want to. If it keeps an innocent child out of the clutches of a monster, then that's the way it's going to be." James rasped.

Well, shit. Isn't that part of who I am as well? To make sure that children are always put first? Why would this be any different? Then the truth hit me. If he had another baby, he wouldn't want another one to deal with...would he?

"What happened?"

My head was hurting from our conversation and my aching mouth, but if James was willing to talk, I would listen. I did let go of his beard though, and he buried his nose into my hair.

"She's been attacked. She'd filed with the lawyer she contacted that I was the father, and left my information down in case of emergency. Well there was an emergency, in the form of him nearly beating her to death at a stoplight, and I have power of attorney now that she's clinically brain dead. Her ex-husband found her, I'm assuming, but the man was never apprehended. She's not doing well at all, and they haven't gotten any brain activity from her in over three days. They're only keeping her alive at this point because of the baby." He said sadly.

"Jesus." I whispered.

"Yeah, that's only the beginning. We have the other thirty-four women to worry about that we've relocated. Unless Teal fucked up, which I know damn sure she didn't, we've got a leak. They're about ten people besides ourselves that know that information, and the locations of all of them, as well as their new identities, aren't even kept on record."

"Who makes the new identification for you?" I asked.

"IDs?" He clarified.

At my nod, he answered. "I don't know. That's something that Sam's taken care of. I do know that we have more than one man who does it. We change after every three women. However, Sam's already aware of what's happened, and he's looking into it. If it turns out that it was the man we went to for Teal, we'll have to relocate the other two women just in case. I have a feeling that Teal's ex was looking for her specifically, and he has a lot more reach than she'd told us about. She knew that, knew that he'd find her. That's why she went to so much trouble to name me the father."

"Fuck."

"I agree," James rumbled, sounding sleepy.

However, in the next instant, his body tensed, and I knew something was wrong by the way he froze against me. All his muscles tensed

"Mr. Allen? I'm Roderick, would you like me to help you..."

I don't know how it happened, nor what happened, but in the next moment, the report of gunfire echoed throughout the tiny hospital room. A nice little hole, the size of a penny, entered into the man's chest almost exactly where James had been shot just a few short weeks ago.

The gun in James hand lowered slowly, and screaming started in the hallway.

Somewhere in the aftermath of James shooting the man, Sebastian showed and pried the gun from James' hand. Wiping the gun off on the black t-shirt he wore, he fired once more into the man in nearly the same place, ejected the clip, removed the bullet from the chamber, and tossed them all into the bathroom before closing the door.

"Knew he'd come here, stupid bastard. Just meant to be here in time." Sebastian smiled at the two of us.

James cursed and made it to his feet slowly before peering at the man who was bleeding out on the floor.

I took a closer look at the man on the floor and finally noticed the numerous tattoos on the man's forearms, neck and head. "What the fuck?" I asked.

Oh, and did I mention the huge ass shotgun?

"Now's not the time for that, Shiloh." James said distractedly.

Jesus Christ, I really had to work on this talking thing. Then again, I would think that two grown men would think more of me than to say 'want to fuck' in the middle of this kind of dilemma. I mean I was kinky, but I wasn't into doing it with dead people in the room.

"Everybody on the ground! No excuses. Get the fuck down." A man's voice called from the hallway.

Was that expected of me? Because if it was, I'd hurt myself. So would James. However, that turned out to be an unnecessary thought when Sebastian scooped me up from the bed and laid me gently down on the ground, following me down once he had me there comfortably.

"Keep your mouth shut." Sebastian whispered.

James' body hit the floor beside us way less graceful than I would've thought, and he grunted in pain, which was the only thing that kept me from punching my brother in the gut. Son of a bitch thought he was funny, too, if the smile on his face was anything to go by.

My perch on the floor was all kinds of precarious.

Texas Tornado

I couldn't lay my face down because my jaw hurt too badly. I couldn't use one of my hands because it was in an L shape plastered against my body, and my foot was stuck underneath me.

I had no traction to do anything to try to get comfortable, and when men rushed into the room, some dressed in police uniforms, and others dressed in hospital security uniforms wielding guns, it became very uncomfortable, very fast.

"Get off her, you piece of shit. She should still be in bed. She's about four hours post-surgery on her leg and jaw, if you hurt her any more than she is right now, I will have your goddamn badge." James snarled from beside me as he was restrained by another officer.

The hands on my back lightened, and I was supremely grateful.

"Help her in to bed. She's no threat to you." James snarled again.

I couldn't see him because of the officer standing beside my head, but I could see Sebastian as he was rolled over onto his back, cuffed arms underneath him. He had a twinkle in his eyes, as if he had a secret.

"Alright, boys. Back away from these men and my daughter. I'm Silas Mackenzie with the CIA. My credentials are..."

My father's voice surprised me, but the man's boots at my face twisted in surprise, accidentally kicking me in the process.

And you guessed it. Right in the kisser.

The burst of pain flashed through me, vomit rose in my throat, poured out of my mouth, burst through my clenched teeth, my nose, and maybe even out my ears.

I puked and then dry heaved for nearly a minute before the pain in my jaw calmed down enough.

I was proud to see that the man that kicked me in the face now had puke on his shoes, as well as a new bruise on his face. He looked incredibly remorseful, but that didn't help the waves of agony that were rolling through me with each pulse of my heart.

"Goddammit! I told you to fucking watch her you stupid piece of shit. You're fucking done." James snarled from his back, straining to get to me.

The arms that were wrapped around me were my father's as he smoothed the hair from my face, wiping my face off gently with a cool towel.

"Page the nurse. Tell her to bring some medication in here for her pain." My father demanded of someone.

I was crying, but the look on James' face had my tears slowing until I was looking at him with wet cheeks only. He looked agonized, as if what he'd done inadvertently caused me to be hurt. Once my tears had stopped though, he calmed, somehow composing himself enough to stop struggling himself.

The sharp pinch of a needle entering my arm brought my attention to the nurse, the same one that hated me for some reason, punched a needle into my arm a little too hard, and I lost the battle with consciousness.

Texas Tornado

***

James

"Simmons is gone. I don't care what you have to do, but you make him gone. He did that on purpose. He was standing a little more than a foot away from her face. He didn't kick her on accident." I hissed to Silas, and then turned to The Captain, making sure they both understood my standpoint.

"We'll look into it..." The Captain started to say before I interrupted him.

"No. He will be gone. It's either him or me. You decide." I gritted out between clenched teeth.

Partly because I was in a lot of pain from my own gunshot wound, and secondly, I didn't trust myself to start yelling the rooftops down.

When I'd seen Glen entering the room, at first my eyes didn't quite comprehend what I was seeing.

I'd been lying in bed with Shiloh for a little over two hours when she'd finally woken. I'd been getting the run around by the nurse for going on half a day about Shiloh's progress, and the nurse kept telling me that she was still asleep.

Since I was in no place to argue with the woman, I let her be, knowing she'd get a hold of me as soon as she was able. Which she'd done, but I'd promptly screwed up by not acknowledging her. I was in shock. I hadn't believed Teal when she'd said that she was too important to be let go. That her ex-husband would find her no matter what she did.

I'd been naïve. I'd thought I knew this world. Thought I knew the kind of scum that inhabited this earth. Teal had been an innocent, and to know that she'd been beaten to within an inch of her life, absolutely shredded me. I'd brought the concerns to Sam, but we'd done everything we could possibly do, short of killing off the ex, which wasn't what we did.

Until now.

With Shiloh asleep on the bed next to me, and Teal being kept alive halfway across the country, I knew that I wouldn't stand by and let this happen anymore. Something had to change.

I'd been thinking about the changes that needed to take place when Glen walked in. Although dressed as an orderly, the shotgun in his hand was unmistakable.

It was gut instinct, on top of raw need to protect the woman I loved, that made my hand act. The gun became an extension of me. It took all of six seconds to get the gun in my hand, aim, and fire. It was only divine justice that the bullet had hit Glen in the same spot as he'd had a sniper take me.

The Captain's vehement speech to Detective Howell brought me out of my musings. "Larson's wanted on attempted murder of a police officer, kidnapping of a woman, attempted kidnapping of a child, and numerous other things, Officer Howell. We have the testimony of his brother and his girlfriend. The man is guilty. What Mr. Mackenzie did was acceptable."

Texas Tornado

"Jesus Christ. You realize this is a colossal clusterfuck. This facility prohibits firearms on the premises. He had to get a gun in here someway without passing through a metal detector. Which means he entered illegally, and purposefully carried a firearm into the facility. That's a violation of the law, and the hospital has the right to press charges, which they are doing." Detective Howell gritted out through clenched teeth.

Technically, me and every other member of my team had done the same in the past week, as well as the past four years all together. I didn't go anywhere unarmed, and that includes lying flat on my back in a hospital bed.

It was another two hours before they moved us to my room, the charge nurse opting to let Shiloh and I share a room until our stay was over with, since Shiloh's was now a crime scene.

Sebastian was arrested for the possession of a firearm, and since he had priors, they kept him, denying him bail.

Shiloh slept.

I guess it was good that at least one of us could. I was fucking exhausted, but my mind was on a hundred different things, going in one hundred different directions.

***

Two days later

"They're releasing you, but not me?" Shiloh asked.

Well, to the best of my knowledge, that's what she asked. "Yeah, but I'm not going anywhere, honey. I'll be here until you get to go home, too."

"Good," she hesitated. "You should go home anyway, spend some time with Janie. Get her used to having a new sister."

I looked at her. I was thinking the same thing myself. Nonetheless, I knew something was bothering Shiloh, minus the fact that her brother was still in jail.

Pressing the button on the side of the bed, I waited for it to lift me up fully before I turned completely towards Shiloh, who was laid back in her own bed, looking even more pitiful than she had two days ago. I couldn't wait to cuddle her, hold her close to my chest, and feel her sleeping next to me again.

"Tell me what's wrong, honey." I said softly.

Instead of talking, she started to type on her phone in a furious burst of motion. Moments later, my phone buzzed.

Shiloh: I scared that I'm going to be a bad mother.

I read the message, and then looked up into her eyes. "You're kidding me, right? Just four days ago, you kept my own daughter safe from a man that broke your jaw, leg, and arm. How do you think Janie would've faired if you hadn't been there, made sure that she was all right?"

I waited for her to reply, but she didn't, only staying silent.

"What about when Lyle and his mother died. I distinctly remembered you being so upset, so outraged, that you wrote a letter to the editor. Which, might I add, everyone and their brother cut out and framed." I stated.

Shiloh: What if I don't love that baby as much as he or she deserves?

At that absurd statement, I burst out laughing. Her scowl only making me laugh all the harder.

"You'll love the baby as much as our own, as much as Janie, when we finally have it." I managed to wheeze.

She threw her empty water pitcher at me, and I caught it reflexively.

Painfully, I stood, and walked to the edge of her bed, clutching my discharge papers in my hand.

Thankfully, she was propped up into a seated position, enabling me to reach her mouth, which I captured with my own.

"Ewww," Janie squealed from the doorway, making my lips lift into a grin before I pulled my lips away.

Shiloh's eyes were dancing with mirth at being caught by my six year old, but she looked excited, too.

She hadn't seen Janie since the day she was taken. Both of us felt that it'd be better until some of the bruises faded from her face, and she was able to take a full shower to wash away the blood from her hair. We'd felt that Janie would be better off if Shiloh looked better, and was dealing with her pain level better.

Because, let's face it, Janie was a very active six year old, and she wasn't easy on injured people. She didn't know how to be. Which was why when she launched herself at me, Silas caught her in midair and twirled her around his head.

"Easy there, midget. Your daddy just had a hole put through his body. He hurts. You'll have to be gentle with him for a few days." Silas explained patiently.

Janie looked at me, and then over to Shiloh. "What's with that cast color? Who picks white?" She finally asked.

Shiloh snickered, and then looked over to me, waiting for me to explain. "Shiloh didn't get to pick it. Guess you'll have to decorate it for her to make it pretty."

"I can do that. I'll need my Sharpie's." She said with a determined expression. "Daddy said you broke your arm again. I told him he should buy you a horse so you didn't have to walk and fall anymore."

I closed my eyes, thinking how nice it would be to have the innocence of a child, and the ability to recover from a traumatizing event only days after it happened.

Sadly, I knew I would remember this for a while. Maybe even the rest of my lifetime.

Although I knew I could bear it. Having Shiloh and Janie would make anybody question their sanity, but that was my life. I looked forward to hearing what new cuss words Janie learned while helping the guys at the shop. Or what would come out of Shiloh's mouth next. I only had one thing I had to make sure to do. That was to embrace the crazy.

Texas Tornado

***

Later that night

My door opened.

Thinking it was only the nurse, I didn't react to the intrusion. I was used to it. Frankly, I didn't think it was even possible to 'recover' well in the hospital. How does one get better when they don't even let you sleep and eat properly?

Turning my head, I was startled to see a frightened, tiny form slipping into the room, and doing her best to close it behind her, despite the little mechanism at the top that kept you from closing it except at the speed it wanted.

"Jolie?" I rasped with sleep still clinging to my voice.

She turned sharply, gasping. Why would she be surprised when she was the one to enter my room?

"Are you okay?" I finally asked as she stood there like a frightened rabbit.

"I'm sorry. I'm just not used to not being afraid all the time. You startled me. I thought you'd be asleep." She finally answered.

"Can you explain that?" I asked.

She walked slowly over to the chair that was beside my bed and sat.

"I don't know if James ever told you about the bullying I'd received in high school..." She asked, looking over to me for confirmation. At the shake of my head she continued.

"I was bullied quite badly after the accident with James' best friend. After a while, I just couldn't take it anymore and left. There was a small incident of an older senior nearly raping me, and I just broke. I left, ran. Lived on the streets in Austin for over eight months before a man found me."

She swallowed hard.

"I was young and impressionable. I thought the man loved me. Then the man loaned me out, bet me like a fucking stack of chips at a poker game to pay, I guess you could say. Glen Larson was one of the ones at the table, and once that bet was made, he made it a mission to win. And win he did. I wasn't too in the know, to be honest, of what kind of person the man I'd been living with for about four months was, but I learned quickly in that week I had to spend with Glen Larson. Stole some money from Glen to get away, and left. I've been running for about six years now. I thought that after five years of no one even looking for me, that it would be safe to come home when my Aunt died and left me her house. I couldn't have been more wrong."

I absorbed that news for a minute. "So, what was all that shit you were trying to do with James?"

She shrugged. "Glen. He wanted you. Told me if I got you alone that he'd consider the money I stole from him paid in full. But I didn't want James hurt, so I tried to wiggle myself between the two of you. Once I learned what they were planning to do to you, I backed off. That's when I truly started to try to get a hold of the police, but James just kept telling me to go away. Same with Max. I didn't know whom to trust. God I was so fucking scared."

Texas Tornado

She seemed to slump, and she looked totally defeated.

"That's why you brought the wrecked bike to Free?" I questioned.

She nodded. "That was one of Larson's men's old bikes. It was just a way in."

"How did you come to be where James was shot?" I asked.

I was burning with questions. The need to know more about what happened with James was absolutely killing me.

"I overheard Glen talking about a new gun before I left the last time and didn't come back. I'd learned from working at The Gun Doctor what you would use that kind of gun for. I followed him; saw where he set himself up. I'd never intended to let anything happen. I was over confident. James came flying down the street before I could even react, tell him, and warn him. It all happened so fast, and I couldn't let anything else happen to him, so I pulled him into my rental and took off. Dropped the car and him at the ER entrance, yelled like a frantic woman that someone was in trouble, and took off."

I couldn't even begin to tell her how humbled I was that she'd do that. Put herself in the line of fire when I was sure she'd been scared shitless.

There was only one thing I could think to say. "Thank you."

"It wasn't enough. It will never be enough." She sniffled, trying her hardest not to cry. "Tell him I'm sorry. He was always so good to me."

"You already told him." I said, nodding my head towards the doorway where James was now leaning quietly, head down.

When I pointed out his presence, he looked up, eyes hard.

"You're about to disappear." He said with no emotion in his voice.

She rose, nodding. "I know. Thank you."

When she tried to slip past him out the door, he grabbed a hold of her arm. "No, we're making you disappear. We'll give you a new identity. Money. A place to live. You'll keep your head down. And you'll never contact us again."

Tears poured down Jolie's face. "Thank you."

He nodded. "Should have contacted me before it got this bad. You're welcome."

Chapter 26

To make sure we always have a happy marriage, I promise to always cop a feel when you get ready in the morning.

-Life Lesson

Shiloh

"Where are we going, Sebastian?" I asked my brother, who had to be high to take me out in this shit.

When he didn't answer, I kept up my ranting.

"It's fucking seventeen degrees, and raining ice. We really shouldn't be outside." I chastised.

"Shut up. Cheyenne has a surprise for you." He growled, fed up with my bad attitude.

It wasn't my fault my jaw was sore.

Nor was it my fault he had to wear an ankle bracelet that monitored his whereabouts. But he did, and he bitched about it constantly.

"What's your problem anyway?" He snapped.

I glared at his back as we exited James' old place, where we stayed on and off throughout the week depending on if he had to work the next morning.

My problem was that James left for a SWAT conference the night before, and I wouldn't see him for another three days.

He missed my jaw being unwired. He missed my casts coming off. And, he took my cat to the groomers, and they'd shaved him like a lion. An honest to God lion. Why do you ask? Because my fiancé is a shit head, and I lost a bet.

"We made a bet. I bet him that Janie would like my present better, and he did the same for his. She chose his, and he shaved my cat like Mufasa." I explained.

"What'd you get her?" He asked in surprise.

I know, I was surprised, too!

I gave great gifts. I always did. I took a lot of time planning each what to get everyone. It started months in advance for the big day. Which was good for me that I'd finished all of my Christmas shopping since I was in the hospital over Christmas. We ended up celebrating Christmas on the first of January.

"I got her a bicycle. It was shaped like a Harley. I mean how freaking awesome is that?" I asked vehemently.

"That's pretty cool. What'd James get her?" He asked as he opened the door to the garage that led us into the down room.

At first, I didn't quite comprehend what I was seeing, and then I gasped at the beauty of it. Twinkle lights shone everywhere. All in the LED white lights that made them look faintly bluish in color.

Sparkly snowflakes hung from the rafters, as well as fake ice crystals. Inside, in the middle of the room, was a dress. My dress. The one I'd cut out of a magazine when I was sixteen and fantasizing about my dream wedding.

Texas Tornado

I turned to study Sebastian, and his surly attitude, his shadowed eyes, and flung myself into his arms. "Oh, Sue. I love you."

His arms tightened in warning, but they were warm and comfortable as he held me close to his chest. "Had your shit packed up by the boys about a month ago, and found that in the closet. Showed it to Cheyenne, and she made it happen. Do you like it?"

"I love it, thank you." I whispered with tears in my eyes.

He grunted, pecked me on the forehead, and unceremoniously dropped me to my feet. I promptly returned the favor by punching him in the stomach, and then turning away to the ladies who'd stayed quiet during my moment with my brother.

"Y'all are fabulous." I proclaimed with gusto.

They laughed.

"We had a little longer than planned, but hey, at least you don't have to worry about fitting into the dress. Getting measurements the first time wasn't so hard, but you've lost a lot of weight over the past six weeks. The second measurements weren't so easy, but it should fit you perfectly." Cheyenne confirmed with a nod of her head.

That was the God's honest truth. I'd lost so much weight, over thirty pounds, that I looked almost sickly. Where before my body was well rounded and muscled, now it was skinny and bony. I did not look good, no matter how much James told me otherwise.

Which was to be expected with nearly six weeks of smoothies. Yes, I could ground up a cookie, but why bother? What was the point in blending that up when I couldn't get the chocolate chunks through my clenched teeth?

I resumed my job, because for the most part, I could be heard and understood. James resumed his job with the SWAT team about a week ago, much to his chagrin. He hated the fact that he had to be one hundred percent healed, but it was understandable when the SWAT team had to be in perfect shape. The lives of others could very well depend on it.

He'd argued that all he did was lay there and shoot people, but the Captain was adamant, and wouldn't let him back until he passed the physical in the same amount of time it'd taken him the first time. He'd argued with that one, too. However, that was the only way the Captain could play it since it was obvious to everyone that James could've passed the test in enough time even with a hole in his chest. His pain tolerance was very high, and that was why he pushed himself sometimes further than he should have.

"At least you still have good boobs." Ember supplied helpfully from across the room where she was shoving cheese whiz into her mouth directly from the squirt can.

That was true also. Out of everything I'd lost, mostly muscle, the fat stubbornly remained. I looked horrible. I really did. My boobs were fat and healthy looking. The stubborn pooch of my belly remained. Then there was the jiggly stuff on my thighs that used be lean muscle. No more. My arms jiggled when I waved, and I couldn't help but stare at them every time I did so, making sure to wave extra-long, just so I could stare at the hideous flap of skin.

James always made sure to smack my ass when I got too carried away though. He was helpful like that.

Texas Tornado

Which always seemed to get us in to trouble, but he'd never finish the act, which was another source of my bad attitude. He'd refused to have sex with me. He'd told me that we both needed to heal, and I couldn't disagree with him, but it was still rather frustrating.

He'd promised me that we only had to wait until all my casts came off, and then all bets were off. I'd been so extremely upset that the day I was to get them off, he'd be gone, that I'd cried myself to sleep. Then he had to go and plan my mother fucking dream wedding, and my anger had evaporated.

"That big shit." I said, shaking my head.

Cheyenne, Blaine, Winter, Ember and Payton all laughed, knowing exactly what it was like to have a man like James to deal with. Each and every one of them had been in my shoes at some point or another. They knew how the alpha male mind worked, just as well as I did.

It was their way, or their way. No excuses.

"Okay, so we have about an hour to get your hair washed and styled, your makeup on, and your dress cinched up. Are you ready?" Blaine asked, clapping her hands in glee.

I smiled at her, nodded my head, and started walking towards them.

"Alright, if you ladies don't need my assistance anymore, I'll be in the garage with everyone else. Okay?" Sebastian asked, clearly uncomfortable seeing all the girl stuff going on.

I waved him out with a dismissive hand, and he exhaled in relief before practically gunning it out the door.

Which promptly reopened when Janie came barreling inside wearing skinny jeans, biker boots, and a hoodie that said, 'Got wind?' Her hair was up in a ponytail high up on top of her head, and she had a single black ribbon tied around the ponytail so it hung equally on both sides.

Those were my doing. She'd finally consented to having a ribbon in her hair, but that's where she drew the line. She did *not* do bows. Period. James only laughed when I'd tried to get her to wear a bow one day, which was why he'd won the present contest in the first place.

He knew his kid. Which was why he got her a small mini bike. She fucking adored it. She's on that thing at least once a day for an hour. The bike I got her sat in the garage gathering dust, sad to say.

"'Loh! Daddy said to give this to you." Janie squealed and handed me a letter just as I'd taken a seat at the kitchen table.

Blaine and Ember immediately went to work on my hair while I sat there and let it happen.

"You should read that now. When we start on your makeup, there will be no more crying." Blaine told me before yanking my hair out of its ponytail.

The first sheet that was folded up was a bunch of numbers, percentages, and really a bunch of gibberish. If I was reading the sheet correctly, the number was nearly 110 million.

What the hell?

Then I got to the letter.

Texas Tornado

Shiloh "Speedy" June Mackenzie, fixing to be Allen,

So I assume you opened up the other letter first. Let me tell you what it means, since I'm sure you're asking yourself....what the fuck?

Stop shaking your head. I know you were.

Two days before I was shot, I had my vasectomy reversed. I know, I know, you're wondering why I didn't tell you. Well it's simple. I didn't want to. I wanted to make sure it was successful before I told you. I wanted to be able to tell you that it worked, and that we could start trying before I got your hopes up. Since I'm telling you now, you know that it was successful. That number says my boy's count is fucking perfect. Boom!

Well, then the kidnapping, followed by our recovery happened, which actually worked out in my favor since I was supposed to withhold from sex for four weeks.

Which would've worked out perfectly because I'd asked Cheyenne to start planning your dream wedding. Your brother helped there, describing a scrapbook you'd made your senior year in high school that held all your hopes and dreams for the future.

Let me tell you, I plan on making every one of those things, and then some, come true. I want you to be the mother of my children. I want you to grow old with me. I want you on the back of my bike when we're sixty years old, having the time of your life with me.

But first, I want to make your first dream come true. Your wedding.

Which is where we're at right now. I hope I've made it all perfect for you. I want this to be everything you've ever dreamed of. Even if I have to wear a tux.

I love you.

See you at the alter.

J.

I wiped tears from my eyes as I finished the letter.

"Good news?" Cheyenne asked in her chair across from me.

My eyes snapped up from the letter to Cheyenne's face. "The best."

When we'd discussed this in the hospital five weeks ago, I'd been optimistic. Now, though, I wasn't so sure that this was a good thing.

We'd been following Teal's progress since her attack, and it was overly apparent that Teal was never going to recover. Teal's ex-husband was indeed more connected than we'd ever thought possible, but sadly, wasn't something the men of Free had even thought to check for before. One tiny little tracking device, implanted without her knowledge, was enough to find her halfway across the world.

Although the situation in and of itself was truly horrible, it was good for the rest of the Freebirds. It meant that their identities hadn't been compromised. They were safe to go about living their lives. Though a new plan of scanning for tracking devices was a protocol on the men's to-do list as soon as the women were picked up to be sent on to their new lives.

Hindsight is twenty-twenty, and it was horrible that a woman had to die for that new protocol to be put into effect.

Texas Tornado

"Any news on Teal's baby?" Winter asked with a small smile on her face.

"She's very close to being full term. They think it'll be another week and a half or so. We plan to go up there within the next week to stay. Teal's ex was identified by not only the traffic light cameras, but also by fifteen motorists and seven pedestrians. He won't be able to challenge the child's paternity. He'll be in prison for well over thirty years." I explained.

"That's so sad. How are y'all going to explain this?" Cheyenne ventured into shark territory.

James had been adamant about making sure the baby would be accepted. He shouldn't have been worried though, everyone was one hundred percent supportive, and couldn't wait for the new arrival, even if the circumstances were horrid.

"The baby's ours. What is there to explain?" Janie asked, breaking into the conversation.

Sometimes, a child's perspective was all that it would take to humble anyone. Possibly, that was all that anyone every needed to hear.

"That's right, sweetie. Is that what you're wearing to watch us get married in?" I asked.

"Yes." She scowled.

I nodded. "Okay.

I wasn't about to tell her what she should wear. I'd seen that battle when James tried to get her to change her jeans because they had too many holes in them. It'd gone so well that I'd promised myself to never question here dressing choices. Plus, I didn't want to have to spank her like James had that day. She was exactly like him, and how could I punish her for being just like the father I loved so much?

She looked at me skeptically, but only until Ember interrupted me by telling me to close my eyes. Which is how I spent my next thirty minutes.

"Alright. That's done. Now, this is something we're going to go do in the back room. You'll want to get it done. I promise you you'll love it. After the hard part's done, that is." Cheyenne said cryptically.

I went with her, leaving everyone behind as they wore shit eating grins that I didn't like at all. "Alright, what exactly are we doing?"

"We're waxing your girly bits." She exclaimed. "Take your panties off."

My shoulders straightened, and I looked at her cautiously. "You've got to be kidding...right?"

"Absolutely not. Now, take those bad boys off, hop up here, and we'll start on the festivities." She said with a bright light in her eyes.

"I don't know that I'm comfortable taking my clothes off and spreading my legs for you." I finally replied after we sat there staring at each other for a few short moments.

"Listen," she said, placing her hand on her hip. "I've seen so many vaginas that I could describe them to you in such minute detail that you'd beg me to stop. Trust me. You ain't got nothing that I haven't seen before. Promise."

Texas Tornado

    Reluctantly I slipped out of my underwear, and blocked the next thirty minutes out of my mind completely. All I had to say was that James better love this, or I'd be doing the same to his pubic hair while he slept. That was even more painful than breaking my leg. All those things from Forty Year Old Virgin were true, only the words that came out of my mouth were much worse than *Kelly Clarkson*.

    "I'm telling you, he's going to love it." Cheyenne enthused as she opened the door that led back out into the down room.

    "Oh, he's going to love it. He came running in here ready to go all Hulk on us when we explained that she was just getting her taco waxed." Ember explained. "He left here with a dreamy look on his face."

    My face flamed. "I wasn't being that loud!"

    They laughed. In fact, they laughed so hard that Payton and Blaine were in tears. "Oh, really? My hoo haa burns. Make it stop. Blow on it. Get it off. Oh my God! Don't you go near my asshole. Jesus, Mary and Joseph. He doesn't even look at my asshole. It's fine. Oh my God! Make it stop. You get that wand near my ass one more time and I'm going to shove it up your nose." Blaine managed to squeeze out in between laughs.

    My face burned even more. "Okay, well it hurt!" I said to the gremlin twins.

    "Oh, we know. Don't worry. We've all let Cheyenne talk us into this before. Now I just let the beast grow. God wouldn't make women grow bushes if they weren't meant to be there." Ember said as she licked her fingers free of the salt from the potato chips.

"Okay, here's your something borrowed. Your something new. Your something old, and your something blue. Go put all this on, and come back out here so we can get you into your dress." Winter insisted, while placing packages into my hands and ushering me back into the torture chamber.

I did as instructed. Dropping the boxes on the padded bench I'd just been mauled on.

The first box I opened held my something new (I hoped), a simple white pair of silk panties and a strapless bra. They'd done well, because the fit was excellent, cupping my breasts and ass perfectly.

The note I found warmed my heart, as well as other unmentionables.

To keep those places covered until I'm ready for them.-- J

The second box I opened held my something blue. Blue fuzzy socks that were so super soft that I wanted to wrap myself up in them. When I pulled them free, a note tumbled to the floor, which I promptly read.

To keep your feet warm when I'm away.—J.

Slipping the fuzzy beauties onto my feet, I sighed in ecstasy, and went for the third box.

It was my something borrowed. Which made me laugh. I had to read the note first.

These are only for tonight. I'm going to need them back. –J

They were his department issued handcuffs, and his police badge. Oh dear, the possibilities were endless.

Texas Tornado

The fourth and final box made my heart nearly stop. James had told me about them only twice, each time bringing them up because I'd asked about them. His father's dog tags. I'd noticed the extra dog tag the day we'd first made love. He hadn't told me about it though, changing the subject with an ease and swiftness that spoke of skill at evading that particular question.

They'd been the only thing they'd found the day he was killed. That was all I knew though, because he didn't like talking about it. I knew it was important regardless of whether he spoke about it or not.

I'd learned more from Daina than I had from James and Cheyenne combined.

Apparently, James had been at an impressionable age, just six years old, when his father had died. He still remembered him, but since he was so young, he'd turned his father into a superhero of sorts. A man who was bigger than the world itself. Who was selfless and kind. Who was the king among kings, and I was happy that he had that.

Daina liked to tell stories of how he'd sit for hours staring at his father's portrait or when he'd tell Cheyenne all the wonderful things about his dad. Although those stories have slowed considerably, his father was still his idol. Someone so important to him that I was honored and blessed that he'd let me wear the dog tags, even for today. There wasn't a need for a note. I didn't need him to explain, I already knew the significance of the act.

Slipping the necklace on over my neck, I tucked the tags down in between my cleavage so only the chain was exposed, then exited the room with my something old, something new, something borrowed, and something blue.

"Holy crap! Your boobs look amazing in that!" Payton declared.

Luckily, Janie had joined the boys, because that would just be incredibly awkward to have to explain what Payton meant when she said my boobs looked amazing.

I rolled my eyes at Payton, and walked towards the women who were now holding the dress up over their heads so they could slip it on over my own.

The dress reminded me more of a princess's dress. High empire waist that went from very fitted in the bodice to poofy and full in the bottom. The train, just as I'd described it to James, was well over eight feet in length.

Finally, they fit the veil over my head, situating it so I could see. I didn't want it impeding my eyesight. Not only did I want to see the man I was marrying clearly, but I also didn't want to fall flat on my face in front of everyone and their brother. Which reminded me.

"Who all is here?" I asked curiously.

Ember answered as she fixed a flyaway hair that had come free from the clip that held it away from my face. She'd gathered it into a clip that resembled a snowflake at the side of my head, and then used bobby pins to keep it in place. In the back, she'd curled my long hair into large loops, and then sprayed so much fucking hair spray on it that a quarter would bounce off it.

Ember laughed. "Well, pretty much everyone. Sebastian, your father, their MC, your ladies from work, all of us, and a few others. So about ninety people or so."

"Holy crap! They aren't all going to fit into the shop, are they?" I asked as they started to hook the million and one tiny hooks at my back.

"Suck in, you've got about ten hooks back here that I can't get," Cheyenne instructed.

A few more minutes of effort on Cheyenne's part, she finally bowed out in defeat.

"I can't get it. Someone else try it." Cheyenne panted.

"Jesus, this is tight, are you sure you have more to go?" I asked concerned for my breathing.

Payton tried, followed shortly by Ember, Blaine, and finally Winter. None of which could fasten my hooks. "Well this is embarrassing." I said dryly.

"Oh, it's going to get done. Too bad you can't suck in your boobs. Let me go get reinforcements." Cheyenne said before leaving the room.

Everybody who was left in the room tried again to hook me up, but it ended with the same results.

Ember looked at my boobs, and then back at my dress. "When we finally do get this done, it's going to make those puppies pop the fuck out."

I laughed. "Yeah, they aren't really that big, Ember. Size 36C is standard size."

"I want your boobs when I grow up." She said wistfully.

***

Sam

"I can't believe you're making me wear this." I said as I pulled the bowtie away from my neck. "What's wrong with our dress blues? At least those are comfortable."

"Because she said tux. So I'm doing a tux. If I have to wear a tux, so do y'all." James said, pulling on his tie.

"Aww, aren't y'all just the cutest little things I've ever seen." Cheyenne teased.

I turned and glared at her. "Watch your mouth."

"That's physically impossible unless you have a mirror, which I don't happen to have right now. I need your big strong hands for a moment please. Then we'll be ready." Cheyenne smiled at me.

"What's going on?" James asked as he sat down to slip socks on.

"You can't wear those." Cheyenne said with horror in her voice.

"What?" James and I asked at the same time.

Ember came out the door muttering about boobs and what she wanted to be when she grew up, stopping with a look of horror on her face. "You cannot wear your motorcycle boots with that, James."

I looked down at my own boots and grimaced. There was a line that was drawn somewhere in the man's code, and that line was that we'd wear the stupid fucking tuxes, but the line was drawn at silly shoes that not only weren't water proof, but were uncomfortable as hell.

Texas Tornado

"The boots are staying. It's colder than a witch's tit outside, and I'll be standing in wet slush for a good twenty minutes at least. Now, what's wrong that you need Sam?" James' voice booked no room for argument.

Ember and Cheyenne's lips pursed as if they'd sucked on a sour lemon. They were so much alike sometimes that it was unreal.

"We need the last five hooks done up on Shiloh's dress, and it's going to take more muscle than all of us combined." Ember explained finally.

I started heading towards the door that Ember and Cheyenne had exited, laughing when I heard James mutter about it not being hard to do, that women were weaklings.

My breath stalled in my chest as I opened the door and saw Shiloh in her dress. She looked stunning.

Her hair hung down her back in golden brown curls, and the dress she had on was massive, with a train that was likely to trip damn near anyone that came within ten feet of her.

"You look beautiful," I said as I entered the room.

"Wait, daddy." Pru ran up from behind me and squeezed in before I could close the door.

I waited patiently, and then closed the door once she was inside.

"Aunt Shiloh! You look like Elsa from Frozen!" Pru squealed.

Everybody got a good chuckle out of that fact from my three and a half year old, but quickly sobered. She did indeed look like Elsa, but I wasn't confirming the fact that I've watched a Disney animated princess movie at least once a day. I'd have to have my man card revoked. Especially if they knew I actually enjoyed it.

"Alright, Shiloh. We're going to go get dressed ourselves. We'll be back once we've done that, and then we can start." Payton said as she exited the room, followed by Winter and Blaine.

Shiloh watched them go with a small smile on her face and then turned to give me her back. "Let's see if you can do this. They tried, but I don't think it will go. It's too tight as it is."

I walked up to her and proceeded to hook the buttons without effort, stepping away slightly as soon as she was done. "Anything else?"

"I can't breathe." She panted.

I laughed as she started panting. "It's not really that bad... is it?"

"I'll get used to it. I may not be able to wear it for long though. Go tell everyone to hurry the hell up." She demanded.

"Just one second," I said stepping close to her and enfolding her in my arms.

Her own arms wrapped around my waist, hammering home the fact that I'd almost screwed this up before I even knew what I'd be missing.

"I don't think I ever actually apologized to you." I whispered into her hair. "I'm sorry for being such an ass, Shiloh. I'm not going to offer up any excuses, either. I should've known better. I love you sweet girl, and I'm proud of all that you've accomplished."

When I leaned back, she grabbed the white handkerchief in my breast pocket and started dabbing at her eyes. "Thank you, Sam. I love you, too. There's no need to apologize. I think we've both done that enough. You've more than made up for everything."

I nodded, taking the handkerchief back from her when she handed it to me. "I'll send our father in. See you soon."

I went out the door, hailed down my father, and sent him to Shiloh before I went to my spot outside in the subzero temperatures.

It was actually fucking snowing. Holy Shit. That was a miracle in and of itself for Texas. I hadn't seen snow since I was younger. I'd been in Texas for going on five years now, and this was the first time I'd seen it snow more than a few seconds. It was actually collecting on all the empty chairs as it floated out of the sky in flurries.

"Can you believe this?" James asked as I reached his side.

"No. Not at all." I said, agreeing that it was a small miracle.

"How'd she look?" He asked me.

The smile on my face said it all, but I answered him anyway. "Stunning."

And when she came out of the side door twenty minutes later on my father's arm, I realized I'd misspoken. She looked absolutely striking.

James' breath hissed when he saw her, and his smile lit his face like a 1000 watt light bulb. However, there was one thing that needed to be said before we went any further.

"If you hurt her, I'll fucking kill you. I'll shred the meat off your bones with a goddamn box cutter and feed it to you." I said, never looking away from my sister as she made it down the aisle.

"Returning the favor?" He asked.

I glanced at him, but he only had eyes for Shiloh. "Just as you said to me five years ago, buddy."

Chapter 27

It's not us, it's them. Them and their stupid boy penises.

-Meredith Grey, Grey's Anatomy

Shiloh

"Please, please. Do it now. Quick J." I panted.

"Settle down, I can't get a good hold on it with you squirming around like that." James growled.

I couldn't help it. It needed to happen now, or I was sure I would die. "Please, James. Hurry."

He growled and threw me to the bed, straddled my thighs and pinned me to the bed with all of his strength.

Satisfaction poured through me as he eased the hooks down until not a one was left clasped, and finally I could breathe again. "Thank you so much." I sighed wistfully.

He growled, yanked the dress off the rest of the way, and tossed it unceremoniously into the corner. "Now, are the panties and bra too tight, too? Do I need to remove those next?" He teased.

"Yep, they're super tight. So tight that I think you need to check my body for proper circulation." I giggled.

Yep, that was me, giggling. I might or might not have been slightly tipsy, too.

I'd had a blast at the wedding, and it was everything I could have ever hoped for and more. James and Cheyenne, as well as everyone, had done a wonderful job, and I would remember this day for the rest of my life.

"Turn over." He said gruffly.

I flipped over, turning from my stomach to my back, and smiled when I saw his nostrils flare before he leaned down, popped the front clasp of my bra, and my breasts spilled free.

"Those look like they're going to need some attention. Let me see if I can breathe some life back into them." He quipped right before swiping his tongue along the sensitive peak of my nipple.

I groaned, tugging on his closely trimmed beard, holding him closer to my breast, urging him on.

The hand that wasn't full of my breast went down lower until he reached the hem of my panties. He slowed for all of two seconds before he slipped beneath the elastic band, freezing completely when he felt the bare skin of my sex.

His mouth pulled away from my aching breast, releasing the nipple almost regretfully before rising up to his knees and staring down at my silk covered sex.

"Did you wax that completely, or it just my overactive imagination? I thought it was only being trimmed." James wheezed.

I smiled, and then shimmied out of my panties while he watched.

"Oh, Jesus. We're never going to make it out of the bed," he said as he went down onto his knees beside the bed, yanking my body close until it was on the very edge.

Texas Tornado

He rested my feet, still encased in my three-inch heels, on his shoulder, and then gave one leisurely lick of my overheated core. Then another. And another.

He continued the pattern, until I was lifting my hips, urging him with my hips to do something other than that, when he thrust three fingers into me, making my body bow off the bed with the suddenness.

However, he didn't stop there, he continued to thrust his fingers, and attacked my clit with hopeless ferocity until I was ready to burst.

Sadly, he stopped before I could tumble over the edge, bringing himself to his feet to watch my body continue to writhe and squirm on top of the bed.

When my hand snuck down to finish the job he'd left, he growled, and moved both hands in one of his while he worked the zipper of his pants with the other. "Hold still, sweetheart."

Then his cock was kissing the entrance of my womb in one hard thrust. "Fuck, but I've been waiting too long for this."

"My hand just doesn't feel the same." I panted as he worked his thick cock inside of me.

He stilled, glancing down into my eyes. "You've used your hand to get yourself off?"

At my nod, he asked, "When?"

"Every night when you were asleep." I answered.

"Where?" He growled against my lips.

I smiled against his lips. "Right next to you. Every single time."

"Minx." He snarled, and then plunged further into me, pumping his hips hard.

The head of his cock was bumping up against my cervix.

Usually it caused a little bit of discomfort when he'd do that so quickly, but today, I was so worked up, that anything felt good. "Yes, harder."

He ignored me, slowing down instead.

The head of his cock pulled free of my clasping channel, reluctant to let him leave. He used the slickened head of his cock to rub against my overheated clit, running the length of himself through my labia.

The feeling was exquisite, and I didn't know if I wanted him to continue what he was doing, or start fucking me again.

"Please," I cried, wanting him to give me that final push I needed to achieve orgasm.

He ignored me again, continuing to work his heavy dick through my slippery folds.

Then I cheated. On his next withdraw, I canted my hips and placed the palm of my hand right before my entrance, forcing his fat cock to tunnel deep inside me, causing us both to groan.

"Cheater." He panted, but didn't withdraw again.

No, instead, he worked his length deep inside of me in slow, deep pushes. Each plunge and withdraw brought me closer and closer to the pinnacle, to where I was sure with just one hard thrust, he would send me over.

His pace never alternated though. Building up the pressure higher and higher.

Texas Tornado

He controlled my hips with laughable ease, refusing to let me have any resistance that he didn't want me to have. So I used the only other tool in my arsenal. My vaginal muscles.

Everybody's done kegals at some point in their life, tightening and loosening those muscles, testing the feelings, the way it made everything feel so super tight. Well, that's exactly what I did. I clamped down on his cock, tightening the muscles of my core so tight that even my abdominals ached, and he exploded.

Everything seemed to happen at once.

My muscles clamped down, he groaned loudly, withdrew, and then slammed back home so hard that I swore I felt him deep inside my belly. He held off just long enough to feel me detonate, which lit his own fuse, causing him to explode only milliseconds after me.

Hot jets of his semen filled me. So much so that he started seeping out of the side, and down onto the bed below our bodies.

"Holy fuck," he panted as he disengaged himself from me, dropping into a heap right beside me.

I didn't move much from my own position, only collapsing my elbows and laying my face flat against the cool sheets of our bed. "Your control sucks." I panted.

He groaned. "I wanted it to be special. I was doing good too until you used those muscles of yours, and then I was a goner."

"Yeah," I agreed, and then promptly fell asleep, ass in the air and all.

***

"Hello?" I heard James voice as if from a distance.

My eyes blinked reluctantly open, and I saw the room was completely dark except for the blue numbers blinking 3:37 A.M. on the alarm clock.

"Yeah?" James voice changed from sleepy to completely alert with the blink of an eye.

"Oh, no. Is it too early?" James asked; panic tinging the edge of his voice.

I rolled over, sitting up and swinging my legs over the side of the bed. Then I went to the bathroom, showered quickly, dressed, and started picking our bags up from the closet when he came in from the kitchen with two travel mugs of coffee.

"Guess you figured out the baby was on the way. They're pretty sure they'll have to do surgery, but they're going to wait and see. Are you ready?"

The thing was...I was. I was married to him. He was the love of my life. The father of one of the most well rounded children on earth.

He held me up when I needed him the most.

There were many things that scared me on this earth, but I well and truly believed that, with James, I could accomplish anything. Be anyone.

James took me on the wildest ride of my life, and I couldn't wait to start this brand new journey with him.

Seriously. Could. Not. Wait.

Epilogue

Marrying you was the best thing I've ever done for my vagina.

-Anniversary card

James

"Please everyone, quiet. Kayla, Janie, do you mind?" The principal of Kilgore High School asked.

Through his microphone.

In front of five hundred students, twice as many parents, family of the students, and the entire teaching staff.

Kayla and Janie's graduation.

Perfect.

Everyone chuckled around me, but I swear that if that girl were not eighteen years old, I would've spanked her in front of the entire graduating class if I could have gotten away with it.

There are many things I've learned over the years by being a father of three and that was that a strong hand was needed. To hold my beer. Or on those rare occasions, sometimes even whiskey. Because when you live in a household of women, something's got to take the edge off. Otherwise, a man, such as myself, would go crazy.

"Daddy, you need to lighten up. Janie's finally graduating. You're lucky she's not pregnant and on that reality show 'Sixteen and Pregnant.'" Scout, our brainiac of a middle child, informed me.

"She'd be on Dateline before I allowed her to be on that show." I grumbled.

Although Scout wasn't of my blood, I'd treated her as my own from the very minute that she was brought into my life. I still remember that day as if it was yesterday. But most importantly, I remember how our family gathered around the newest member of the Free family, and cherished her like she was always meant to be cherished.

***

Twelve years ago

First night home with the new baby

"You know. That looks an awful lot like Cat. Are you sure you're not going to mix the two up?" Janie asked me from her perch at my side.

I looked down at the sleeping infant, Scout, in my arms and smiled.

"She does look a lot like Cat, doesn't she?" I agreed.

"Don't let Jack take the baby though. She's ours." Janie said, narrowing her eyes at Jack as he laughed at what my daughter had just said.

Janie was very protective of Scout.

As soon as we'd pulled into the driveway, Janie had rushed forward, eager to meet the newest member of our family. She'd even been the one to pick out Scout's name.

Texas Tornado

"We'll make sure he stays on the straight and narrow. Don't worry." I said, handing the baby off to Cheyenne as she cooed and cawed at her.

"Jesus, Cheyenne. You sound like a motherfucking bird. Can't you keep your sounds straight?" Ember growled as she stared at the baby. "Let me hold her, you've had her long enough."

"She fits in great." Shiloh exclaimed from my side.

I held my arm up, and she fit her body into mine, encircling her arms around my torso. "Yep. Knew she would."

"Me too." She joked.

"Who's next?" Elliott asked the group.

"Next as in next to have a kid... or next as in next to get pregnant?" Blaine clarified.

"Pregnant. Gabe already knocked Ember up. So she doesn't count." Elliott quipped.

"That would be me. Found out this morning. Congratulations, honey." Blaine said mirthfully.

Elliott paled. "Oh, shit."

Champagne was uncorked, and a celebration commenced. Not only for the newest member of Free, but also for the members to be. I was glad that my children had this to grow up around, because they would always have the love and protection of any one of the people in this room, no matter what.

A person needed that, regardless of age, and I valued it for what it was.

Happiness.

***

Present day

"Janie Allen, our salutatorian, graduates with honors with thirty two college semester hours, a 3.97 GPA, perfect attendance, and will be attending the University of A&M in College Station, Texas." The principal called through the microphone.

At the mention of Janie's name, our entire group roared. Shiloh was up on her feet, standing on top of the bleachers, stomping and yelling for all she was worth.

"That's my girl!" Shiloh screamed.

I smiled, hooking my arm around Shiloh's waist just in case she decided to slip off the bleacher and break her arm for a fifth time.

And yes, I do mean fifth. She not only did it one more time since she was kidnapped, but twice, once at the beginning of her pregnancy with Rebel, and once at the end.

The fifth time she broke her arm was the night she'd gone into labor with Rebel. Emmaline was my baby. She was ten years old, and our last child. We'd originally planned to try for more, but sadly, it wasn't meant to be.

The memory of the day Emmaline, AKA Rebel, was born was still ingrained in my mind. Like a hot brand that would forever be a reminder of a time in my life that I literally felt like everything was falling apart.

Texas Tornado

***

Ten years ago

October

It was Halloween.

The day I dreaded the most out of any day of the year.

For some reason, this was the night that every single irrational person in the small city of Kilgore decided to let their crazy out to play. I'd been introduced to the night three years ago when I'd started with the Kilgore SWAT team, and each subsequent year got worse and worse. Somehow topping the year before it.

I'd managed to get out the door with the kids dressed in their matching Raggedy Anne outfits, and even to the first house before my pager went off.

I'd left a very pregnant Shiloh in the hands of her brothers, Cheyenne, and my mother, before jogging all the way back home, hopping onto my bike, and arriving at the station, only to turn around and head back home. It'd been a false alarm, and I was annoyed with damn near everyone who crossed my path.

I didn't want to leave Shiloh, not with her four days past her due date and walking around the city. Before I'd left the station to head back home, I'd informed the Captain that I would be taking my leave effective immediately.

When I got home, I'd checked with Sam, and met back up with the group at a very old home that was one of the oldest in our neighborhood.

It was the type of house that you had to practically climb up a hill to get to the front door.

Cheyenne had Janie in front of her, and her youngest child's hand in one of hers while the other held the hand of Scout. Sam was sandwiched between the twins, and Shiloh followed up in the rear.

Just as Shiloh approached midway down, two teenagers came barreling down the steps with the entire bowl of candy from the house, with the owner yelling at them about their rude behavior.

Instead of avoiding our slow moving group, they'd decided to plow straight through them. I watched in horror as the two teenagers blasted through them, causing not only the kids to fall, but to my utter horror, Shiloh as well.

Where the kids had been lucky, having the parents right there to catch them, Shiloh hadn't been as fortunate. The massive weight of her belly altered her balance, and she teetered forward, and then backward before her heels slipped out from underneath of her.

She'd managed to control her fall somewhat by throwing her arm out and maneuvering her body to the side so she didn't fall on the children, but endangered herself more in the process.

She'd hit the rock pathway first, causing the same arm she'd broken so many times before to break like like a match stick. Then she rolled down the steep slope until she came to rest at the very bottom in a crumpled mess.

It all took no less than thirty seconds, but in that thirty seconds, time felt like it slowed down to a crawl.

Texas Tornado

I'd watched in dismay as she fell, and I'd moved, but there was nothing I could do but witness the entire ordeal.

She'd been in a lot of pain once she came to a standstill and covered from head to toe in blood. In the ambulance, she'd coded twice, and as soon as she was rushed to the hospital, I was informed that the placenta had detached from the uterine wall during her fall. She was rushed into surgery ruthlessly fast in a vain attempt to save the baby's life, even though nobody was optimistic, not even myself.

I'd collapsed into the closest chair that allowed me to see the operating room they'd taken her into, and waited for over an hour before I was given any news.

A nurse was the first to exit, and in her arms, she held a precious bundle of pink swaddled closely to her chest. She deposited the baby into my arms before telling me the outcome.

"Your wife is currently still being operated on. They were able to get the baby out in time; however, due to the damage caused by the abruption, the bleeding couldn't be stopped. The doctor's in the process of removing Shiloh's uterus in an attempt to get the bleeding under control." The nurse explained

The baby and I waited another forty-five minutes for news.

I felt like Kevin Bacon in that movie She's Having A Baby. I was totally and utterly lost. I had a baby, but no Shiloh. And although the baby was absolutely beautiful, I couldn't celebrate yet, which made me feel like a big pile of shit.

I berated myself for hours on what I could've done differently, what I should be doing differently even now, but only managed to grab a hold of my overloaded emotions when the same nurse returned with a wide smile on my face.

I took a deep breath, and thanked the nurse, waited for her to round the corner, and then promptly fell apart.

I knew I was being watched.

I knew my brothers, as well as family and friends were just down the hall, and that nurses were watching me lose it, but I couldn't help it.

I looked at that baby, the one that had Shiloh's beautiful brown hair, and her big precious eyes, and I wept.

Or like Shiloh liked to say, watered my beard.

The good news was my wife was okay. My baby was okay. The bad news? My heart would never be the same.

***

Present

Rebel scooted closer into my side, burrowing in behind me, holding on while we all cheered for Janie.

At ten years old, she was hell on wheels, and she was daddy's little girl for sure.

She lived for the opportunity to watch daddy shoot, work on motorcycles, wash the car, or even play a video game.

Where I was, she was, much to Shiloh's annoyance.

In Rebel's eyes, I could do no wrong.

"Daddy, lift me up. I can't see Janie." She yelled.

Texas Tornado

I did as instructed, and we all watched as Janie crossed the stage, biker boots and all, to accept her diploma.

"Thank God." Shiloh muttered quietly from beside me.

I looked down into her beautiful face.

She was a little older now, a little more curvy. Her hair had pale silver strands that threaded through her brown locks here and there, but not in one single way did it detract from her beauty.

She was still just as loving and caring now, if not more so, than she'd been when I'd met her twelve years ago. "You can say that again." I declared, smiling down at her.

Her eyes warmed as she looked from my smile to my daughter that was perched on the top of my shoulders. "One down, two to go." She said, eyes twinkling.

"And now, I'd like to present to you the 2026 class Valedictorian, Kayla Nash!" The principal cheered.

Around us, our little family roared.

Kayla hadn't led an easy life.

At the age of two, she'd lost her father, and one of my best friends, to the war in Iraq.

Eight years later, she lost her only other living relative, to cancer.

She'd moved in with us a couple of months before her grandmother had gotten too sick, where she'd remained for the last eight years. Each Sunday, like clockwork, she'd visit her father and grandmother, who were buried next to Kayla's grandfather. There, she'd tell them her hopes and dreams, and goal of becoming the valedictorian, and then on to become a doctor that searched for a cure for cancer.

Every bit of instinct I possessed knew she'd accomplish that goal, too.

"Hello, class of 2026!" Kayla yelled into the microphone.

She was beautiful, and to see her standing there, wearing her yellow sash that declared her at the top of her class, I got a little teary eyed thinking about all that Dougie had missed when he'd died.

"One of my biggest motivators to be where I am today is because of one man." She said, swallowing thickly. "He's in heaven, and I call him daddy."

Silence reined at her announcement, and I heard Cheyenne lose her battle with tears next to me.

"Sixteen years ago, he died protecting his country. He died doing what he loved. He died being a hero. My hero." Kayla finished on a whisper.

Her tears spilled over her cheeks, but the waver in her voice didn't stop her.

"He wrote me a letter while he was over there, and had one of his best friends in the world bring it home to me, to keep it safe until I was old enough to understand it." Kayla said. "I'm going to read it to you, and maybe you'll find inspiration in what he's written to me, too. Or maybe once you leave here, there won't be one single thing you enjoyed about my speech, but you'll forever remember this letter. You'll remember it when you need it the most, just like I have."

She cleared her throat, and then started reading.

Texas Tornado

Pumpkin,

I'm writing this letter on a beautiful sunny day in the middle of an open desert.

Although you might not know it, I loved you very much. You were my world. From the moment I first saw you, I knew you'd become something great. Something this world has never experienced before.

I've been instructed to carry out one final mission before I come home. I have one of the greatest men the world has ever been blessed with at my side, and we're going into hostile territory. Although it's supposed to be routine, I want to write this letter to you, just in case. Which means, that if this letter is currently in your hands right now, I didn't make it.

I want to impart on you some wisdom that I've learned.

The world is not a very nice place.

There are people in this world who will constantly bring you down. However, there are also people in this world that will help raise you up. Make you a person that you are proud to be.

You will find, many times in your life, things do not go your way.

During those times, I want you to take a step back, and analyze the situation. I want you to notice, not only with your eyes, but also with all your other senses, the root of the situation. I want you to be aware. I want you to be prepared. And I want you to be forgiving.

The world can use more forgiveness.

I've learned those things too late in life to put them to use, but you, my bright, young daughter, have the whole world ahead of you. You can do anything you want to. Be anything you want to be.

Although I'm gone, I will never stray far from your side. I will forever be watching you, holding you up in times of need, laughing with you when you see a funny movie, and holding your hand when you need to just cry.

It tears my heart in two that you are going to marry someday, and I won't be there to witness it. That I won't have that opportunity to walk you down the aisle. However, someday, you will find that perfect someone, and you will make a life with him. You will have children of your own someday and only then will you know the feeling of your heart walking around outside your body.

Only then will you know that it takes compassion and sacrifice to get to where you want to be, be who you want to be.

Remember to always follow the Golden Rule- Treat others the way you wish to be treated.

Lastly, do not forget that I love you. I will always be proud of you, and I will never think that you are anything less than perfect.

Always put your trust in God, because he will never steer you wrong.

Love, Daddy.

I found myself burying my head into Shiloh's neck, trying my hardest to stem the flow of tears, but it didn't work.

That man, Dougie, was one of the best men in the world, and it still made my heart ache each and every day to think about him not being here. To see his daughter bloom into a beautiful young woman. To know that he won't ever be there to witness her accomplishments.

Texas Tornado

However, to this day, I still remember the last thing that Dougie ever said to me.

Ride like the wind. Know what it feels like to be free. That's where I'll be.

***

"James!" Shiloh yelled from the kitchen.

"What?" I yelled back, not getting up from my recliner in the basement.

My haven.

My vacation from the estrogen factory.

I'd declared it mine about five years after Scout was born.

I loved the shit out of the women in my life, but about eight years of dealing with endless girl shit, I declared the basement a girl free zone. This was my territory. A place where I could leave my shit around, cuss, spill my beer without cleaning it up, and watch a cop show without my girls bitching about missing Project fucking Runway.

Shiloh showed at the top of the stairs a few moments later.

She was in a pair of extremely short pajama shorts, and an old SWAT t-shirt of mine.

My blood heated at the sight of her. She was even more beautiful now than she was when I met her all those years ago.

"Kayla went to go visit Dougie." She said.

My eyes watched the play of emotions that came and went on my wife's face. "When?"

I knew she'd go. I just hadn't expected her to do it on her graduation night.

"She left about five minutes ago." Shiloh explained.

Sighing, I stood up, grabbed the t-shirt that was laying on the back of the recliner, and tugged it on over my head. Walking up the stairs, I gave Shiloh a peck on the lips and a smack on the ass as I passed, and walked through the back door and out into the night.

It wasn't until I was passing the damn thing that I realized that Kayla and Kayla's car were still in the driveway.

She was sitting in the driver's seat with her head resting on the steering wheel. Her hair was still curly from her graduation ceremony, covering her face from my view.

I stopped next to the door, opened it, and crouched down. "What's wrong, pretty girl?"

Kayla's eyes met mine, and I realized she was crying.

I knew why, too. It didn't take a genius. Today was a big day for her. It was life changing. And life changing events make you realize what you do and don't have any longer.

"I miss my dad." She sniffled.

Knowing what she needed, I stood and offered my hand.

"You want to go visit him?" I asked, looking into her watery eyes.

She nodded, handed me her keys, which I pocketed, and followed me to the bike.

Texas Tornado

An hour later, I heard Kayla's hesitant voice in my ear. "Not that I don't love riding with you, but we're not going the right way. The cemetery's that way." She said, pointing in the opposite direction.

Before I answered, I pulled over, wanting to explain a little better without the distraction of road noise before we continued.

I didn't turn around though. Instead, I stared out at the sun setting low in the sky. The pink, orange, and bluish hues of the sky making the perfect backdrop for what I had in mind.

"I don't think of your dad being buried in that cemetery. That's not really where he's at. Sure, that's where his remains are, but I feel him the most when I'm out riding. Remembering the laughter in his voice when he told a stupid joke. Remembering how much he loved you, and bragged about you when you were a little girl. The way he protected us during our missions. The way he treated his mother like a queen."

"That why you don't visit the grave anymore, J?" Kayla whispered, leaning her head against my back.

"I visit. I just don't want anybody watching when I water my beard, so I go alone." I teased.

Kayla snorted. "Show me more of my dad."

So I did, telling old goofy stories of him through the headset built in to the helmet.

We drove until I could feel Kayla's head leaning so heavily against my back that I knew she'd be asleep soon if I didn't take her home.

I hadn't intended to drive so long, but it was nice to show Kayla how I remembered her dad. Commemorated his existence.

I pulled the old Harley into the driveway and got Kayla settled into her room before I ran a check over the house. I locked the doors, checked the windows, fed the dog, and checked on the kids, before heading in to my own room and stripping my clothes off.

I eased down in the bed as carefully as possible, but as always, I woke her when I looped my arms around her.

"What time is it?" She asked as I pulled her warm body closer into my arms.

"Little after three." I murmured, running my face along her naked, exposed neck.

"What took so long?" She asked.

"I was showing Shiloh how I visited Dougie." I rasped, snuggling even closer into her soft pliant body.

"As long as you didn't show her how fast you normally visit him, we're good." She snorted softly.

"I'd never do that with Kayla. Only with you, baby."

"Yeah, I'm sure Dougie wouldn't like you showing her how to ride it like you stole it." She laughed quietly.

The woman always knew the right thing to say. I'd be lost without her.

"No, he definitely would not." He said, closing his eyes and drifting off, knowing he'd wake in the morning to another beautiful day with his little slice of heaven.

My Texas Tornado.

The End

Printed in Great Britain
by Amazon